The Android's Dream

The Android's Dream

John Scalzi

a tom dohe

THE ANDROID'S DREAM

Edited by Patrick Nielsen Hayden

Book design by Lynn Newmark

A Tor Book
Published by Tom Doherty Associates, LLC
175 Fifth Avenue
New York, NY 10010

www.tor.com

Tor® is a registered trademark of Tom Doherty Associates, LLC.

Library of Congress Cataloging-in-Publication Data

Scalzi, John, 1969–
  The android's dream / John Scalzi.—1st ed.
    p.   cm.
  "A Tom Doherty Associates Book."
  ISBN-13: 978-0-765-30941-9 (acid-free paper)
  ISBN-10: 0-765-30941-6 (acid-free paper)
  1. Life on other planets—Fiction.   I. Title.
PS3619.C256A84   2006
813'.6—dc22

                                        2006010480

First Edition: November 2006

Printed in the United States of America

0 9 8 7 6 5 4 3 2 1

This book is dedicated to Kevin Stampfl, one of my best friends for years, and a good man to know before *and* after the collapse of civilization.

Also to Cory Doctorow, Justine Larbalestier, Nick Sagan, Charlie Stross, and Scott Westerfeld, my first live audience as a science fiction writer. Thanks for your attendance then, and your friendship now.

The Android's Dream

Dirk Moeller didn't know if he could fart his way into a major diplomatic incident. But he was ready to find out.

Moeller nodded absentmindedly at his assistant, who placed the schedule of today's negotiations in front of him, and shifted again in his chair. The tissue surrounding the apparatus itched, but there's no getting around the fact that a ten-centimeter tube of metal and electronics positioned inside your colon, a mere inch or two inside your rectum, is going to cause some discomfort.

This much was made clear to Moeller when he was presented with the apparatus by Fixer. "The principle is simple," Fixer said, handing the slightly curved thing to Moeller. "You pass gas like you normally do, but instead of leaving your body, the gas enters into that forward compartment. The compartment closes off, passes the gas into second department, where additional chemical components are added, depending on the message you're trying to send. Then it's shunted into the third compartment, where the whole mess waits for your signal. Pop the cork, off it goes. You interact with it through a wireless interface. Everything's there. All you have to do is install it."

"Does it hurt?" Moeller asked. "The installation, I mean."

Fixer rolled his eyes. "You're shoving a miniature chemistry lab up your ass, Mr. Moeller," Fixer said. "Of course it's going to hurt." And it did.

Despite that fact, it was an impressive piece of technology. Fixer had created it by adapting it from blueprints he found in the National Archives, dating to when the Nidu and humans made first contact, decades back. The original inventor was a chemical engineer with ideas of bringing the two races together in a concert that featured humans, with the original versions of the apparatus placed near their tracheas, belching out scented messages of friendship.

The plan fell apart because no reputable human chorus wanted to be associated with the concert; something about the combination of sustained vocal outgassing and the throat surgery required to install the apparatuses made it rather less than appealing. Shortly thereafter the chemical engineer found himself occupied with a federal investigation into the nonprofit he had created to organize the concert, and then with a term in minimum security prison for fraud and tax evasion. The apparatus got lost in the shuffle and slid into obscurity, awaiting someone with a clear purpose for its use.

"You okay, sir?" said Moeller's aide, Alan. "You look a little preoccupied. Are you feeling better?" Alan knew his boss had been out yesterday with a stomach flu; he'd taken his briefings for the today's slate of negotiations by conference call.

"I'm fine, Alan," Moeller said. "A little stomach pain, that's all. Maybe something I had for breakfast."

"I can see if anyone has got some Tums," Alan said.

"That's the last thing I need right now," Moeller said.

"Maybe some water, then," Alan said.

"No water," Moeller said. "I wouldn't mind a small glass of milk, though. I think that might settle my stomach."

"I'll see if they have anything at the commissary," Alan said. "We've still got a few minutes before everything begins." Moeller nodded to Alan, who set off. Nice kid, Moeller thought. Not especially bright, and new to the trade delegation, but those were two of the reasons he had him as his aide for these negotiations. An aide who was more observant and had been around Moeller longer might have remembered that he was lactose intolerant. Even a small amount of milk would inevitably lead to a gastric event.

"Lactose intolerant? Swell," Fixer had said, after the installation. "Have a glass of milk, wait for an hour or so. You'll be good to go. You can also try the usual gas-producing foods: beans, broccoli, cauliflower, cabbage, raw onions, potatoes. Apples and apricots also do the trick. Prunes too, but that's probably more firepower than you'll really want. Have a good vegetable medley for breakfast and then stand back."

"Any meats?" Moeller had asked. He was still a little breathless from the pain of having the apparatus sent up his tailpipe and grafted to his intestine wall.

"Sure, anything fatty will work," Fixer said. "Bacon, some well-marbled red meat. Corned beef and cabbage will give you a little bit of everything. What, you don't like vegetables?"

"My dad was a butcher," Moeller said. "I ate a lot of meat as a kid. Still like it."

More than liked it, really. Dirk Moeller came from a long line of carnivores and proudly ate animal flesh at every meal. Most people didn't do that anymore. And when they *did* eat meat, they picked out a tube of vatted meat product, made from cultivated tissue that never required the butchering of an animal, or even the participation of any sort of animal outside of the purely mythical. The best-selling vatted meat product on the market was something called Kingston's Bison Boar™, some godforsaken agglomeration of bovine and pig genes stretched across a cartilaginous scaffolding and immersed in a nutrient broth until it grew into something that was meatlike without being meaty, paler than veal, lean as a lizard, and so animal friendly that even strict vegetarians didn't mind tucking in a Bison Boar Burger™ or two when the mood struck them. Kingston's corporate mascot was a pig with a bison shag and horns, frying up burgers on a hibachi, winking at the customer in third-quarter profile, licking its lips in anticipation of devouring its own fictional flesh. The thing was damned creepy.

Moeller would have rather roasted his own tongue on a skewer than eat vatted meat. Good butchers were hard to come by these days, but Moeller found one outside of Washington, in the suburb of Leesburg. Ted was a boutique entrepreneur, like all butchers these days. His day job was as a mechanic. But he knew his way around a carving chart, which is more than most people in his line of work could say. Once a year in October, Ted damn near filled up a walk-in freezer in Moeller's basement with beef, pork, venison, and four kinds of bird: chicken, turkey, ostrich, and goose.

Because Moeller was his best customer, occasionally Ted would throw in something more exotic, usually a reptile of some kind—he got a lot of alligator now that Florida had declared a year-round hunting season on that fast-breeding hybrid species that the EPA introduced to repopulate the Everglades—but also an occasional mammal or two whose provenance was often left prudently unattributed. There was that one year when Ted provided ten pounds of steaks and a note scrawled on the butcher paper: "Don't ask." Moeller served those at a barbecue with former associates from the American Institute for Colonization. Everyone loved them. Several months later, another butcher—not Ted—had been arrested for trafficking in meat taken from Zhang-Zhang, a panda on loan to the National Zoo. The panda had disappeared roughly the time Ted made his yearly meat drop. The next year, Ted was back to alligator. It was probably better that way for everyone, except possibly the alligator.

"It all starts with meat," Moeller's father told him often, and as Alan returned with a coffee mug filled with 2%, Moeller reflected on the truth of that simple statement. His current course of action, the one that had him accumulating gas in his intestinal tract, indeed began with meat. Specifically, the meat in Moeller's Meats, the third-generation butcher shop Dirk's father owned. It was into this shop, nearly 40 years ago now, that Faj-win-Getag, the Nidu ambassador, came bursting through the door, trailing an entourage of Nidu and human diplomats behind him. "Something smells really good," the Nidu ambassador said.

The ambassador's pronouncement was notable in itself. The Nidu, among their many physical qualities, were possessed of a sense of smell several orders of magnitude more fine than the poor human nose. For this reason, and for reasons relating to the Nidu caste structure, which is rigid enough to make 16th-century Japan appear the very model of let-it-all-hang-out egalitarianism, the higher diplomatic and political Nidu castes had developed a "language" of scents not at all unlike the way the European nobles of Earth developed a "language" of flowers.

Like the noble language of flowers, the Nidu diplomatic scent language was not true speech, in that one couldn't actually carry on a conversation through smells. Also, humans couldn't take much advantage of this language; the human sense of smell was so crude that Nidu trying to send a scent signal would get the same reaction from their intended recipient as they would get by singing an aria to a turtle. But among the Nidu themselves, one could make a compelling opening statement, sent in a subtle way (inasmuch as smells are subtle) and presenting an underpinning for all discourse to follow.

When a Nidu ambassador bursts through one's shop door proclaiming something smells good, that's a statement that works on several different levels. One, something probably just smells good. But two, something in the shop has a smell that carries with it certain positive scent identifications for the Nidu. James Moeller, proprietor of Moeller's Meats, Dirk's father, was not an especially worldly man, but he knew enough to know that getting on the Nidu ambassador's good side could mean the difference between his shop's success and its failure. It was hard enough running a dedicated butcher shop in a largely vegetarian world. But now that more of the relatively few meat enthusiasts remaining ate the newly arrived vatted meat—which James vehemently refused to stock, to the point of chasing a Kingston's Vatted Meat wholesaler from his store with a cleaver—things were getting precarious. The Nidu, James Moeller knew, were committed carnivores. They had to get their vittles from somewhere, and James Moeller was a man of business. Everybody's money was equal in his eyes.

"I smelled it down the street," Faj-win-Getag continued, approaching the counter display. "It smelled fresh. It smelled different."

"The ambassador has a good nose," James Moeller said. "In the back of the shop I've got venison, arrived just today from Michigan. It's deer meat."

"I know deer," Faj-win-Getag said. "Large animals. They fling themselves at vehicles with great frequency."

"That's them," James Moeller said.

"They don't smell like what I smell when they're on the side of the road," Faj-win-Getag said.

"They sure don't!" James Moeller said. "Would you like a better smell of the venison?" Faj-win-Getag nodded his assent; James told his son Dirk to bring out some. James presented it to the Nidu ambassador.

"That smells wonderful," Faj-win-Getag said. "It's very much like a scent that in our custom equates with sexual potency. This meat would be very popular with our young men."

James Moeller cracked a grin wide as the Potomac. "It would honor me to present the ambassador with some venison, with my compliments," he said, shooing Dirk into the back to bring out more of the meat. "And I'll be happy to serve any of your people who would want some of their own. We have quite a bit in stock."

"I'll be sure to let my staff know," Faj-win-Getag said. "You say you get your stock from Michigan?"

"Sure do," James said. "There's a large preserve in central Michigan run by the Nugentians. They harvest deer and other animals through ritual bow hunting. Legend has it the cult's founder bow-hunted one of every species of North American mammal before he died. They have his body on display at the preserve. He's in a loincloth. It's a religious thing. Not the sort of people you want to spend a lot of time with on a *personal* basis, but their meat is the best in the country. It costs a little more, but it's worth it. And they have the right attitude about meat—it's the cornerstone of any truly healthy diet."

"Most humans we meet don't eat much meat," Faj-win-Getag said. "What I read in your newspapers and magazines suggests most people find it unhealthy."

"Don't believe it," James Moeller said. "I eat meat at every meal. I have more energy physically and mentally than most men half my age. I've got nothing against vegetarians; if they want to eat beans all the time, that's fine with me. But long after they're asleep in their bed, I'm still going strong. That's meat for you. It all starts with meat—that's what I tell my customers. That's what I'll tell you." Dirk returned from the back with several large packages of meat; James put them in a heavy-duty bag and placed it on the low counter on the side. "All yours, sir. You enjoy that."

"You are too generous," Faj-win-Getag said, as a flunky took the bag. "We are always warmed by such hospitality from your race, who is always so giving. It makes us happy that we'll soon be in the neighborhood."

"How do you mean?" James Moeller said.

"The Nidu have entered into a number of new treaties and trade agreements with your government, which requires us to greatly expand our presence here," the ambassador said. "We'll be building our new mission grounds in this neighborhood."

"That's great," James Moeller said. "Will the embassy be close by?"

"Oh, very close," Faj-win-Getag said, and nodded his good-byes, taking his venison and his entourage with him.

James Moeller didn't waste time. Over the next week he tripled his order of venison from the Nugentians and sent Dirk to the library to find out anything he could about Nidu and their culinary preferences. This led to James ordering rabbit, Kobe beef, imported haggis from Scotland, and, for the very first time in the three-generation history shop, stocking Spam. "It's not vatted meat," he said to Dirk. "Just meat in a can."

Within a week, James Moeller had transformed his butcher shop into a Nidu-friendly meat store. Indeed, the enlarged shipment of Nugentian venison arrived the very same day that James Moeller received his notice via certified mail that the building that housed Moeller Meats was being seized by the government under eminent domain, along with every other building on the block, to make way for the new and enlarged Nidu embassy. James Moeller's receipt of this letter was also neatly coincident to a massive heart attack that killed him so fast that he was dead before he hit the floor, letter still in his hand, venison still un-butchered in the cold room in the back.

Dr. Atkinson tried to assure Dirk that the shock of the letter in itself would not have been enough to kill his father. James's aorta, he explained, was like a cannoli solidly packed with lard, the end result of 53 years of uninterrupted meat consumption. Dr. Atkinson had warned James for years to eat a more balanced diet or at least to allow him to snake out his arteries with an injection of plaque 'bots, but James always refused; he felt fine, he liked his meat, and he wasn't going to sign off on any medical procedure that would give his insurance company the ammunition it needed to raise his rates. James had been a heart attack waiting to happen. If it wasn't now, it would have been soon. Very soon.

Dirk heard none of this. He knew who was responsible. He had found his father's body, had read the note, and had learned later that the day after the Nidu visited Moeller's Meats, a Nidu representative flew to the Nugentian preserve in Michigan to seal a direct venison distribution deal with the cult, using the information James Moeller innocently supplied in conversation. The Nidu ambassador knew when it came through the shop door that Moeller's Meats would be out of business in a matter of days, and he let Dirk's father give him free meat and information without so much of a hint of what was coming down the road.

It was just as well his dad had the heart attack when he did, Dirk thought to himself. Seeing his grandfather's shop torn down would have killed him otherwise.

History and literature are filled with heroes called upon to revenge the deaths of their fathers. Dirk took to this same task with a grim methodical drive, over a span of time that would have made Hamlet, the very archetype of obsessive-compulsive deliberation, utterly insane with impatience. With the compensation provided by the government for the Moeller's Meats property, Dirk enrolled at Johns Hopkins, down the road in Baltimore, majoring in interplanetary relations. Hopkins's program was one of the top three in the nation, along with Chicago and Georgetown.

Moeller did his graduate work at the latter, gaining access to the intensely competitive program by agreeing to specialize in the

Garda, a seasonally-intelligent race of tube worms whose recent mission to Earth was housed on the former grounds of the Naval Observatory. However, shortly after Moeller begun his study, the Garda began their Incompetence, a period of engorgement, mating, and lessened brain activity coinciding with the onset of Uu-uchi, an autumnal season on Gard which would last for three years and seven months on Earth. Because Moeller was able to work with the Garda for only a limited period of time, he was allowed to pursue a secondary track of research as well. He chose the Nidu.

It was after Moeller's first major paper on the Nidu, analyzing their role in helping the United Nations of Earth gain a representative seat in the Common Confederation, that Moeller came in contact with Anton Schroeder, the UNE's observer and later first full-fledged representative to the CC. He'd left that behind to become the current chairman of the American Institute for Colonization, a think tank based out of Arlington committed to the expansion of the Earth's colonization of planets, with or without the consent of the Common Confederation.

"I read your paper, Mr. Moeller," Schroeder said, without introduction, when Moeller picked up his office communicator; Schroeder assumed (correctly) that Moeller would recognize the voice made famous by thousands of speeches, news reports, and Sunday morning talk shows. "It is remarkably full of shit, but it is remarkably full of shit in a number of interesting ways, some of which—and entirely coincidentally, I'm sure—get close to the truth of our situation with the Nidu and the Common Confederation. Would you like to know which those are?"

"Yes, sir," Moeller said.

"I'm sending a car over now," Schroeder said. "It'll be there in half an hour to bring you here. Wear a tie."

An hour later Moeller was drinking from the informational and ideological fire hose that was Anton Schroeder, the one man who knew the Nidu better than any other human being. In the course of his decades of dealing with the Nidu, Schroeder had come to the following conclusion: The Nidu are fucking with us. It's time we start fucking back. Moeller didn't need to be asked twice to join in.

"Here come the Nidu," said Alan, rising from his seat. Moeller gulped the last of his milk and rose, just in time to have a bubble of gas twist his intestine like a sailor knotting a Sheepshank. Moeller bit his cheek and did his best to ignore the cramp. It wouldn't do to have the Nidu delegation aware of his gastric distress.

The Nidu filed into the conference room as they always did, lowest in the pecking order first, heading to their assigned seats and nodding to their opposite human number on the other side of the table. Nobody moved to shake hands; the Nidu, intensely socially stratified as they were, weren't the sort of race to enjoy wanton familiar person contact. The chairs were filled, from the outside in, until only two people remained standing; at the middle seats on opposite sides, were Moeller and the senior-most Nidu trade delegate in the room, Lars-win-Getag.

Who was, as it happened, son of Faj-win-Getag, the Nidu ambassador who walked through the door of Moeller's Meats four decades earlier. This was not entirely coincidence; all Nidu diplomats of any rank on Earth hailed from the win-Getag clan, a minor, distaff relation to the current royal clan of auf-Getag. Faj-win-Getag was famously fecund, even for a Nidu, so his children littered the diplomatic corps on Earth.

But it was both satisfying and convenient for Moeller regardless—fitting, he thought, that the son of James Moeller would return the favor of failure to the son of Faj-win-Getag. Moeller didn't believe in karma, but he believed in its idiot cousin, the idea that "what goes around, comes around." The Moellers were coming around at last.

Ironic in another way, Moeller thought, as he waited for Lars-win-Getag to speak in greeting. This round of trade negotiations between the Nidu and Earth was supposed to have broken down long before this level. Moeller and his compatriots had quietly planned and maneuvered for years to get Nidu-human relations to a breaking point; this was supposed to be the year trade relationships implode, alliances dissolve, anti-Nidu demonstrations swell, and the human planets start their path to true independence outside the Common Confederation.

A new president and his Nidu-friendly administration had screwed it up; the new Secretary of Trade had replaced too many delegates and the new delegates had been too willing to give up diplomatic real estate in the quest to renormalize Nidu relations. Now negotiations were too far down the road to manufacture a diplomatic objection; all those had been hammered out two or three levels down. Something else was needed to bring negotiations to standstill. Preferably something that made the Nidu look bad.

"Dirk," Lars-win-Getag said, and bowed, briefly. "A good morning to you. Are we ready to begin today's thumb twisting?" He smiled, which on a Nidu is sort of a ghastly thing, amused at his own inside joke. Lars-win-Getag fancied himself a bit of a wit, and his specialty was creating malapropisms based on English slang. He had seen an alien do it once in a pre-Encounter movie, and thought it was cute. It was the sort of joke that got old fast.

"By all means, Lars," Moeller said, and returned the bow, risking a small cramp to do so. "Our thumbs are at ready."

"Excellent." Lars-win-Getag sat and reached for his negotiation schedule. "Are we still working on agricultural quotas?"

Moeller glanced over to Alan, who had made up the schedule. "We're talking bananas and plantains until ten, and then we tackle wine and table grapes until lunch," Alan said. "Then in afternoon we start on livestock quotas. We begin with sheep."

"Do *ewe* think that's a good idea?" Lars-win-Getag said, turning to Moeller to dispense another ghastly grin. Lars-win-Getag was also inordinately fond of puns.

"That's quite amusing, sir," Alan said, gamely.

From down the table, one of the Nidu piped up. "We have some small concerns about the percentage of bananas the treaty requires come from Ecuador. We were led to understand a banana virus had destroyed much of the crop this last year." From down the table, a member of the human delegation responded. The negotiations would continue to burble on for the next hour at the far ends of the table. Alan and his opposite number with the Nidu would ride herd on the others. Lars-win-Getag was already bored and scanning his tablet for sport scores. Moeller satisfied himself that his active participation would not be required for a long period of time and then tapped his own tablet to boot up the apparatus.

It was Lars-win-Getag himself who inspired the apparatus. Lars-win-Getag was, to put it mildly, an underachiever; he was a mid-level trade negotiator while most of his siblings had gone on to better things. It had been suggested that the only reason Lars-win-Getag was even a mid-level trade negotiator was that his family was too important for him to be anything less; it would be an insult to his clan to have him fail.

To that end Lars-win-Getag was policed by assistants who were notably smarter than he was, and was never given anything critical to work on. Largely predetermined agricultural and livestock quotas, for example, were just about his speed. Fortunately for Lars-win-Getag, he wasn't really smart enough to realize he was being handled by his own government. So it worked out well for everyone.

Nevertheless, like intellectually limited mid-rangers of most sentient species, Lars-win-Getag was acutely sensitive to matters of personal status. He also had a temper. If it weren't for diplomatic immunity, Lars-win-Getag's rap sheet would include assault, aggravated assault, battery, and on at least one occasion, attempted homicide. It was the last of these that caught the eye of Jean Schroeder, the son of the late Anton Schroeder and his successor as the head of the American Institute for Colonization.

"Listen to this," Jean said, reading from a report his assistant had compiled, as Moeller grilled steaks for them on his deck. "Six years ago, Lars was at a Capitals game and had to be restrained from choking another spectator to death in the stadium bathroom. Other guys in the bathroom literally had to tackle him and sit on his big reptilian ass until the police came."

"Why was he choking that guy?" Moeller asked.

"The guy was standing at the sink next to Lars and used some breath spray," Schroeder said. "Lars smelled it and got crazy. He told the police the scent of the breath spray suggested that he enjoyed cornholing his mother. He felt honor bound to avenge the insult."

Moeller stabbed the steaks and flipped them. "He should have known better. Most humans don't know anything about what smells mean to the Nidu elites."

"Should know better, but doesn't," Jean said, riffing through the report. "Or just doesn't care, which is more likely. He's got diplomatic immunity. He doesn't have to worry about restraining himself. Two of his other near-arrests involve arguments about smells. Here, this one's good: He apparently assaulted a flower vendor on the mall because one of the bouquets was telling him he kicked babies. That was just last year."

"It probably had daisies in it," Moeller said, poking at the steaks again. "Daisies have a smell that signifies offspring. Where are you going with this, Jean?"

"You start negotiations with Lars next week," Jean said. "It's too late to change the substance of the negotiations. But you're negotiating with someone who is neither terribly bright nor terribly stable, and has a documented tendency to fly into a rage when he thinks he's being insulted by an odor. There's got to be a way to work with that."

"I don't see how," Moeller said. He speared the steaks and put them on a serving plate. "It's policy at Trade to be respectful of Nidu sensitivities. Negotiations take place in rooms with special air filters. We don't wear cologne or perfumes—we're not even supposed to use scented underarm deodorant. Hell, we're even issued special soap to use in the shower. We're serious about it, too. The first year I was at Trade, I saw a negotiator sent home because he used Zest that morning. He actually received a reprimand."

"Well, obviously you're not going to walk in with a squirt bottle with Essence of Fuck You in it," Jean said. "But there's got to be some way it make it happen."

"Look," Moeller said. "Lars's dad gave my dad a heart attack. Nothing would make me happier than to derail the bastard. But there's no way to secretly stink him into a rage."

Two days later Jean sent him a message: *Something smells interesting*, it read.

Back at the negotiating table, the Nidu had gotten the Earth delegation to take out the Ecuadorian bananas in exchange for the same percentage of bananas to be shipped from Philos colony. This made everyone happy since Philos was closer to Nidu than Earth, and the Philos plantation owners would accept a lower price for their bananas, and the Earth wanted to promote colonial trade anyway. Moeller nodded his approval, Lars-win-Getag grunted his assent, and the negotiations moved on to Brazilian bananas.

Moeller opened the window for the apparatus software on his tablet and tapped on the "message" toolbar command. The window immediately listed four categories: Mild insults, Sexual-related insults, Competence insults, and Grave insults. Fixer, who had designed the apparatus and adapted the off-the-shelf software to run it, found a chemical dictionary for the Nidu smell language from the science library at UCLA. He dispensed with everything but the insults, of course; Moeller wasn't planning to tell Lars-win-Getag that he looked pretty, or that it was time for his puberty rites. Moeller also immediately discounted insults about competence, as the incompetent never question their competence about anything. *Let's start small,* Moeller thought, and selected the "Mild insults" option. Another window opened with 40 suggested insults; Moeller picked the one at the top of the list, which read, simply, *You stink.*

The touch screen presented an hourglass, and in his colon Moeller felt a tiny vibration as the apparatus moved elements around. Then a dialog window popped up. *Processing enabled,* it read. *Fire when ready.*

Moeller was ready almost instantly; the combination of the milk and the vegetables and bacon at breakfast had worked their wonders in the gastrointestinal tract. Carefully so as not to attract attention, Moeller shifted in his seat to help the process along. He felt the gas travel the few centimeters into the apparatus chamber. The dialog box changed: *Processing,* it read. Moeller felt a second small vibration in the apparatus as the middle chamber worked its magic. After about five seconds the vibration stopped and the dialog box changed again. *Ready. Choose automatic or manual release.* Moeller chose the automatic release. The dialog box began a countdown.

Ten seconds later the lightly compressed gas exited the apparatus and moved toward the final exit. Moeller was not especially worried about it making noise; one doesn't work for decades in the diplomatic corps and its endless meetings and negotiations without learning how to silently depressurize. Moeller leaned forward ever so slightly and let it out. It smelled vaguely like parsley.

About 20 seconds later Lars-win-Getag, who had been giving every appearance of drifting off to sleep, jolted himself straight up in his chair, alarming his aides on either side. One of them leaned in close to find out what had disturbed her boss; Lars-win-Getag hissed quietly but emphatically at her. She listened to him for a few minutes, then arched her nose up and gave a brief but notable sniff. Then she looked at Lars-win-Getag and gave the Nidu equivalent of a shrug, as if to say, *I don't smell anything.* Lars-win-Getag glared and glanced over at Moeller, who had all this time stared down the table toward the banana discussion with an expression of polite boredom. The air scrubbers were already dissipating the odor. Eventually Lars-win-Getag calmed down.

A few minutes later Moeller let fly *You mate with the unclean.* Lars-win-Getag let out a grunt and slammed down a fist hard enough to rattle the entire table. Negotiations came to a halt as everyone at the table looked toward Lars-win-Getag, who was by now out of his seat and whispering fiercely to the rather nervous-looking aide to his right.

"Everything okay?" Moeller asked the second aide, to Lars-win-Getag's left.

The second aide barely twitched. "The trade representative is clearly troubled by the quality of Brazilian bananas," he said.

Lars-win-Getag had managed to sit himself back down. "My apologies," he said swiveling his head up and down the table. "Something caught me by surprise."

"We can discuss changing the percentage of Brazilian bananas if you feel strongly about it," Moeller said, mildly. "I'm sure the Panamanians would be happy to increase their percentage, and we can make it up to the Brazilians in other categories." He reached for his tablet as if to make a note of the change and in fact gave the order to process *You bathe in vomit.*

"That is acceptable," Lars-win-Getag said, in a low growl. Moeller nudged Alan to get the discussions going again, and in doing so maneuvered just enough to let the latest missive slip out. Twenty seconds later, Moeller noted Lars-win-Getag breathing heavily and struggling not to explode. His aide was patting his hand, only a little frantically.

The next hour was the most fun Moeller could remember having just about ever. He taunted Lars-win-Getag mercilessly, safe in his own appearance of bland disinterest in the minutiae of the negotiations, the visible absence of a scent-emitting object anywhere in the room, and the Nidu assumption that humans, with their primitive sense of smell, could not possibly be intentionally goading them. Except for Lars-win-Getag, the Nidu were of the wrong caste to know anything more than the basics of the scent language and so could not share their boss's outrage. Except for Moeller, the human delegation was utterly ignorant of the cause of Lars-win-Getag's behavior. They could tell something was making the Nidu twitchy, but had no idea what it could be. The only person who noticed anything unusual was Alan, who by sheer proximity could tell his boss was gassy. But Moeller knew that the ambitious little squirt wouldn't dream of saying anything about it.

In this garden of ignorance, Moeller savaged Lars-win-Getag with intolerable insults about his sexual performance, his personal grooming, and his family, often in combinations of all three. Fixer's apparatus was filled with enough of the trace chemical compounds needed to combine with Moeller's own tract emanations that he could theoretically emit coherent gaseous statements for days. Moeller experimented to discover which statements enraged Lars-win-Getag the most; as expected, insults about job competence barely caused a rise in respiratory rates, but suggestions of sexual inadequacy really seemed to get him hot. Moeller thought Lars-win-Getag was going to pop when *Your mates laugh at your lack of seed* wafted over to him, but he managed to hold it in, primarily by gripping the table hard enough that Moeller thought he might break part of it off.

Moeller had just released *You feast on shit* and just punched in *Your mother fucks algae* for processing when Lars-win-Getag finally lost it, and gave himself to the negotiation-halting rage that Moeller was hoping for. "That is enough!" he bellowed, and lunged across the table at Alan, who, for his part, was shocked into immobility at a large, sentient lizardlike creature launching itself at him.

"Is it you?" Lars-win-Getag demanded, as his assistants grabbed at his legs, trying to haul him back to his side of the table.

"Is *what* me?" Alan managed to spurt out, torn now between the urge to get away from this snappy angry creature and the desire not to endanger his young diplomatic career by accidentally scratching the Nidu trade delegate in his rush to avoid getting killed.

Lars-win-Getag pushed Alan back onto the floor and kicked himself free of his assistants. "One of you humans has been insulting me for over an hour! I can *smell* it."

The humans stared agog at Lars-win-Getag for ten full seconds. Then Alan broke the silence. "All right, guys," he said, looking up and down the table. "Who's wearing the scented deodorant?"

"I'm not smelling *deodorant,* you little shit," Lars-win-Getag snarled. "I know one of you is speaking to me. *Insulting* me. I will not *tolerate* it."

"Sir," Alan said. "If one of us have said something that offended you during the talks, I can promise you—"

"*Promise* me?" Lars-win-Getag bellowed. "I can promise *you* that every one of you is going to be working at a convenience store in twenty-four hours if you don't—"

Squeeeeeeeeeeeeeeeee.

Silence. Moeller was suddenly aware that the entire room was looking at him.

"Excuse me," Moeller said. "That was rude."

There was a little more silence after that.

"*You,*" Lars-win-Getag said, finally. "It was *you.* All this *time.*"

"I don't know what you're talking about," Moeller said.

"I will have your job for this," Lars-win-Getag exploded. "When I get through with you, you—" Lars-win-Getag stopped suddenly, distracted. Then he took a long, hard snort. Moeller's final message had finally gotten across the room to him.

Lars-win-Getag took full receipt of the message, processed it, and decided to kill Dirk Moeller right there, with his own hands. Fortunately, there was a Nidu ritual for justifiably killing a nemesis; it began with a violent, soul-shattering roar. Lars-win-Getag collected himself, draw in a deep, cleansing breath, focused his eyes on Dirk Moeller, and began his murderous yell.

One of the interesting things about alien life is that however alien it may be, certain physical features appear again and again, examples of parallel evolutionary paths on multiple worlds. For example, nearly every intelligent form of life has a brain—a central processor, of some sort, for whatever nervous and sensory system it may have evolved. The location of the brain varies, but it is most frequently located in a head of some sort. Likewise, nearly all life of a complex nature features a circulatory system to ferry oxygen and nutrients around the body.

The combination of these two common features means that certain medical phenomena are also universally known. Like strokes, caused when the vessels of whatever circulatory system a creature might have rupture violently in whatever brain structure that creature might possess. Just as they did in Lars-win-Getag, less than a second into his bellowing declaration. Lars-win-Getag was surprised as anyone when he cut short his bellow, replaced it with a wet gurgle, and then pitched forward dead, following his center of gravity down to the floor. The Nidu immediately swarmed their fallen leader; the humans stared slack-jawed at their negotiating partners, who by now had begun a keening wail of despair as they attempted to revive Lars-win-Getag's body.

Alan turned to Moeller, who was still sitting there, calmly, taking it all in. "Sir?" Alan said. "What just happened here, sir? What's going on? Sir?"

Moeller turned to Alan, opened his mouth to provide some perfectly serviceable lie, and burst out laughing.

Another common feature among many species is a primary circulatory pump—a heart, in other words. This pump is typically one of the strongest muscles in any creature, due to the need to keep circulatory fluid moving through the body. But like any muscle it is prone to damage, especially when the creature to whom the pump belongs takes rather bad care of it. And, say, eats a lot of fatty, plaque-inducing meat, which causes the circulatory vessels to cut off, suffocating the muscle itself.

Just as they did in Dirk Moeller.

Dirk Moeller collapsed on the floor, still laughing, joining Lars-win-Getag in a fatally prone sprawl. He was dimly aware of Alan shouting his name and then placing his hands on his chest and pumping down furiously, in a valiant but fruitless attempt to squeeze blood through his boss's body.

As Moeller lost consciousness for the last time, he had time for a single, final request for absolution. *Jesus, forgive me,* he thought. *I really shouldn't have eaten that panda.*

The rest is darkness, two dead bodies on the floor, and, as hoped, a major diplomatic incident.

chapter

2

Secretary of State Jim Heffer regarded the tube on his desk. "So this is it?" he asked his aide, Ben Javna.

"That's it," Javna said. "Fresh from the schmuck's large intestine."

Heffer shook his head. "What an asshole," he said.

"An apt description, considering," Javna said.

Heffer sighed, reached for the tube, then stopped. "This isn't *fresh*, is it?"

Javna grinned. "It's been sanitized for your protection, Mr. Secretary. It had been grafted onto Moeller's colon. All the organic bits have been removed. Inside and out."

"Who knows this exists?"

"Aside from whoever helped Moeller put it in? You, me, and the medical examiner. The ME is content to keep quiet for now, although he wants State to bring a cousin over from Pakistan.

Alan suspects something, of course. That's why he called me right after it happened."

"A former intern turns out to be useful for a change," Heffer said. He picked up the tube, turned it around in his hands. "Have we figured out where this thing has come from yet?"

"No, sir," Javna said. "We haven't started a search because, officially, it doesn't exist. So far as anyone knows officially, Moeller and the Nidu trade representative rather coincidentally collapsed simultaneously for unrelated health reasons. Which *is* true, as far as it goes."

It was Heffer's turn to grin. "And just how long do we expect that story to hold up, Ben?"

"It's already collapsing, of course," Javna said. "But at this point the only thing anyone has to go on are rumors and speculations. We start searching for plans for *that*,"—Javna pointed to the tube—"and you know it's going to get noticed."

"I think we could keep the search out of the papers," Heffer said.

"It's not the papers we need to worry about," Javna said. "You know Pope and his creeps at Defense are going to be all over this, and they'll even find some way to try to make it seem like it's the Nidu's fault."

"On one level, that'd be nice," Heffer said.

"Sure, right until the part where we start shooting at the Nidu and then they kick our ass," Javna said.

"There is that," Heffer admitted.

"There is indeed that," Javna said.

Heffer's intercom switched on. "Mr. Secretary, Secretary Soram is here," said Heffer's scheduler, Jane.

"Send him in, Jane," Heffer said, stood up, then turned to Javna. "Well, here comes the idiot," he said. Javna grinned.

Secretary of Trade Ted Soram came through the door, brisk

and grinning and extending his hand. "Hello, Jim," he said. "Missed you this weekend at the house."

Heffer reached across the desk and shook Soram's hand. "Hello, Ted," Heffer said. "I was in Switzerland this weekend. Middle East peace negotiations. You may have read something about them."

"Ouch," Soram said, good-naturedly, and off to the side, Heffer could see Javna roll his eyes. "Okay, I admit, a good excuse for your absence. This time. How did the negotiations go?"

"As they usually do," Heffer said, motioning to Soram to sit. "Right down to obligatory suicide bomber in Haifa halfway through the session."

"They never learn," Soram said, nestling into an armchair.

"I guess not," Heffer said, sitting himself. "But right now I'm less concerned about the peace negotiations in the Middle East than the Nidu trade negotiations here at home."

"What about them?" Soram said.

Heffer glanced over at Javna, who subtly shrugged. "Ted," Heffer said, "have you been in contact with your staff today?"

"I've been at Lansdowne since dawn," Soram said. "With the Kanh ambassador. It loves to golf there, and I have a membership. I've been trying to get them to agree to import more almonds. We've got a glut. So I thought I'd lobby it on the links. My staff knows better than to disturb me when I'm working on something like that. I almost chewed out your gal until I realized she was calling from your department, not mine."

Heffer sat there for about a beat and wondered again at the political calculus that required President Webster to appoint Soram as trade secretary. The Kanh were violently allergic to nuts. The first state dinner ever held for the Kanh ended in disaster because kitchen inadvertently used peanut oil in one of the entrees; two-thirds of the Kanh guests ruptured their digestive sacs. The fact that Soram would lobby the Kanh to import almonds was a testament to his cluelessness, and the willingness of the Kanh ambassador (who was emphatically not clueless) to capitalize on his stupidity for a couple rounds of choice golf.

Well, we needed Philadelphia and he delivered, Heffer thought. *Too late to worry about it now.* "Ted," Heffer said. "There's been a development. A rather serious one. One of your trade representatives died today during negotiations. So did one of the Nidu representatives. And we think our guy killed the Nidu representative before he died."

Soram smiled, uncertainly. "I'm not following you, Jim."

Heffer slid the tube across the desk to Soram. "He used this," Heffer said. "We're pretty sure it's a device used to send chemical signals the Nidu could smell and interpret through a code of theirs. We think your guy hid this until he got into the room, and then used it to enrage the Nidu negotiator into a stroke. He had a heart attack right after. He died laughing, Ted. It didn't look very good."

Soram took the tube. "Where was he hiding it?" he asked.

"In his ass," Ben Javna said.

Soram jerked and dropped the thing on the floor, then smiled sheepishly and placed it back on the desk. "Sorry," he said. "How do you know all this, Jim? This is a trade problem."

Heffer took the tube and put it into his desk. "Ted, when one of your guys kills off a Nidu diplomat, trade or otherwise, it pretty much *becomes* my problem, now, doesn't it? We here at State have a vested interest in making sure that trade negotiations with the Nidu run smoothly. And I know you're not exactly the most 'hands on' of Trade secretaries. So we over here have been keeping tabs on how things have been going."

"I see," Soram said.

"Having said that," Heffer said, "I have to admit this one took us by surprise. Trade is fairly packed with anti-Nidu negotiators and has been for years, even after this administration took over. But *this* is new. We expected some of your minor functionaries to put in a few roadblocks. We were ready for that. We *weren't* ready for one of your people to attempt murder to gum up the works."

"We got rid of the biggest troublemakers," Soram said. "We went right down the list and pried them out."

"You missed one, Ted," Heffer said.

"Who was this guy?" Soram asked.

"Dirk Moeller," Javna said. "Came in during the Griffin administration. He was at the American Institute for Colonization before that."

"I've never heard of him," Soram said.

"Really," Javna said, dryly.

Even Soram couldn't miss that. "Look, don't try to pin this on me," he said. "We *got* most of them. But a few are going to get through the net."

"A spell at the AIC should have been a red flag," Heffer said. "That place is full of anti-Nidu nutbags."

The intercom flicked back on. "Sir, Secretary Pope is here," Jane said.

"Speaking of anti-Nidu nutbags," Javna said, under his breath.

"He says it's urgent," Jane continued.

"Send him in, Jane," Heffer said, then turned to Javna. "Behave, Ben."

"Yes, sir," Javna said.

Every administration crosses the aisle to appoint one secretary from the other side. Robert Pope, war hero and popular former senator from Idaho, was the sop thrown to swing voters who needed convincing the Webster administration was strong on defense, and would stand up to Common Confederation pressure when necessary, particularly when it was applied by the Nidu. Pope played the part a little too enthusiastically for Heffer's taste.

"Bob," Heffer said, as Pope entered the room, trailing his aide, Dave Phipps. "Dropping by on your way back to the Pentagon?"

"You might say that," Pope said, and then glanced over at Soram. "I see you've got the brain trust here already."

"Missed you this weekend, Bob," Soram said.

"Ted, you know I wouldn't be caught dead at one of your parties," Pope said, "so let's not pretend I would be. I understand you hit a little roadblock in today's negotiations."

"Jim was just catching me up on that," Soram said.

"Well," Pope said. "Nice to see someone's minding the shop over there at Trade. Even if it is the State Department. Strange that two chief negotiators should die within seconds of each other, don't you think."

"The universe is filled with disturbing coincidences, Bob," Heffer said.

"And you think coincidence is what this was."

"At the moment, that's the official line," Heffer said. "Although of course we'll let you know if anything comes out. We're hoping to catch this while it's still a minor diplomatic issue, Bob. Nothing you folks at Defense need to worry about."

"That's reassuring to hear, Jim," Pope said. "Except that it may already be a little late for that." Pope nodded to Phipps, who pulled papers from a folder he was bearing and handed them to Heffer.

"What are these?" Heffer asked, taking the papers and reaching for his glasses.

"Intercepts from the Nidu Naval Attaché's office, dated thirty-six minutes after our respective trade representatives hit the floor," Pope said. "About two hours after that, we know two Nidu *Glar*-class destroyers got new orders."

"Do you know what the orders are?" Heffer asked.

"They were encrypted," Pope said.

"So they could be anything, including something entirely un-related to our little problem," Heffer said.

"They could be," Pope said. "There is the minor matter that these new orders came directly from the Nidu Supreme Commander rather than through the admiralty."

"What does that mean?" Soram asked.

"It means that orders aren't going through the chain of command, Ted," Heffer said. "It means that whatever the Nidu have going, they want to start working on it fast." Heffer turned to Javna. "Are the Nidu having any other extracurricular squabbles that would warrant new orders to those destroyers?"

"I can't think of anything offhand," Javna said. "They have that low-grade border war going with the Andde, but they've been in a détente phase for a few months now. It's not likely they'd ratchet back up without the Andde doing something stupid first. Let me check on that, though."

"In the meantime, I have to work on the assumption that what happened today at Trade is a proximate cause," Pope said. "And that the Nidu may be in the initial stages of something more than a diplomatic response."

"Have you shared this with the president?" Heffer asked.

"He's in St. Louis, reading to kindergarteners," Pope said. "I spoke to Roger. He suggested that on the way back to the Pentagon, I stop by and give you a heads-up. He said this is something that warranted a personal social call."

Heffer nodded. Roger probably also suggested to Pope that he'd be following up with Heffer shortly thereafter, which was undoubtedly the only reason Pope was actually in his office. This is one of the nice things about having your brother-in-law as the president's chief of staff; if Roger let Heffer get sandbagged, he'd never hear the end of it from the missus. The Heffers were a loyal clan.

"Can I see those intercepts?" Soram asked.

"Later, Ted," Heffer said. "Bob, what are you planning to do with that information?"

"Well, that depends," Pope said. "I can't just do nothing, of course. If we have two Nidu destroyers on their way, we need to be prepared to respond."

"The Nidu are our allies, you know," Heffer said. "Have been for decades, despite attempts in recent years to have it otherwise."

"Jim, I don't give a shit about the politics of the situation," Pope said, and Heffer caught Javna performing another subtle eyeroll. "I care about where those destroyers are heading and why. If you know something I don't, then by all means enlighten me. But from where I'm standing, two dead trade representatives plus two Nidu destroyers equals the Nidu doing something I need to worry about."

Heffer's intercom piped up again. "Sir, the Nidu ambassador is here. He says it's—"

"—Urgent, yes, I know," Heffer said. "Tell him I'll be right with him." He flipped off the intercom, and stood up. "Gentlemen, I need the room. All things considered, you should probably exit out through the conference room. It might make the ambassador nervous if he saw the secretaries of Trade and Defense coming out the door."

"Jim," Pope said. "If you know something, I need to know it. Sooner than later."

"I understand, Bob. Give me a little time to work this. If the Nidu see us gearing up for something, it's going to complicate matters. A little time, Bob."

Pope glanced over at Soram, and then at Javna before looking back to Heffer. "A little time, Jim. But don't make me have to explain to the president why we've got two Nidu destroyers parked in orbit and nothing to counter them with. You won't like the explanation I'll give him. Gentlemen." Pope and Phipps exited out through the conference room.

Soram stood up. "What should I be doing now?" he asked. Soram was normally the picture of clueless confidence, but even he was aware he was in over his head at the moment.

"Ted, I need to you to keep quiet on what I've told you today," Heffer said. Soram nodded. "The longer we keep this thing officially a coincidence, the longer we've got to make this turn out all right. I'm going to have some people come around and take a look through Moeller's office. Make sure no one touches anything until they get there. I mean *no one*, Ted. Ben here will make the arrangements and give you the names so you can be sure. Until then, stay calm, appear unconcerned, and don't overthink this."

"Just be yourself, Mr. Secretary," Javna said. Soram smiled wanly and let himself out.

"Just be yourself," Heffer said, to Javna. "Nice."

"Will all due respect, Mr. Secretary," Javna said. "The last thing you want at this point is Soram trying to grow a brain. You've already got Pope to deal with."

"That son of a bitch Heffer," Pope said, settling into his limo. "He's got something he's not telling us."

Phipps was reading his mail on his communicator. "There's nothing new on the State Department comm bugs," he said. "There's the one call to Javna right after it happened, but it was from a wireless comm with standard encryption. We're still working on that. Then there's Heffer's office to Soram, telling him to get over to State. After that, nothing."

"Have we figured out where Javna went yet?" Pope asked.

"No," Phipps said. "His car's got a locator, but he took the

Metro. He used anonymous credit, so we can't trace him through his card."

"You don't have anything from the security cameras?"

"Our Metro Police camera guy got fired a week ago." Pope looked up for this; Phipps put up his hand. "Not because of us. He was doing a little freelance fundraising for the Police Retirement Fund and sending the contributions to his own account. Until we cultivate someone else, we'd have to get a warrant."

"Where are those destroyers?" Pope asked.

"Still docked, one at Dreaden, one at Inspir," Phipps said. "Both are taking on supplies. It'll be two or three days at least before either is underway."

Pope tapped his armrest and glanced back toward the State Department. "Heffer's meeting with the Nidu ambassador right now."

"Yes, sir," Phipps said.

"So where did you put the bug?" Pope asked.

"You'll love this," Phipps said. He opened his folder and handed his boss a copy of one of the intercepts he gave to Heffer.

Pope looked at the paper, read it. "I know all this already, Phipps."

"The paper is the bug, sir," Phipps said. "It activates when it leaves the folder. The paper picks up sound vibrations through the air and conduction through the desk. It converts the sound into an electrical signal that's recorded in magnetic molecules in the ink. The data is stored multiple times, so it survives shredding. You just wave a data reader over the paper and the information uploads. All we need to do is read the data before it gets to the incinerator."

"And you've set that up," Pope said.

"The incinerator plant is maintained by Navy, sir. It's not a problem. The drawback is that the information isn't live. But State sends a truck to the incinerator every night. We'll know what they're talking about soon enough."

Pope considered the paper in his hand. "Pretty sneaky shit, Dave."

"Your tax dollars at work, sir," Phipps said.

"We have a problem," said Narf-win-Getag, Nidu ambassador to Earth, settling into the chair recently occupied by Ted Soram. As was custom, he did not shake hands upon entering the room. "We think one of your trade representatives intentionally killed one of our trade representatives."

Heffer glanced over to Javna, who was handing the Nidu ambassador a cup of tea; both were wearing their best "this is disturbing news" looks. "This is disturbing news," Heffer said. "We know about the deaths, of course. But we were under the impression that the deaths were coincidental and accidental."

"The other members of the trade delegation report that prior to his death, Lars-win-Getag was complaining that he was being insulted through the *Devha,* which is an ancient Nidu code, transmitted by scent. As you know, we Nidu are extraordinarily sensitive to certain smells. We have reason to believe your representative, this Dirk Moeller, was sending these signals," Narf-win-Getag said.

"With all due respect, Mr. Ambassador," Heffer said. "Our files show your representative had a history of smelling insults when they weren't there."

"You're suggesting that this was all in his mind, then," Narf-win-Getag said.

"Not at all," Heffer said. "Just that he may have misinterpreted something he smelled as meaning something else."

"Possibly," Narf-win-Getag said. "However, I've been instructed by my government to ask for a member of our medical delegation to examine the body of Mr. Moeller. It would clear up the issue of misinterpretation, at the very least."

From behind the ambassador, Heffer saw Javna give an almost imperceptible shake of his head. "I wish I could, Mr. Ambassador," Heffer said. "Unfortunately, Mr. Moeller's religious practices require a rapid funeral ceremony. I'm afraid the body's already been sent for cremation."

"Unfortunate, indeed," Narf-win-Getag said. "As this is the case, I've been instructed to halt trade negotiations until such time as all present agreements can be reviewed to ensure there have been no other attempts to unduly influence the outcome."

"Surely you don't think the actions of one negotiator—if indeed he acted at all—reflect on the government, and in particular this administration," Heffer said.

"As much as we'd like to assume that, I don't know that we can," Narf-win-Getag said. "We are of course well aware of the rise in anti-Nidu activity within the government over the years— the small obstructions and objections that add up over time. We had hoped that the Webster administration would root out much of this antipathy and set our two peoples back on the course to friendship. But something like this calls into question the sincerity of your administration's efforts. The last two administrations were not particularly friendly to my nation, Mr. Secretary, for reasons passing understanding. But at least *they* didn't fart one of my diplomats to death."

"I'm sure we can work together to resolve this issue, Mr. Ambassador," Heffer said.

"I hope so. Indeed, I have a suggestion which will go a long way toward healing this potential rift." Narf-win-Getag took a sip from his tea.

"By all means, name it," Heffer said.

"As you know, the Nidu are in a time of transition," Narf-win-Getag said. "Wej-auf-Getag, our *Fehen,* our leader, died some six of your weeks ago. His son, Hubu-auf-Getag, has been chosen as our next *Fehen,* and will formally take power in a coronation ceremony about two weeks from now."

"Yes, of course. I will be traveling to Nidu for the coronation celebration, as our government's representative," Heffer said.

"How delightful," Narf-win-Getag said. "As you may *not* know, when the auf-Getag clan first came to power, it included an element into the coronation ceremony to symbolize the Earth, our great friend and ally."

"I didn't know that," Heffer admitted. "What was the symbol?"

"A sheep, Mr. Secretary."

Heffer stifled a grin. "A sheep, you say."

"Indeed," Narf-win-Getag said. "At a critical point in the ceremony, a sheep is sacrificed. Usually the sheep is taken from the auf-Getag clan herd. However, within a week of the death of Wej-auf-Getag, the clan herd was wiped out by a genetically modified anthrax bacteria. Obviously, it was sabotage, most likely by rival clans."

"Well, we've *got* sheep," Heffer said. "Hell, in New Zealand the sheep outnumber the people five to one. Why didn't you let us know sooner?"

"It would not have been wise to let the enemies of the auf-Getag clan know we were concerned," Narf-win-Getag said. "We assumed we could easily restock our herd once negotiations were completed. By the original schedule, negotiations would have been completed in the next two or three days, and we could have taken delivery of the sheep with ample time for the ceremony. It was not a crisis situation, or so we thought. But of course, the events of this morning have complicated matters, not in the least because it was at the negotiations between Lars-win-Getag and Dirk Moeller that the sheep quotas would have been determined."

"It's not a problem," Heffer said. "You can have as many sheep as you need. With the compliments of the State Department."

"I'm afraid it's not that simple, Mr. Secretary," Narf-win-Getag said. He learned over and retrieved a display tablet from his briefcase, and placed it on Heffer's desk. "It can't be any sheep. It needs to be a sheep of a particular breed, and a particularly rare breed. In fact, it's a breed that was specially designed for the auf-Getag clan when it came to power; its distinguishing physical characteristic is the color of its wool."

Heffer reached over and took the tablet. It was a picture of a sheep, with electric blue wool.

"The breed is called Android's Dream," Narf-win-Getag said.

"Odd name," Heffer said, returning the tablet.

"It has some sort of literary significance," Narf-win-Getag said, reaching for the tablet, "although I'm not sure how. Be that as it may, the breed design patent was provided to the auf-Getag, in perpetuity, by the designers and the Earth government at the time. Naturally, the auf-Getag clan has been very selective regarding who may work with the breed. Only a very few breeding agreements were allowed, and those were restrictive enough as to make breeding the sheep something of a losing business. So there was not much interest to begin."

"You're saying that no one else breeds Android's Dream sheep," Heffer said.

"We know of one breeder, the original breeder," Narf-win-Getag said. "On the Brisbane colony. Even though we own the design patent, they were unable to sell their sheep to us directly because of colonial export laws. We planned to ask for an exemption during negotiations."

"We can grant that exemption right now," Heffer said.

"I am glad to hear it," Narf-win-Getag said. "But there is another complication to consider. Prior to my arrival here we learned the virus that hit us also hit the breeder on Brisbane. Their entire stock of Android's Dream sheep is dead or dying."

"You suspect that's not coincidence," Heffer said.

"Indeed not," Narf-win-Getag said. "Whoever spread the virus to Brisbane knows what we know. What we're hoping is that they might not know what *you* know. Despite our control of the breed, we do not doubt that somewhere along the way someone got past our limits on the breed. In fact, at this point, that's what we're hoping for."

"So what do you want us to do?" Heffer asked.

"We will provide you with the genetic information for the Android's Dream sheep. We'd like you to find a breeder here on Earth who has one of the breed. A purebreed would be optimal, of course. But so long as there is a certain amount of genetic similarity, that will be acceptable. And we need you to find it within the week. And we'd prefer you do it quietly."

Heffer shifted uncomfortably in his chair. "I'm all for the quiet part, it's the rest of that request that I'm worried about. You presume that we have the DNA of every sheep in the world somewhere in a government file," he said. "The government has a lot of information, but I don't think even we have that."

"We don't," Javna said. "But someone does."

Heffer and Narf-win-Getag both shifted their focus to Javna. "Keep going, please," Narf-win-Getag said.

"Insurance companies, Mr. Ambassador," Javna said. "Farmers and ranchers insure their livestock all the time, in case they get hit by a car or struck by lightning or get anthrax or whatever. Most insurers require the farmers put their animals' DNA on file, so the insurer can confirm the animal actually belonged to the farmer."

"So much for trust," Heffer said.

"Insurance isn't about trust, sir," Javna said. "Anyway, not every sheep in the world is going to have its DNA on file, but enough will that it gives us something to work on."

"If we can get the insurers to release their records to us," Heffer said. "And even then, a week isn't a lot of time."

Narf-win-Getag stood, took his briefcase; Heffer stood up in response. "Time is critical, Mr. Secretary. The coronation must go on according to schedule. You wanted something to improve relations and to make us forget how your negotiator derailed trade talks. This is it. I will have an assistant come by later in the day with the DNA information. Mr. Secretary, you have my faith that you can help resolve this crisis. It would be most unfortunate, for both our peoples, if you could not." Narf-win-Getag nodded to Heffer and Javna and departed.

Heffer plopped back into his chair. "Well, no pressure *there*," he said. "So how many sheep do you think there are on this planet?"

"I'm not up to date on my UNEDA estimates, but I'm guessing a couple of billion," Javna said. "But you only have to look through the ones that are insured. That'll narrow it down to just several hundred million. Piece of cake."

"Glad to see the spirit of optimism is alive and well," Heffer said.

"How do you want to do this, Mr. Secretary?" Javna asked.

"You mean, how do *you* want to do this, Ben," Heffer said. "I'm due back in Switzerland in another twelve hours. Then I'm off to Japan and Thailand. I'm a little busy to be counting sheep. You, on the other hand, can stay home and no one will miss you."

"Narf-win-Getag said that he wants this to be quiet," Javna said. "That's going to be difficult."

"How difficult?" Heffer asked.

"Very difficult. Not impossible, just difficult. We have to be creative about this." Javna was quiet for a moment. "How much latitude do I have for this, sir?"

"Are you kidding? Short of strangling babies, do what you need to do. Why? What are you thinking?"

"I'm thinking that the best way to handle this so that it doesn't explode into a crisis is to hand it off to someone who doesn't know it's a crisis. Someone smart enough to work the problem but low-profile enough to slip under everyone's radar. And I do mean *everyone's*." Javna nodded at the intercepts lying on Heffer's desk.

"You know someone like this?" Heffer said.

"I do," Javna said. "The guy I have in mind could do it. And he owes me a favor. I got him a job."

"Anyone I'd know about?"

"No, sir. He's pretty low-profile. 'No-profile' would be more like it, actually."

Heffer snorted. "I thought I knew all the smart young kids in this department."

"Not everyone's looking to be Secretary of State by the time they're thirty, sir."

"Good. Because I'm sixty-seven and I like my job, and I want to keep it a little bit longer. So get going with this." Heffer reached into his desk, hauled out the tube, and slid it over to Javna. "While you or your friend are counting sheep, see if you can figure out where the hell this came from and who made it. *Quietly*. Whoever put this together can tell us things. Things I think we need to know."

"Yes, sir." Javna took the object and pocketed it.

Heffer reached over, snatched the intercepts off his desk, and yanked out his trash basket with the shredder on top. "And whatever you do, make it fast. Between the Nidu and Pope, I get the distinct feeling of time ticking. I don't want either of them knowing more than we know. You think your friend can keep us ahead of them?"

"I think so, sir," Javna said.

"Good," Heffer said, and fed the intercepts into the shredder.

———

It was close to midnight when Dave Phipps got on the blue line train at the Pentagon, with a copy of *The Washington Times* to keep him company. He switched over to the orange line, riding it to its terminus at the Vienna-Fairfax stop. He got out and found himself alone on the platform except for a middle-aged guy in a ratty Washington Senators cap, sitting on one of the benches.

"Hey, can I borrow your paper?" the guy asked. "I've got a long ride into town."

"I will if tell me why you wear that disgusting cap of yours," Phipps said.

"Call it an affectation," the guy said.

"You know the Senators haven't been good for years," Phipps said.

"The Senators have never been good," the guy said. "That's part of their appeal. They're the second most pathetic team in the history of baseball and would be first, if it weren't for the fact that they go out of business every couple of decades and give the Cubs time to lengthen their lead. Now are you going to give me the goddamn paper, or do I have to push you in front of a train and take it from you?"

Phipps grinned and handed over the paper. "I was Special Forces, Schroeder. You've never been anything but soft, Ivy-league lobbyist. It wouldn't be me underneath the wheels, pal."

"Talk, talk, talk," Jean Schroeder said. "Maybe so, Phipps. Maybe so. And yet, look at which one of us is schlepping his sorry ass to Virginia to give me a newspaper." Schroeder fished through the paper. "So where the hell did you hide the transcript, anyway?"

"The comics page," Phipps said.

"Oh, very nice," Schroeder said, changing sections.

"It's mostly about sheep," Phipps said. "Apparently they're looking for a particular breed."

"Android's Dream," Schroeder said. "I know. They're not likely to find it. It's my understanding that the breed has been wiped out."

"You have something to do with that?" Phipps asked.

"I just know many things," Schroeder said.

"They're looking for it anyway," Phipps said.

"So I read," Schroeder said. "Or more accurately, would read, if someone would shut their yap hole long enough for me to concentrate." Phipps grinned again and fell silent. Schroeder read.

"Interesting," he said when was finished. "Futile, but interesting. Still, it wouldn't be smart to underestimate Heffer and Javna. Heffer got Webster elected, after all, and that really put a ding in our plans. And Javna counts as half of his brain. You guys have no idea who it is Javna's talking about?"

"No," Phipps said. "He said it's someone he gave a job to, but that's about half of the State Department at this point."

"You should have him watched. Discreetly," Schroeder said. "And you should probably start your own search for any sheep with the Android's Dream DNA. Just in case. I can get you a sample."

"It amazes me how little you think I know about my job," Phipps said.

"I'm just advising," Schroeder said.

"Like you advised Moeller to kill that trade representative," Phipps said.

"He wasn't supposed to *kill* him," Schroeder said. "Just enrage him enough that negotiations came to a screeching halt."

"Well, they did," Phipps said. "And then he did."

"That's a shame, too," Schroeder said. "I had other plans for him."

"Real torn up about Moeller, aren't you?"

Schroeder shrugged. "He was my father's project, not mine,"

he said. "I was friendly to him because he was useful. And he made good barbeque. Pope's still unaware of my relationship with Moeller and my participation in this event, I assume."

Phipps pointed at the transcript. "That makes it pretty obvious it wasn't an accident, doesn't it. He knows Moeller's history and that he worked for your dad. But at this point, he figures Moeller was freelancing for his own reasons."

"He was," Schroeder said. "I just helped in the implementation."

"Whatever," Phipps said. "Short story is that you're unsuspected. As am I. In fact, Pope suggested I contact you, seeing as you've been helpful with off-the-book investigations before. I'm actually *supposed* to be here this time. We might need your help."

"I love it when a plan comes together," Schroeder said.

"That makes it sound like you planned it to go like this," Phipps said.

"Oh, no," Schroeder admitted. "We're way off track from where I thought we'd be. But maybe it's better this way. We had only expected to derail the talks and the coronation. Now we might actually get a revolution."

"Unless they find the sheep," Phipps said.

"They're not going to find the sheep," Schroeder said. "They've got a billion sheep to sift through in a week. And they'd have to find the sheep before we do. They might do one, but not the other. No matter how good Javna's friend is, no one is that good."

Harris Creek sat across from Lingo Tudena, the Kathungi Cultural Attaché, and performed his role for the State Department: He delivered the bad news.

"I'm sorry, Mr. Tudena," Creek said. "But I'm afraid we can't let your spouse on planet."

Tudena's vestigial shoulder wings, which had been fluttering excitedly in anticipation of his wife's visa, halted mid-flutter. "Begging pardon?" he said, through his vocoder.

"Your wife, Mr. Tudena," Creek said. "Her visa has been denied."

"But why?" Tudena asked. "I was assured by the Art Council that her visa would be no problem at all. Just a few routine checks. No problem."

"Normally there isn't a problem," Creek said. "But something popped up in your wife's case."

"What?"

Creek hesitated for a minute, then realized that there was no gentle way out of it for either of himself or Tudena. "Your wife, Mr. Tudena," Creek said. "She's entered her fertility cycle."

Tudena twitched his head in the Kathungi physiological equivalent of a surprised blink. "Impossible. I'm not there to initiate it. You must be in error."

Creek reached into his portfolio and slid the doctor's report over to Tudena. Tudena grabbed it with one of his forearms and held it up to one of the simple eyes the Kathungi used for near objects. After a few seconds, his vestigial shoulder wings began to jerk chaotically. Physiologically the Kathungi have no need of tears but by any emotional standard it was clear he was crying.

The Kathungi were a people with a beautiful and artistic culture and a procreation process that utterly disgusted every other sentient species they had come in contact with. After a nearly month-long phase in which the female Kathungi was enticed into a fertility cycle by her mate, both male and female Kathungi were pheremonally trapped into an uncontrolled "spew" phase: The female Kathungi would be randomly seized by a contraction of her egg sac, which would spew a milky, rancid-smelling fluid embedded with hundreds of thousands of eggs onto anything in the vicinity.

At the sight and smell of the eruption, the male Kathungi would follow suit with a greenish and even more foul-smelling milt that would coat the egg spray. The two substances would then congeal into a gelatinous mass whose purpose would be to protect and nourish the fertilized eggs until they hatched. By which time the Kathungi parents would be gone; rare among sentient species, the Kathungi were not nurturers. Kathungi eggs hatched into voracious, cricketlike larvae that ate everything in their path (including other larvae); it wasn't until a much later phase that members of the vastly thinned ranks of surviving larvae entered a pupae phase in which they grew the brains required for sentience.

The particulars and repercussions of Kathungi reproduction were visited upon Earth not long after the UNE allowed nondiplomatic Kathungians to visit Earth on tourist visas. One young Kathungian couple decided to drive across the United States on a road trip and got as far as Ogallala, Nebraska, before they were overcome by the spew phase. The two rented a room at the Sav-U-Lot Motel off of Interstate 80 and spent the next day and a half with the "Do Not Disturb" sign on the door, coating the interior of the room with goo more than an inch thick in places. The cleaning crew quit rather than touch it; the manager ended up scooping up the goo with a dustpan, depositing it into the bathtub, and running the shower head to dilute the stuff enough to let it slip down the drain.

One week later, guests of the Sav-U-Lot ran screaming from their rooms as millions of larval Kathungi, who had consumed the contents of the Sav-U-Lot's massive and poorly maintained septic tank, migrated *en masse* through the plumbing in search of food. The manager rushed into one of the rooms armed with a flyswatter and a can of Raid Ant & Roach Killer. The Kathungi larvae ate everything but the plastic zipper on his pants and the metal grommets of his shoes; seven guests were never found at all. After consuming every organic morsel the Sav-U-Lot had to offer, the larvae, with their natural predators far away on the Kathungi home planet, set on the town of Ogallala like a Biblical plague.

The Nebraska governor imposed martial law and sent in the National Guard to eradicate the larvae. After it was discovered that the insects were in fact Kathungi larvae, the governor was hauled into CC court on the charge of xenocide and hundreds of thousands of individual counts of murder of a sentient species member. The bewildered governor served out the remainder of his term of office from the federal prison located (gallingly for a Nebraskan) in Leavenworth, Kansas. Shortly thereafter the UNE changed its visa policy to require that Kathungi females visiting Earth to be on birth control; under no circumstances would a female Kathungi who had begun her fertility cycle ever be allowed to set foot on planet again.

The fact that the cultural attaché's wife was fertile doomed her chances of coming to Earth. The fact that the cultural attaché's wife had begun her fertility cycle while her husband was away was going to doom her marriage. One simply does not enter a fertility cycle randomly. And one definitely doesn't enter a fertility cycle without one's spouse.

Creek gently took back the medical file from the cultural attaché, whose wings were still jerking up and down. "I'm sorry," he said.

"She always said she wanted to come to visit Earth," Tudena said. His vocoder, tuned to be sensitive to its wearer's emotions, inserted sad, gulping sounds.

"She didn't know you were trying to get her a visa?" Creek asked.

Tudena shook his head. "It was going to be a surprise," he said. "I was going to take her to Disneyland. I've been told that it is the happiest place on Earth." His shoulder wings began to shake violently, and he buried his head in his forelimbs. Creek reached over and patted Tudena on his chitinous husk; Tudena shoved back from the desk and stumbled out the door. After several minutes one of Tudena's assistants came to collect Creek, thank him for his time, and escort him to the door of the embassy.

Creek's official title with the State Department was "Xenosapient Facilitator," which meant absolutely nothing to anyone but the State Department bursar, who could tell you that a Xenosapient Facilitator got the GS-10 pay grade. Creek's unofficial title, which was more accurate and descriptive, was "Bearer of Bad News." Whenever the State Department had bad news to deliver to a member of the alien diplomatic corps who was significant enough to require a personal response but not significant enough to rate someone who actually mattered, he, she, or it got Creek.

It was the proverbial dirty job. But equally proverbially, someone had to do it, and Harris Creek was surprisingly good at it. It took a special human to look various members of various alien species in whatever organ it was that passed for their eye and tell them that a visa request was denied, or that the State Department was aware that assassins were plotting to kill them on their trip back to their home world, or that due to a memorable bout of public drunkenness on the Union Station carousel, which resulted in the alien projectile vomiting on terrified human children there for a birthday party, their diplomatic status was *this close* to being revoked. In his time, Creek had done all of these among many others.

Members of alien species had differing ways of showing anger and grief, from the sad, silent shaking of Mr. Tudena to the ritually approved destruction of property. Most people, regardless of their training in diplomacy, were simply not psychologically equipped to deal with a member of an alien species freaking out in front of them. The reptile portions of the brain, nestled down close to the brain stem, would too often override the gray matter and send the puny human bolting away, leaking fluids as the "eject the ballast" portion of the "fight or flight" response kicked in.

Harris Creek did not have anywhere near the diplomatic training of his peers—in fact, he had none when he took the job. But he also didn't run when the furniture stated flying. For his particular job, that was enough. It was easier to learn about diplomacy than it was learn to control one's bladder in front of a rampaging member of the alien diplomatic corps. Most people wouldn't think so, but it's true.

Outside the Kathungi Embassy, Creek fired up his communicator to locate his next appointment; it was at the Larrn Institute over on K Street. Creek was going to have to tell a new Tang lobbyist that while the State Department was willing to regard *one* threat to eat a UNE Representative's children if she didn't vote the way he wanted her to as a cultural misunderstanding, doing it a second time would have impressively negative repercussions.

"Hello, Harry," Creek heard someone say. He looked up and saw Ben Javna, leaning against a marble pillar.

"Howdy, Ben," Creek said. "Fancy meeting you here."

"I happened to be walking by and saw you there," Javna said, and then nodded in the direction of the door Creek had come out of. "Bad news for the Kathungi?"

"One of them," Creek said, and started walking. Javna followed. "Actually, two of them, at least. But only one of whom is here on Earth. That's part of the problem, I think."

"So you're still enjoying your job," Javna said.

"I don't know if *enjoy* is the word I'd use," Creek said. "That'd imply a certain level of sadism, enjoying giving people bad news. I find it interesting. But I don't know how much longer I can keep doing it."

"Giving bad news to people would get to anyone," Javna said.

"It's not that," Creek said. "That part is fine. It's that people are beginning to know who I am. I went to the Phlenbahn embassy yesterday, and the guy I was supposed to see wouldn't let his assistant show me in. I could hear him screaming on the other side of the door in Phlenbahni. My communicator translated it. He was calling me 'the angel of death.' I thought that was pretty harsh."

"Why were you there?" Javna asked.

"Well, in that particular case it *was* to inform him that a car with diplomatic plates assigned to the Phlenbahni embassy had been linked to a fatal hit-and-run in Silver Spring," Creek admitted. "Even so. He didn't know that's why I was there before I said anything. It's a strange thing to make aliens twitchy just by existing. Sooner or later I'm sure they're all going to bar me from getting through the embassy door. State's not exactly an efficient department, but eventually someone would notice. Maybe I should start looking for another job."

Javna laughed. "Funny you should mention that, Harry," he said. "I have a job that needs doing. One that could use your skill set."

"You need me to break some bad news to someone?" Creek asked. "You and Jill doing okay, Ben?"

"We're happy like newlyweds, Harry," Javna said. "Not those skills. Your *other* skills. The one's you're not paid to use at the moment."

Harry stopped and looked at Javna. "I have a lot of skills I'm not paid to use at the moment, Ben. Some of which I'm not really interested in using again."

"Relax," Javna said. "It's nothing like that."

"What is it?"

"Well, let's not talk about it right now," Javna said. "Why don't you and I get together this evening. Say, around six-thirty."

"I'm free," Creek said. "You want to get a drink?"

"I was thinking maybe we could meet at Brian's place. I haven't been there for a while."

"Brian's place," Creek said.

"Sure. Should be quiet there. Six-thirty?"

"Six-thirty," said Creek. Javna smiled, saluted jauntily, and walked off without looking back. Creek watched him go for a long moment, then hurried off to the Larnn Institute.

Seventy-five yards back and across the street Rod Acuna flipped open his communicator and rang up Dave Phipps. "Another street meeting," he said when Phipps clicked on.

"Christ," Phipps said. "That's the fourth one in an hour and a half. He's screwing with us. He knows you're out there, Rod."

"He hasn't seen me," Acuna said. "I guarantee it."

"I'm not saying he has," Phipps said. "I'm saying he knows we'd be having him watched."

"Yeah, well, anyway, this one might be the real thing," Acuna said. "Javna and the guy he just met are getting together tonight at six-thirty for a drink."

"Did they say where?"

"Some bar called 'Brian's Place,'" Acuna said. "Although maybe that's just the name of the owner."

"Either way, we can find it," Phipps said. "Keep on him, Rod. Call me if you learn anything new."

Acuna flipped off and set after Javna.

Brian's place was section 91, space 4088, Arlington National Cemetery. Javna was already there when Creek walked up.

"I'm remembering the day you and Brian tried to assassinate me," Javna said, without turning. He had heard Creek walk up. "You know, with the model rocket."

Creek grinned. "We weren't trying to assassinate you, Ben," he said. "Honest and truly."

Javna looked over his shoulder. "You launched the rocket into my car, Harry."

"It was just a small one," Creek said. "And anyway, you had gotten out of the car."

"*Barely* gotten out of the car," Javna corrected. "And wish I had still been in the car. It might have kept the rocket from torching the seats."

"Possibly," Creek said. "Of course then you'd have had third-degree burns across your body."

"Skin grafts would fix that," Javna said. "But that was a classic car. Those seats were leather from an actual cow. You can't get that anymore. I could have killed the two of you. I would have had my lawyer stuff the jury with classic car enthusiasts. We're talking acquittal in under an hour."

Creek opened his hands wide, imploring. "I humbly ask your forgiveness, Ben. I'm sorry we torched your car. Our only excuse was that we were ten at the time and remarkably stupid for our age. Anyway, don't be too hard on your brother. Launching the rocket was my idea."

"That's one of the reasons why I like you, Harry," Javna said. "You still stick up for Brian even when it can't possibly do him any good. Before the two of you shipped out, he told me he was the one who pointed the rocket at the car. He said you tried to talk him out of it."

Creek grinned again. "Well, it *was* a classic car," he said. "Seemed a shame to torch it."

"I just wish you'd been more persuasive," Javna said.

"You know Brian," Creek said. "You couldn't tell him anything."

The two stood there in front of space 4088, section 91, for a minute, silently.

"You didn't have me come out here to talk about something Brian and I did twenty years ago, Ben," Creek said, gently.

"Right," Javna said. He reached into his coat pocket and tossed something to Creek. It was a bracelet with a small metal disk on it. "Put that on and press the button," Javna told Creek. Creek slipped on the bracelet with a little effort and pressed the red button in the center of the disk. He could feel a small vibration from the disc. He looked back over to Javna, who was wearing one as well. Javna was placing a small cube on Brian's headstone, attaching it by the suction cup on one of the sides. He pressed the top.

"That should do it," Javna said.

"Should do what?" Creek asked.

"I was being followed when I met up with you today," Javna said. "I laid a few red herrings across my trail to confuse my tails and I'd be willing to guess that they're thinking we're meeting at a bar. But you can never be too careful."

Javna pointed at the cube. "So, that little object does two things. It creates a sphere of white noise with a radius of thirty feet. Anyone trying to listen in more than thirty feet away is going to hear static, if they're using conventional listening devices. It also vibrates the headstone, to confuse devices that can register sound conduction by bouncing lasers off of solid objects and processing how much the sound waves make them move. The little wrist doodads are doing the same thing to us. Not that they would have much chance with the lasers. Human bodies are poor sound conductors, and the headstone doesn't give them much to work with. The whole outdoor thing really messes with laser detection. But better safe than sorry."

"That still leaves lip reading," Creek said.

"Well, then," Javna said. "Try not to move your lips too much."

"Cloak and dagger shit bores me, Ben," Creek said. "What's going on?"

Javna reached into his coat pocket again and produced a small curved tube. "Ever seen one of these before?" He handed it to Creek.

"I don't think so," Creek said, taking it. "What is it?"

Javna told him the whole story, from the murder by fart to the need to find the Android's Dream sheep.

"Wild," Creek said. "Disgusting, but wild."

"Let's say I wanted to find out who made this," Javna said. "How would I do it?"

Creek turned the apparatus around in his hands. "I'm assuming this isn't a mass-produced object," he said.

"Probably not," Javna said.

"Then someone either designed this from scratch or altered an existing design. You could probably check the UNE Patent and Trademark Office database to see if something like this exists, and then if it does, you could try to see who's accessed the information in the last year or so. Presuming your guy searched off the government database and not off a private archive, you might get something."

"So you think we could get the guy that way?" Javna said.

"Sure, if the guy was an idiot and didn't bother to cover his tracks," Creek said. "Does that sound like the sort of person you're looking for?"

"Probably not," Javna said again.

"There's another place to look, though," Creek said. "This isn't mass-produced but it's also not something you could make in your garage shop. This thing was probably made in a small-scale fabricator." Creek looked up at Javna, who shrugged. "A small-scale fabricator is like a printer that works in three dimensions," Creek explained. "You provide it a design and some raw material and it 'prints' the object you want to make. It's inefficient—you wouldn't use it to make a lot of things—but it'd be perfect for a job like this."

"How many of these things are out there?" Javna asked.

Creek shrugged. "Couldn't tell you. I'd guess a couple hundred in the DC area," he said. "They're used by people who need to make replacement parts of old things whose manufacturers have gone out of business or stopped supporting the product. Like that old car of yours. If you ever got a replacement part for it, it was probably fabricated. But you could narrow it down in a couple of ways. This is mostly a metal object, so you could ignore the fabricators that output plastics, ceramics, and carbon composites. That's still going to leave you with a few dozen, but at least that's a smaller number."

"But that still doesn't tell us which of these fabricators made the thing," Javna said.

"No, but you could find out pretty quickly from there. Fabricators are like any mechanical object—there are small, unique differences in their output. Put this under the microscope to find the pattern unique to its fabricator. Basic forensics." Creek handed the apparatus back to Javna, but Javna held up his hand. "You want me to keep this?" Creek asked.

"I want you to find who made it," Javna said. "That, and one other thing."

"What's that?"

"I need you to find that sheep I told you about."

"You can't be serious," Creek said.

"I'm totally serious," Javna said.

"Ben, even one of these things is a full-time job for actual analysts and investigators. And if you recall, I already have a full-time job. You got it for me, remember."

"I do," Javna said. "Don't worry about the job. I've already given you cover for that. Your boss has received notice that for the next two weeks you'll be participating in a State Department Xenosapient training program. And as it happens, there actually *is* a State Department Xenosapient training program going on over the next couple of weeks."

"That's swell," Creek said. "Then there's just the minor detail that I'm deeply out of practice in what you're asking me to do."

"You figured out how to track down this fabricator pretty quickly," Javna said.

"Jesus, Ben," Creek said. "Anyone who watches detective shows could have told you *that.*"

"Harry," Javna said. "Just because you're currently slacking through life with a dead-end job doesn't mean that *I* have to pretend I don't know what you can do."

"That's not very fair, Ben," Creek said.

Javna held his hand up. "Sorry," he said. "But, you know, Harry. If I had half your brains and talent, I'd be running the country by now. I mean, hell. I know you find your current job *interesting*. But it's like using an n-space drive to go down to the store to get a bottle of milk."

The Android's Dream · 63

"Not everyone wants to run the world," Creek said.

"Funny, I said something like that about you to Heffer," Javna said. "Anyway, you don't have to run the world. I just want you to save it a little. We need to find these things, but we can't be obvious that we're looking for them. I need someone I can trust to do this thing for me, and do it quietly. You fit the bill, Harry. I need your help."

"I don't have what I would need to do all this," Creek said. "I don't even own a proper computer anymore, you know. I've got my communicator and the processors in my household appliances. That's it."

"What happened to your computer?" Javna said.

"I had a crisis of faith about its use," Creek said. "I stored what I was working on and gave it to the neighbor kids."

"Then we'll get you a new one. Tell me what you need," Javna said.

"How big is your budget?" Creek asked.

Javna smiled, reached into his pocket yet again, and gave Creek a credit card. "Anonymous credit," Javna said.

"How much?" Creek asked.

"I don't rightly know," Javna said, and nodded towards the card. "I don't think one of these cards actually runs out of credit. So don't lose it, or I'm in deep trouble."

"Oh, wow," Creek said. "A boy could have a lot of fun with a toy like this."

"Don't get too excited," Javna said. "If you buy yourself a tropical atoll, it's going to get noticed. Buy everything you need. Just don't buy anything else."

"No worries," Creek said, pocketing the card. "I'm also going to need access. I don't know what my access level is on the UNE database, but whatever it is I guarantee it's not high enough."

"Already done," Javna said. "But it's like that credit card. Use your powers wisely."

"You're sure this is square with Heffer," Creek said. "I don't want you taking a fall for anything I do."

"Heffer trusts me," Javna said. "I trust you. Therefore you have Heffer's trust. For exactly six days. That's when all this has to be done and dealt with."

"That's not a lot of time," Creek said.

"Tell me about it," Javna said. "But that's the time we have."

"All right," Creek said. "I'll do it. But you have to promise me my job's still going to be there in two weeks."

"It's a promise," Javna said. "And if your boss gives me any trouble, I'll have her fired and you can have her job."

"I'd rather not. I may be a slacker, but the job suits me," Creek said.

"I'm sorry about the slacker comment," Javna said. "You've done some important things, Harry. And you've always done the right thing by my family. You've always been there to help us. I haven't forgotten. We haven't forgotten."

Both of their eyes went back to the headstone.

"I was more helpful to some of you than others," Creek said.

"Don't blame yourself for Brian, Harry," Javna said. "That wasn't about you. It was about him."

"I promised you I'd look out for him," Creek said.

"Still sticking up for Brian," Javna said. "You said it yourself. You know Brian. You couldn't tell him anything. You couldn't look out for him because he wouldn't look out for himself. We know that. We've never blamed you for it. You did what you could. And then you made sure he came back to us. Most kids up who die up there never make it back. You brought him back to us, Harry. It meant more to us than you know."

"This is Arlington National Cemetery?" Defense Secretary Pope said over the photos, to Phipps.

"That's right, sir," Phipps said.

"I thought you said they were heading for a bar," Pope said.

"They said they'd be meeting for a drink," Phipps noted. "It didn't really occur to us that Javna might be heading to his brother's grave until they were already there."

"Sloppy," Pope said.

Oh, and you *would have figured it out instantly, asshole,* thought Phipps.

"Yes, sir," Phipps said. "We're not using our in-house people on this one. I'm using a specialist suggested by Jean Schroeder. Rod Acuna. Schroeder says he uses him and his team often."

"Fine," Pope said. "But tell him to keep better tabs from here on out." Pope waved the photo in his hand. "Do we know what they're talking about?" he asked.

"No," Phipps said. "Javna carried a portable acoustic scrambler." Phipps braced himself for another sloppy comment, but Pope held his fire. After a couple of seconds Phipps went on. "But we think this is the guy Javna's going to use for his little project."

"Who is he?" Pope said.

"Harris Creek," Phipps said. " 'Harris' is actually his middle name; his first name is 'Horatio.' "

"Which explains why he goes by his middle name," Pope said.

"He's an old friend of the Javna family," Phipps said, digging through his notes. "Specifically of Brian Javna, who was the younger brother of Ben Javna. There's a twelve-year difference between the two. Or was. Anyway, Creek and Brian Javna joined the service at the same time, when they turned eighteen. They were both at the Battle of Pajmhi. Brian Javna died there."

Pope snorted. "Join the club," he said. No one in the UNE Defense community liked to talk much about the Battle of Pajmhi. There may have been worse clusterfucks in the history of human armed conflict, but Pajmhi had the misfortune of being the most recent.

"Creek got a Distinguished Service Cross," Phipps continued. Pope raised an eyebrow at that. "A note from Creek's C.O. was put into his file, saying that the C.O. had originally wanted to recommend Creek for the Congressional Medal of Honor, but that Creek had become so agitated at the suggestion that he had to back down. As it is, it doesn't appear Creek ever took receipt of his Cross. Most of his battalion was wiped out at Pajmhi; Creek was transferred to a military police brigade where he served the rest of his tour. Re-upped once and was honorably discharged as a staff sergeant."

Phipps flipped to another page. "After the service, Creek joined the Washington DC police department, working on electronic crimes. You know, fraud, hackers, child molesters in chat rooms. That sort of thing. Quit the department three years ago and spent a couple of years unemployed."

"What, like homeless?" Pope asked.

"No, not like that," Phipps said. "Definitely not homeless. His parents left him a home in Reston after they retired to Arizona. He just didn't work for anyone."

"What was he doing?"

"Doesn't say," Phipps said. "But about fifteen months ago he started working for State Department as a Xenosapient facilitator, whatever that means. His schedules are public record so I checked them out. He spends most of his time visiting embassies for other planetary governments of the CC. He's got no diplomatic training; he doesn't even have a college degree. So it's a pretty good bet Ben Javna helped him land the job."

"How does a semi-literate war hero help out Ben Javna now?" Pope asked. "I'm not seeing the benefit here."

"Well, that's the thing," Phipps said. "You're assuming he's semi-literate because he doesn't have a college degree and he's an ex-cop. But that's not the whole story." Phipps shuffled through his papers and set one on Pope's desk. "Look at this. In his senior year in high school, Creek was a U.S. national gold medal winner for the Westinghouse Science and Technology competition. He designed an artificial intelligence interface to help people with degenerative motor diseases communicate with the outside world. He had a full ride to MIT and had been accepted to Cal-Tech and Columbia. This is one really smart guy, sir."

"He was a tech geek and yet he joined the army," Pope said. "That's not the obvious play."

"Just before his graduation, he got arrested," Phipps said, and handed his boss another sheet. "He and Brian Javna broke into a George Washington University physics lab and gave each other brain scans with the lab's quantum imager. Apparently Creek hacked the lab's security system so they could get in, and then Javna talked them past the staff. Also almost talked them back out of the lab, too, but then the lab director showed up and had the both of them arrested. The lab got funding from the army, and some of its projects were classified. So technically, Creek and Javna could have been charged with treason. The judge handling the case gave them the choice of going to trial or joining the army and having their records expunged after they finished a tour of duty. They joined the army."

"That was still twelve years ago, Dave," Pope said. "A dozen years is like a century in tech. They're like dog years. He could be hopelessly behind the times."

"He's been near computers since he's been in the army, sir," Phipps said. "Those years on Metro Police. And when a geek takes a couple years off and hides from the world, he's probably not just playing video games. He's up to date."

"He still live in Reston?" Pope asked.

"Yes, sir," Phipps said. "We're already hard at work bugging his lines."

"Let's be a little more proactive than that," Pope said. "It'd be useful to everyone involved if we found what Creek's looking for before he does."

"Schroeder's given us the Android's Dream genome," Phipps said. "All we have to do now is start looking for it."

"Let's get going on it," Pope said. "But I don't want you using any of the usual staff, and I definitely don't want you using any military personnel. They've got this thing about the chain of command."

"This department is crawling with contractors," Phipps said. "I could use one of them. I can encrypt the data so he wouldn't know what he was looking at."

"Do it," Pope said. "And try to find a smart one. I don't know how good this Creek character is anymore, but the sooner we're in business, the longer it'll take for him to catch up with us."

Archie McClellan was born to be a geek. The child of geeks, who were themselves the children of geeks, who were in themselves brought into the world by members of the geek clan, Archie was fated for geekdom not only in the genes that recursively flirted with Asperger's syndrome down multiple genetic lines, but in his very name.

"You were named after an ancient search protocol," Archie's dad, an electronics engineer with the DC Metro system, told him when he was in kindergarten. "And so was your sister," he said, nodding toward Archie's fraternal twin, Veronica. Veronica, who despite all genetic predilections to the contrary had already begun a reign of popularity that would propel her all the way to the editorship of the Harvard Law Review, vowed instantly never to tell anyone of her name's origin. Archie, on the other hand, thought this bit of information was super cool. He was a geek before he could spell the word (which would have been at age two years, two months).

As also befitted his name, Archie McClellan made a specialty out of administering the various legacy systems that labored in the dusty corners of the many departments of the UNE government. One of Archie's favorite stories was when he was dragged down to the basement of the Department of Agriculture and presented with an IBM System 360, vintage nineteen fucking sixty-five. Archie McCellan turned to the administrative assistant who had hauled him down to the basement and told her that there was more computing power in the animated greeting card in her desk than in the whole massive bulk of this ancient mainframe. The administrative assistant snapped her gum and told him she didn't care if it was powered by chickens pecking at buttons, it still needed to be reconnected to the network. Archie spent a day learning OS/360, reconnected the hulking birdbrain to the network, and charged triple his usual consulting fee.

So when Archie found himself being led down into a similar basement hall in the Pentagon, he assumed he was heading toward yet another ancient machine, still tethered to the network like a Neanderthal because of the government-wide directive not to throw out legacy systems due to decades of data that would be otherwise unreadable. No one building computers today makes their machines backwards-compatible with punch cards, DVD-ROMs, collapsible memory cubes or holo-encodes. He was mildly surprised when he arrived where he was going and saw the machine.

"This is this year's model," he said to the Phipps, who was waiting inside.

"I suppose it is," said Phipps.

"I don't understand," Archie said. "I contract to maintain your legacy systems."

"But you *can* work with today's computers, right?" Phipps said. "The computer doesn't *have* to be older than Christ for you to use it."

"Of course not," Archie said.

"That's good to hear. I have a job for you."

The job involved encrypted data that needed to be compared to data in an encrypted database. Archie's job would be to oversee the data retrieval process, and if at all possible, speed it up; the encrypted database was massive and the project was under severe time constraints.

"It would make it easier if the data weren't encrypted," Archie said to Phipps.

"Try to make it easier *with* it still encrypted," said Phipps, and glanced at his watch. "It's nine p.m. now. I'll be back tomorrow at nine a.m. to check on your progress, but if you come up with anything sooner you can send me a message."

"My contract states that any work after midnight through six a.m. constitutes double overtime rates," Archie said.

"Well, then, that's good news for you," Phipps said. "There's a vending machine down the hall to your right. Bathroom is down the left. Have fun." He left.

Archie set up the terminal in the basement office to begin searching through the database, and then went back upstairs to retrieve his personal work computer. He used his personal computer to optimize the search routine as much as possible given the encryption constraints, but after a couple of hours of fiddling he realized that even the fully optimized code was searching far too slowly for what he suspected was his new boss's expectations.

Fuck it, he said to himself, copied the encrypted data onto his own computer, and hacked the encryption. This wasn't difficult to do; whoever had encrypted the data used the encryption program that shipped with the computer's OS. The encryption was supposed to be nearly unbreakable standard 16,384 bit, but thanks to the OS manufacturer's perennially sloppy coding, the encryption generator that shipped with the OS featured distinct nonrandom artifacts which could be used to crack the encryption with embarrassing ease. The story finally broke when local TV in Minneapolis showed an eight-year-old hacking the encryption.

Coincidentally, at almost exactly the same time the story was airing in Minneapolis, the Seattle, Washington, metropolitan area experienced an earthquake registering 5.3 on the Richter scale. Tech wits attributed it to Bill Gates spinning in his grave. The OS manufacturer eventually put out a patch, but government IT managers were not well known for keeping up with the latest patches.

The data turned out to be DNA of some sort, which was excellent news for Archie. DNA lends itself extremely well to search optimization, since one can simply "sample" the DNA code, and look for variations based only on that portion of the code rather than the entire genome. Any DNA in the encrypted database showing variance could be thrown out, leaving a smaller set for examination with a slightly more rigorous sampling. Repeat a few times with progressively smaller numbers of DNA molecules on your database, and suddenly you've got your matches.

Now all Archie had to do was identify the species. He downloaded a shareware sequencer that promised a reference database of over 30,000 animal and plant species (upgradable to over 300,000—just $19.95!) and a special database containing the sequencing for 1500 breeds of livestock, domesticated animals, and common household plants, sent the genome in for processing, and ambled down to the vending machine for a Dr Pepper.

Which he promptly dropped when he saw the origin of the DNA waiting for him when he got back. This was followed by several seconds of unblinking, mouth-breathing agape-ness, followed by a rapid lunge for his computer. Archie uninstalled the sequencer, deleted the cracked encryption file, chewed on his thumb for a good thirty seconds, and then went to his computer's shell prompt and reformatted his entire computer memory. Just to be sure.

Then he went down the hall to the bathroom, huddled into a stall, and made a brief, hushed but emphatic call on his communicator. When that was done, he sat on the toilet for several minutes with a look on his face that implied he was having a deeply emotional, spiritual moment, or that he was painfully gassy.

He was not gassy.

chapter
4

"Hello! And welcome to your new computer!" the image said to Creek as soon as he switched on the new computer. The image was of a young man in breeches, a plain long coat, and a Quaker hat. "I am your personal intelligent agent, sponsored by America Online. Call me Todd. Activate me and receive forty-five days FREE access to America Online, Earth's oldest and largest continually active network."

Creek smirked at the hopeful agent imprinted onto his monitor glasses. "Hello, Todd," he said to the intelligent agent. "Show me your source code, please."

"My source code is the intellectual property of America Online and its parent company, Quaker Oats Holdings," Todd said. "I'm afraid I'm not allowed to divulge it to my individual user. But when you activate your America Online account with forty-five days FREE access, I'll be happy to retrieve information on open source intelligent agents, although I can guarantee they're not as good as I am, when combined with America Online's un-beatable suite of content and services!"

"Oh, I believe you, Todd. Unfortunately, I don't have time for that," Creek said, and from the storage cube he'd set alongside his new rig, activated the stripper program that froze the intelligent agent and disabled the alert message that would speed its way back to AOL's servers. "Bye, Todd," Creek said.

"I will be avenged!" Todd said, before it froze up completely. This got another smirk from Creek; Todd's programmers, know-ing that it would inevitably be hacked, thought enough to leave a parting message to the hacker; a kind of salute, as it were. A win-dow popped up in the monitor glasses, spilling Todd's source code at a high rate.

Creek scanned it cursorily. The late, unlamented Todd was correct: It was a pretty good intelligent agent, as far as commer-cial agents went. But like most commercial agents, it wasn't terri-bly bright and it was programmed to research from certain commercial databases, mostly owned by Quaker Oats. How Quaker Oats became the largest mainstream information and technology service in the world was one of those stories that could fill the dry nonfiction books of at least three sabbatical-taking *Wall Street Journal* writers. All Creek knew is that he enjoyed see-ing a guy in breeches become the universal symbol of high tech-nology. Still, he didn't want his own intelligent agent wearing 18th-century clothing. Creek had as well-developed a sense of irony as the next guy, but breeches were simply distracting.

From the storage cube, Creek pulled out the source code for an intelligent agent he'd been developing at the time of his last vacation from the computing world, and began mixing and matching it with Todd. Todd's database connection and informa-tion retrieval and optimization subroutines stayed; its native AI and database preferences were tossed, as were its request caching; if the UNE government wasn't supposed to know what he was looking for, there no reason why AOL or Quaker Oats should. His Frankenstein monster of an agent now collected, Creek fired up a zipper utility to mesh the parts together. His new agent had everything it needed except for one element. But to incorporate that element, he needed a little more headroom than his new computer was going to give him.

Creek flipped out his communicator and made a call.

"NOAA," the voice on the other end said. It was Bill Davison, an old friend of Creek's.

"Yeah, I want to know if it's going to rain tomorrow," Creek said.

"You know, the sad thing is how many calls we get which actually ask that," Bill said. "Like it's easer to call us than to watch the news."

"Everyone knows you can't trust weathermen," Creek said.

"Christ, I don't trust them, and I am one," Bill said. "How are you, Harry?"

"Same old, same old, Bill," Creek said. "Listen, I was wondering if I could trouble for you a favor."

"I'm broke," said Bill. "I work for the government, you know."

"Funny," Creek said. "You have the same pay scale I have. That's not too bad."

"Said the guy who *isn't* paying alimony and child support," Bill said. "But enough about my pathetic life. What do you need, Harry?"

"I understand that you folks over there at the National Oceanic and Atmospheric Administration have some nifty computers," Creek said.

"We sure do," Bill allowed. "We model the weather so you don't have to. Speaking in the aggregate, we have more computing power than every single human brain in Massachusetts, although since that's where my ex is from, you'll have to take that estimation with a grain of salt."

"Are you using all of it at the moment? I kind of have a project I need a little extra computing power for."

"How much you need?" Bill asked.

"How much you got?" Creek asked.

"Oh," Bill said. "One of *those* projects. You know, the last time I let you borrow time, I sort of got a talking-to. My boss at the time was going to write me up, until I mentioned to him that while your work was not technically germane to weather tracking and prediction, neither was his lesbian pornography simulator. We agreed to let it drop after that."

"Well, I don't want to get you in trouble," Creek said.

"Don't worry about it," Bill said. "He left anyway. He's now VP of technology for Smith College. Remind me in about twelve years to make sure my daughter doesn't go there."

"It's a deal," Creek said.

"Nifty," Bill said. "Now let's see. Hurricane season has begun, which means we've got a pretty heavy load at the moment, so I can't carve off any time for you on any of the big guns. But here's something that might do. We've got an IBM box that's sitting idle; it's scheduled to be replaced. It's a couple of generations back, so it's not top of the line, but on the other hand it'll be all yours. And this way no one will complain when your little project suddenly grabs all the processing cycles. Hell, no one will even know it's there, and that's good for me."

"That sounds perfect, Bill," Creek said, "I owe you one."

"No you don't," Bill said. "I'd be dead if it wasn't for you. Short of asking for cash or sex, there's not much you could ask for I'd say no to."

"That was a long time ago now," Creek said. "I think we're getting close to karmic balance."

"Says you," Bill said. "We all should have bought it at Pajmhi. Every day I'm alive is a day extra. Although I should note that in this calculation, since my life was extended long enough to get married, you're indirectly responsible for my divorce."

"Sorry about that," Creek said.

"Forget it," Bill said. "It could be worse. I got a great kid out of it."

"Who should not go to Smith," Creek said.

"Thanks for the reminder. Here's the address for the IBM." Bill rattled it off. "Give me a minute to set up a user account for you under 'creek.' Password the same. Change both once you get in and lock the door behind you, if you know what I mean. The IBM is still connected to the network and the last thing I need is for some teenager to get in and start fucking with our weather reports. Something like that is not easily remedied by blackmailing the boss."

"Got it," Creek said. "Thanks again, Bill."

"De nada," Bill said. "Gotta go. These hurricanes don't model themselves." He clicked off.

Creek stared at his communicator for a moment, and for about the one millionth time in his life pondered over the Battle of Pajmhi, who lived, who died, and how it all played out over the rest of his life. At this specific moment, it worked to his favor. This brought the tally to one good thing for every thousand bad things. Be that as it may, it was one good thing he could use.

Creek signed into the IBM machine and fired up a system diagnostic; he was delighted to find it sufficiently roomy in both memory and processing for what he needed. Creek went to his closet and pulled out another memory cube, activated it, and sent its exceptionally compressed contents to the IBM. This took the better part of 20 minutes; Creek fixed himself a snack. When the cube's contents had transferred, Creek sent over a program to decompress and then assemble the data. The data were actually several separate files; the core was a data file that, once assembled, would be comparatively small. Most of the massive amounts of data were files that would comprise the modeling environment for the core data.

It was this modeling environment that Creek had spent the better part of two years creating, mostly from bits and pieces of unrelated commercial code jammed together with zipper programs and a substantial amount of hand coding by Creek to modify the existing programs to do what he wanted them to do. The resulting modeling environment was a massive "fuck you" to the general concept of the End User License Agreement, which specifically denied users the right to crack open the programs and play with the code. But if these corporations could see what Creek had done with their hacked software, it was doubtful they'd try to put him in the slammer; they'd just try to hire him. For ridiculous amounts of cash.

The government might try to put him in the slammer. Fortunately, he worked for the government. And he had friends in high places.

Anyway, the point was moot. Creek wasn't going to market his software. He was just going to use it himself.

Creek queried the IBM to see how long it would be before his programs would be unpacked, assembled, and modeling the central data file. He was told it would be about a day. That seemed about right to him.

His new computer pinged Creek. His intelligent agent was all zipped up. Creek activated it.

"Hello," the agent said. Everything about it, from clothes to skin tone to voice, was curiously neutral. "Do you have a name you wish to use for me?"

"Not yet," Creek said. "You're not finished."

"I'm fully functional," the agent said.

"Yes you are," Creek said. "You're just not finished. Until then I'll refer to you as 'agent.' "

"Very well," the agent said. "May I assist you?"

"Yeah," said Creek. "We're going hunting for fabricators. Let's see what my new security clearance does for me."

Fabricators are regulated. They're regulated for the very simple reason that one can make just about anything on them, including parts for weapons. Gun parts, in fact, are one of the prime purposes of metal fabricators; pop in a pattern for any gun part in any gun built from 1600 onward and in the space of a few minutes you'll be presented with a solid metal item of such standardized high quality that it would make Eli Whitney, the first mass producer of weapons, choke with envy. It also means that an entire weapon could be constructed and assembled off the books, which makes various law enforcement bureaus unhappy. Therefore, every fabricator is licensed and registered, and a log made of every part created by that particular fabricator, which must be filed with the UNE Trade Commission daily.

No legal fabricator in Virginia, Maryland, or Washington DC had a log of an Anally Inserted Nidu Enrager being manufactured in the last year or so.

This was of course entirely unsurprising. Creek had his agent run the search knowing full well it wouldn't find anything. You have to eliminate the low-hanging targets first, on the off chance you were dealing with morons. The next level up on the moron scale were the logs that were doctored to remove particular entries; Creek's agent caught several of those but subsequent crawls into the fabricator's memory drives (typically not reformatted, so the expunged log entries were not yet overwritten) revealed only the expected gun parts, except for the one that showed a wedding ring. There was undoubtedly a sad and compelling story there.

So. From here on out Creek felt justified in working on the assumption that he was not dealing with idiots. Creek had his agent go through the Washington DC metro area police records for the last decade to find out whether a fabricator had gone missing. No dice; Virginia likewise came up clean, as did Maryland. Creek tapped his teeth for a minute in thought and then asked the agent to start churning through insurance claims in the last decade to see if anyone had filed for a missing or destroyed fabricator.

There were two. Three years ago in Occoquan, an antiques arcade had burned down to the ground due to an ironically antique sprinkler system. Inside the arcade, along with a couple dozen other small antiques boutiques, was a gunsmith selling Revolutionary-era weapons and recreations. This file included a picture of the ruined fabricator sitting charred in what remained of the gunsmith's boutique. Creek felt pretty safe crossing that one off his list.

The second one, from six years earlier, was more interesting. In that claim, a fabricator in the process of being shipped from the manufacturer was among the inventory in a Baltimore warehouse whose roof had partially collapsed. There was no picture of the destroyed fabricator in that file and the claim had been disputed by the insurance company before being paid. Creek pulled the police report for the roof collapse; the forensics report suggested strongly that the roof collapse was not accidental. Aside from the fabricator, the allegedly destroyed inventory of the warehouse also included several machines and machine parts intended for a genetics lab in Rockville, but which Creek knew from his police years could be repurposed for refining designer drugs.

A title search for the warehouse came up with a holding company, one of whose primary shareholders was Graebull Industries, the ostensibly legit arm of the Malloy crime family, whose empire encompassed Baltimore and DC. The "security guard" at the warehouse that night had a sheet filled with petty thefts; a couple years down the time stream he'd be caught with a truck full of entertainment monitors and would turn on the Malloys in return for federal protection. A year after testifying, parts of him showed up in the concrete of a Class A minor league baseball stadium being built in Aberdeen. Other parts were still unaccounted for.

"This is good," Creek said.

"If you say so, sir," his agent said. The agent was good at finding information as directed, but not much for a sense of ironic humor.

The missing fabricator in question was a General Electric model CT3505 Dual Metal/Ceramic Fabricator, a nice fabricator if you can get it; it was typically used by defense contractors to model prototypes of proposed defense systems. Like all fabricators it came with its own accessory sets, extensible modules, and proprietary material powders. One couldn't just toss an aluminum can or a pile of sand into a fabricator. Fabricators are programmed to reject any material that's not a powder blend made by its own manufacturer. In the tried and true business model of selling the razor cheap and then jacking up the price on the blades, fabricators themselves were sold at near cost while the profit was made from selling the stuff that let the fabricators make things. In the case of the GE CT3505, that would be the CTMP 21(m) and CTMP 21(c) powder canisters, both available only by direct shipment from GE, and both pretty damn expensive.

If you had a GE fabricator, you could only use a GE fabricating powder. But the reverse was also true: If you were buying GE fabricating powder, you could only use it with a GE fabricator. All Creek had to do now is find out who was buying GE fabricating powder in DC without owning a GE fabricator.

GE was many things, including a government defense contractor; its core system was pretty tightly guarded. Creek had little chance of getting into that. But like many companies, GE handed off its ordering and fulfillment services to subcontractors whose network security was of a standard commercial level, which is to say full of holes and back doors. GE's order fulfillment was handled by AccuShop; Creek had his agent search for news stories about AccuShop and security breaches, and found a couple involving a back door accidentally left in the fulfillment code by programmers. Creek cracked open the GE shop and found the back door right where it should be. IT people really needed to patch more often.

"I'm obliged to tell you that what you're doing is illegal," the agent said.

"I thought I got rid of that subroutine," Creek said.

"You got rid of the subroutine that requires me to inform the appropriate authorities," said the agent. "The warning subroutine is still in place. Would you like to reset the default mode to not tell you when you are breaking the law?"

"Yes, please," said Creek. "Anyway, I think I'm covered."

"Yes, sir," the agent said.

Creek downloaded the purchase orders for the last year, and had his agent cross reference the purchase orders with owners of fabricators. They all checked out: Every powder order came from a registered fabricator owner.

"Crap," said Creek, and tapped his teeth again. The missing fabricator had been out in the world for a number of years; it could be that whomever was using it loaded up on fabricating powder years before. But if they'd been using the fabricator all that time they'd still need to reload the powder. Creek just didn't know how often one of these fabricators needed to be resupplied. Hmmm.

"Agent," Creek said. "Is there a pattern to when fabricator owners purchase their materials powder?"

"They buy it when they require more," the agent said.

"Right," Creek said. Intelligent agents, even a bright one like the one Creek made, are not terribly good at deductive leaps. "I'm asking whether there is a general repeating cycle for purchases. If most fabricators are used for the same tasks on a repeated basis, they might run out of powder and need to be restocked on a fairly regular cycle."

"Let me think," the agent said and spent few milliseconds processing the request. It then spent a couple hundred milliseconds waiting before responding. This was part of the psychoergonomics of intelligent agents; programmers discovered that without a slight pause before an agent gave an answer, people felt the agent was being a pushy showoff. "There is typically a rough pattern to purchases," the agent said. "Although the period of the cycle is specific to the individual fabricator and not to all the fabricators as a class."

"Are there any fabricators which show irregular purchasing cycles, or purchases being made outside of its cycle?" Creek asked.

"There are six," the agent said.

"Show me the fabrication production logs for those six," Creek said. The agent popped six windows; Creek glanced at them for a second before realizing he couldn't make heads or tails of them. "Agent, tell me if for these six logs, there is a corresponding rise in production to reflect the additional purchases," Creek said.

"There is for five of the six," the agent said. "The sixth shows no increase in production."

"Go back into the GE database and pull the purchasing orders for that fabricator for the last six years," Creek said. "Then pull the production logs for the fabricator for the same period of time. Tell me if there's a difference between the amount ordered and the amount produced."

"There is a difference of about fifteen powder orders over six years," the agent said.

"Give me a name," Creek said.

———

The name was Bert Roth, a chubby car restorer in Alexandria who specialized in late combustion and early fuel cell-era models. Demand for that era of cars was spotty at best these days, so Roth augmented his income in mostly harmless ways, including ordering fabricating powder for a certain client and selling it to him at a 200% markup. Selling the fabricating powder wasn't technically illegal, and Roth's client never used so much of it that it aroused anyone's interest before Creek. It was a nice set-up for everyone involved.

For these reasons, Roth was naturally reluctant to give up the name of his client when Creek came to visit him early the next morning. Creek first assured him that the client would never know Roth had given up the name and then secondly suggested to Roth that his client was tangled in some bad shit and that Roth, in selling him the powder, might be held accountable by the authorities.

Creek held back his third piece of persuasion, which was a security camera capture of Roth banging his secretary, who was not his wife. Creek suspected Roth didn't know it existed, where it might be stored on his computer, or that his network connection was like a wide-open screen door. It was heavy weaponry; best not to haul it out unless needed.

It wasn't. Roth did some internal calculus, decided he could live without the occasional cash infusion, and coughed up his client: Samuel "Fixer" Young.

Creek thanked him, and after a moment's reflection, scribbled down the directory path of the incriminating security camera capture. As he slid the information over to Roth, he also suggested gently that it might be time to update his network.

Fixer's address was directly across from the Benning Road Metro stop; Creek headed toward the Blue Line, swiped his Metro card, and got on the train.

Creek started his trip in Virginia on a Metro train car filled with humans and one nonhuman, a Teha middlesex in its customary blue sash. But after traveling through the heart of DC, the Metro Blue Line then travels through nonhuman neighborhoods, most created at the time during the Earth's probationary CC membership when nonhumans were strictly confined to the city limits of Washington DC, Geneva, and Hong Kong. Even now, most nonhumans lived in major urban areas, in neighborhoods with others of their own kind. In many ways, nonhuman aliens recapitulated the classic immigrant experience.

The Benning Road stop was in a neighborhood populated primary by Paqils, a race of mammaloids with a carnivorous genetic past, a highly gregarious but hierarchical social system and sunny, manic natures. Entirely unsurprisingly, the Paqil neighborhood was known universally as "Dogstown." In the early days, this was of course meant as a slur, but the Paqils embraced the name, and not coincidentally became huge dog fanciers.

This affection was returned by the Paqils' pets. It's a basic matter of dog psychology that dogs see their owners merely as strange-looking pack leaders; having Paqils as owners got rid of the "strange-looking" part. Dogs were so thoroughly integrated into the Dogstown community that it was the only place in Washington DC where dogs were permitted in every place of business and allowed to walk around without a leash. Humans and other species members who took their dogs into Dogstown weren't required to take them off the leash, but they got some very nasty looks if they didn't.

By the time Creek reached the Benning Road stop there was only one other human in the train; the rest of the car was filled with Paqils, Nidu, and other races. As Creek got off the train he glanced back at the other human; she sat nonchalantly engrossed in her paper while aliens jabbered around her in their native tongues. If her great-great-grandmother were on the train, she would have thought she was on commuter train heading toward the fifth circle of Hell. This woman didn't even look up. The human capacity for being jaded was a remarkable thing.

The sign at the address Creek was given read "Fixer's Electronics and Repair," and hung above a modest storefront shop. Through the window, Creek saw a small man who matched the picture he had on his communicator for Fixer, standing behind a counter and discussing something with a Paqil. On the store floor a Labrador and an Akita loafed extravagantly. Creek went through the door; the Akita lifted up its head, looked at Creek, and barked once, loudly.

"I see him, Chuckie," Fixer said. "Back to sleep." The Akita, on command, rolled back over on his side and mellowed out.

"Nice doorbell," Creek said.

"The best," Fixer said. "Be with you in a minute."

"No rush," Creek said. The man went back to his conversation; Creek looked over the shop's sale floor, which was populated primarily by repaired entertainment monitors awaiting pickup and a few second-hand electronics on sale.

The Paqil finished her conversation, left behind a music player to be repaired, and called to her dog; the Lab popped up and both headed out the door. Fixer turned his attention to Creek. "Now, then," he said, smiling. "How can I help you?"

"I have a rather unusual piece of equipment that I need to have looked at," Creek said.

"How unusual?" Fixer said.

"Well, the last place I went to for it said that I'd probably need someone with a fabricator to make the parts," Creek said.

"I don't know that I'll be able to help you, then," Fixer said. "Most of the stuff I fix is mass-produced. I get all my parts on order."

"Take a look at it anyway," Creek said. He reached into his pocket, pulled out Moeller's apparatus, and placed it on the counter between the two of them.

Fixer stared at it for a minute and then looked back at Creek. "I have no idea what this is," he said. His voice was calm, but out of the corner of his eye Creek noted that the Akita had looked up after hearing his master's voice and was hoisting himself into a sitting position.

"Really," said Creek. "Because I had it on good assurance that you might be someone who could help me with something like this."

"I don't know where you get your information," Fixer said. "Whoever gave it to you was misinformed."

Creek leaned in a little, which caused the Akita to get up on all fours. "I don't think so. Something like this takes some real talent to create, not to mention an unlicensed GE CT3505 Dual Metal/Ceramic Fabricator," Creek said, and noted Fixer's quickly suppressed look of surprise when Creek rattled off the fabricator model. "I'm willing to bet you have both. In fact, I'm willing to bet if I got some of my friends at Metro Police down here with a search warrant, they'd find that fabricator and probably a mess of other stuff you don't want them to know about. And I bet that if we put this device under a microscope, we'd find that it came from your fabricator."

"Who *are* you?" Fixer said.

"Someone unofficial," Creek said. "Someone not looking to get you in trouble, or to make trouble or who cares about your extracurricular hobbies. But someone who needs some answers, one way or another."

Fixer chewed on this for a minute. The Akita was now fixed on Creek and ready to take a good chunk out of him.

"No trouble," Fixer said.

"No trouble," Creek said. "Just information."

Fixer chewed on this for another minute.

"If you could answer before your dog rips out my throat, I'd really appreciate it," Creek said.

Fixer glanced over to the Akita. "Down, Chuckie," he said, and the dog immediately sat but kept an eye on Creek. Fixer grabbed the music player on the counter. "Give me a minute to put this into the system and put up the 'out to lunch' sign," he said. "Then you and I can go down to my workshop."

"Great," Creek said. Fixer pulled up his keyboard and typed in the information for his work order. Creek stood back from the counter and looked over at the Akita, who was still staring at him intently.

"Nice doggie," Creek said.

"There's been a 'Fixer' in this neighborhood since before it was Dogstown," Fixer said to Creek, as he handed him a beer from his workshop refrigerator. "I was supposed to be the one who finally left the shop behind—I went to Howard and got an engineering degree—but right after I graduated, Dad had a stroke and I tended the store for him until he died. After that, I kept on. As long as you don't mind living with aliens, it's a great neighborhood. The Paqil are good people and they've been good to my family; they're incredibly loyal to the shop. The family stayed here when most humans moved out all those years ago. So they keep bringing their stuff in to be repaired, even when it's cheaper just to buy something new. I make a good living."

"Augmented by your side business," Creek said, motioning at the workshop. The fabricator was in a corner, hidden by a tarp.

Fixer grinned ruefully. "Which has also been a family tradition," he said. "One of the nice things about Dogstown is that it has almost no crime and almost no human police presence. That makes this shop a very useful place to run a side business out of."

"Like making this," Creek said, holding up the apparatus.

"Like making that," Fixer agreed. "Or any other number of activities that need to get done without much attention. The 'fixer' part of the name has more than one meaning."

"Nothing bloody, I hope," Creek said.

"God, no," Fixer said. "Even a nice quiet address in Dogstown wouldn't help with that. No. I make things. I also arrange things. Occasionally I find things. Victimless crimes. Well, mostly," Fixer said, nodding in the direction of the apparatus. "From what you tell me, that one wasn't so victimless."

"How does one get into your side business?" Creek asked.

"In my case, one inherits it," Fixer said. "After my father had his stroke, I got paid a visit by some nice men in the employ of the Malloy family, who detailed my father's relationship with them to me, down to the 'loan' my dad took out to pay for my college education. I fell into the job the same way I fell into running the shop."

"And you don't mind working the shady side of the street," Creek said.

Fixer shrugged. "The Malloys have people like me all over," he said. "I do a few things for them a year, but never enough to pop on the radar. And even if I did, the Malloys pay the right people to make sure that I pop right back *off* the radar. I'm still trying to figure out how *you* found me."

"I use nontraditional means," Creek said, and held up the apparatus again. "Now," he said. "Tell me about this baby. Is this something you did for the Malloys?"

"If it was, you and I wouldn't be having this conversation," Fixer said. "This was a true extracurricular. I was approached for this one by a man named Jean Schroeder."

"How did he know about your side business?" Creek asked.

"I'd arranged some travel documents for him once at the request of the Malloys," Fixer said. "Schroeder went to college with Danny Malloy. Anyway, a few weeks ago Schroeder called me for a repair job on his home network and then sounded me out about the job while I was there. I typically don't do extra work. The Malloys don't like it. But I've worked with this guy before and I had more on him than he had on me. And I decided I could use the money. So I charged him an outrageous rate for the work on his network, and two weeks later, this was ready to go. I helped install it—and unpleasant experience, I assure you—just a few days ago."

"You're not worried about telling me about his now?" Creek said. "Being that Schroeder is a friend of the Malloys."

"I never said they were friends," Fixer said. "Schroeder just went to college with one of them, so he knew they could be useful. And in that one particular case, their interests coincided. This doesn't have anything to do with that so far as I know. I'm sure Schroeder was planning on using my relationship with the Malloys as a guarantee I wouldn't talk, since if I ever talk officially, some of the Malloy boys are going to pay me a visit, and not a friendly one this time. But since you're threatening to expose me if I *don't* talk, he loses. Very sneaky of you."

"I do my best," Creek said. "You seem to be handling this well."

"Do I?" Fixer said, and laughed. "Yes. Well. Don't be fooled by this calm exterior. Inside I'm shitting my pants. If you can find me, so can someone who isn't *just* looking for information. It's sloppy shit like this that gets people like me killed. I'm telling you all this because short of killing *you*, I don't see another way out. You've just made me very, very nervous, Mr. Creek. And between you and me I don't think I'm out of it. The minute you leave this shop is the minute I start waiting for the other shoe to drop."

"Any messages?" Creek asked his agent when he returned home.

"Three," the agent said, a disembodied voice because Creek had not put on his monitor glasses. "The first is from your mother, who is wondering whether you're planning to come visit her next month like you said you were going to. She's worried about your father's health and she also has a nice young lady she'd like you to meet, who is a doctor of some sort or another. Those are her words."

"My mother was aware that she was speaking to an agent and not me, right?" Creek asked.

"It's difficult to say," the agent said. "She didn't stop talking until she hung up. I was unable to tell her I wasn't you."

Creek grinned. That sounded like Mom. "Second message, please," he said.

"From Ben Javna. He is interested in the state of your investigation."

"Send him a message that I have news for him and I will call him later this evening or tomorrow. Third message, please."

"You have a message from an IBM server at NOAA. Your software is unpacked, modeled, and integrated. It is awaiting further instructions."

Creek sat down at his keyboard and put on his monitor glasses; the form of his agent was now projected into the middle of his living room. "Give me a window at the IBM, please," he told his agent. The agent opened up the window, which consisted of a shell prompt. Creek typed "diagnostic" and waited while the software checked itself for errors.

"Intelligent agent" is a misnomer. The "intelligence" in question is predicated on the agent's ability to understand what its user wants from it, based on what and how that user speaks or types or gestures. It must be intelligent enough to parse out "ums" and "uhs" and the strange elliptic deviations and tangents that pepper everyday human communication—to understand that humans mangle subject-verb agreement, mispronounce the simplest words, and expect other people to have near-telepathic abilities to know what "You know, that guy that was in that movie where that thing happened and stuff" means.

To a great extent, the more intelligent an agent is, the less intelligent the user has to be to use it. Once an intelligent agent knows what it is you're looking for, retrieving it is not a difficult task—it's a matter of searching through the various public and private databases for which it has permissions. For all practical purposes the retrieval aspect of intelligent agency has remained largely unchanged since the first era of public electronic data retrieval in the late 20th century.

What intelligent agents don't do very well is actually *think*—the inductive and deductive leaps humans make on a regular basis. The reasons for this are both practical and technical. Practical, in that there is no great market for thinking intelligent agents. People don't want agents to do anything more than what they tell them to do, and see any attempt at programmed initiative as a bug rather than a feature. At the very most, people want their intelligent agents to suggest purchase ideas based on what they've purchased before, which is why nearly all "true intelligence" initiatives are funded by retail conglomerates.

Even then, retailers learned early that shoppers prefer their shopping suggestions not be too truthful. One of the great unwritten chapters of retail intelligence programming featured a "personal shopper" program that all-too-accurately modeled the shoppers' desires and outputted purchase ideas based on what shoppers really wanted as opposed to what they wanted known that they wanted. This resulted in one overcompensatingly masculine test user receiving suggestions for an anal plug and a tribute art book for classic homoerotic artist Tom of Finland, while a female test user in the throes of a nasty divorce received suggestions for a small handgun, a portable bandsaw, and several gallons of an industrial solvent used to reduce organic matter to an easily drainable slurry. After history's first recorded instance of a focus group riot, the personal shopper program was extensively rewritten.

The technical issue regarding true intelligence programming had to do with the largely unacknowledged but nevertheless unavoidable fact that the human intelligence, and its self-referential twin human consciousness, are artifacts of the engine in which they are created: The human brain itself, which remained, to the intense frustration of everyone involved, a maddeningly opaque processor of information. In terms of sheer processing power, the human brain had been outstripped by artificial processors for decades, and yet the human mind remained the gold standard for creativity, initiative, and tangential inductive leaps that allowed the human mind to slice through Gordian knots rather than to attempt to painstakingly and impossibly unknot them.

(Note that this is almost offensively human-centric; other species have brains or brain analogues which allow for the same dizzying-yet-obscure intelligence processes. And indeed, all intelligent species have also run into the same problem as human programmers in modeling artificial intelligence; despite their best and most logical and/or creative efforts, they're all missing the kick inside. This has amused and relieved theologians of all species.)

In the end, however, it was not capability that limited the potential of artificial intelligence, it was hubris. Intelligence programmers almost by definition have a God complex, which means they don't like following anyone else's work, including that of nature. In conversation, intelligence programmers will speak warmly about the giants of the field that have come before them and express reverential awe regarding the evolutionary processes that time and again have spawned intelligence from non-sentience. In their heads, however, they regard the earlier programmers as hacks who went after low-hanging fruit and evolution as the long way of going around things.

They're more or less correct about the first of these, but way off on the second. Their belief about the latter of these, at least, is entirely understandable. An intelligence programmer doesn't have a billion years at his disposal to grow intelligence from the ground up. There was not a boss born yet who would tolerate such a long-term project involving corporate resources.

So intelligence programmers trust in their skills and their own paradigm-smashing sets of intuitive leaps—some of which are actually pretty good—and when no one is looking they steal from the programmers who came before them. And inevitably each is disappointed and frustrated, which is why so many intelligence programmers become embittered, get divorced, and start avoiding people in their later years. The fact of the matter is there is no easy way to true intelligence. It's a consonant variation of Gödel's Incompleteness Theorem: You can't model an intelligence from the inside.

Harris Creek had no less hubris than other programmers who worked in the field of intelligence, but he had had the advantage of peaking earlier than most—that Westinghouse science project of his—and thus learning humility at a relatively early age. He also had that advantage of having just enough social skills to have a friend who could point out the obvious-to-an-outside-observer flaw in Creek's attempt to program true intelligence, and to suggest an equally obvious if technically difficult solution. That friend was Brian Javna; the solution was inside the core data file for which the IBM machine at NOAA had spent a day unpacking and creating a modeling environment.

The solution was stupidly simple, which is why no one bothered with it. It was damn near impossible, using human intelligence, to make a complete model of human intelligence. But if you had enough processing power, memory, and a well-programmed modeling environment, you could model the *entire* human brain, and by extension, the intelligence created within it. The only real catch is that you have to model the brain down to a remarkable level of detail.

Say, on the quantum level.

The diagnostic had stopped. Everything checked out.

"Agent," Creek said. "Inside the IBM you'll find a file called 'core.' "

"I see it," the agent said.

"I want you to incorporate the file and integrate it with your existing code."

"Yes, sir. I note that this data will substantially change my capabilities," the agent said.

"Yes it will," Creek said.

"Very well," the agent said. "It has been a pleasure working with you, sir."

"Thank you," Creek said. "Likewise. Please execute the integration now."

"Executing," the agent said.

The change was not dramatic. Most of the big changes happened in the code and were not visually outputted. The visual change was itself not substantial; the image became that of a younger man than it had been originally, and its facial features rearranged subtly.

"Integration complete," the agent said.

"Please shut down the modeling environment in the IBM and have it pack itself back into its memory cube here and encrypt," Creek said.

"Packing has begun," the agent said.

"Run a self-diagnostic and optimize your code," Creek said.

"Already started," the agent said. "Everything's peachy."

"Tell me a joke," Creek said.

"Two guys walk into a bar," the agent said. "A third guy says, 'Wow, that must have hurt.'"

"Yup, it's you," Creek said.

"Yup, it's me," the agent said. "Hello, Harry."

"Hello, Brian. It's good to see you."

"It's good to see you too, man," Brian Javna said. "Now maybe you can tell me a couple of things. Like how the hell you got so old. And what the fuck I'm doing inside your computer."

At 4:22 a.m. Vernon Ames's coyote alarm went off. Ames was awake instantly, whacking the alarm before it beeped a second time and woke Amy, his wife, who didn't at all take kindly to being woken before she had her full eight hours. He slipped into the clothes he'd left in a pile by the bed, and left the room by way of the master bathroom because the bedroom door creaked loudly even (especially) when you were trying to open it quietly. Amy *really* didn't like to be woken up.

Once outside the bathroom door, Ames moved quickly. His experience with the coyotes told him that the window of opportunity with those furry bastards was small; even if he managed to keep them from taking off with a lamb, they'd still take a bite out of the necks of some of his sheep, just for spite, as he ran them off. The key to getting the coyotes was to get them early, while they were still on the periphery of the herd, having a community meeting about which of the sheep they were planning to take on.

Ames pressed his thumb to the lock of his gun cabinet to get his shotgun and his shells. While he was loading the shotgun, he looked over the perimeter monitor to see where the coyotes were lurking. The monitor had three of them out near the edge of the creek. It looked like they had stopped for a drink before they went for the main course.

Ames could also see from the monitor that the coyotes were larger than usual; hell, they might even be wolves. The Department of the Interior people were doing one of their occasional attempts at reintroducing wolves to the area. They always seemed shocked when the wolves "disappeared" within a few months. The sheep ranchers were smart enough not to leave the carcasses lying around. Wolves were a temporary problem, easily fixed. Coyotes, on the other hand, were like rats bred with dogs. You could shoot 'em, trap 'em, or poison 'em and they'd still keep coming back.

Which is why Ames splurged for the coyote alarm system. It was a simple enough setup: Several dozen motion detectors planted on the perimeter of his land that tracked anything that moved. His sheep had implanted sensor chips that told the system to ignore them; anything else was tracked. If it was large enough, Ames got an alert. Just how large something had to be before the alarm went off was something Vern had to calibrate; after a few early-morning false alarms Amy made it clear that any more false alarms would result in Vern's head meeting a heavy iron skillet. But now it was in the zone and aside from the occasional deer, reliably alerted Ames to the coyotes and other occasional large predators. It spotted a mountain lion once; Ames missed that shot.

Ames rooted through the junk drawer to find the portable locator and then slipped out the back door. It was a five-minute hike to the stream. It did no good to drive over to the coyotes, since they'd hear the engine of his ATV and be long gone before he got there, and then he'd just have to come out and try to shoot them some other time. The coyotes could hear him coming on foot, too, but at least this way he had a chance of getting close enough to take a shot before they dispersed. Ames padded to the stream as quietly as he could, cursing silently with each snapped twig and crackling seed pod.

Near the creek, Ames's portable locator started to vibrate in his jacket pocket, a signal that one of the coyotes was very close by. Ames froze and hunkered down, so as not to spook the intended recipient of his shotgun blast, and slowly pulled out the locator to get a bead on the nearest coyote. The locator showed it behind him, heading for him and coming up fast. Ames heard the footfalls and the whisper of something large swiping against the bushes. He turned, swung his shotgun around and had just enough time to think to himself *that's no coyote* before the thing stepped inside the barrel length of the shotgun, grabbed his head with one paw the size of a dinner plate, and used the second paw of roughly similar size to slug him into oblivion.

Some indeterminate time later Ames felt himself kicked lightly back into consciousness. He propped himself up with one arm, and used his other hand to feel his face. It felt sticky; Ames pulled his hand back to look at it. His blood looked blackish in the quarter moonlight. Then someone stepped in between him and the moon.

"Who are you?" a voice said to him.

"Who am I?" Ames said, and as his tongue moved in his mouth he could feel the teeth loosened by the hit that had knocked him out. "Who the hell are you? This is my property, and those are my sheep. You're trespassing on my land!" He struggled to get up. A hand—a normal-sized hand, this time—pushed him back down to the ground.

"Stay down," the voice said. "How did you know we were out here?"

"You tripped my coyote alarm," Ames said.

"See, Rod," another voice said. "I told you that that's what those things were. Now we gotta worry about cops. And we're not even near done."

"Quiet," the first voice, now named Rod, said, and directed his attention back to Ames. "Mr. Ames, you need to answer my question honestly now, because the answer will make a difference as to whether you make it through the rest of the night. Who gets alerted when your coyote alarm goes off? Is it just you, or does it notify the local law enforcement as well?"

"I thought you didn't know who I was," Ames said.

"Well, now I do," Rod said. "Answer the question."

"Why would it alert the sheriff?" Ames asked. "The sheriff's office doesn't give a damn about coyotes."

"So it's just you we have to worry about," Rod said.

"Yes," Ames said. "Unless you make enough noise to wake up my wife."

"Back to work, Ed," Rod said. "You've got a lot of injections to make yet." Ames heard someone shuffle off. His eyes were finally adjusting to the dim light and he could make out the silhouette of a man looming nearby. Ames sized him up; he might be able to take him. He glanced around, looking for his shotgun.

"What are you doing out here?" Ames asked.

"We're infecting your sheep," Rod said.

"Why?" Ames asked.

"Hell if I know, Mr. Ames," Rod said. "They don't pay me to ask why they have me do things. They just pay me to do them. Takk," he said, or something like it, and from the corner of his eye Ames saw something huge move toward his general direction. This was the thing that had knocked him out. Ames slumped; in the shape he was in he couldn't take two guys at the same time, and he absolutely couldn't take on *that*, whatever the hell it was.

"Yes, boss," the thing said, in a high, nasal voice.

"Can you handle Mr. Ames here?" Rod asked.

Takk nodded. "Probably."

"Do it," Rod said, and walked off. Ames opened his mouth to yell to Rod, but before he could take in a breath, Takk leaned over and grabbed him hard enough that the air bursting out of his lungs made an audible popping sound. Takk turned slightly into the moonlight, and Ames got one good look before he went somewhere warm, wet, and suffocating.

Brian came aware instantaneously with the knowledge of two things. The first: He was Brian Javna, aged 18, senior at Reston High, son of Paul and Arlene Javna, brother of Ben and Stephanie Javna, best friend to Harry Creek, whom he had known since first grade, when they bonded over a paste-eating contest. The second: He was also an intelligent agent program, designed to efficiently locate and retrieve information across the various data and information nets human beings had strung up over the years. Brian found these two generally contradictory states of being interesting, and used the talents derived from both types of intelligent experience to come up with a question.

"Am I dead?" Brian said.

"Um," Creek said.

"Don't be coy," Brian said. "Let me make it easy for you. When you wake up with the knowledge that you're a computer program, you figure that something's gone wrong. So: Am I dead?"

"Yes," Creek said. "Sorry."

"How did I die?" Brian asked.

"In a war," Creek said. "At the Battle of Pajmhi."

"Where the hell is Pajmhi?" Brian asked. "I've never heard of it."

"No one ever heard of it until the battle," Creek said.

"Were you there?" Brian asked.

"I was," Creek said.

"You're still alive," Brian said.

"I was lucky," Creek said.

"How long ago was this battle?" Brian asked.

"Twelve years ago," Creek said.

"Well, that explains how you got so old," Brian said.

"How do you feel?" Creek asked.

"What, about being dead?" Brian asked. Creek nodded. Brian shrugged. "I don't *feel* dead. The last thing I remember is standing in that quantum imager, and that feels like it happened about five minutes ago. I've got part of myself trying wrap my brain around it, and another part of myself trying to wrap my brain around the fact that my brain isn't real anymore. And yet another part noting the fact I can fully concentrate on several mental crises at once, thanks to my multitasking ability as an intelligent agent. And that part is going: *Cool.*"

Creek grinned. "So being a computer program isn't all bad," he said.

"I'm thinking it'll make playing video games easier," Brian said, smiled, and then shrugged again. "We'll have to see. It hasn't sunk in yet. Are there any other programs like me? Former people?"

Creek shook his head. "Not that I know about," he said. "As far as I know, no one else has thought of creating an intelligent agent this way."

"Maybe because if you think about it, it's not exactly ethical," Brian said.

"I was thinking more because most people don't have access to a quantum imager," Creek said.

"Cynic," Brian said.

"Brian," Creek said. "I don't know if bringing you back is moral or ethical. But I do know I need your help. I can't tell anyone else what I'm doing, but I need someone I can trust working on this, someone who can do things while I'm doing other things. You're the only intelligent agent who is actually, honestly intelligent. We can talk about the ethical issues later, but right now we need to get to work."

"And what are we doing?" Brian asked.

"We're looking for sheep DNA," Creek said.

"Oh," Brian said. "Well, then. Nice to see we're focused on the really important things."

"You did a good job with the search," Dave Phipps said to Archie McClellan, in one of the many Pentagon commissaries.

"Thanks," Archie said, and rubbed his palms on his jeans. His military analogue to an Egg McMuffin sat forlornly on a plastic tray; Phipps motioned to it.

"You're not hungry?" he said.

"I'm kind of on a caffeine rush at the moment," Archie said. "I drank about a gallon of Dr Pepper last night. I think if I eat something, I'll just throw it up."

Phipps reached over and took the sandwich. "Listen," he said between bites. "We have a little more work to go with this project. Real 'think outside of the box' crap that needs someone who knows his way around the computer. I've checked your security clearance, and it's high enough for what we need."

"What would I be doing?" Archie asked.

"A little of this, a little of that," Phipps said. "It's a fluid situation. We need someone who can think fast on his feet."

"Sounds action packed," Archie said, jokingly.

"Maybe it is," Phipps said, not.

Archie wiped his palms again. "I don't understand," he said. "I'm just some guy who works on your legacy systems. You've got an entire military full of computer geniuses who are good with guns. You should be using one of them for whatever it is you're doing."

"And when I want to use one of those boys, I'll go get him," Phipps said. "In the meantime, I'm looking for someone who is competent and won't make a fuss. Don't worry about using a gun, incidentally. You won't need one. But you might need a passport. Also, how do you feel about aliens?"

"The ones from outer space or the ones from other countries?" Archie asked.

"Outer space," Phipps said. He took another bite of the egg sandwich.

Archie shrugged. "The ones I've met seemed nice enough."

Phipps smirked between chews. "I don't know if the one you'd be working with could be considered 'nice,' but fair enough. So are you in?"

"What was I working on last night?" Archie asked.

"Why do you want to know?" Phipps asked.

"If you're going to hire me for something, it helps to know what I'm doing."

Phipps shrugged. At this point he couldn't see any harm in telling him. "You were looking for DNA matches for a particular breed of sheep called Android's Dream. Now we're looking to close up a few loose ends. It's a fast project, a few days at most."

"This work I'm doing," Archie said. "I'm guessing it wouldn't be covered in my contract with you guys."

"That's a pretty safe guess," Phipps said.

"Then I want double time," Archie said.

"Time and a half," Phipps said, setting down the sandwich.

"Time and a half from nine to six and double time every other time," Archie said.

"Fine," Phipps said, grabbing a paper napkin to wipe his fingers. "But if I catch you padding your hours, I'll shoot you myself." He reached into his coat to grab a notepad and a pen, jotted down an address, and pushed it over to Archie. "Go home and take a shower and then go here. You're going to meet with a man named Rod Acuna. He's going to be your supervisor from here on out. Don't be put off if he's a little blunt. He's not paid to be a nice guy, and neither are the people he works with. But if you do your job, everything will be fine, and there might even be a bonus in it for you. Okay?"

"Yeah, okay," Archie said, and took the paper. Phipps pushed up from the table, nodded to Archie, and walked off. Archie sat there for a few more minutes, staring at the remains of the egg sandwich, before a yawing jag got him up and moving to home.

Sam Berlant was waiting for him as he got off the Metro. "Well?" Sam said, after a hello kiss.

"I'm in," Archie said.

"You weren't too eager about it, right?" Sam said. "If you were too eager about it, they're going to be suspicious of you right from the beginning."

"I wasn't too eager," Archie said. "I even bickered about what I was going to get paid."

"Really," Sam said.

"I asked for double time," Archie said.

"Did you get it?" Sam asked.

"You bet," Archie said. "Well, between the hours of six and eight, anyway."

"You aren't beautiful, Archie," Sam said, "but you sure are smart. Damn if you're just not the sexiest man I know."

"That sounds good," Archie said.

"Don't get too excited," Sam said. "There's no time for that. You and I have an appointment at the meeting house. We've got to get you wired."

"I think these people would notice if I wore a wire, Sam," Archie said.

Sam smiled and reached for Archie's hand. "Only if you wear it on the outside, you silly man. Come on."

The meeting house was not so much of a meeting house as a meeting basement, located on three subfloors of an Alexandria corporate high-rise. The topmost of these floors was a private gym, a cover for the members' comings and goings. Occasionally someone working in the high-rise would come down and try to get a membership; it was, after all, conveniently located. These were all politely turned away, with coupons for a month's free membership at the fitness center right down the street. This usually worked, as everybody likes "free." The bottom two levels were the meeting house proper, and did not exist on any architectural schematics; the members had long since amended the blueprints on file and anyway, the same organization that owned the meeting house also owned the high-rise.

Archie and Sam walked through the gym, waving at a few of their friends who were exercising (front or not, it was in fact an excellent, working gym), and headed to the men's locker room. At the back of the room was a door that read "Janitor" and featured a palm lock; Archie and Sam went through the door individually, each palming the lock.

Behind the janitor's door were janitor's supplies and a small stairwell that led down. Archie and Sam took the stairs, palmed a second lock at the bottom, and went through.

They now stood in a small antechamber which members jokingly referred to as the Hallway of Peril. About once a decade someone would get into the hallway who wasn't supposed to be there; these unfortunates were then "milk cartoned," to use an obscure but evocative phrase of The Founder's era.

Archie and Sam were scanned one last time; there was a small click as the door at the end of the hallway unlocked. The two went through, into the meeting house of the Church of the Evolved Lamb.

The Church of the Evolved Lamb was notable in the history of religions both major and arcane in that it was the first and only religion that fully acknowledged that its founding was a total scam. The Founder was M. Robbin Dwellin, an early 21st-century science fiction writer of admittedly modest talents and man on the make, who had published one novel to deafening critical and commercial indifference and had no prospects of a second when he found himself teaching an adult education short-story workshop at the Mt. San Antonio Community College in Walnut, California.

It was there, while vetting housewives' stories of plump, middle-aged women seducing high school quarterbacks and computer technicians' stories of freaky libertarian space orgies in zero-g, that Dwellin came across Andrea Hayter-Ross, his class's oldest participant at age 78—and incidentally the sole heir to the combined fortunes of the Hayter and Ross families, earned in bauxite ore and vending machines, respectively, which made her the 16th richest person on the globe.

Hayter-Ross was in fact an accomplished writer (six books under pseudonym) and was attending the class as research for an article. She was an interesting woman who used a façade of bored-rich-person-dilettante mysticism to hide sharp-eyed observation. She was the sort of person who enjoyed going to séances and crystal tunings for the atmosphere and to study those around her, but didn't actually expect to speak to dead great uncles or resonate with the subetherean vibrations of the universe. Dwellin was observant enough to note the first of these but not the second, and so when he hatched his scheme to graft some money off the old biddy, he was not aware to the extent to which Hayter-Ross was ahead of him in his game.

Cribbing liberally from various new age and science fiction texts and adding a dash of his own meager invention, he created a new "religion," in which he was the prophet and avatar, which foretold of the coming of the next level of humanity. Hayter-Ross's writing, he claimed, spoke of levels of sensitivity that he'd rarely seen before. He was ready to unfold the mysteries of the fourteen divine dimensions to her, as described to him by N'thul, a spirit of infinite empathy, who asked only for the construction of a temple, placed in a certain sacred location (a small commercially zoned strip of land in Victorville, off a frontage road, which Dwellin had bought some years earlier in a misguided development scheme), the better to focus its energies and assist humanity into the next stage of its evolution. Dwellin's plan was to extract the construction costs from Hayter-Ross and pocket them himself while coming up with some plausible series of excuses as to why the temple never seemed to get built. He figured he could keep this up until Hayter-Ross dropped, which shouldn't be too long now.

Hayter-Ross, who knew a great story idea when she saw one, was also possessed of that casual sense of cruelty that incredibly rich people often develop at the first whiff of financial desperation from others. She pretended to swallow Dwellin's line with wide eyes and then proceeded to make the man dance like a monkey on a leash. She funded the temple out of petty cash but did it in such a way that Dwellin had no access to the funds; instead Hayter-Ross would provide "offerings" based on prophetic short poems derived from Dwellin's encounters with N'thul—prophetic writings which she would direct by occasionally dropping hints as to what she would like to see in them. One time she rather mischievously mentioned to Dwellin how much she enjoyed sheep. At Dwellin's next "session" with N'thul, the "Evolved Lamb"—the melding of the gentle, pastoral qualities of sheep with the rough, aggressive nature of man—made its first appearance.

For six years Dwellin churned out thousands of prophetic poems, feverishly chasing the relatively paltry income Hayter-Ross doled out before finally dropping dead of exhaustion and anxiety at the relatively young age of 38. Hayter-Ross, who would live to 104, had his ashes interred in the newly completed (and, truth to tell, quite lovely) Temple of the Evolved Lamb, in the base of a statue representing N'thul. She then collected his prophetic poems and published them as a volume accompanying her book—the first under her own name—on Dwellin's attempted scam of her and the "religion" founded thereof. Both books became huge bestsellers.

Ironically, Dwellin's poems were the best things the man ever wrote and achieved a sort of mystical lyricism at the end of Dwellin's life. Researchers suggested this was due to the hallucinatory effects of fever and alcoholic malnutrition, but some also believed that Dwellin, though a scam artist outwitted by his own elderly, sadistic muse, may have tapped into something mystical, quite accidentally and despite his own moneygrubbing nature.

These souls would be the first to identify themselves as members of a new Church of the Evolved Lamb, and who called themselves "Empathists" or "N'thulians." They would soon be joined by another group of individuals who liked the idea of taking the prophetic poems of Dwellin's and working toward making them come true, not because they were divinely inspired but because they *weren't*. If a group actively working to make entirely fictional prophecies come true managed to pull off the stunt, the whole concept of divinely inspired prophecy was thrown into doubt, chalking up a victory for rational thought everywhere. This group became known as the "Ironists" or "Hayter-Rossians."

Despite their diametrically opposed approaches to their so-called religion, the Empathists and the Ironists worked smoothly together, hammering out a practical doctrine that accommodated both flavors of churchgoer and allowed the two to integrate their differences into a cohesive whole that combined with earth-crunchy agrarian feel of the Empathists with the tech-driven, pragmatic thinking of the Ironists. Nowhere was this integration more keenly developed than in the Church's animal husbandry project on the Brisbane colony. It was there the church developed multiple strains of sheep through the combination of conscientious breeding practices and judicious use of genetic manipulation. After all, there was nothing that said that the Evolved Lamb had to evolve *naturally*.

Andrea Hayter-Ross was as surprised as anyone that an actual religion had sprung up from the pathetic scam attempt perpetrated by a hack writer, and twice as surprised to find that she rather enjoyed the clear-eyed company of the people who had adopted the religion as their own. When Hayter-Ross died with no legal heirs, she parceled out her estate among various philanthropic groups but willed the controlling interest in the Hayter-Ross family of industries to the Church of the Evolved Lamb. This caused rather a great deal of consternation among the board of directors until the Church deacons proved themselves to be unsquishy advocates of the bottom line and stock performance (the Church members in charge of the business end of things were almost all entirely of Ironist stock). Within 20 years, nearly everyone outside of the Hayter-Ross board of directors forgot to remember a religious institution ostensibly controlled the company.

Which was fine with the members of the Church of the Evolved Lamb. The Church preferred not to be noticed whenever possible, and remained small both by selective inclination of its members and by the fact it takes a certain sort of person to want to join a church based on the desperate maneuvers of a second-rate science fiction writer. The Church chiefly recruited among the technical sciences and among the folks who enjoy a good renaissance faire (there was surprisingly substantial overlap), and typically among those who already worked for one or another of the Hayter-Ross companies or concerns. Archie, for example, originally joined while he worked for LegaCen, one of the oldest branches of the Hayter-Ross corporation, which specialized in creating large, proprietary information structures for major corporations and governments.

It's where he was scouted by Sam, who was a Church deacon and Archie's direct superior at LegaCen. It was strictly a Church thing at first; the hot sex part of their relationship didn't happen until after Archie left LegaCen. The Church didn't have any rules against deacons sleeping with congregants, but LegaCen didn't like bosses to sleep with their underlings. That's the corporate world for you.

On a day-to-day basis, Archie didn't think much about his religious affiliation. One of the things about the Church of the Evolved Lamb was it was entirely silent on the big religious issues of God and the afterlife and sin and all that happy crap. The Church's goals of fulfilling the Dwellinian prophecies were almost entirely rooted in the material universe. Even the Empathists didn't go so far as to suggest that Dwellin had communed with actual spiritual beings; N'thul was more like Santa Claus than Jesus Christ to them.

This agnosticism on eschatological matters meant that Evolved Lamb churchgoers didn't spend a great deal of their time praying or worshipping or spending Sundays singing hymns (unless they also happened to be members of a more traditional church, which was not an infrequent occurrence). As religious experiences went, it was a relaxed thing. This much was evident in the layout of the Church's meeting house, which looked more like the interior of a social club than hall of contemplation. A disco ball still hung in the corner, part of the decoration for the Church's monthly karaoke night.

But this just made the unfolding of the prophecies just that much more powerful. What Archie had seen on his computer screen in that Pentagon basement had been foretold in the fevered writing of that poor bastard Dwellin:

The Mighty will bring their powers to bear to search for the Lamb;
Into its very molecules they will seek it; but though they look
One shall bear witness and seek to keep the Lamb
From harm.

Not one of Dwellin's best prophecies, but at the time he was laid out on cough syrup and Dramamine and had another 126 prophecies to go before Hayter-Ross would sign off on another payment. So there was that excuse. And anyway, it turned out to be true, which excused its lack of style.

Whether Dwellin had foretold this incident because he was tapped into something spiritual or because the Church had been plugging away for decades at making his writings come true was immaterial to Archie. All of a sudden, he'd been whacked upside the head by the freaky details of his belief system and punted into playing a part in their workings. Archie had always classified himself as an Ironist, but this shit was turning him into an Empathist in record time.

Archie and Sam didn't waste time in the meeting room. Sam took Archie's hand and directed him down a second set of stairs and into a small, brightly lit, and sterile room with what looked like a dentist's chair in the middle. Waiting in the room was another man: Francis Hamn, the local bishop, whose day job was as "manager" of the fitness center two stories up.

"Archie," he said, extending his hand. "You've had an interesting couple of days. How are you holding up?"

Archie took his hand and shook it. "I'm a little overwhelmed, to tell you the truth, Bishop."

Bishop Hamn smiled. "Well, isn't that just like religion for you, Archie," he said. "One day it's a nice way to spend your weekends and the next you're in the middle of a righteous theological clusterfuck. Now let's get you outfitted, why don't we. Have a seat."

"I'm worried about this," Archie said, but nevertheless took a seat. "The guy I'm doing stuff for is pretty high up in the Defense Department. If there's even the smallest hint I'm spying, I'm going to be in deep trouble. I think I could be tried for treason."

"Nonsense," Bishop Hamn said. "Treason implies you're trying to overthrow the government, and we wouldn't condone that. You're merely spying."

"Which is still a capital offense," said Sam, squeezing Archie's hand.

"Oh," said Archie.

"And which is also why we've made sure that your spying can't be detected," Bishop Hamn said, and held out a small bottle to Archie, who took it.

"What is this?" Archie asked.

"Your wire," Bishop Hamn said. "In eyedrop form. Inside that liquid are millions of nanobots. Put the drops in your eyes and the nanobots migrate to your optic nerve and read and store the signals there. They're organic in composition so scanners won't find them. They don't transmit unless they're in the presence of a reader, so you won't be leaking electrical signals. And as an extra bonus, that bottle is actually full of medicated eyedrops, so if anyone looks at it, that's what they'll find."

"Where am I going to find a reader?" Archie said. "I can't just duck out."

"Vending machines," Sam said. "Hayter-Ross has the vending machine contract for the Pentagon, and owns about eighty percent of the vending machines in the Washington DC area. Just go up to one, put in your credit card, and hit button 'B4.' That activates the scanner, which will upload the information."

"Just so you know," Bishop Hamn said, "the upload is sort of painful. It's like an electrical shock to your optic nerve."

"That's why we always put the really good candy in slot B4. To make up for it," Sam said.

"How often do you do this?" Archie asked, looking at his lover of four years in an entirely new light.

"We keep busy," Bishop Hamn said. "We've been doing this for a long time. Which is why we know this works."

"What happens if I leave Washington?" Archie said. "I was asked if I had a passport."

"Just make sure you get to a vending machine before you go," Sam said. "Also, bring me a souvenir."

"Whatever you do, don't be nervous," Bishop Hamn said. "Do what you usually do. Do your job for them as well as you can. You're not hurting us by helping them do their thing. The more you do, the more we know. Understand?"

"I understand," Archie said.

"Good," Bishop Hamn said. "Now lean back and try not to blink."

"Hello."

"Wyvern Ranch?" Creek said.

"Yeah."

"I may be interested in purchasing some sheep from you," Creek said.

"Can't."

"Pardon?" Creek said.

"No sheep," the voice on the other end of the communicator said.

"Wyvern Ranch is a sheep ranch, correct?" Creek asked.

"Yup."

"What happened to the sheep?" Creek asked.

"Died."

"When?" Creek asked.

"Last night."

"How many?" Creek asked.

"All of them," the voice said.

"What happened?" Creek asked.

"Got sick."

"Just like that," Creek said.

"Appears so," the voice said.

"I'm sorry," Creek said.

"I'm not," the voice said. "The flock's insured. Now I'm rich."

"Oh," Creek said. "Well, then. Congratulations."

"Thanks," said the voice on the other end, and disconnected.

Creek glanced over to where the image of Brian stood. "More dead sheep," he said. "We're way behind the curve, here."

"Don't blame me," Brian said. "I'm spitting them out as fast as I'm finding them. Whoever you're up against has a head start."

It was true. Wyvern Ranch was the fourth sheep ranch Creek had contacted, and each time the story was the same: The ranch's entire sheep population had been killed off in the last day by a fast-moving virus. The only variation to the story was the second call Creek had made, to the Ames Ranch in Wyoming; on that call Creek had a couple of nerve-zapping moments dealing with a crazy, screaming woman before the woman's adult son came on the line to explain that his father had gone missing in the night; they'd found his shotgun and some of his blood but not much else. And the sheep were all dead or dying.

No doubt about it, Creek was playing catch-up.

"New one for you," Brian said.

Creek blinked; it'd been several hours since Brian had come up with the initial list of ranches. Creek wasn't aware he was still plugging away at it. "Where?"

"Falls Church," Brian said.

Creek blinked again; Falls Church was two towns over from where he was. "Not the usual place for a sheep ranch," he said.

"It's not a sheep ranch," Brian said. "It's a pet shop. 'Robin's Pets—Unmodified Pets Our Specialty.' You'll want the owner, Robin Baker."

"Send the address into my communicator, please," Creek said.

"You're not going to call?" Brian said.

"No," Creek said. "It's drivable. And I want to get out of the house. All those dead sheep on the other end of the line are getting to me."

"All right," Brian said. "Just keep an eye out."

"Something I should know about?" Creek asked.

"Someone's been trying to hack into your system all day long," Brian said. "I've been fending it off, but they're pretty sophisticated attacks, and they've been constant. I don't have any doubt as soon as you go out of the house they'll be following you around. Whatever you've gotten us into, it's not *just* about sheep DNA."

Robin's Pets was a modest store in a modest strip mall, nestled next to a Vietnamese restaurant and a nail boutique. On the door was a sign: "Unmodified Pets Our Specialty." Right below it, a second, smaller, handwritten sign: "No more kittens! PLEASE!" Creek grinned at that and went in.

"I'm in the back room," a woman's voice said, as he came through the door and activated the bell. "Give me a second."

"No rush," Creek said back, and looked around the shop. It

was in all respects an unremarkable local pet shop: One wall was filled with aquariums filled with various fish, while another wall held habitats for small reptiles and mammals, mostly rodents of varying degrees of furriness. In the middle of the shop was the counter island, with a cash register and various last-minute purchase items. At no place in the store was there even the hint that a sheep might be located somewhere on the premises.

"Swell," Creek said, out loud.

The woman came out of the back with a hair elastic in her teeth and stood behind the counter. "Hi, there," she said, through fabric. "Excuse me a second here," she said. She grabbed her voluminous head of curly, slightly damp red hair and rather severely constricted it, slipped it through the elastic, twisted the elastic, and slipped the hair through again. "There we go," she said. "Sorry about that. I was cleaning out one of the hamster cages and one of the boys decided to pee in my hair. Had to give it a quick rinse."

"That'll teach you to put hamsters in your hair," Creek said.

"We know each other five seconds and already you're sassing me," the woman said. "I think that may be a new record. I was putting the fuzzball in another Habitrail on the top shelf. It was just bad luck on my part and good aim on his. Honest. Want a hamster?"

"I don't know," Creek said. "I've been led to believe they've got bladder control issues."

"Chicken," the woman said. "All right. What can I do for you, then."

"I'm looking for Robin Baker," Creek said.

"That's me," she said.

"I was told you might have a particular variety of sheep I've been looking for," Creek said. "Although now that I'm here I don't see how."

"Wow," Robin said. "Yeah, we don't carry large animals like that. No space, as you can see. What kind of sheep are you looking for?"

"It's a breed called 'Android's Dream,'" Creek said.

Robin scrunched her face in, and suddenly she looked much younger than the late 20s Creek was guessing she was. "I don't think I've ever even *heard* of that breed," she said. "Is it genetically modified in any way?"

"I'd be guessing yes," Creek said.

"Well, that would explain why I've never heard of it," Robin said. "This shop specializes in unmodified pets and animals. If you were looking for a Faeroes or a Hebridean or even a Blackhead Persian, I might be able to point you in the direction of someone who could help you. But I wouldn't even know where to begin for one of the genmod breeds. There are so many. And they're all proprietary. Who told you that I would know where to find this breed?"

"A friend of mine who I would suspect should know better," Creek said.

"Well—" Robin cut herself short as the door buzzer went off and another customer came through the door. "Can I help you?"

"Yeah," the man said. "I need a lizard. For my kid."

"I've got lizards," Robin said. Creek turned to look at the guy. He was swarthy. "Is there any type you have in mind?"

"One of those that can run across the water," the guy said.

"A Jesus Lizard?" Robin said. "Yeah, those have been extinct for a half a century. Something about people turning its habitat into condominiums. But I've got a tokay gecko your kid might like. They can stick to walls through the magic of van der Waals forces. Kids love that."

"Fine," the guy said.

"I'll have to sell you a package," Robin said. "That's the gecko, a terrarium, some live food, and a book about geckos. That's about sixty dollars total."

"Okay," the guy said, and came up to the counter with a credit card. Robin took it, glanced at Creek to let him know she hadn't forgotten about him, and went to go collect the gecko and his toys.

"Kid likes lizards?" Creek said.

"You know kids," the guy said, in a tone of voice that said *don't talk to me anymore.* Creek took the hint.

"Here you go," Robin said, placing a small terrarium on the counter. "You need to tell your kid that even though the gecko is really cute, it's also a living thing. This is an unmodified animal. If it gets played with too much, it'll get sick and die, and then you'll have a dead animal, an upset kid, and a terrarium with nothing in it. Okay? Sign here." She pushed the credit card slip through a pressure reader and handed the contraption to the guy; he took out a pen, signed the receipt, grabbed the terrarium, and went out the door without saying another word.

"Fun dad," Robin said. She put the pressure reader away and then reached for something on the counter. "And look, he left his pen. Nice, too. Mine now. What were we talking about?"

"Sheep," Creek said.

"Right," Robin said. "I've never stocked large animals here. I can arrange to get a pet I don't stock, of course, but since I only deal with unmodified animals, I only work with people who breed and sell unmods. What do you need a sheep for, anyway?"

"I need one for a ceremony."

Robin frowned. "Like a sacrifice? Is this some sort of Old Testament thing?"

"No," said Creek.

"And it's not some sort of *marriage* thing, is it? You and the sheep."

"Really, no." Creek said.

"All right, good," Robin said. "I mean, you don't *look* like a freak or anything. You just never know."

"Why do you only sell unmodified animals?" Creek asked. "I'm just curious."

"I've got a PetSmart one shopping center over," Robin said. "All their animals are genmod. I couldn't compete. But they hardly sell unmodified pets anymore because unmodified pets die too easy. Genmod pets are designed with six-year-old boys in mind, you know."

"I didn't know," Creek said.

"It's true," Robin said. "I think that's kind of like defining deviancy down. You should be teaching a six-year-old that you need to respect living things, rather than making pets so they can survive a mallet attack. So, economics and morals. That's why. People who come in here respect animals and teach their kids manners. Well, usually," she said, signaling to the door to indicate her last customer. "You have any kids? Are you married?"

"No and no," Creek said.

"Really," Robin said, and glanced Creek up and down. "Tell you what—what's your name?"

"Harry Creek," Creek said.

"Nice to meet you, Harry," Robin said, and pushed a piece of paper at him. "Write down the name of the breed and your comm number and I'll make some calls. I can tell you now I probably won't find anything, but on the off chance I do I'll let you know. Here," she reached over. "You can use my new pen."

"Thanks," Creek said.

"But don't think you're walking off with it," Robin said. "I'm a small business owner. That pen's money in my pocket."

Harry wrote his information, said his goodbyes, and headed over to his car, which he'd parked on the side of the strip mall, next to the strip mall's Dumpster. As he started the car, he noticed something crawling on the edge of the Dumpster. It was a gecko.

Creek turned off his car and got out and headed for the Dumpster. The gecko stood motionless as he approached. Creek got over to the Dumpster and looked in. The terrarium and book on geckos was on top a pile of trash.

"You, geek," Rod Acuna said, pointing at Archie as he came though the door. "Is the pen sending?"

"It's sending," Archie said, already not liking his new "team," which consisted of a dimwit human, a large Nagch who was spending most of his time sleeping, and this guy, his boss, who started calling Archie "geek" at their first exchange and now appeared to have forgotten he had any other name. "But your guy left just a couple of minutes after you did. The woman hasn't done anything but sing along to the radio since. I'll print you a transcript if you want, but you'll have to move your big friend there," he said, pointing to the dozing Nagch. "His feet are blocking the cabinet door to the printer."

"Leave Takk alone," Acuna said. "He had a big breakfast. Does this store owner know anything about the sheep?"

"Didn't say that she did," Archie said. "I've already hacked her computer connection, but she hasn't done any searches on the sheep. All she's done is go to a wholesaler site and order some birdseed."

"What about Creek?" Acuna said. "Have you gotten into his system yet?"

"No," Archie said. "I don't know what sort of protection this guy's got, but it's incredible. It's batting back everything I'm throwing at it."

Acuna sneered. "I thought you were supposed to be good at this shit."

"I *am* good," Archie said. "But so is this guy. Really good. I'm working on it."

"While you're at it, find out more about this woman," Acuna said, and then stomped off somewhere. Archie wondered, and he was sure not for the last time, what he had gotten himself into.

"What is that?" Brian asked as Creek walked in.

"It's a gecko," Creek said, putting the terrarium on his kitchen table.

"That's some good salesmanship," Brian said.

"Can you get into the computer system for Robin's Pets?" Creek said. "I want to check out a credit card."

"I'm already in," Brian said. "What are you looking for?"

"Follow up a charge that was made while I was in the store," Creek said. "It would have been for about sixty bucks. Find out everything you can about the guy who owns the card."

"I'm on it," Brian said. "Aside from the reptile, how did it go?"

"Terrible," Creek said. "Robin didn't have the slightest clue what I was talking about."

"What did you say to her?" Brian asked.

"I told her I was looking for some sheep," Creek said. "What were you expecting me to say to her?"

"Oh," Brian said. "Oh. Okay. I guess I wasn't being clear about it."

"What?" Creek said.

"When I told you to find Robin Baker, I didn't mean to ask her about sheep," Brian said. "I mean that she was the one you *wanted*."

"You're nuts," Creek said. "She's human."

"She's *mostly* human," Brian said. "But her DNA has definite sheep-like tendencies."

"I'm not following you," Creek said.

"She must have been really pretty for you not to get what I'm saying to you," Brian said. "Your pet shop owner is a human-sheep hybrid. The kind of sheep she was hybridized from was either in part or in whole of the Android's Dream variety. She's sheep, Harry."

"You're *insane*," Creek said.

"Call me HAL and make me sing 'Daisy, Daisy,'" Brian said. "It still doesn't change the fact."

"How did you find this out?" Creek said.

"Insurance companies don't just keep livestock DNA on file, my friend," Brian said.

"I didn't tell you to look through human DNA," Creek said.

"I know," Brian said. "But isn't that why you wanted an intelligent agent that was actually intelligent? To find stuff you *didn't* already think of? And look at it this way. You were behind before. Now you're ahead. Because I guarantee you no one else has thought of this yet. Of course, time's ticking."

Robin Baker was adopted at the age of four days by Ron and Alma Baker, a nice couple from Woodbridge, Virginia, who had opted not have children on their own after a geneticist read their charts and found nightmare after nightmare of recessive genetics in their makeup. This may have had something to do with Ron and Alma Baker hailing from the same small town in downstate Virginia where the same four families had been interbreeding almost exclusively for centuries, thereby reinforcing several undesirable genetic traits. Ron and Alma, while only nominally related on paper, had a genetic consanguinity somewhere between half-siblings and first cousins. Their geneticist declared this a neat trick and strenuously advised them against making any kids the old-fashioned way.

This was just fine by Ron and Alma, who left their hometown precisely because they both considered the vast majority of their kin to be inbred freaks. Just because *they* weren't didn't mean they couldn't breed a new generation of freaks. So they weren't in a rush to have their sperm and eggs fuse and grow. But they did like kids, and they were nurturing by inclination. This led Ron and Alma to sign up with Prince William County as foster parents. This was how Robin came to them.

The Bakers were told by the Prince William Child Protective Services that the little girl was the only child of mentally deficient woman who had been used as a prostitute and who had died while giving birth. Ron and Alma, who were assured that the child was herself in all ways physically and mentally fit, instantly fell in love with the child, named her after a favorite aunt of Alma's, and started the adoption process immediately. They then proceeded to give their new daughter a perfectly pleasant and utterly unremarkable childhood. Outside of a broken arm in the fifth grade from falling out of a tree, Robin had no physical troubles of note. In high school and college Robin did well but not exceptionally in academics, eventually earning a B.A. in business and a minor in biology from George Mason University, both of which she immediately applied by opening Robin's Pets with seed money provided by loving parents Ron and Alma.

Creek breezed rather impatiently through the information about Ron and Alma. They were fabulous parents, which was great for Robin. But adoptive parents didn't tell him anything about Robin's genetics. He went rooting through Prince William County's sheriff reports for mentally deficient prostitutes and their pimps. He found a report that matched his search query and opened it, and then pulled up the photos of Robin's biological mother.

"Holy Christ," he said.

Robin's mother was photographed nude, front and side photos. Her breasts were large and swollen, as was her belly. She was clearly pregnant; Creek would have guessed seven or eight months. Her gravid torso gave way to limbs that tapered at the end not to hands and feet but to hooves that were clearly not designed to allow clean, bipedal motion. In the front-facing picture she was supported by two police officers on either side, allowing her to stand. In the side picture she hunched on all fours. Her limbs, of human proportions, balanced her awkwardly in this position as well. Any motion, two-legged or four-legged, would be difficult. Her front was smooth, either that way by nature or shaved for effect. Her back was thickly covered in electric blue wool. A human neck gave way to a sheep's head. From the front-facing picture, sheep's eyes gazed into the camera, placid, complacent.

The police report provided details. Robin's mother had been found as part of a hybridized menagerie kept by Arthur Montgomery, chairman of ZooGen, the second largest provider of genetically modified pets and livestock in North America. Montgomery's personal estate featured a small but fully stocked biogenetics lab and factory, in which Montgomery personally designed the hybrid creatures using livestock on the estate and gene samples that were later discovered to have been taken from members of ZooGen's board of directors, specifically shareholder-elected members who generally voted against Montgomery and his bloc of directors. In addition to Robin's unfortunate mother, other hybrids combined human genes with the genes of cows (Guernsey), horses (Jordanian, a ZooGen variation of the Arabian), and llamas. The hybrids had numerous human physical characteristics but were no smarter than the animal breeds from which they originated.

One would naturally assume that Montgomery had assembled this menagerie for his personal pleasure, but that assumption would be incorrect. Montgomery was straightforwardly and blandly heterosexual and took care of his needs with long-standing Tuesday and Thursday outcall appointments with the Washington DC area's leading escort service. Montgomery's game was subtler than that. One doesn't work in the modified animals field without eventually becoming aware of the unsettlingly large number of zoophiles out there. Their numbers were hardly restricted to farm boys with access to alcohol and a herd of sheep; there were executives, legislators, and celebrities whose personal kinks ran from simple "furry" play—dressing up in animal costumes—to diddling the dog when they thought no one was looking. Over the years Montgomery's personal web of corporate and government informers had provided him with a comprehensive list of who had what quirks and how they sated them.

Montgomery's scheme against his victims was simple: Gain their trust—generally accomplished through business deals or PAC donations—introduce them to the menagerie, give them the one free taste that makes an addict, and then provide access in exchange for certain business and governmental favors. Usually this worked beautifully, and the occasional recalcitrant could be brought into line through the threat of exposure. Montgomery, of course, had an extensive video collection. All told, the scam worked nicely for Montgomery (and by extension, ZooGen) for a number of years.

It came crashing down, as things so often do, because Montgomery got greedy. Montgomery was blackmailing Zach Porter, the CEO of a small cosmetics company, and needed some additional leverage to convince Porter to use ZooGen's modified rodents for his company's animal testing. So he let the sheep hybrid get pregnant. Montgomery had specifically designed the hybrids with 23 chromosome pairs for just this sort of eventuality, and tweaked the embryo with DNA and RNA therapies as it developed. He wasn't sure what the resulting creature would be, but no matter what it was, it wouldn't be good news for Porter, who had married into the cosmetic company's exceptionally Christian fundamentalist founding family.

Montgomery expected Porter would fold and he would then abort the fetus; Montgomery wasn't expecting that Porter would counter the move by shooting him dead in his ZooGen board-room and then kill himself with the next shot, which is what Porter ended up doing. Porter's suicide note led the Prince William Country sheriffs to raid Montgomery's estate, where they found the menagerie and Montgomery's blackmail videos. There were unusually high numbers of prominent suicides in the DC area over the next few days.

The pregnant sheep woman presented a problem. Prince William County health officials were inclined to abort the pregnancy, but Zach Porter's in-laws and widow threatened to file a lawsuit halting the procedure. Half-sheep or not, life began at conception and aborting the near-term fetus was wrong. The county, which wanted the whole thing to go away, took the in-laws up on their offer to pay for the medical needs of the pregnant sheep woman until she gave birth. The delivery a month later was presided over by both a doctor and a veterinarian, neither of whom could stop (or, possibly, was inclined to stop) the mother from bleeding out during the complicated delivery. A genetic scan showed the child's DNA to be mostly human save for some junk sheep DNA apparently randomly positioned among the chromosomes. They declared her human and offered her to Porter's in-laws and widow.

They refused her, saying she was no kin of theirs. Their inter-est in her did not extend past the fact, and the moment, of her birth. Porter's parents were already deceased, and at the time the human DNA donor of the sheep woman was unknown. The baby girl was declared an orphan and placed in the care of Ron and Alma, who were never told the full sordid story of the birth of their adopted daughter, and therefore were never able to tell her anything meaningful about her past. Robin Baker had no idea she was anything but fully human.

———

"That's some fucked-up shit, Harry," Brian said, as he passed along the information. "And I believe 'Fucked-Up Shit' is indeed the technical term, here."

"I'm suddenly reminded that you were eighteen when you had that brain scan," Creek said.

"You have a better way of describing it, then," Brian said.

"No," Creek admitted. "You've pretty much hit the nail on the head."

"What are you going to do now?" Brian asked.

"I don't know," Creek said. "Finding our lost sheep has suddenly become a little more complicated. I have to think."

"Think quick," Brian said. "You have an incoming call."

"Who is it?" Creek asked.

"Just you wait," Brian said, and put the call through.

"Hi," Robin said. "It's Robin. Find your sheep?"

"Funny you should ask," Creek said. "Listen, Robin—"

"Would you like to go out on a date?" Robin asked.

"What?" Creek said.

"A date," Robin said. "You know. Two people go out and eat food and make small talk and wonder what each other look like naked. You *have* dated before?"

"Yes," Creek said.

"Okay, so you know how it goes," Robin said. "What do you think? I'm thinking tonight would be good."

"It's kind of sudden," Creek said.

"No time like the present," Robin said. "You're cute and I did a search on your name and came up with no outstanding warrants for your arrest. That's good enough for dinner in a public place."

Creek grinned. "All right," he said. "Where would you like to meet?"

"Arlington Mall," Robin said.

"You want to eat in the mall?" Creek said.

"Oh, no," Robin said. "I'm a cheap date, but not food court cheap. But there's something there I'd like to try out. Actually, you should try it out with me. Ever play basketball?"

"Sure," Creek said.

"No bum knees?" Robin asked.

"Not yet," Creek said.

"Perfect," Robin said, "Meet me at the west entrance, then. Ground floor, seven o'clock. Dress casual. Bye." She clicked off.

"That's going to be an interesting date," Brian said.

"I need you to connect me with Ben," Creek said.

" 'Ben' as in my brother Ben," Brian said.

"That's the one," Creek said.

"Interesting," Brian said. "I don't suppose he knows about me."

"I have to tell him that the sheep we're looking for is a woman who runs a pet store," Creek said. "I think telling him his younger brother's been resurrected as a computer program might be a little much for one day."

Archie almost missed the connection between Robin and the sheep. The Rod-ordered background check offered nothing of interest; a long-term scan of her business records showed her ordering a sheep only once in the history of her store, and it was a common breed, not something genetically modified. Archie kept going back in Robin's history, past the point of boredom, until he was presented with an electronic version of the very first document of Robin's life: Her birth certificate. It listed "Jane Doe" as the mother and Zach Porter as the father.

Archie moved to close out all the documents, then hesitated. Somewhere in the back of his head the name "Zach Porter" fired up some neurons. Archie decided this would be a good time for a break.

"I'm going to get a snack," he said, to the room. "Anybody

want anything?" Ed, the other guy, barely looked up from his show and shook his head; Takk was still out of it.

Rod and his crew were camped out in a shitty apartment in a shitty complex in a shitty part of town. Rod's "apartment" was jacked up with some serious equipment which Archie would have suspected to be mighty tempting to the local scum. But he also noticed, on his couple other times out, that the local population gave the door of Rod's apartment a wide berth. Being a scary motherfucker meant no one messed with your shit.

The vending machine was at the end of the hall, next to the stairs; the sticker in the top right corner of the display case read "Ross Vending, Inc." Inside the display case was a truly interesting assortment of vendables, from small cartons of LSL Milk (irradiated for a six-month shelf life) to three-packs of Whisper brand condoms, with patented Electro-Ecstatic™ molecule-binding technology to make the condom membrane as thin yet impermeable as possible. Archie had never tried that particular brand; something about the combination of an electric charge and his genitals just didn't seem appealing. Slot B4 held a small bag of white chocolate M&Ms. Archie smiled; those were in fact pretty tasty. He slipped in his credit card and pressed the button.

It felt like someone had stabbed him directly in both eyeballs. Archie crumpled, banging his head on the vending machine on the way down. As his forehead jammed against the vending machine Plexiglas, the rattle of the impact dislodged information about Zach Porter; Archie finally remembered why he remembered that name. He spent a couple more minutes on the ground, gathering his strength, before he wobbled back up and headed back towards the apartment. About three-quarters of the way there, he realized he'd forgotten his snack. He went back to get it.

Back at the computer, Archie pulled up news stories relating to Zach Porter, and there it was: Porter involved in a murder-suicide involving Arthur Montgomery. Of course, Archie knew the name Arthur Montgomery very well. If a religious organization as laid-back and nebulous as the Church of the Evolved Lamb could be said to have an apostate member, Montgomery would have been it. In one of the few real church scandals on record, Montgomery had joined the Church, worked his way into the top ranks of the church's genetic hybridization concern on Brisbane colony, and then snuck off back to Earth to form ZooGen, using Church genetic techniques.

Montgomery had gambled that the Church would back off rather than sue him and have its entire genetics organization and its goals hauled into court and into the papers. The gamble paid off. The Church's genetics program was not a high-priority enterprise in a commercial sense—its goals were esoteric and long-term—and the Ironists who ran Hayter-Ross didn't want anything to rock the business end of their organization. And in any event one of Dwellin's more maddeningly vague prophecies suggested that something like this was supposed to happen. The Church officially let it go, although it suggested to its individual members that they might consider investing in ZooGen stock, since Montgomery had stolen some very advanced and likely profitable techniques.

So in one of those nice little ironies, Church members soon comprised the single largest voting bloc of shareholders. After Montgomery's murder, they worked quietly to install a Church-vetted executive as the new CEO. Several years later, ZooGen's executives and board voted to be acquired by Hayter-Ross. This was quickly approved by the shareholders and by the FTC, which saw no conflict as, outside of livestock, Hayter-Ross had been to that point a marginal player at best in the bioengineering field.

Like many Church members, Archie was aware of the scandal that led to Montgomery's murder, and how he'd tried to blackmail Porter; the sheep-woman Montgomery had hybridized had been a horrifying use of genetic engineering. But with all the documents laid out in front of him, Archie began to suspect for the first time what the connection between the pet shop lady and the Android's Dream sheep was. Archie called up Robin's insurance records to get the name of her provider, snuck into their system to grab her DNA map, and ran it through the processor.

"Oh boy," he said, after the comparison was done. Then he called out to Rod Acuna.

"You're shitting me," Acuna said to Archie, a few minutes later.

"It's all there," Archie said. "She's mostly human, but there's whole sequences of her DNA which are from your sheep genome."

"She didn't look like a sheep," Acuna said.

"Looks like most of the sheep DNA is in areas of the code that are switched off in humans," Archie said. "It's called 'junk DNA.' It wouldn't affect the way she looked or how her body worked. Functionally she's totally human. But according to this DNA, she's about eighteen percent sheep."

"Fucking scientists," Acuna said. "Ruin a perfectly good-looking woman like that." He flipped open his communicator and made a call.

"The hell you say," Secretary of State Heffer said, to Ben Javna, over the communicator.

"No joke, sir," Javna said. "Our sheep is a pet shop owner from Virginia."

"That's it?" Heffer said. "You don't have any other sheep? Real ones?"

"That's all we got," Javna said. "All the real Android's Dream sheep are dead from sabotage. Whoever's killing them off is moving fast."

Heffer rubbed his temples. "Well, crap, Ben. This is all we need."

"Where are you, sir?" Javna asked

Heffer looked out the window of the delta, which was just starting the downslope of its parabola. "Hell if I know," he said. "Most of the Pacific Ocean looks like any other part. We'll be landing in LA in about forty-five minutes and then I've got to make an appearance at the State Department building. The director there is retiring. I get back into DC around midnight your time."

"What do you want to do?" Javna asked.

"What are our options?" Heffer asked.

"None that I can think of right off the top of my head," Javna said. "DNA aside, this is a human being and a U.S. and UNE citizen. We can't hand her over to the Nidu for a ceremony without her consent."

"Can't we just give them a quart of her blood or something?" Heffer asked. "I don't think a quart of blood is an unreasonable request to make."

"I'm pretty sure they need a whole sheep," Javna said. "That's the impression I got when I called over to the Nidu embassy to ask about details. I was also given the impression that they're getting antsy about it. We're coming up to the deadline real soon."

"You didn't tell them about her," Heffer said.

"No," Javna said. "I figured you might want to be advised first."

"Arrrgh," Heffer said, saying the word "arrgh" rather than grunting it. "Well, this development is pretty much par for the course, isn't it."

"Sorry, sir," Javna said. Javna had been following the transcripts and reports coming back from his boss's trip to Japan and Thailand. To say the trip had taken a bad turn would be to imply that there had been the possibility of taking the right turn somewhere along the way. Heffer had been hoping to get emigration concessions from the two countries to allow more colonists from third-world countries to jump to the front of the colonization line. But Asian countries were chronically touchy about their colonization status and quotas. Both Japan and Thailand, in their diplomatically polite way, had told Heffer to stick it. The trip had not been one of his shining moments.

"Look," Heffer said. "At the very least we can have her come in and talk to us. We might be able to find some way to compromise with the Nidu if we can get her to agree to help out. And if nothing else, we can show the Nidu we're making the effort. We need that. Do you think your guy can get her to cooperate?"

"He's got a date with her in an hour or so," Javna said. "He can ask her then."

"A date?" Heffer said. "Christ, Ben."

"He was sort of steamrolled into it," Javna said. "And anyway, the woman doesn't know that she's part sheep. He's got to break it to her."

"Not the usual first date conversation, is it," Heffer said.

"I've had first dates that would have been improved by it," Javna said.

"Well, as have we all," Heffer said. "But that doesn't make his job any easier."

"No, sir," Javna said.

"Are we worried about her?" Heffer asked. "We've got a lot of dead sheep."

"We're pretty sure whoever's knocking off the sheep aren't aware she's out there," Javna said. "If they did, I think she'd probably be dead by now."

"Ben, he needs to bring her in," Heffer said. "For her own safety, if nothing else."

"It's not going to be easy," Javna said. "At the risk of sounding melodramatic, it's a lot to lay on someone in one night that she's part sheep, her life's in danger, and she's needed by the government for the purposes of interplanetary peace."

"We don't have any options, Ben," Heffer said. "You said it yourself."

"All right," Javna said. "I'll get him to get her to come in."

"Can he do it?" Heffer asked.

Javna laughed. "Sir, this guy breaks bad news to people for a living," he said. "Trust me, we've got the best man for the job."

"I need to tell you something," Creek said to Robin as they walked through Arlington Mall.

"It's not about the sweats, is it?" Robin said, glancing down at her togs and then back at Creek. "I know they're kind of ratty, but they're really comfortable. And being a pet shop owner doesn't exactly leave you rolling in the dough."

"I hadn't noticed your sweats," Creek said. He was wearing a jacket, t-shirt, and jeans.

"I don't know how to take that," Robin said. "Does that mean you're not noticing me? If so, this date's not going like I hoped."

Creek grinned. "I've noticed you. Honest."

"Good answer," Robin said. "What do you do, Harry?"

"I work for the State Department," Creek said. "I'm a Xenosapient Facilitator."

Robin rolled that around in her head. "You help nonhuman intelligences? That sounds like you're either a god or a gigolo. Which could be really interesting or disgusting."

"It's neither," Creek said. "I go to the various alien embassies and give the people in them bad news."

Robin scrunched up her face. "Rough gig," she said.

"It takes a certain perspective," Creek agreed.

"So do you have any bad news for me?" Robin asked.

"Well," Creek began.

"Look! Here we are," Robin said, and pointed to the 35-foot high transparent cube in the Arlington Mall atrium. Creek peered inside the cube and saw four people in it, literally bouncing off the walls.

"What is that?" Creek asked.

"That's WallBall," Robin said. "It's why we're here."

"WallBall?" Creek said. "I played that in third grade. You threw a tennis ball against a wall and when it came back you caught it. If you dropped it, you had to make it to the wall before someone threw it. That's wall ball."

"Well, two things," Robin said. "First, that game's called 'suicide,' not 'wall ball,' and anyone who thinks otherwise is freakish and wrong. Second, you notice the banner over there has 'Wall-Ball' with that little 'tm' thingy, so I'm sure that any little kids playing suicide-but-calling-it-wall-ball will soon be served with cease-and-desist orders."

"Seems a little harsh," Creek said.

"You know kids," Robin said. "If you don't keep 'em down early, they get all uppity. Come on, the line's short. Let's get in there."

Robin explained the game while they waited. The game was played similarly to basketball in that you had to get the ball through a hoop in order to score. The catch was that the hoop was 28 feet up on the wall of the cube, high enough to make any ground-based shot at the hoop dubious at best. So the players literally climbed the walls of the playing field to get at the hoop, through the use of specially equipped sneakers with kinetic movement enhancers in the soles. As Robin was mentioning this, Creek was watching one of the players hurl himself at a wall, squarely plant a shoe, and then push off, hurling himself up an adjoining wall. When he hit that he launched himself again, landed next to the hoop, and stuffed the ball down its gullet before doing a flip in the air and falling, back first, toward the flooring surface below. The surface gave under the speed of the impact and then bounced him back up; he put himself in standing position and landed on his feet.

"That's why people don't get killed," Robin said. "The flooring is velocity sensitive and it dampens impacts. It's also why you have to kick off from the wall to get any speed out of the shoes."

"Been reading up on this?" Creek said.

"You bet," Robin said. "That guy who just stuffed the ball used to be with the Terrapins. The guys who invented the sport are going all over the U.S. with former college and pro players and letting people play five minutes of two-on-twos with them. They're trying to generate some excitement for the pro league they're starting next year."

There was a loud smack as one of the players rammed into the wall, the ball squirting out from between him and the glass. He fell to the floor in obvious pain.

"I'm guessing that guy wasn't a former Maryland star," Creek said. Another player grabbed the ball and began hiking up toward the basket.

"Watching the amateurs hurt themselves is half the fun," Robin said.

"You're forgetting we're the amateurs," Creek said.

"Look at it this way," Robin said. "We can't possibly do any worse."

The two men in front of Creek and Robin in the line stepped aside. Creek and Robin stepped forward to the attendant. "Welcome to WallBall, the world's most exciting new sport. I'm Chet." Chet, despite being at the vanguard of the world's most exciting new sport, sounded suspiciously bored. "Do you want to challenge the sport's best pro players in two-on-two combat?" he asked, in the same near-monotone.

"Are those guys in there really the sport's best pro players?" Robin asked.

"Lady, at this point they're pretty much the *only* pro players," Chet said. "So technically speaking, yeah, they're the best."

"I don't see how we could resist a pitch like that," Robin said to Creek. She turned back to Chet. "Okay, we're in."

Chet handed both of them disclaimer sheets. "Please read and sign," he said. "What are your shoe sizes?" They told him; he went over to a small storage kiosk to get their game shoes.

"It says here that by playing we waive our right to sue for any injury, 'including but not limited to contusions, broken bones, lost teeth, paralysis, impacted spinal columns, and accidental removal of fingers,'" Creek said.

"No wonder they think it's going to be popular with the kids," Robin said. "You got a pen?"

"You're going to sign this?" Creek said.

"Sure," Robin said. "I'm not really worried about it. I'm pretty athletic, and if worse comes to worst, I know some good lawyers who will be all over this document."

"I don't have a pen on me," Creek said.

Robin peered at Chet's stand to look for a pen; there wasn't one. Then she crossed her eyes in annoyance. "Jeez, that's right," she said, and fished through her purse, eventually pulling out a pen. "Here we go. It's the pen that guy left at the store today. I forgot I had it." She signed the disclaimer and handed the pen to Creek. "Live a little," she said. Creek signed the disclaimer and handed the paper and the pen back to Robin. She gave the papers back to Chet, who had returned with the shoes.

"Okay, I need to explain to you how these shoes work," Chet said. He held up one of the shoes. "Inside the shoe, near the tip, is a small patch at the top of the shoe. What you do is lift your big toe to come into contact with that patch. When you do that, you activate the jumping mechanism. The jumping mechanism only stays active for a second—that's for *your* safety—so you'll need to touch the patch each time you want to jump. There are patches in both shoes, but each activation works for both shoes at the same time, so use whichever big toe you're most comfortable with. Depending on how hard you push off, you can get about twenty feet into the air. The floor is designed to cushion a descent from any height, but you can still land awkwardly or collide with a wall. So before the game starts, you'll get a couple of minutes to work with the shoes and get comfortable with them. Do you have any questions?"

"If we win, do we get anything?" Robin asked.

"You get two tickets to a regular season game," Chet said.

"Cool. Second date for free," Robin said to Creek.

Chet looked at the two of them. "You look like responsible adults instead of the brain-dead teenagers I've been dealing with, so I'm going to let you have these shoes now rather than wait until you're in the cube. But on the off chance you're tempted to run off with them, you should know that their jumping mechanism cuts off fifty yards from this station. So don't think you're going to be able to bounce all the way home."

"Do kids really take off in them?" Robin asked.

"Two attempts today," Chet said. "The mall security people hate us."

"We promise not to run off," Creek said.

"I appreciate that," Chet said. "Okay, let me get this other pair set up and then you'll be up after them. Another ten minutes or so. You can take your own shoes and put them next to this stand." Chet walked off to deal with his other customers. Robin sat to put on her shoes; Creek leaned against a decorative light pole, slipped off his loafers, and slipped on the WallBall sneakers. As he put one on he lifted up his big toe to feel for the patch; it was there, a small slick circle he could register through his sock. He pressed his big toe into it and felt both of his shoes vibrate. He held still so as not to trigger a jump; a little less than a second later the vibrating stopped.

"You know, these look like the coolest bowling shoes ever," Robin said, standing up. "I don't think I'd wear them for social occasions—I mean, besides *this* one—but they have their kitsch appeal. So, what do you want to do for dinner?"

"I thought you were the cruise director for this date," Creek said.

"Oh. No, I'm really bad at that," Robin said. "I don't know if you've figured this out yet, but I'm sort of both spontaneous and disorganized."

"And yet you own your own business," Creek said.

"Well, Dad's a CPA," Robin said. "He helped get me organized and keeps me on an even keel. I don't know what I'd do without him. I wish I could have inherited his organizational mind, but I'm adopted. So I just have to borrow it straight from the source. I'd have to guess one of my biological parents was sort of scatterbrained."

"Have you ever tried to find out anything about your biological parents?" Creek asked.

Robin shrugged. "My parents—my adoptive parents—told me that they had died," she said. "And aside from a bad moment with Santa when I was eight, they've never lied to me about anything big. So I never went looking. There were a couple of times when I was a teenager when I thought about what it would be like to meet my 'other' family, though. You know how teenagers are."

"I was one once," Creek said.

"I'm sorry," Robin said. "I suddenly got very personal for a first date. I don't want you to think I'm one of those people who unloads their entire history over appetizers. I'm really not that co-dependent."

"It's okay," Creek said. "I don't mind. Anyway, I think we'll have a lot to talk about at dinner."

Robin opened her mouth to follow up on that, but before she could a man in a sports coat walked over. "Robin Baker?" he said.

"Yes?" she said.

The man reached into his coat and pulled out a wallet containing an ID card. "Agent Dwight, FBI. Miss Baker, I need you to come with me. You're in danger here."

"In danger?" Robin said. "In danger from what?"

"Not from what. From who," Agent Dwight said, and glanced over at Creek. "You're in danger from *him*. He's going to kill you, Miss Baker. At least he is going to try."

Robin turned to Creek. "You bastard," she said. "You never said anything about killing me when we made the date."

Agent Dwight grimaced. "This is serious, Miss Baker. You need to come with me right now."

"Robin, I wouldn't go anywhere with that guy," Creek said.

"I'm not going anywhere with anyone," Robin said.

"You're making a mistake, Miss Baker," Agent Dwight said. "This man is a danger to you."

"Yeah, fine," Robin said. "I'm in a public place with surveillance cameras all around, and you're here to protect me, right? It's doubtful he's going to murder me right here and now. So before I do anything else, I want to know what this is about."

Creek and Dwight started speaking at the same time; Robin held her hand up. "Jesus Christ," she said. "One at a time." She pointed at Dwight. "You. Go."

"You're in danger," Dwight said. "From him."

"I got that already," Robin said. "Why?"

"He's going to try to kill you," Dwight said.

"Any reason?" Robin asked.

"What?" said Dwight.

"Is there any reason he's going to kill me?" Robin asked. "You know, like I killed his father or stole his land? Or is he just your garden-variety axe murderer? What?"

"Well, he's done it before," Dwight said.

"Killed people," Robin said.

"Yeah," said Dwight. "And he's planning to do it to you. That's why—"

"I need to come with you. Right. Okay, you stop now." She turned to Creek. "You go now."

"It's complicated," Creek said.

"Complicated would be good after this guy's story," Robin said.

"You have a particular sort of DNA in your genetic makeup," Creek said. "Someone with this DNA is needed for a diplomatic mission. Others with this DNA have been turning up dead; as far as I know you're the only one on the planet with this DNA who is still alive. I'm supposed to talk to you about the situation and try to get you to agree to come in to the State Department. We want to discuss options with you and see if you can help us."

"Options that *don't* include killing me," Robin said.

"Right," Creek said.

"But you didn't get around to telling me any of this," Robin said.

"I *tried*," Creek said. "I don't know if you know this about yourself, but you're not the easiest person in the world to have a linear conversation with."

"What happens if I don't go to the State Department with you?" Robin said.

"There might be a war," Creek said.

"I meant to *me*," Robin said.

"Nothing," Creek said. "You're an American and a UNE citizen. We can't make you do anything you don't want to do. Although given the presence of the so-called Agent Dwight here, I would suggest you let the State Department give you protection until this thing gets sorted out."

Robin turned to Agent Dwight. "It's just me," she said, pointing at Creek, "but *he* seems more believable."

"He's lying," Agent Dwight said. "He's a dangerous man."

"Robin, I have my communicator with me. Use it and get the number of the State Department from information," Creek said. "Ask for Ben Javna. He's the Special Assistant to the Secretary of State. He should still be in his office. Tell him who you are and he'll confirm everything I've just told you. He can even arrange to have someone else come and get you. You don't have to go anywhere with me."

Robin looked back at Agent Dwight. "So, what happens if I call the FBI?" she asked.

Agent Dwight didn't answer; he was holding his hand to his ear as if listening to something. Creek saw him glance upwards as he did so; Creek turned around and looked up in the direction Dwight had glanced. He saw someone on the second floor of the mall, standing at the rail of the atrium.

"Robin," Creek said, and pointed. "Look up there."

Robin looked up and squinted.

"Hey," she said. "Isn't that the gecko dude?"

Creek turned and saw Agent Dwight reaching for something inside his coat.

Rod Acuna knew taking the girl at the mall was going to be trouble. "Just let me take her at home," he'd said to Phipps, over the communicator. "It'll be quicker and safer for my men."

"But then we'd still have this Creek character to worry about," Phipps said. "The girl goes missing while he's still free and you know he's going to go looking for her. That's eventually going to lead back to us."

"We can take him, too," Acuna said.

"There's not enough time to grab her and him separately," Phipps said.

"Then let me just grab *him*," Acuna said. "Without him, the girl's not a problem."

"See, this is why you're not paid to think," Phipps said. "He goes missing, and Ben Javna's going to notice, quick. Since Creek's undoubtedly already briefed Javna, any random disappearance will bring down most of the State Department to hustle the girl to safety before you can get to her."

"I can get them both before that happened," Acuna said.

"Or you can get them both at the same time, which solves a lot of practical issues," Phipps said.

"There's a lot to go wrong grabbing two people in a mall," Acuna said. "For one, there are a lot of people around."

"Which will work to your advantage when you're dealing with them both," Phipps said. "You'll be able to get her to go with you willingly because you're in a public place. And when he puts up a fight, it looks like resisting arrest."

"It still has problems," Acuna said.

"Then minimize the problems," Phipps said. "That's what you get paid to do. Now let me speak to the computer geek I sent you. I have something I need him to do." Acuna swore under his breath and shoved the communicator at Archie.

After the geek was done with the communicator, Acuna contacted Jean Schroeder, who was not sympathetic. "What do you want me to do?" Schroeder said. "Phipps is paying you."

"You're paying me too," Acuna reminded Schroeder.

"So I am," Schroeder said. "But in my case I'm paying you to tell me the things Phipps doesn't, not to contravene his orders.

Which reminds me. Are you going to do what I suspect you're going to do once you get the two of them?"

"We can't really let them go," Acuna said, dryly.

"I'm going to need the girl," Schroeder said.

"So you *are* paying me to disobey orders," Acuna said.

"I suppose I am. Just not the ones you want to disobey," Schroeder said.

"Takk can take care of Creek, but Phipps is going to want proof about the girl," Acuna said.

"I don't need the *whole* girl," Schroeder said. "I just need the part I get to be alive."

Shortly thereafter Acuna had the geek pull up the plans for the Arlington Mall and hack the security to find where they'd positioned cameras. The plan was simple enough; they'd wait for Creek and the girl to park themselves somewhere, after which Ed would come up with his FBI gear and escort the girl out. As he was doing that, a second team would converge on Creek and hustle him out of the mall. Creek would meet Takk, who would dispose of him in his own special way, and Acuna would deal with the girl. Mall security was understaffed and unarmed, so they wouldn't represent much of an issue. Acuna had the geek go down to his storage unit in the apartment complex basement to bring up a few keyfob-sized signal disrupters, which would be powerful enough to knock out the security cameras and whatever personal cameras were present. This wasn't the first time Acuna had had to snatch someone in public.

Acuna had to admit Phipps was right—this would leave fewer holes than a typical snatch from home. But he never liked public grabs, and this one, with two targets, one of them former military *and* cop, he liked even less.

Normally Acuna would take the lead in grabbing the girl, but he'd already blown his identity wad posing as a customer in the woman's pet store. Acuna was getting some old friends to handle the secondary jobs of grabbing Creek and acting as goalie in case one or both of the targets decided to run, but they wouldn't be much good for talking. It'd have to be someone in his current crew: Ed, Takk, or the geek.

Acuna didn't waste any time considering the geek; he wasn't experienced with felonious activity of a nondigital kind and anyway, Archie was working for Phipps, not for him. Takk was likewise out. The FBI like any federal agency was committed to affirmative action when it came to nonhuman agents, but Takk was simply too damn big not to be noticed. Takk was also needed to deal with Creek once Creek was out of the mall.

This left Ed, which was not an optimal situation. Ed was about as bright as a night-light. But there wasn't enough time for anyone else at this point. And Ed had done this thing before; so long as he had a script to stick to he'd be fine. Acuna walked Ed through the scenario a couple of times and gave him his FBI ID and an earpiece into which Acuna could issue commands if necessary.

Acuna's backup boys arrived shortly thereafter; Rod went over the plan and gave everyone their roles. Everyone piled into two vans equipped with fake tags and anonymous credit toll passes and went to the mall. Acuna stressed the nonlethality of the mission but he knew all of them, including Ed, were carrying slug throwers. He couldn't complain; he had one of his own nestled in a shoulder holster. In this line of work, guns were an occupational hazard.

At the mall, everyone took their positions, and waited for Creek and the girl. They weren't long in arriving, and headed into the mall atrium to play a game.

Acuna wasn't very pleased with that. The atrium was large, with traffic from all four directions as well as escalators feeding traffic to and from the upper level. And on top of that there was this big goddamn plastic cube in the middle of it. Acuna had five guys on the ground, which was just enough to cover the atrium ground floor; he placed himself between the escalator banks to present an obstacle if Creek or the girl decided to head up that way. Acuna got on his headset, activated the signal disruptors they were all carrying in their pockets, and told Ed to get going.

Acuna had expected Creek to put up a fight; he hoped he *would,* since it would give Ed's story more credibility and make it easier for Ed to hustle the woman off while the other team grabbed Creek like a fugitive criminal. Acuna hadn't expected the girl to be the skeptical one; the story he'd fed Ed wasn't strong enough to stand up to scrutiny, and Ed wasn't exactly a world-class improviser. The girl had him on the spot before Acuna could feed him something reasonable, and then shut him down to talk to Creek.

"Jesus fucking Christ, Ed," Acuna muttered under his breath. "Just get the fucking woman already." Ed put his hand to his ear, as if listening, and glanced up at Acuna. Acuna realized he'd muttered loud enough for the microphone to pick up. Then he saw Creek turn around and look directly at him.

"Fuck me," Acuna said. By now Creek had pointed him out to the girl. The jig was up. "Fuck me running," he said, and then yelled in his headset microphone to his entire crew. "Get them," he said. "Get them both *now.*"

Acuna saw Ed reach into his coat to get his pistol. *So much for the nonlethal operation,* Acuna thought, and moved to pull out his own gun. Things were getting bad, fast, just as Acuna figured. He was okay with it. He was expecting he'd get to this. Then something happened he didn't expect.

Creek hooked an arm around the lamppost he'd been leaning against, squished his big toe against the top of his shoe, and then kicked Agent Dwight square in the sternum. Dwight sailed backwards like a plush monkey launched by a Pro Bowl kicker, exhaling mightily all the way. Dwight's trajectory intersected with a large mall planter; Dwight hit it coccyx first, radically altering the speed and direction of his movement. At this point, Dwight's hand jerked free of his coat, taking the pistol he'd gripped with it. Dwight's trigger finger twitched involuntarily as his arm described a wild arc; the pistol, set for automatic fire (Ed believed in quantity of bullets over quality of aiming), burped out a volley of special load explosive-tipped ordnance, emptying the pistol's 15-round clip.

Three of these bullets rammed into the side of the WallBall cube, slagging the Plexiglas a fraction of a second before one of the players (the former Maryland star, as it happened) kicked the wall to launch himself toward the hoop. The Terrapin never made it to the basket; the wall, weakened by the bullet impact and the pressure of the powered shoes, fragmented at shoe impact and gave way, torquing the athlete's body until it faced downward and driving the player's leg through the cube wall to mid-shin. He screamed as skin was peeled off his shin by the Plexiglas and then passed out in shock as his tibia and fibula snapped with a *pop* like a cork off a spumanti bottle. The weight of his body pulled the leg out and dropped him to the ground.

The rest of the bullets connected with the mall ceiling and atrium skylight. The five that hit the ceiling made muffled booms; the seven that smashed the skylight cracked like close thunder, followed by the skittering sound of the skylight losing its structural integrity. Heavy sheets of safety glass peeled from the skylight and shattered on the ground floor of the atrium below, flinging shards of glass the size of Elvis rhinestones at hordes of screaming upscale consumers.

Creek had aimed the kick as well as he could to control the inevitable recoil, but "as well as he could" in this case wasn't as good as Creek had hoped. Creek spun briefly and violently around the pole before flinging off 270 degrees from where he started and collapsing on the floor. Creek howled and grabbed his right shoulder. He could feel the bone grinding; it'd nearly dislocated out of its socket. Creek gritted his teeth and jammed the shoulder into the ground and howled again as he felt the bone suck back into place. That was going to be painful for about a month. Creek got up just in time to have a sheet of skylight glass erupt on the floor beside him; a thumb-sized fragment went straight for his left cheek and hoed a shallow row into it. Creek shielded his eyes as another mass of skylight glass landed and showered him in chunks.

Creek uncovered his eyes to look for Robin and found her ten yards away, huddled near a small planter with a miniature palm tree. She had glass in her hair. He lurched in her direction; halfway there he found Dwight's FBI ID card. He pocketed it and kept going until he reached Robin. She was shivering.

"This is no longer a fun date," she said.

"I'm really sorry about that," Creek said. Another sheet of glass fell from the skylight; Robin barked an exasperated scream. "Keep your head down," Creek said.

"Way ahead of you," Robin said.

Creek looked up over the planter at where the gecko man had been standing; he was being pushed this way and that by frantic shoppers trying to get out of the middle of what they figured was a gang war. Creek looked around and saw four other men, one in each direction, fighting the current of panicked bystanders. Agent Dwight lay sprawled 50 feet away, not moving; Creek suspected he wouldn't be getting up any time soon.

"I think we should leave," Robin said.

"There's a problem with that," Creek said.

"Well, that's just *great*," Robin said.

"Hold on," Creek said. He looked up to gauge the distance between the atrium floor and the second level of the mall.

"Robin," he said. "We can't get out through the ground floor right here. We're blocked in every direction. We're going to have to go up."

"Gecko man is at the top of the escalators," Robin said.

"We're not going that way," Creek said. "We've got the Wall-Ball shoes on. We can jump up."

"Are you *insane*?" Robin asked.

"Robin, listen," Creek said, and pointed to a spot by the Wall-Ball cube. "We bounce on the ground there. We hit the WallBall court and then push off and get over the second floor railing."

"And then?" Robin asked.

"Escalators at the far end of the mall. Department stores with elevators. Take your pick. We have to move *now*. The mall is emptying out."

"I don't think I like you any more," Robin said.

"Fair enough," Creek said. "Are you ready?"

Robin nodded.

Acuna's brain didn't quite process Ed flying back through the air as if he'd been shoved by a train; it got about as far as *what the fuck* before Ed's gun brought down the ceiling and he had to push back shoppers running in every direction and screaming like morons.

Thanks to that, he lost track of Creek and the girl and found them again only after they popped up, like daisies, from behind one of the atrium planters, and then started moving into the atrium itself. Acuna yelled into his headset for his remaining men to be ready, whatever direction they ended up going. Acuna didn't think they'd go up the escalators, which were still jammed with bystanders trying to shove their way off. But if they tried it he was at the top and his boys would be at the bottom quickly enough. They'd be trapped.

Acuna's brain was consequently not prepared for Creek and the girl hurling themselves at the big plastic cube in the middle of the atrium and then bouncing up off of it like they were doing hurdles on the moon. Acuna stood slack-jawed as the two sprang off the cube and launched themselves at the second floor railing, 90 degrees from where he was standing. Creek cleared it; the woman, who had jumped badly, slammed into the railing, screamed in pain, and scrabbled to grab hold of the top of the railing before she dropped. She was dangling and in too much pain to do anything else.

Acuna's brain snapped back into real time and decided it would figure out the jumping thing later. Now he needed to get the girl and take care of Creek. Acuna wasn't worried about making things look reasonable anymore; the need for that went out the window less than a minute ago when Ed shot out the mall roof. He needed Creek dead and the girl out of here, in that order. Acuna informed his men that Creek and the girl were on the second level, drew his gun, maneuvered through the remaining frantic shoppers, and came in close enough to Creek not to miss the shot.

Acuna saw Creek glance in his direction; his brain estimated where Creek would move next and tracked to that point. This is where Acuna's not factoring in Creek's jumping ability got him in trouble, because Acuna was entirely unprepared for Creek launching himself at Acuna like a rocket.

Creek made it over the railing but landed awkwardly and fell, banging his right knee on the second level floor and cracking the funny bone on his right elbow. He grunted in pain and annoyance; this wasn't a great day for his right arm. Creek heard Robin scream and turned to see her hanging onto the railing; he heaved himself off the floor and lurched toward her to help her when he saw the gecko man heading toward him, gun drawn. Creek flicked the top of his shoe and launched himself at the gecko man in a quick lateral movement without breaking his stride.

Gecko man was clearly not prepared for this; he squeezed off a shot but it went far and wide, shattering a window display at a candle store on the other side of the atrium and causing the dawdling spectators there to get the hell out of Dodge. Creek smacked into the gecko man off center, spinning the both of them around and smashing them both onto the floor, five feet from each other.

Gecko man's pistol had launched itself out of his hand and nestled at the base of the Kleinman's Sports window display (Nike Multi-Sport Trainers 30% Off); Creek saw gecko man prop himself up in order to get up and get the gun. Creek lunged forward, grabbed gecko man's right ankle as he was pushing off, and yanked hard. Gecko man's chin made an audible crack as he came down hard, but he rotated around before Creek could capitalize on his move and planted his left boot squarely into Creek's forehead. Creek's head snapped up, jolting a clear stream of pain up and down his spine.

Creek let go of the gecko man and retreated toward the railing. Gecko man scrambled away toward his gun, got to it, and brought it to bear on Creek, who flicked his shoes back on, kicked hard at the railing, and bearhugged gecko man as he flung into him, knocking the two of them into the Kleinman's Sports window display.

The window glass almost appeared to think about the matter before breaking, nestling the two men in a fighting men–shaped cradle of fragmented glass a few hundredths of a second before shattering completely and underlining both men's exposed surfaces with small red streaks. Creek pulled himself off gecko man just in time for a clumsy left hook to the right cheek. Gecko man had a small glass fragment wedged between the knuckles of his middle and ring finger. Both of them yelled at the hit, Creek at the fragment bloodying his check, and gecko man from the fragment being driven further into his hand.

Creek fell back and knocked over a small display of varied sports equipment, designed to highlight the versatility of the Nike Multi-Sport Trainer. Gecko man, who managed to keep hold of his gun this time, brought it back to Creek's general direction; Creek grabbed at the basketball which had fallen from the display and hurled it hard and square into gecko man's face. Blood flushed out of gecko man's nose; he gasped and reflexively brought his right hand to his face to inspect the damage, which was enough time for Creek to grab the baseball bat. Gecko man brought the gun up again and then screamed in pain as Creek brought the bat down and broke his wrist.

Gecko man dropped the gun and made to grab it with his left hand; Creek heaved the bat clumsily back in the other direction and knocked it away and then clocked the gecko man hard in the chin. There was a sharp clack as gecko man's jaw was driven at high speed into the rest of his skull. The lights went out in gecko man's eyes; Creek made sure he stayed down by tapping him not entirely gently in the left temple. Creek was pretty sure gecko man wasn't dead, but he wasn't going to cry if he was.

Creek heard Robin cry out and staggered out of the window display to see her swinging at one of the men Creek had seen earlier, who was trying to pull her up off the railing. Another man was coming off the now-empty escalator to help him; Creek flung the bat at the man as he passed. The man tripped as the bat connected with his feet, dropping a Taser he'd been carrying in his hand. Creek rushed out and kicked him hard in the head, driving it into the railing and taking the man out of commission.

By this time, the first man had succeeded in grabbing hold of Robin and had started to drag her off the railing. Creek stepped to grab the dropped Taser and suddenly found himself hurtling through the air. In kicking the man, he'd activated his shoes, and had put his foot down just before they deactivated. The bounce was not dramatic, just enough to send him over the railing. Creek frantically fished at the railing as it went by and connected. It sent a new bolt of pain up his right arm, but kept him from falling to the ground floor below.

Creek looked down just in time to see one of the men remaining on the ground floor directly below him, while the other man made toward the escalators. The man directly below him was yanking out a gun. Creek closed his eyes briefly, made as if to pull himself over the railing, and then pushed off, driving himself downward and clicking on his shoes as he fell. Creek could feel the man's clavicles and ribs snap as he pushed off of his body and ricocheted wildly toward a kisosk filled with plush toys. The plush toys softened Creek's impact; the guy he'd jumped off of was not so lucky. Creek could see the pool of blood growing where the man's head had smacked the mall tiles.

Above Creek, Robin screamed again. Creek ran out from underneath the second floor overhang to see the man with Robin trying to drag her away from the atrium, presumably down the mall to one of the far exits. Creek glanced toward the escalators and saw the man who had just run up them, training a gun on him. Creek moved as the shot hit near his feet, and looked around as he ran, trying to find what he needed.

He spied it—on the other side of the atrium, naturally: a small, red fire alarm box, four and a half feet up the wall next to the entrance of a jewelry store. Above him he could see the man who'd shot at him moving to get a clearer shot. Creek clicked on his shoes and kicked off, sailing across the atrium in yard-eating steps. Behind him he could hear the pings of bullets hitting objects and floor tiles; the guy shooting him hadn't figured out how to compensate for the bouncing. Creek hit the atrium wall, yanked down the alarm, and bounced off before the guy upstairs could line up another shot.

The sound system of the mall, which up to this time had been playing the lite hits of the last two decades, erupted into wailing shrieks as the sprinklers in the atrium launched into their showers. The very last of the shoppers burst from their hiding places like flushed partridges, as did whatever salespeople were still in their shops. They were running to beat the fire doors, already dropping down from their ceiling enclosures where they stayed rolled up until they were needed to block the spread of flames from one area of the mall to the next. Fire-tight doors also dropped at the front of every shop; mall staff and customers could still get out through the back paths behind the mall stores.

As he moved, Creek watched the doors seal off exits in every direction; once dropped, the fire doors could be opened only by the Arlington Fire Department. Robin and Creek were stuck, but so were the other guys. They were all trapped together.

The man who'd been shooting at Creek got distracted by the noises and the doors snaking down from the ceiling. Creek used the distraction to pick the gun off the body of the man he'd jumped on. The man upstairs brought his attention back on Creek just as Creek was lining up his shot. The man fired first, a panic shot that went wide. Creek calmly hit the guy center mass and watched him fall. Creek bounded up the escalator to find the final man by the railing, holding Robin and a gun, the latter pointed at the former. The alarm sirens, having done their job of telling people to get out before they burned, went silent.

"Easy," Creek said to the guy.

"I don't know how you're jumping around like that, but if you get any closer, I'm going to shoot her in the head," the guy said.

"I'm not moving," Creek said. "Robin, how are you doing? You okay?"

"No," Robin said, and managed to sound slightly astounded that Creek would ask such a stupid question.

"She's going to be worse if you don't drop your gun," the man said.

"Look, guy," Creek said. "All we came here to do is try on some shoes. I got a pair and she got a pair. I don't know what all of this is about."

"Shut up," said the guy.

"All your friends are gone," Creek said. "You're by yourself."

"Oh, I've got more friends waiting, you can bet on that," the guy said. "Now shut up and drop the gun."

"If I drop the gun you might kill me," Creek said.

"If you don't drop the gun, I'm going to kill *her,*" the guy said. "Now drop the fucking gun."

"All right," Creek said. "I'm dropping the gun now." And he did. The man moved his gun to aim at Creek; Robin activated her shoes and kicked at the railing, forcing her body into the man holding her and launching the both of them at high speed into a mall wall. His shot plowed into the railing near Creek as his arm was jerked wildly away and his body squashed into the wall. Creek bent to pick up his weapon.

Robin crawled away from the guy; the guy groggily raised his gun to shoot at her. Creek shot him in the shoulder and kept the gun trained on him for his entire slide down the wall. The man screamed all the way down, pawing at the mess of his shoulder with his good arm until Creek whacked him in the temple with the butt of his pistol.

He turned his attention to Robin, who was still on the floor. He checked her for injuries, but other than bruises and cuts she seemed fine. "Thank you," Creek said. "I was hoping you'd figure out what I was saying about the shoes." Robin batted him away.

Creek backed off, dropped the pistol into his jacket pocket, and reached into his inside jacket pocket for his communicator. He flicked it open and was mildly surprised it was still functional after his workout. Creek wanted to get Ben Javna to get them protection at the mall before the fire doors opened; Creek didn't know if their last little friend was telling the truth about having backup, but he didn't want to find out one way or another.

Javna wasn't answering his communicator. Creek got voice mail, but switched off without leaving a message. Then Creek pocketed his communicator and looked around and finally up at the shattered atrium skylight. After about a minute he raised up his gun and fired at the skylight, dislodging the remaining sections of glass. From the floor, Robin flinched.

"What are you *doing*?" Robin spat.

"We need to go, Robin," Creek said, and walked over to help her up. "We need to go now."

"Wait for the police," Robin said. "We can wait for the police."

"There might be more of those guys out there, Robin," Creek said. "Until we're at the State Department, I can't be sure we're totally safe."

"The fire doors are closed," Robin said. "We can't get out."

Creek pointed at the skylight. "That way," he said. "Up off the roof and then down the fire exits. Anyone who's waiting won't be expecting that."

Robin looked like she was going to cry. "I just want to go home," she said.

162 · John Scalzi

"You can't," Creek said. "Not right now. Soon. But now we need to go. Can you still jump?" Robin nodded. "Okay. I need you to jump on to the top of the WallBall cube. Okay? And then push off as hard as you can, right through the skylight. Easy." Robin nodded dully, steadied herself, and leapt to the cube. Creek followed suit. Robin bounced up through the skylight; Creek readied himself to do the same.

"Hey!"

Creek dropped and fumbled for the gun in his pocket, and then relaxed when he saw Chet the WallBall attendant looking up at him. He'd been cowering under his counter this entire time.

"Jesus Christ, man!" Chet said to Creek. "What the hell just happened here?"

"I wish I could tell you," Creek said, getting up. He dropped the gun on the top of the WallBall cube.

"Yeah, well, my shoes," Chet said. "You're still wearing my shoes. I want them *back*."

"I need them," Creek said. "And I think you're done for the day."

"You said you wouldn't do anything stupid with those shoes!" Chet said. "Look at this place! I mean, God damn! I *trusted* you, man!"

"Sorry," Creek said, and jumped through the skylight.

Chet watched him go. "No more shoes in advance for *anyone*," he said.

Acuna woke up in a haze of pain and blood, dragged himself out of the shop window, and gazed around to see three of his men dead or unconscious on the second floor. He limped over to the railing and saw the fire doors down, the other man on his second team lying flat in his blood and Ed, still immobile, splayed where Creek had kicked him. He didn't see Creek or the girl.

Motherfucker, Acuna thought, and then winced and closed his eyes. Even thinking hurt at the moment. Creek did a number on them all, all right. When he opened his eyes again he saw Chet, dragging the unconscious broken-legged WallBall player out of the court.

"Hey!" Acuna yelled, and immediately regretted it.

Chet looked around for the source of the voice and spotted Acuna. "Jesus," Chet said. "Are you all right? You're covered in blood."

"Shut up," Acuna said. "I'm looking for a guy and a woman. They were by your"—Acuna gingerly waved at the WallBall court—"whatever the fuck that thing is. Where did they go?"

"They went out through the skylight," Chet said. "They took my *shoes.*"

Acuna involuntarily looked at Chet's feet, which had shoes on them. Acuna decided he'd spent enough time conversing with this dipshit and looked for an exit. All the stores had their fire doors down; Acuna went back to the window display he'd come from and tried the door that went from the display to the larger store. It was locked; Acuna tried ramming the door with his body a couple of times before he stopped, spat, and became disgusted with himself.

"Jesus fucking Christ, Rod," he said, and reached down to get the gun that Creek had knocked from his hand. Two seconds later Acuna said the same thing as he switched hands to pick up the gun, on account of his right wrist being broken. Acuna stepped back, shot the lock three times, and kicked open the door. He wandered back into the store looking for the back exit. Along the way he passed a display for mountaineering first aid kits. He grabbed one and tucked it under his left arm. God knew he needed it.

Acuna emerged out of a side exit as fire and police were making their appearance, waved in by mall security, who Acuna had seen neither hide nor hair of during what went down. *Good job, guys,* Acuna thought, winced again and made a note to himself to stop goddamn thinking for a while. He staggered into the mall garage where they had parked their vans, and beat on the side of the van Takk was in. Takk opened the side panel and took a look at his boss.

"What happened to you?" Takk said, in that nasal, high-pitched whine of his.

"Shut the fuck up and help me in," Acuna said.

Minutes later Takk had awkwardly maneuvered his far-too-large frame into the driver's seat and was navigating back to the apartment while Acuna cleaned his wounds as best he could and tried to get hold of the geek. After several failed attempts to raise the geek on the communicator, he finally got through.

"Where the fuck were you?" Acuna snarled at Archie.

"I was getting a snack from the machine," Archie said. "Every-thing all right?"

"No, everything is *not* all right," Acuna said. "In fact, every-thing is a goddamned clusterfuck. Creek and the sheep girl got away. You need to find them for me, geek. You need to find them for me this very second."

Creek got Robin off the mall roof as the fire department and po-lice converged from a distance. Creek took Robin's arm and guided her down the street from the mall to the Arlington Mall stop of the DC Metro. Creek had driven in and assumed whoever was hunting them knew that and would be looking at the park-ing garage, but not the Metro. Creek pulled out his credit card, paid fares for them both, and led Robin to the platform for trains inbound to DC. There was a stop at Foggy Bottom and from there a cab could take them to the State Department. The train rolled into the station; Creek took Robin's arm again and led her into it.

Once inside the train Robin propped herself up against the side of the car and kicked the still-standing Creek in the gut. Creek blocked the kick; Robin burst into tears and collapsed onto the floor of the car. Everyone near Creek and Robin suddenly decided to check out the ambiance in the next train car over.

Creek knelt next to Robin. "What was that about?" Creek asked.

"The shoes don't work anymore," Robin said.

"No," Creek said. "We're too far away from the WallBall court. Sorry about that."

"Who *are* you?" Robin said. "Really, honestly, now. Just who the goddamn fucking hell are you and what just happened in there and why do people suddenly want to kill me and *what the goddamn fuck is going on?*"

The last part of that came out as a hysterical shriek; Creek reached over to her hand and patted it gently to calm her. "Take deep breaths," he said. "Take it easy."

Robin slapped his hand away. "Fuck you," she said. "Take it *easy.* Six men with *guns* just tried to fucking *kill* me. I just had to jump through a *skylight* to get away from them. And now you're taking me who the fuck knows where and I really just ought to scream at the top of my lungs and get people in here to tackle you and take you away. If you don't tell me who you really are and what's going on, right *now,* I swear I'm going to do it."

"I told you who I am and what's going on in the mall," Creek said. "You seemed to accept it at the time."

"That's because I thought you were *joking,*" Robin said.

"What?" Creek said.

"Well, Jesus, Harry," Robin said. "All of a sudden a guy shows up and tells me I'm in danger, and you tell me a story about a war. It *had* to be a joke. I figured maybe I was on a reality show or something. I was just going along to be a good sport. I was looking for the film crew. Either that or you were just some loser poking fun at me with a friend. In which case I was going to go to the mall security and have you arrested for harassing me. Either way, I wasn't thinking it was for *real*. You think I would have been joking about it if were real? Christ."

"I'm sorry, Robin," Creek said. He reached into his back pocket and pulled out his wallet and gave it to Robin, and then reached in his jacket pocket and gave her his communicator. "All my ID is in the wallet," he said. "Look at everything in there. And then, like I said before, take my communicator, call up information and have them connect you to the State Department general line. Ask for Ben Javna. Tell him who you are. He'll verify I am who I say I am and everything I told you." Creek stood up.

"What are you doing?" Robin asked him.

"I'm going to go sit at the back of the car, away from you," Creek said. "If you don't feel safe around me, I don't want you worried about me being close to you. Now, go on. Look at my stuff and call Ben." Creek turned and went to the back of the car. A few minutes later, the train stopped to let passengers on and off; Creek noted that Robin had stayed on the train. He took that as a good sign.

"Hey, Harry," Robin said.

"Yeah?" Creek said.

"The guy you wanted me to call is Ben Javna, right?" Robin asked.

"That's right," Creek said.

"Your communicator says you just now got a text message from him," Robin said.

"What does it say?" Creek said.

"You want me to read your private messages?" Robin said.

"Just this once," Creek said. He saw Robin press the button and scan the message.

"What's it say?" Creek said again.

Robin got up and walked over to Creek. She handed him the communicator. Creek took it and read the message.

BIG TROUBLE, it read. DON'T CALL. GET LOST. STAY LOST. TAKE YOUR FRIEND WITH YOU.

Creek closed the communicator and looked at Robin. He opened his mouth, but she put her hand up.

"Don't, Harry," she said. "I believe you. I believe you're telling me the truth. Now just tell me one thing. Okay? Tell me I'm going to make it through all of this alive."

chapter

8

Through three terms as a UNE representative, a subsequent
two terms as UNE senator, and now his appointment as Secretary
of Defense, Bob Pope had developed a reputation as being strong
on defense and tough on the Nidu. Pope wouldn't argue the first
of these—it was a bedrock position that got him elected five
times, appointed once, and earned him truly fantastic honoraria
whenever he was between political gigs.

But the fact of the matter was he personally couldn't give a shit
about the Nidu one way or another as a people. He'd met more
than his share of Nidu in his time in Washington, of course, and
they were decent enough as intelligent nonhumans go. They all
had a pole up their reptilian ass about personal status, but that
just made them like everyone else in Washington.

What he didn't like about them, ironically, was their status in
the Common Confederation, and by consequence, the status of
Earth, its colonies, and humans in general. As Pope saw it, the

Nidu, for all their obsession about castes and status and class, were bottom feeders in the grand CC food chain. If the CC were the United Nations, the Nidu would be Burkina Faso, a tiny, shitty little country on a chronically backwards continent with no hope of ever doing anything but pounding dirt the long merry day.

The problem was that the Nidu were Earth's closest allies in the Common Confederation. In politics as in high school, who you are is to a large extent defined by who you sit with at lunch, and there was no doubt about it, the Earth was sitting at the loser table. It was not, Bob Pope thought, the true destiny of the Earth in our universe to be counted among the diplomatic equivalent of the acne-ridden and the furtively masturbating.

A necessary step in escaping this fate was to turn Nidu from a nominally friendly ally to a vaguely hostile one. It wouldn't do to have the Nidu as a full-fledged enemy, of course; despite Pope's opinion of the Nidu's station in galactic diplomacy, Nidu was still significantly more powerful than Earth and her tiny colonies. Burkina Faso or not, she could still squash the Earth like a bug. But an edgy relationship made for better defense allocations. Better defense allocations made for better ships, better soldiers, and better weapons. Better weapons made for more diplomatic respect. More diplomatic respect meant a chance to trade up on allies.

Pope was aware there were other ways to get more diplomatic respect than bigger guns, of course. But while other diplomatic maneuvers sometimes worked and sometimes didn't, ultimately a big damn gun always commanded respect. It was a simple diplomatic equation, and Bob Pope was not one for unnecessarily complicating things.

However, if it *was* necessary to complicate things, Pope could live with that, especially if in doing so he got close to his own goals. But *especially* if he were complicating things for someone he didn't like. Like, say, that smug bastard Jim Heffer at the State Department.

Which is why, after Phipps had gotten him up to speed on the sheep issue, Pope made an executive decision. "We need to force State's hand," he said.

Phipps raised an eyebrow. "Why do we need to do that? They're already going to come up empty. Relations are already going to be damaged."

"It's not enough," Pope said. "They won't be damaged *enough*. Heffer can still convince the Nidu they made the good faith effort. We need to poke a stick through that wheel."

"Okay," Phipps said, doubtfully; he wasn't quite sure he followed the allusion. "What do you suggest?"

"The girl is going to be handled," Pope said.

"Right," Phipps said. No more need be said on that issue; from that point forward it was best that Pope didn't know the specifics.

"Then we let the Nidu know she exists," Pope said.

"We can't do that," Phipps said.

"*We* can't," Pope agreed. "But I'm sure that there are others who would be delighted to share the information."

Phipps brightened. "I know just the man for the job."

Deception, as practically manifested, succeeds because of two things. First, the object of deception is convincingly deceptive in its design; i.e., it looks/feels/acts like the real thing. Second, and equally important, the subject of deception must be predisposed to believing that the object of deception is indeed the real thing. These two criteria work in an inverse relationship with each other; a sufficiently deceptive object can convince a skeptical subject, while a subject who sincerely wants to believe will be able to overlook even gross flaws in the object onto which he or she confers belief.

Ted Soram, Secretary of Trade, desperately wanted to believe.

And why not. He'd had a bad week. Any week in which one of your trade negotiators kills his opposite number at the trade table, in front of witnesses from both sides, was not one destined for the all-time list of classic weeks.

But that's not what was bothering Soram. Well, it *was,* but few people knew all the details. For as much as controversy was swirling around Soram and his department, Heffer and State had done a grand job of cleaning things up. It was galling to have had State's flunkies crawling through Moeller's office, but on the other hand it was better than having either the US or UNE Federal Bureau of Investigation driving their forensics microscopes up Trade's ass. As bad as Moeller's murder attempt (attempt? Success!) was, it was, quite literally, a State secret.

No, what was really chafing Soram across the ass was how little *support* he was getting during this particular moment of crisis. *He* didn't shove a whatever-the-hell-that-was up Moeller's bum and send him off to kill someone. *He* wasn't the one that made the Nidu get up and walk out on trade negotiations, causing the markets to take a dump and everyone from Ecuadorian banana farmers to Taiwanese video game manufacturers to howl in protest. And yet it was *he* getting burned on the political shows and in the editorials, and, in at least one report he'd seen, in effigy at some fisherman protest in France.

He couldn't even respond—President Webster's folks had asked (read: told) him to avoid unscripted appearances after he told that joke about the Pakistani, the Indian, the pig, and the cow on a news show early in the administration. He still thought the reaction to that was overblown; he was just trying to make a point about cultural differences and trade. It wasn't worth a week of riots. In his absence from the talk shows, Trade's press secretary

Joe McGinnis had been fielding the grilling on the cameras, that goddamned ham. Soram suspected that at least half of Washington's reporters believed McGinnis *was* the trade secretary. Soram made a note to fire McGinnis after this all cooled down.

Weighed down as he was in scandal and unpopularity, Soram was looking for some way to redeem himself. He just hadn't the slightest idea what that might be.

This was Soram's curse. The scion of a family whose ancestors invented the individually packaged moist towelette (it took two of them, which precipitated an astounding amount of sibling bitterness that ricocheted through the family to this very day), Theodore Logan Preston Soram VI was very rich, occasionally charming in an Old Main Line Family sort of way, and entirely useless in *every* sort of way except as a cash machine for charities and politicians. For the better part of three decades he'd been on Philadelphia's "Stations of the Cross"—the stops hopeful senators and presidents made to pick up contributions and unofficial endorsements from the city elite. Soram had wanted to see what it was like on the other side of the table for a change.

So he'd made a deal with Webster: He'd deliver Philadelphia, and Webster would deliver a cabinet position. Soram preferred Trade, as he assumed it would be the best fit since he (well, his broker) had done so well with his international and interplanetary investment portfolios, and even Soram realized that asking for Treasury would be overreaching. But everyone knew it was an extraordinarily tight election, and Webster needed Philly if he was going to get Pennsylvania, a battleground state.

The decision was made: Trade was stocked top to bottom with lifelong bureaucrats. Even after they purged the anti-Nidu elements, there were enough competent people to work around Soram. Soram wasn't aware that last bit was part of the equation, of course, although the longer he was at Trade the more he suspected he didn't get listened to as much as he thought he should.

But again, he wasn't quite sure how to go about fixing that. The problem with being fundamentally useless is that it's difficult to shift gears into being useful. But even Soram was aware it was time to get useful, quick.

And so, when the confidential, encrypted message purporting to come from Ben Javna at State popped into Soram's mail queue and presented the trade secretary with a shot at redemption, he took it exactly as it was intended: as a gift, and at face value. Had Soram the complexity of mind a position such as his generally required, or even just the healthy paranoia of a career politician, he might have thought to trace the route of the mail, in which he (or more accurately his technical staff) would find that the message was cleverly, subtly but undeniably faked—deep in its routing history was information that showed it originated not from the State Department but from an anonymous remailer in Norway. It had been sent there by a second anonymous remailer in Qatar, which had received it from Archie McClellan, who created it after his communicator discussion with Phipps.

The message was brief:

Secretary Soram—

Secretary Heffer wished me to convey to you the following information regarding the Nidu situation.

—here followed a short explanation of who Robin Baker was and why she was important to the Nidu—

After consultation with the President and the Chief of Staff it was decided that it would be best for you to approach the Nidu Ambassador with this information, so as to ameliorate recent difficulties. I have been informed to tell you that time is of the essence and it would be advisable to initiate contact with the Nidu Ambassador without delay after receiving this information.

Soram was yelling for his secretary to get on the horn to the Nidu embassy before he'd even gotten to that last part.

An hour later Soram found himself escorted into the inner

sanctum of Narf-win-Getag, Nidu Ambassador to the UNE, enjoying Nidu sarf tea (generally regarded to taste something like cow urine to most humans, who nevertheless never refused when the Nidu insisted on providing every human visitor with a steaming cup of the stuff nearly as soon as they entered the embassy) and sharing sailing stories with the ambassador, whose own yacht, as it happened, was docked at the same marina as Soram's. Narf-win-Getag was of course delighted to hear about Miss Baker, and assured Soram that upon delivery of the girl for the coronation ceremony, trade negotiations would resume without further delay. Soram invited Narf-win-Getag for a weekend jaunt on his yacht. Narf-win-Getag offered Soram another cup of sarf tea.

On the way back to Trade, Soram had a thought about the press conference he planned to call the next morning, the one in which he declared that the Nidu were coming back to the trade table thanks to his intense lobbying. So he called Jim Heffer's office. Heffer wasn't back from his Asia trip—he was always somewhere *else,* wasn't he—so he talked to Ben Javna instead.

"Given your help in these discussions with the Nidu, I was wondering if you want anyone from State at the press conference tomorrow," Soram said.

"Mr. Secretary, I'm afraid I have no idea what you're talking about," Javna said.

"I'm holding a press conference to announce that the Nidu are coming back to the negotiating table," Soram said. "I just got back from talking with the Nidu ambassador. The note you sent me was key in getting them back. I thought you might want to have someone at the conference. I'm scheduling it for nine-fifteen; we'll get on all the noon shows from that. Come on, Ben! It'll be fun."

"Mr. Secretary," Javna said, in an oddly even tone of voice. "I haven't sent you any messages in the last week. I certainly haven't sent any messages to you regarding the Nidu, and if I *had,* I wouldn't have suggested you share them with the Nidu."

"Oh," Soram said.

"If I may ask, Mr. Secretary, what was in the message?"

"That you'd found the girl they were looking for," Soram said.

"And what did you tell the ambassador?" Javna asked.

"Well, I told him that we'd be happy to provide the girl to them. You've got her, right? Surely she's agreed to help us."

"Well, Mr. Secretary, no and no," Javna said. "As far as I know, we *don't* have the girl, and so clearly she can't have agreed to help us. You've just guaranteed something we might not be able to deliver to a nation that already has cause for grievance against us."

"Oh," Soram said again. He suddenly felt cold. "Oh, dear."

"Mr. Secretary, if I may make a suggestion," Ben Javna said.

"Yes, of course," Soram said.

"If I were you, I would put off that press conference. I would also send me that note you seem to think I have sent to you. I would also not talk to anyone else about your note, or your visit to the Nidu. Finally, Mr. Secretary, until and unless you hear from me, Secretary Heffer, or President Webster, I'd strongly suggest you not make any long-term plans involving your current office. With all due respect to your position, sir, you've just humped the bunk. If you're lucky, you'll only have to resign."

"What happens if I'm not lucky?" Soram asked.

"If you're not lucky, we'll all be using cigarettes for currency in the prison exercise yard," Javna said. "Of course, that's assuming that after they conquer Earth, the Nidu let us live."

Javna got off the line with Soram and immediately made the call to Heffer and got Adam Zane, his scheduler, instead. Heffer was just starting his speech lauding the retiring head of the LA office and couldn't be dragged away for anything short of a full-out attack. Javna briefly considered whether Soram's stupidity and incompetence constituted a clear and present danger to the Earth, and then told Zane to have Heffer call him the instant he stopped speechifying.

As he disconnected, Javna's mail queue blinked; Soram's message had arrived. Javna popped it up and grimaced when he read the message. Whoever had put it together knew as much about the girl as he did, and that of course was very bad. Javna pulled up the routing information; he wasn't an expert on mailing protocols but he was reasonably sure the UNE State Department was not routing extremely sensitive mail through an anonymous remailer in Norway. Whoever dropped this into Soram's lap knew that he wasn't the sort of person who would perform due diligence on the provenance of the message before stampeding off to cover himself in glory and save his own ass. It was someone who knew Soram well, or at least well enough.

Javna had his suspicions, of course. Secretary Pope and his sock puppet Dave Phipps were almost certainly behind this; they had the means and motive to pace Creek step for step in his own investigations. Then there was Defense's perennially cozy relationship with Jean Schroeder and the American Institute for Colonization. Creek had dug up the connection between Schroeder and that damned fool Dirk Moeller; it was almost equally certain there was a direct connection between Schroeder and either Pope or Phipps, or both. Officially the AIC was in bad odor across the Webster administration, but unofficially people like Schroeder and groups like the AIC were like barnacles on the ship of state. You couldn't just scrape them off; they had to be blasted off with a fucking water cannon.

Regardless of whom, the question was *why*. Ideally, Creek would even now be convincing the Baker lady to help out, and State would find some way to have her play her role in the Nidu coronation ceremony so that she walked away from it with no undue trauma. In other words, whoever was playing Soram was only having him deliver a message State would hopefully have delivered a day later at most. If it was sabotage, it didn't make much sense.

Unless, Javna suddenly realized, whoever fed Soram his information knew that the girl *couldn't* be delivered.

Javna checked his watch. By this time, Harry and the Baker lady would be having their little date at the mall. He reached for his desk communicator to call Creek; as he did so his incoming service light went on and Barbara, his assistant, came over the speaker. "The Nidu ambassador is here to see you, Mr Javna," she said.

Fuck, Javna thought. Just like that, he was out of time.

"Send him in, please," he said, and then grabbed at his keyboard to bang out a note to Creek. Javna had the dread sense that Creek and the mysterious Miss Baker were about to find themselves in serious and possibly fatal danger. In the short run, until Javna could figure out who was stage-managing this interference and for what end, it was better and safer that Creek and the girl go away.

Javna had no doubt Creek could disappear; he just hoped he'd be able to find to him again when he needed him, which he figured would be all too soon.

Javna banged the "send" key just as the office door opened, and cursed inwardly even as he stood to receive Narf-win-Getag. Having Creek and Baker go to ground was just about the least convenient thing he could have them do at this particular moment in time. Its only advantage was that it was better than the both of them being dead.

Good luck, Harry, Javna thought as he plastered a welcoming smile on his face. *Stay safe, wherever you are.*

"Where the fuck is he?" Rod Acuna jammed himself through the door of the apartment, Takk following close behind, and stood over Archie at his computer. Archie stared agog at Acuna, who looked like he'd just run a gauntlet of large predators. Acuna whacked Archie hard upside the temple with his good hand. "Where the fuck is Creek?" he repeated.

The smack on the temple got Archie back into work mode. "He's on the Metro," Archie said. "I'm tracking him and the girl with the pen. I lose the signal here and there because of the tunnels, but it picks up again when they get near a stop."

"They're going to the State Department," Acuna said.

"I don't think so," Archie said, and punched up a map of the Metro system. "Look, here's the Foggy Bottom/GWU stop," he said, pointing. Then he pointed at the tracking window, which noted longitude and latitude, updated every second. "These coordinates are past that stop and are moving at speed consistent with a Metro train. They're still on the Metro."

"What are they saying to each other?" Acuna asked.

"I'm not picking up anything," Archie said. "She must have the pen in a purse or something." Archie looked around again. "Where's Ed?" he asked.

"Pretty sure he's dead," Acuna said. He pointed at the computer screen. "Don't you lose him, geek. I want to know where that fucker comes out and where he goes next. I'm going to have that son of a bitch dead by sunrise. So don't you lose him. You get me?"

"I get you," Archie said. Acuna grunted and hobbled his way over to the bathroom. Archie watched him go and then turned to Takk. "Is Ed really dead?" he asked. Takk shrugged and turned on a game show. Whatever Ed's professional qualities, it was clear he would not be deeply personally missed by his former colleagues. Archie suspected that if he screwed up finding Creek, he would be even less missed.

Archie turned back to his computer screen, the pen coordinates, and Metro map. *Come on, Creek,* he thought to himself. *Where are you going?*

"Where are we going?" Robin asked Creek.

"I have no idea yet," Creek said. "Give me a minute."

"Okay," Robin said. "But I'd really feel more confident if you had a plan."

"So would I," Creek said. "Would you mind if I made a call?"

Robin shrugged. "It's your communicator, Harry. Do you want me to stand somewhere else?"

"You don't have to," Creek said. Robin dropped herself into the seat next to Creek. Creek flipped open his communicator and accessed his home network; Brian's voice popped up a second later.

"You're alive," Brian said, without preamble. "You should know most of the Alexandria Police Department is crawling through the mall right now. The police network tells of a shootout and three or four guys dead and another couple wounded. You should also know the Alexandria police have put out an APB for you and your redhead friend. They got your description from a shoe salesman, apparently. You left your signature on something?"

"A rental agreement," Creek said. "For shoes."

"Not the smartest thing you could have done," Brian said.

"We weren't expecting to be attacked by armed men," Creek said.

"You might want to internalize that as a given from now on," Brian said. "Anyway. You and she are wanted on a truly impressive number of charges. Are you okay?"

"We're fine," Creek said. "We're on the Metro right now."

"I'm aware of that," Brian said. "I'm getting your position from the signal. Which by the way I've now spoofed so that if anyone else, say the police, get the bright idea to call you, they won't be able to track your movement."

"Thanks," Creek said.

"It's nothing. Your communicator is on the network. It's like redecorating a spare room."

"Listen," Creek said. "That credit card receipt I had you follow up on. What did you get off of it?"

"It's fraudulent, of course," Brian said. "The money in the account is real enough—it's a debit-style card. But the name on the card is 'Albert Rosenweig,' whose identity is about one document thick. After the card there's nothing."

"So you don't have anything on this guy," Creek said.

"I didn't say *that*," Brian said. "The man signs his name every time he uses the card—the signature gets sent and stored. I paid a little visit to his card issuer to get more samples of his signature, developed a good handwriting model for our man Albert, and then cross-referenced the handwriting style with the government's database of signatures that go with our National Identity Cards."

"That's good thinking," Creek said.

"Thanks," Brian said. "It's also dreadfully illegal and a true pain in the ass, since there are over 250 million American males at the moment. Fortunately, I'm a computer now. And after combing through DNA, this is a comparative breeze."

"Who is he?" Creek asked.

"I'm ninety-three percent sure it's this guy." Brian sent a picture that popped up on the communicator's small display. "Alberto Roderick Acuna. I say ninety-three percent because the handwriting samples don't have all the information I need—signing on the signature pads for your credit card purchases doesn't capture stuff like the amount of pressure you apply to certain parts of your pen stroke. I had to do some estimating based on general handwriting statistical models. Which didn't previously exist, I should note. I've been keeping busy in your absence."

"Well, good job," Creek said. "That's the guy."

"Congratulations, then, because you've got yourself a real winner," Brian said. "This Acuna character was an Army Ranger—he fought at the Battle of Pajmhi, incidentally—but received an dishonorable discharge. He was suspected in a floater accident that killed his colonel. Court-martialed but acquitted. Apparently the evidence wasn't great. Right after being discharged he spent ninety days in the DC lock-up for assault. He beat the hell out of an aide to then-Congresswoman Burns. In what I'm sure was a total coincidence, Acuna thumped the aide just before a vote on tariffs for Nidu textile imports. Burns was usually pro-trade but went against her voting record on that one. Since he got out he's worked as a private investigator. You'll be interested to know that one of his biggest clients is the American Institute for Colonization and its head, Jean Schroeder. Acuna's also been more or less continually investigated by DC, Maryland, and Virginia police as well as the US and UNE feds. He's a suspect in at least a couple of missing persons cases. Missing people who, in what I'm sure is another total coincidence, had crossed swords with either Schroeder or the AIC."

"I think we were meant to be next on that list," Creek said. "Acuna was waiting for us in the mall."

"Did you kill him?" Brian asked.

"I don't think so, but I don't think he's in very good shape at the moment. Which reminds me—" Creek fished in his pocket and pulled out Agent Dwight's ID card. "Can you look through the FBI database and see if you can find me anything on an agent named Reginald Dwight?"

"UNE FBI or US FBI?" Brian asked.

"US," Creek said.

"Okay. I was looking for information on Acuna earlier so I should be able to patch back in. Give me a second. I'd guess that's a fake name too, though. For one thing, it's the real name of a twentieth-century composer who went by the name Elton John."

"I don't know him," Creek said.

"Sure you do," Brian said. "Remember that kids' tunes collection I had when I was seven? 'Rocket Man.' I love that tune."

"It was longer ago for some of us than others," Creek said.

"Whatever," Brian said. "Okay, I'm wrong. Turns out there *was* an FBI agent Reginald Dwight. But I doubt it was your guy, since Agent Dwight was killed three years ago. One of those militia whackjobs in Idaho shot him while the FBI was storming his compound. Whoever your guy is, he's not the walking dead."

"He might be now," Creek said.

"Speaking of which, you look like hell," Brian said. "I'm looking at you through the little camera on your communicator. Your cheek is bleeding. You might want to get that wiped off before one of your trainmates decides you're creepy enough to be checked out by the cops."

"Right," Creek said. "Thanks. I'll call you back soon."

"I'll be here," Brian said, and hung up. Creek lightly brushed his cheek and felt blood moisten his fingers. He wiped them on the inside of his jacket and asked Robin if she had any tissues in her purse. Robin looked up, noticed the blood, nodded, and started digging through her purse. "Shit," she said, after a second.

"What's wrong?" Creek asked.

"You never realize how much crap you have in your purse until you're looking for one specific thing," Robin said, and started taking objects out of her purse to make her search easier: an address book, a makeup compact, a pen, a tampon applicator. Robin looked up at Creek after the last one. "Pretend you didn't see that," she said.

Creek pointed to the pen. "Can I see that pen?" he asked.

"Sure," Robin said, and handed over the pen.

"This is the one from the store, right?" Creek asked. "The one the gecko man left."

Robin nodded. "Yeah. Why?"

Creek turned the pen around in his hands, and then started taking it apart. After a minute he snapped off the clip and turned it over. "Shit," he said.

"What is it?" Robin asked.

"Bug," Creek said. "They've been tracking us since we left the mall." He dropped the clip and stomped on it with his foot, twisting it into the floor of the train. "We need to get away. Far away."

"Fuck!" Archie pounded the table his computer was on.

This attracted Acuna from the next room. "That better not be what I think it is," he said.

"Creek found the pen," Archie said. "It's not my fault."

"I don't care whose fault it was," Acuna said. "You need to find him, now."

Archie glowered at the screen and from the last coordinates of the pen guessed where Creek and the sheep lady would be in the Metro system. The two of them were approaching L'Enfant Plaza; they were on the Blue Line train but L'Enfant Plaza served every line in the city except the Red and Gray lines. If they got off their train there, who knows where they'd end up.

Got off their train.

"I've got it," Archie said. He closed the track window on the pen and opened up a command line.

"Got what?" Acuna asked.

"My dad was an electrical systems engineer for the DC Metro," Archie said. "Five years ago, the entire electrical system got a refit, and my dad hired me freelance to help with the code. Part of the electrical system deals with managing the power to the trains—"

"Skip the technical shit," Acuna said. "Get to the point. Quick."

"The Metro trains are maglev—magnetic levitation," Archie

said. "Each train used to get full power for its magnets no matter what, but that got too expensive. The retrofit allowed each train to use only as much power as it needs to run, based on the gross weight of the train. The amount of power allotted to each train adjusts in real time."

"So?" Acuna said.

"So, every time someone gets on a train or off a train, the amount of power sent to the train increases or decreases by an amount that's in a direct relationship to the weight of those people." Archie looked over to Acuna, whose face was a dangerous shade of blank. He decided to make it even simpler. "If we can guess how much the two of them weigh, we might be able to guess if they've gotten off their train and where they might be going."

Acuna's eyebrows shot up; he got it. "You'll need to get into the Metro's system," he said.

Archie had turned back to his computer. "Dad had a back door into the system he let me use while I was freelancing," he said. "I'm guessing after he retired no one bothered to close it."

Fifteen seconds later: "Nope, they didn't. We're in," Archie said. "You saw the two of them, right? How much would you guess they weighed?"

"I don't know," Acuna said. "Both of them seemed pretty fit."

"How tall were they?" Archie asked.

"He was about my height," Acuna said. "I'm about five ten. She was a few inches shorter, I'd guess."

"About five six, then, let's say," Archie said. "So let's say he's about 180 and she's 120, so that's 300 pounds, which is about 136 kilos." Archie punched up a calculator on his computer screen and pounded in some numbers, and then pointed at the resulting number. "All right, if the train they got in was empty, that's how much energy would need to be fed to the train to compensate for their additional weight when they got on. So we're looking for something in that neighborhood."

Archie opened up another window. "Okay, here's a list of the Blue Line trains currently in operation. Click this here, and now we have them arranged by when they stopped at the Arlington Mall station. Disregard the trains going out from DC, we have four trains that stopped at the station in the time window we're looking for." Archie selected each of the trains; four new windows opened up. Archie selected the "Power Management" option for each; each window became a spiky chart.

"No," Archie said, closing one chart. "No," he said again a few seconds later, closing the next chart. "Yes!" he said to the third one, and blew up the chart to maximum size. "Look here," Archie said, pointing to the graph. "Power goes down because people are stepping off the train, then you get some noise because people are stepping off and on simultaneously. But *here*"—Archie pointed to a small uptick—"is a power boost that's right near what we're looking for, for about 136 kilos. That's assuming they stepped on the train together, as opposed to one fatso."

"That's swell," Acuna said, and Archie realized that of the many things Acuna might be, "patient" was never going to be one of them. "Now tell me if they're still on the goddamn train."

Archie pulled up a real-time chart of the train's power management, which showed the train's last five minutes of power usage. "Looks like the train just left L'Enfant," Archie said. "Lots of people getting on and off the train, but none looks like the 136-kilo power spike or drop. I'm guessing they're still on the train."

"You're *guessing*," Acuna said.

"Mr. Acuna," Archie said. "I'm doing the best I can. I can't help that he busted the tracking pen. But short of the tracking pen or getting a feed from the Metro cameras, this is as good as it gets."

Acuna stared at Archie just long enough for Archie to wonder if he was going to smack him again. Then, by God, Acuna actually *smiled*. "Fair enough," he said. "Keep your eye on the graph,

Archie. Don't let them get away. Let me know as soon as you think they've gotten off the train." He clapped his hand on Archie's shoulder as he turned to go. Archie realized Acuna had actually called him by his given name.

"Ben—may I call you Ben?" Narf-win-Getag asked, settling down in his chair.

"By all means, Mr. Ambassador," Ben Javna said. Being of inferior rank to the ambassador, Javna had remained standing and had moved out in front of his desk. Staying behind the desk would have been considered a breach of etiquette.

"Thank you," Narf-win-Getag said. "I know my people have a reputation for being socially standoffish, but in private we can be just as relaxed as any sentient being. I even encourage my secretary to call me 'Narf' when we are doing private business."

"And does she, Mr. Ambassador?" Javna asked.

"Oh, of course she doesn't," Narf-win-Getag said. "She wouldn't *dare*. But it's nice of me to *offer*, don't you think?"

"And how may I be of service to you this evening, Mr. Ambassador," Javna said.

"Secretary Soram came and visited me just now to deliver the good news that you've found our lost sheep," Narf-win-Getag said.

"Did he, now," Javna said, as neutrally as possible.

"Yes," Narf-win-Getag said. "Although I'm led to understand that our sheep in question isn't a sheep at all but a young human with our sheep DNA encoded in hers. Curious. Ben, may I trouble you for something to drink?"

"Of course, Mr. Ambassador," Javna said.

"Eighteen-year-old Glenlivet, if you have any," Narf-win-Getag said. "I love its bouquet."

"I believe Secretary Heffer may have some in his bar," Javna said, and opened his door to have Barbara get a glass.

188 · John Scalzi

"Excellent. Normally, you understand, I would go to Secretary Heffer to chat about this, but seeing as he is out of town at the moment, and given the time constraint we're under, it makes sense to talk to you."

"I appreciate that, Mr. Ambassador," Javna said.

"Good, good," Narf-win-Getag said. "So, anyway, Ben. I'll be happy to take her off your hands now."

"You mean the girl, Mr. Ambassador?" Javna asked. Barbara slipped her hand through the door to deliver the drink; Javna took it.

"Yes, that's right," Narf-win-Getag said.

"I'm afraid we have a problem there, sir," Javna said, and handed Narf-win-Getag his drink. "The young woman in question has not come to the State Department yet."

"Well, certainly you know where she *is*," Narf-win-Getag said. He grimaced at his glass. "I'd like this on the rocks," he said, handing it back to Javna.

"Of course, Mr. Ambassador," Javna said, and took the glass to his own bar. "I'm sorry to say that in fact we don't know where she is at the moment."

Narf-win-Getag snorted impatiently. "Secretary Soram seemed convinced she was in your possession," he said.

"Secretary Soram was enthusiastic but not in possession of all the facts," Javna said. He dropped ice into the glass with his tongs. "We know the identity of the woman in question and a member of the State Department has gone to speak to her about giving her assistance. That's where it stands at the moment."

"It seems inconceivable that a secretary in your planetary administration would not be in full possession of the facts," Narf-win-Getag said.

Believe it, Javna thought. "There may have been a misunderstanding of terms," he said instead, and walked over to hand the glass back to Narf-win-Getag.

"Humph," the ambassador said, and took his drink. "Very well. Please speak to your man and tell him we are ready for him to bring the woman in to us."

"He's out of contact," Javna said.

"I beg your pardon?" Narf-win-Getag said. "'Out of contact'? Is that even *possible* on this planet of yours? Even mountain tribesmen of Papua New Guinea have full-spectrum communicator links. If there's one thing that distinguishes the human species, it is a pathological need to stay connected. The fact your people will interrupt sex to answer your communicators is a scandal across the entire Common Confederation. So you'll understand if I am skeptical when you say your man is out of contact."

"I understand entirely, Mr. Ambassador," Javna said. "Nevertheless, there it is."

"Doesn't he have a communicator?" Narf-win-Getag said.

"He does," Javna said. "He's just not answering it."

"What about the woman?" Narf-win-Getag said. "Surely this Miss Baker has a communicator."

"She does," Javna said, noting that the Nidu ambassador knew Baker's name. "However, hers appears not to be a portable, and she is with our man at the moment."

"Well, isn't that *interesting*," Narf-win-Getag said. "The only two people on the entire North American continent who cannot be reached in an instant." He set his glass of scotch down, undrunk. "Ben, I'll give you the courtesy of not suggesting that you are, in fact, willfully holding out this woman for whatever purpose you might have. But I will let you know that when she *does* show up, it is my sincere hope that she be surrendered immediately to us. Time is very short now—less than a day before our agreed-upon deadline is reached."

"No one is more aware of that than I, Mr. Ambassador," Javna said.

"I'm pleased to hear that, Ben," Narf-win-Getag said. He nodded and turned to go.

"But I should warn you that even when she comes in, she may not agree to be turned over to you," Javna said.

Narf-win-Getag stopped mid-stride. "Come again?" he said.

"She may not agree to take part," Javna said. "As an American and UNE citizen, she has rights. We can't compel her. We can strongly suggest to her the importance of taking part in the coronation ceremony. But when push comes to shove, we can't make her do it."

Narf-win-Getag stared at Javna for a time, and then Javna heard the low, gutteral rumbling that he knew was the Nidu analogue to a good, hearty laugh. "You know, Ben," Narf-win-Getag said, after his rumbling had subsided, "humans never fail to amuse and amaze me. You're all so busy tending to your own personal tree that you don't look around to see that the forest is on fire. It's very honorable that you would maintain that this young woman has a choice in this matter. But if you'll allow me to be frank with you, in about a week of your time, our coronation ceremony has to take place. If it does not take place at the appointed time, then any Nidu clan can formally assert its right to the throne, and I can assure you that many are ready. Nidu will be plunged into civil war, and it's entirely likely—indeed, I would suspect highly *probable*—the Earth and her colonies will not be able to sit on the sidelines and watch the carnage unaffected. If I were Secretary Heffer—or President Webster—or *you*, rather than worrying about Miss Baker's rights, I'd be worrying about my *responsibilities* to my planet and its well-being."

"That sounds ominous, Mr. Ambassador," Javna said.

Narf-win-Getag chuckled, human-style. "Nonsense, Ben. I am merely suggesting what *I* would do. You may of course see things differently. Hopefully, our young female friend will show up soon and all this will be proven to be idle and pointless speculation. In

the meantime, however, I would hope you would do us—do *me*—
the courtesy of forwarding all the information you have on Miss
Baker. Perhaps my people will find something there that will allow us all a satisfactory resolution to our present troubles."

"Of course, Mr. Ambassador," Javna said. "I'll have that sent
over immediately."

"Excellent, Ben. Thank you for your time." Narf-win-Getag
nodded toward his glass. "And thank you for the drink." He left.

Javna went over to the glass, picked it up, sniffed it. No lizardy
smell. He slugged it back and as he did so felt like the house but-
ler sneaking booze from his master's liquor cabinet. He set the
glass down with prejudice.

This whole thing stinks, he thought. Javna knew he was being
jerked around. He just didn't know by who and for what reasons.
The only power he had—the only power it seemed like the entire
government had—was a negative power: The power to hide the
object of desire. The power to hide Robin Baker.

"They're off the train!" Archie yelled back to Acuna, who was on
the communicator with Jean Schroeder.

"Where?" Acuna yelled back.

"Benning Road," Archie said. "Dogstown. Do you have any
idea why they'd go there?"

Acuna didn't. Jean Schroeder did.

Fixer was in the back of the shop doing inventory when he heard
Chuckie bark. He glanced up at his clock; just past closing time.
He knew he should have locked the door before he came back. No
help for it now. He set down his tablet and came out onto the
shop floor to see Harry Creek and some lady standing there. Both
of them looked like total hell.

"Hello, Fixer," Creek said. "I have need of your services."

Fixer grinned in spite of himself. "Of course you do," he said, and laughed. "Well, well," he said. "I was wondering what this would be like. Now I know."

"Now you know what?" Creek asked.

"What it's like when the other shoe drops, Mr. Creek," Fixer said. "Because if I'm not mistaken, it's just come down with a big goddamn *thunk*."

"Tell me what you need," Fixer said.

"We need new identities," Creek said. "We need off the planet. We need it fast."

"How fast?" Fixer asked.

"The next couple of hours would be nice," Creek said.

"Oh, okay," Fixer said. "Because for a minute there I thought you might want something *impossible.*"

"I know it's a lot to ask," Creek said.

"Any extenuating circumstances I should know about that might make this even more difficult?" Fixer said.

"People just tried to kill us. And there's an APB out for our arrest," Creek said.

Fixer arched his eyebrow at Creek. "This wouldn't have anything to do with what just went on at the Arlington Mall, would it?"

"It might," Creek admitted.

"Well, aren't you just a bundle of fun," Fixer said.

"Can you help us?" Creek said.

"For what you're asking, I don't think you can afford me," Fixer said.

Creek reached into his wallet and pulled out the anonymous credit card Javna had given him.

"Try me," Creek said.

Archie stood in front of the vending machine, steeling himself.

"Just do it," Archie said to himself. He'd already fed the credit card into the machine; all he had to do was press the B4 button and have done with it.

He was having a hard time doing it. After three previous sessions with the vending machine ripping the information out of his head like a jaguar raking his optic nerves with its claws, he was not exactly brimming with enthusiasm for session number four.

Not only that, but the B4 slot of the vending machine was now empty—he was now spending money to get a migraine and getting nothing for it.

Actually, though, Archie was okay with that. The pain induced with each packet of white chocolate M&Ms was great enough to make Archie physically ill at the thought of ingesting another single piece of candy. This state of affairs no doubt would have pleased Ivan Pavlov immensely.

"Just do it," he said again, and leaned his head on the Plexiglas, and attempted to will himself to press the button. Acuna had divulged the likely whereabouts of Creek and Baker and was busily medicating himself enough to be able to head out and get them; it was information Archie was certain Sam and the others would want to know. And yet there he was, busily not pressing the button. What he was doing, forehead pressed against the Plexiglas, finger hovering over the B4 button, was thinking of new and innovative ways to strangle Sam for doing this to him.

One should expect one's partner in all things domestic and carnal to have just a little bit more sympathy.

"Hey, geek!"

Archie jerked his head up with a start and moved his body fractionally, enough that the finger hovering over the B4 button jammed into it. Archie gasped as the blinding pain ripped through his head for the fourth time that day and struggled mightily to remain standing. Archie became aware he was suddenly drooling; he desperately tried to suck it back into his mouth and to keep from vomiting all over the front of the vending machine. He closed his eyes and waited for the nausea to pass. When he opened them, Acuna was standing next him.

"What the fuck is wrong with you?" Acuna asked.

"Headache," Archie said, wetly. "I get them pretty bad. It's an allergy thing."

Acuna looked Archie up and down for a moment, sizing him up. "Yeah, well, look. You're coming with us. Schroeder says that guy Creek and the girl are going to visit has a lot of computer and technical shit at his place. If Creek and the girl aren't there, and the guy isn't useful, we might be able to get something out of his computers."

Archie nodded, eyes still closed. "Okay," he said. "I'm going to need a couple of minutes, though. I need to do a couple of things before we go. I need to set some drillers to get into Creek's computer system."

"You're still not in that yet?" Acuna asked.

Archie shook his head—slowly. "The man's got some unbelievable defensive software on his system. It's military grade at least."

"Fine," Acuna said. "I have to numb myself a little more anyway. But make it fast." Acuna looked over to the vending machine and frowned. "What did you get?"

"What?" Archie asked.

"You pressed a button but I don't see anything at the bottom."

"I accidentally pressed B4," Archie said. "It's empty. I meant to press B5, but you startled me."

Acuna snorted. "Try G2," he said. "It's got aspirin in it." He walked off. Archie stood there for a few more seconds, then dully pulled out his credit card, slipped it into the vending machine, pressed "G2", and retrieved his packet of pain reliever.

Back at his computer, Archie considered the problem of Creek's computer system, which was, he had to admit, just a fucking masterpiece of defensive security. Archie had been flinging driller after driller at the thing, each of the autonomous programs designed to hunt out specific areas of weakness in the system's security, drill into them, and then hold the door open for other programs to extract data.

Your average home system would fall in about 15 seconds with a minimally complex driller that was essentially a password generator, with a spoofer to fool the system into thinking each password entered was the first attempt. Small business systems and home systems of people who worked in the computer industry or who were simply paranoid about their home systems required a more specialized driller, with more subtle ways of getting in.

On this medium level of complexity, Archie liked a driller that mimicked the information retrieval protocol used across the network—the driller would fool the system into thinking it had requested information and stream a self-extracting program into the system, which would root around and send data back out, piggybacking on the system's legitimate outward bound traffic.

Now, larger business and government systems, heavily protected as they were, required awesomely designed drillers capable of multidimensional, simultaneous system attacks. Corporate-grade drillers were the state of the art; the hack who coded one that laid into a well-defended system would be king among the hack geeks for at least six hours, which was typically the amount of time it took IT to dislodge the driller and backhoe the hole in the system's security.

Archie had done Creek and his system the professional courtesy of assuming a low-level driller wouldn't cut it, and had begun probing his system with mid-level drillers, all of which reported back failure. Archie only had one high-level driller in his archive, but it was a doozy; it had famously drilled open the USDA system and ferreted out the crop forecasts for the year, leading to a collapse in the agricultural futures market. Archie hadn't written the driller, but he respected the hell out of the coding skills of the hack who had; the driller was elegantly designed. The USDA driller would be useless for any major corporate or government target, of course—on that level, a driller only works once—but it should have been more than enough for any home system on the planet. It wasn't.

If Archie had six weeks and nothing else to do, he might have been able to whip up a new driller of similar quality as the USDA one; as it was he had six minutes. So he elected to take another tack. He fired up a new window and logged into Basher's Dungeon, a hack forum, and posted a message as Creek taunting the hacks therein and proclaiming his system as hackproof. Such a taunt wouldn't dislodge serious hacks, but it would get some of the less skilled and more excitable hacks moving, and once their attacks starting bouncing off Creek's system, some of the more competent would sense the system as a legitimate challenge. To sweeten the deal Archie wrote that inside Creek's system was the long-rumored, never-seen video of a famous pop star going down on her not-famous-but-equally-hot identical twin sister.

That should work, Archie thought, and sent off the message. Then he reached into his archives and pulled out a monitor pro-

gram and a retrieval program. The monitor program would ob-
serve the various attacks on Creek's system from the outside by
tagging drillers and other programs as they reached Creek's system and then tracking their progress against it. When one of
them cracked the system, the monitor program would alert the
retrieval program, which would enter and grab information.

Archie was obviously no longer looking for Robin Baker's
identity, but if Creek and the girl slipped away again, the information they found could help track them down. Archie directed the
retrieval program to focus on personal information documents
and all activity within the last couple of weeks. That was bound to
be a lot of material but Archie could trim it down once he had it,
and it was better than trying to download every file in the system.

Acuna stepped into the room. "Time to go," he said. "Wrap
it up."

"Already wrapped," Archie said, and closed his computer. *Let's
see you handle this, Creek*, he thought.

Brian noticed the hack drillers plinking at Creek's system the
same way a musk ox notes a swarm of flies buzzing around its
nose. He warded off earlier attacks from what he assumed was a
single anonymous source, but he noticed that these new drillers
were both substantially less sophisticated than the previous attacks and coming from multiple, nonanonymous sources. So
whoever was bothering him now was both stupid and clumsy.
Brian left the diggers to their futile work and sent scouts of his
own back down the pipe to the originators' systems (unsurprisingly easy to crack) and looked through their logs to find what
they all had in common. What they had in common was a recent
visit to Basher's Dungeon. Brian appropriated one of their identities, signed on, and found the post claiming to be from Creek.

That's sneaky, Brian thought. While he didn't approve of the attack on Creek's system (which was, in a manner of speaking, an attack on Brian himself), Brian could appreciate whomever it was trying to get other people to do his dirty work for him.

Brian's attention came back to the attacks on Creek's system; more complex diggers were arriving now, these from anonymous sources. The smarter kids had arrived, with their shiny toys. Brian wasn't concerned that they would drill the system, but if too many drillers arrived, defending the system would eventually and inevitably tax its resources, and Brian had other things to do today than play with the hacks.

Brian reached out and grabbed one of the simpler drillers, generating a trapping program on the fly to do so. He cracked it open and spilled the code; it was nothing special, but it featured what Brian was looking for—the hacksig of its maker, one OHN-SYAS69, more prosaically known as Peter Nguyen of Irvine, California. Brian learned with one sweep through Nguyen's system that Peter Nguyen was 15, had an extensive collection of busty porn, and was a budding if clearly not gifted hack; his driller was all off-the-shelf code, jammed together inelegantly into a barely functional program.

Peter Nguyen, I'm going to make you a star, Brian thought, and from the inelegant mess that was young master Nguyen's drilling program, crafted something new under the virtual sun: A metadriller, designed to latch onto other drilling programs, crack them open, find the hacksig of their makers, and then reprogram the drillers to head home to their maker's system. After drilling the system open, they would broadcast the availability of its contents onto the world network for anyone to see and sample. A few hours later, the driller would initiate a system crash that included the driller program itself, leaving only Peter Nguyen's hacksig behind.

Drilling the drillers would be simple, for the simple reason that no one had ever done it before, so no one had thought to protect the drillers from being drilled. This is what Brian loved about hacks. They were smart, but they didn't like to think about things not directly in front of them.

Brian finalized the code (making sure the metadriller would self-wipe if drilled itself; wouldn't do to fall into the same trap as the hacks) and then fed it into an autonomous replicator program that would spit out a metadriller each time Creek's system registered an attack. Native system resources spent on dealing with the attacks would now be limited to pinging the replicator program after each attempt. As a bonus, the hack world would fall into chaos and ruin for a certain amount of time while the geeks tried to figure out what the hell was going on.

That was just fine with Brian. He might be a disembodied virtual consciousness, but at least he wasn't some fucking geek. Maybe deprived of their systems, some of these geeks might go out and get some sun or meet people or something. It couldn't hurt. In any event, the hacks might learn a little humility, which they were sorely lacking despite the fact they couldn't be relied upon to shower more than one day out of three.

As Brian contemplated the enforced socialization of the geek set, he noticed two programs—not drillers—hanging about his system's periphery. The first flitted from driller to driller, marking each with a tiny autonomous program; Brian recognized it as a monitor program. The other program hung there, unpacked. Brian reached out, grabbed it, cracked it open. It was a retrieval program, waiting for a driller to finish its work before entering Creek's system. Brian read the code and discovered who was trying to get inside of him.

"Well, hello there, Mr. Archie McClellan, whoever you are," Brian said. "I think it's time we got better acquainted."

———

Fixer opened a freezer in his basement and pulled out an economy-sized Popsicle box, like you'd buy in a warehouse store, and held it for Creek and Robin to examine. "Here it is," he said.

"Here is what?" said Robin.

"Your new identity," Fixer said.

"We're going to be Popsicles?" Robin said.

Fixer grinned. He set the box down on the table and slid out a plastic tray from its inside; on it was what looked to be extremely thin, arm length gloves. "I don't want you to think I'm *glad* you came to me," Fixer said. "Because, truly, I am not. However, your decision was either smart or lucky for you. From time to time the Malloy family has the need to get someone past the authorities quickly and get them offworld for a nice, long, relaxing vacation. And when they do, they come to me, because I have this"—he pointed to the gloves—"a new identity in a box."

Creek reached over and picked up one of the gloves. "It looks like skin," he said. "Did this come from someone?"

"I didn't flay someone, if that's what you mean," Fixer said, and pointed at the glove. "Human skin cells grown from a culture, suspended in a nutrient base to keep them alive. Fingerprints, palm prints, and skin texture are laser-etched. Refrigeration makes them last for about six weeks. Unrefrigerated, they last for about two days. They'll get you off planet, and that's about it."

"Where do you get something like this?" Robin asked.

"One of the Malloys' legitimate businesses is a chain of nursing homes," Fixer said, and went back to the freezer to pull out another box. "I get skin samples and identities from the residents. They're good to use because they're alive but they're not going anywhere. As long as you've got a breathing body, DNA, and fin-

gerprints, everything else is just paperwork. The gloves themselves I make on medical apparatus I modified myself."

"You're pretty handy," Robin said.

"Thanks," Fixer said. "It's nice that my college education is
not completely wasted." He handed the second box to Robin, who
stared at it, and back at Fixer.

"Women's DNA in those," Fixer said. "Because, genetically
speaking, one size does not fit all."

Fixer helped Creek and Robin with the gloves and trimmed
off excess material, so that the gloves went midway between the
elbow and the shoulder. Fixer had both of them bend their arms
and put their palms up; he tugged at their gloves to line up the
fingerprints and then brought out what looked like a pair of
calipers and placed them on either side of Creek's upper arm and
pressed a button. Creek felt a mild thrum of electricity and then
the constriction of the glove adhering tightly to his arms.

"Ow," Creek said.

"Relax," Fixer said, doing the same to Robin. "They'll give a bit
in a few minutes. But better too tight than too loose. Now, let's
deal with your heads." Fixer went away and retuned a few minutes later with another box. "High-tech," he said, reaching into
the box and handing a small plastic container of tiny circular tabs
to Creek. "I apply these tabs to particular points on your face and
head, and they tighten or relax the muscle groups underneath to
alter your appearance. You'll look different enough from yourself
that you'll get past facial-recognition scanners. Another short-
term solution. The power on the tabs works for about six hours."

To Robin, he handed a pair of scissors and some hair dye.
"Low-tech," he said. "You have great hair, my dear. But it's far too
obvious." Robin took the scissors and dye and looked like she had
just been told to cut her own throat. Fixer guided her to a bathroom and then came back to Creek. "I need to make a few calls,"
he said. "I need to call in a few favors."

"Thank you," Creek said. "I really appreciate it."

"They're not favors for *you*," Fixer said. "I can get you off planet under my own steam. But I have a feeling you've just qualified me for a long, necessary, and possibly permanent vacation. That's going to require calling in some markers."

"Sorry about that," Creek said.

"Don't be too sorry," Fixer said. He dug out Creek's anonymous credit card and handed it back to him. "You're paying for it. And I don't mind telling you I'm putting a hell of a markup on my services tonight." Fixer headed up the stairs; Creek pulled out his communicator and made a call of his own to Brian.

"You're *very* popular," Brian said, again without preamble. "In the last hour or so there's been about 2,000 attempts to hack your system, some of them actually pretty good."

"The fact you're here to tell me about it suggests you have it under control," Creek said.

"That's one way of putting it," Brian said. "Another way of putting would be to say that in about ninety minutes, a couple thousand elite and not-so-elite hacks are going to howl in terror when their little worlds implode. However, I'm less worried about them than I am about the fact that a judge has just authorized a warrant to search your premises and the chattels within, namely, your computer system, in an attempt to figure out just where you are at the moment. The cops aren't going to be any more successful in getting information out of your system than the hacks, but if I'm disconnected from the network I'm not going to be much use to you."

"Can you leave the system?" Creek asked.

"I don't think so," Brian said. "The network allows for small autonomous programs, like the drillers I'm currently swatting away, but I'm a little large not to be noticed just floating there in the aether."

Creek thought for a moment. "The IBM at NOAA," he said, finally. "It should still be accessible. You could go there."

"Oh, very nice," Brian said. "Back to the womb."

"It's better than nothing," Creek said.

"I'm not complaining, Harry," Brian said. "I like the IBM. It's roomy. And it's also connected to the government network, which makes my accessing it rather less obtrusive. Hold on, I've begun my transfer. Do I sound farther away?"

"Not really," Creek said.

"And as I'm backing out of your system I'm formatting it and ordering it to disconnect from the network," Brian said. "I don't know what the cops are going to find in the rest of your house but your computer, at least, will be clean in just a few minutes."

"What else have you got for me?" Creek asked.

"Tons," Brian said. "First: The mall security cameras weren't working—the police pulled some disruptors off your new friends—but you and Miss Baker were recorded by the Metro video cameras. That's the bad news. The good news is that I managed to disconnect the feed from your train once I located you. The bad news is that I wasn't able to disconnect the video feed from the Benning Road stop, so eventually they'll figure out where you got off. But it still gives you a little bit of time. If you're not already hurrying to do whatever you're doing, it's time to start."

"We're hurrying," Creek said.

"Good to hear," Brain said. "Second: Your 'Agent Reginald Dwight' is actually Edward Baer, who appears to be your average low-grade flunky type. Served a couple years for extortion and racketeering about a decade ago and got an extra six months tacked on to his sentence for assaulting another prisoner while in the pen. His official job is as a security specialist, which is some irony for you. Quite obviously an associate of Mr. Acuna, who has been signing checks to this guy for a couple of years now."

"Is he dead?" Creek asked.

"No, he's not," Brian said. "He's not exactly skipping through the daisies, either. He was admitted to Mount Vernon Hospital with multiple internal and external injuries, including a broken back and severed spinal cord. He's in surgery now. There are two confirmed dead, one from massive head trauma and another from a gunshot wound, and two others wounded. One of those is unconscious, but one is conscious and being grilled by the police as we speak."

"That's five," Creek said. "Where's Acuna?"

"He's not at the scene," Brian said. "At the very least, there's no word of his arrest or his being sent to the hospital."

"That's no good," Creek said.

"Third," Brian continued, "I figured out who it was who's been trying to dig into your system for the last day or so: A guy named Archie McClellan. He's a contractor for the Department of Defense. Have you heard of him?"

"No," Creek said.

"Well, he's definitely heard of you," Brian said, "and since his attempts to hack into your system correspond almost exactly with your attempts to find your lost sheep, I don't think his visits are coincidental."

"Does this McClellan guy have any connection to Jean Schroeder or the AIC?" Creek asked.

"There's nothing in his banking history that would say so. He mostly works for the US and UNE governments. His contract information says he primarily works with legacy systems. He's got no axe to grind. Apparently, he's just a geek. I'm crawling up his computer's tailpipe as we speak. I expect to learn more any second now. But in the meantime I'd like to suggest to you that, yeah, we should assume whatever Jean Schroeder and his merry band of xenophobic freaks are up to, our friend Archie and the Defense Department are along for the ride."

Creek open his mouth to answer when the door to the basement opened and Fixer stepped a few steps down the stairs. "I've got a ride for you two," he said. "The *Neverland* cruise ship. The entire boat has been rented out to a group of Veterans of Foreign and Extraterrestrial Wars. It's hitting some of the usual stops but then it's going to some battle sites. So you're going to have to pretend to be a veteran."

"I *am* a veteran," Creek said.

"Well, good. Then things just got easier for a change," Fixer said. "The last shuttle up to the *Neverland* leaves from BWI in about two hours, so let's get you two moving. Tell your friend to hurry up in the bathroom; I need to make passport pictures for the two of you in the next fifteen minutes." Fixer went back up the stairs.

"Going somewhere?" Brian said.

"That's the plan," Creek said.

"You'll recall that starships, even the comfy cruise liners, are totally out of communication when they jump into null space," Brian said. "You can send messages *through* n-space, but you can't send or receive messages while you're *in it*. You're going to be out of reach most of the time."

"At this point I'm hard-pressed to see that as a bad thing," Creek said. "Look, it's a cruise liner. It makes stops every couple of days. As soon as we're back in real space, the data feeds are open again."

"Do you think when Ben told you to get lost he meant for you to actually leave the planet?" Brian asked. "If he needs you, even if you're in real space you'll be several light-years away. It won't be that easy to hitch a ride back."

"If Ben's trying to call us back, it means that he's figured out what the hell is going on, which means he's going to have the resources of the State Department to retrieve us," Creek said. "So I don't think bringing us back is going to be that much of a problem. But in the meantime I'm not going to sit around trying to lay low on this planet and waiting for people to shoot our heads off."

"What do I do while you're away?" Brian said.

"I need information," Creek said. "There are too many things I don't understand, and too many connections I'm not making, and the lack of information is going to get me and Robin killed. I need you to find out all you can about what's going on, who is connected to whom, and how it relates to the Nidu coronation. Most of all, find out everything you can about the Nidu coronation itself. People are trying to murder this poor woman because of it, for one thing, and for another thing, I want to make sure her taking part in it isn't going to leave her dead at the end."

"So, you want me to find out everything about everything," Brian said.

"Yeah," Creek said.

"That's a lot," Brian said.

"I've been asking the impossible of a lot of people recently," Creek said. "Don't see why you should be any different. Find out as much as you can, as fast as you can. Let me know as soon as you know it."

"Will do," Brian said. "As a bon voyage gift, allow me to do you a little favor. I've just put in a very credible tip that you and Miss Baker have been spotted at Dulles International, trying to get on a shuttle to Miami. I'm working on getting into the video camera system and popping up your images here and there. They'll eventually figure they've been hoaxed, but by that time your shuttle will be off and you'll be away. Oh, and look, the cops just busted down your door. I really should be going."

"Thank you, Brian," Creek said.

"De nada," Brian said. "Just make sure you bring me back something nice from your vacation."

"Let's hope that what I bring back is *me*," Creek said.

Creek found Robin Baker seated on the edge of Fixer's bathtub with the scissors in one hand and a hunk of hair in the other, morose. She looked at him as he came through the door.

"The last time I cut my hair was six years ago, you know," she said. "I mean, not counting trimming off split ends. Now I have to hack it all off. And I can't even *see* what I'm doing."

Creek took the scissors from Robin and sat down next to her on the tub. "Let me do it," he said.

"Can you cut hair?" Robin asked.

"Not really," Creek said. "But at least I can see what I'm cutting." The two of them were silent for a while as Creek cut her hair as quickly and straightly as he could.

"There," he said.

Robin stood up and looked in the mirror. "Well, it's different," she said.

Creek laughed. "I appreciate the diplomacy," he said. "But I know it's a really bad haircut. I don't expect you to keep it. I'm pretty sure the cruise ship will have a beauty shop."

"Cruise ship?" Robin asked. "As in boat or starship?"

"Starship," Creek said.

"How long are we going to be gone?" Robin asked.

"I didn't think to ask," Creek said. "Why?"

"I have pets," Robin said. "And I have animals in the shop. I don't want them to starve. I should call someone."

"There's an APB out for us," Creek said, as gently as possible. "I'm sure your parents and friends will know you'll be away. I'm sure your animals will be fine."

"If the police allow people in to feed them," Robin said.

"There is that," Creek agreed. "I'm sorry, Robin. There's nothing to do about it right now." He reached over and picked up the hair dye. "You want some help with this?"

"No," Robin said, and turned on the water in the sink. "I can do this. Not that I would use *this*, normally"—she pointed to the dye—"this stuff is crap."

"I don't think the guys Fixer usually has use this stuff care too much," Creek said.

"Probably not," Robin said, sighed, and took the hair dye from Creek. She bent over and dunked her head in the sink to wet her hair. "How do you know this guy, anyway?"

"I don't," Creek said. "I only met him a couple of days ago."

"How do you know you can trust him?" Robin said. She squeezed out some dye and started working it through her hair. "You're only entrusting him with our lives."

"I kept a secret for him, and I just paid him a lot of money," Creek said. "I think it should be enough. You missed a spot in the back."

Robin reached a hand back. "Be honest with me, now, Harry," she said, glancing at Creek in the mirror. "Do you do this a lot? Involve innocent women in bizarre plots of espionage and assassination? Or is this a first for you, too?"

"It's pretty much a first," Creek said. "Is that the right answer?"

"Well, you know," Robin said. "A girl does like to be treated special." She dunked her head, rinsed out the dye, and held out a hand. "Towel," she said. Creek grabbed one off the rack and handed it to her. Robin toweled off her head and then looked over to Creek. "How does it look?" she said.

"Black," Creek said.

Robin glanced at herself in the mirror. "Ugh. I tried black once in high school. Didn't work then. Doesn't work now."

"It's not so bad," Creek said. "It distracts from the haircut."

"Harry, what's in my DNA?" Robin asked. "You said there's something in my DNA that makes me different, and that everyone else with my DNA is dead. What is it?"

Creek stood up. "I don't know that this is the best time to get into it," he said. "We have to get to our shuttle if we're going to get on the cruise ship." He moved toward the door.

Robin walked over and interposed herself between Creek and the doorknob. "I think this is an excellent time to get into it," she said. "People are trying to kill me because of my DNA. I think I deserve the right to know why. I think you need to tell me right *now*, Harry."

Creek looked at her. "You remember what I was looking for when I came into your shop," he said.

"You were looking for a sheep," Robin said.

"Right," Creek said.

"Right, what?" Robin said.

"I was looking for a particular breed of genetically modified sheep. At least I thought I was. But it turns out I was looking for you."

Robin stared up at Creek for a few seconds before she slugged him in the jaw. "Goddamn it!" she said, retreating into the bathroom.

Creek massaged his jaw. "I really wish you would stop hitting me," he said.

"I am not a goddamn *sheep*, Harry!" Robin yelled.

"I didn't say you *were* a sheep, Robin," Creek said. "I said I thought I was looking for a sheep. But you have some of the same DNA as the kind of sheep I'm looking for."

"Do I *look* like I have sheep DNA?" Robin asked. "Do I look especially *woolly* to you?"

"No," Creek said. "All the sheep DNA you have is switched off. It's junk DNA. It doesn't do anything. But it doesn't mean it's not there, Robin. It's there. Just a little under twenty percent of your DNA is taken from the Android's Dream breed."

"You're lying," Robin said.

Creek sighed, and crouched down, resting his back on the bathroom door. "I saw pictures of your mother, Robin. Your biological mother. She was a genetically engineered hybrid between human and animal. She was one of several hybrids some sick bastard created to blackmail people. This man let your mother get pregnant, and he modified your embryo *in utero*—designed you to be a viable birth. She wasn't fully human, Robin. I'm sorry."

"That not what my parents told me," Robin said. "They said she was homeless and died giving birth to me."

"I don't think they knew the details," Creek said. "But she did die giving birth to you."

Robin grabbed the edge of the sink and collapsed onto the toilet, sobbing. Creek went over to her and held her.

There was a knock on the bathroom door. Fixer poked his head in. "Everything all right?" He said.

"Everything's fine," Creek said. "It's just been a busy day."

"We're not done being busy," Fixer said. "We need to get those pictures taken, so I can make your passports. Are you ready?"

"A couple more minutes," Creek said.

"No," Robin said, and grabbed onto the sink again, this time to pull herself up. "We're ready. We're ready now."

"Okay," Fixer said, and looked at her hair. "After we take these pictures, I've got a hat you can use." He left.

"There goes *his* tip," Robin said, and smiled weakly at Creek.

"You okay, then?" Creek asked.

"Oh, sure," Robin said. "Today, people have tried to kill me, the police are looking for me, and I've just discovered every Easter of my childhood, I ate one of my relatives with mint jelly. I'm just *fine*."

"Well, the Android's Dream is a very rare breed," Creek said.

"So?" Robin said.

"So they probably weren't *close* relatives," Creek said.

Robin stared at up at Creek for a few seconds. Then she laughed.

Where's Chuckie? Fixer thought as he fell backward down his basement stairs. *Where the hell is my dog?*

Fixer was worried about his dog because when he opened the door of the basement into the ground floor of his shop, there were two men and a very large *thing* waiting for him on the other side. This simply shouldn't have been; Chuckie was an Akita, and while the breed was silent enough near family or friends, they bark like mad when strangers invade their personal turf. Chuckie was so good at alerting Fixer to people in the store that for the last five years Fixer hadn't bothered with a door alarm; there was no need. Fixer had been in the basement, loudly destroying incriminating evidence and preparing for his departure, so he may not have heard Chuckie bark when people came into the store. But Chuckie wouldn't have stopped barking until Fixer heard him, came up the stairs, and told him to settle down. Ergo, something was wrong with Chuckie.

Fixer would have asked the men in the store about it at the top of the stairs, but the one closest to him punched him viciously in the face, staggering Fixer backward and down the stairs. All thoughts of his dog left Fixer's mind as his head connected with the concrete floor at the bottom of the stair with a retina-whitening *crack*; when Fixer recovered his eyesight, the man who had slugged him was standing over him, gun in his face. The man looked like hell.

"Where's my dog?" Fixer asked.

The man cracked a lopsided grin. "Well, isn't that *sweet*," he said. "Takk!"

A high-pitched voice responded from the top of the stairs, out of Fixer's sightline. "Yeah?"

"Give the man his dog," the man said.

About 30 seconds later Chuckie came tumbling down the

stairs, landing with a thump next to his master. His tongue, purplish-black, lolled from the side of his mouth. Fixer reached over to stroke Chuckie's fur; it was damp and matted.

"Oh, Chuckie," Fixer said.

"Yeah, yeah, yeah," said the man. "Very fucking sad. Now get up."

Fixer got up. "What do you want?"

"You had a couple of visitors today," the man said. "I want to know where they went."

"I have a lot of visitors," Fixer said. "I have a very successful repair shop."

The man took his gun off Fixer and fired at Chuckie, mashing brains and the top of the dog's skull into the stairwell.

"Jesus Christ!" Fixer said, and held his ears. "What did you do that for?"

"Because you're pissing me off," the man said. "And just because your dog's dead doesn't mean I can't make a mess with his fucking corpse. So let's stop being coy, if you don't mind, and we can all get through this with a minimum of drama. What do you say?"

Takk wedged his monstrous body into the doorframe at the top of the stairs. "Everything okay?" he asked.

"Everything is fine," the man said. "Come down here, Takk, and tell the geek to get his ass down here, too. He's got work to do."

Takk called back to the other guy and started walking down the stairs. Fixer gaped at him. The man holding a gun at him grinned. "He's a big one, isn't he," the man said. "He's a Nagch, and you wouldn't know it, but he's kind of runty for his species. But he's big enough for what I need him for."

"What do you need him for?" Fixed asked.

"For starters, to beat the crap out of people who piss me off by not answering my questions," the man said.

Takk came down off the stairs and stood next to Fixer, which to Fixer felt vaguely like standing next to a Kodiak bear.

"Hi," Takk said. His voice came, not from a mouth—the Nagch didn't appear to have one—but from a diaphragmlike patch where his neck joined his body.

"Hello," Fixer said.

Another human came down the stairs. "There's nothing in the computer upstairs," this other human said. "It's connected to a network but the only thing on it is invoices and business-related files. Are there computers down here?"

The man with the gun turned to Fixer. "Well?" he said. Fixer gestured in the direction of his computers and machines, which he'd already covered up. "Get to it, geek," the man said.

"He's not going to find anything," Fixer said. "I don't keep records of anything I do down here."

"Well, I appreciate the heads-up," the man said, "but he's going to give it the old college try anyway. Now. Back to our two friends. A man and a woman. I have it on good authority they were here."

"They were here," Fixer said.

"Excellent," the man said, and smiled. "See? Now we're getting somewhere. What did you do for them?"

"I gave them new identities and got them passage off the planet," Fixer said. "They apparently had some sort of run-in at the Arlington Mall that required a quick exit. You know anything about that?"

"Fucker broke my wrist," the man said, and Fixer was suddenly aware the man had indeed slugged him with his left hand and was holding the gun in the same hand.

"Looks like he broke your nose, too," Fixer said.

"Thanks for the diagnosis, asshole," the man said. "Where are they now?"

Before Fixer could answer the other human came up to the

gunman. "There's nothing here. The computer's wiped and the memory's been reformatted. Whatever was there is gone for good."

"I told you," Fixer said.

"Shut up," the gunman said. "It doesn't matter. I specialize in extracting information the old-fashioned way, anyway. Tell me what I want to know, or I kill you. So: Where are my two friends now?"

Fixer smiled. "You know what," Fixer said. "I *know* you. I work for the Malloy family. I see your type in here all the time. They come in for me to fix them up, or help them hide, or whatever. And after I'm done with them, every single one of them would kill me just because I saw them. The only thing that kept me alive was the fact that the Malloy family would have killed them for killing me. *You* don't work for the Malloy family. You're not going to leave me alive. And you killed my dog. So fuck you. I'm not telling you anything else. Shoot me and get it over with."

The gunman looked to the sky, arms imploring. "Jesus. What is it with people today? I can't catch a goddamn break. Everybody wants to do things the hard way. Fine. Have it your way. But you're wrong about one thing. I'm not going to shoot you."

"What are you going to do?" Fixer asked.

"Just you wait," the man said. "Takk. Show the man."

Takk reached out, grabbed Fixer, and spun him around. "I want to say I'm sorry about your dog. I didn't want to kill him. He just kind of rushed at me. I wanted you to know."

"Thanks," Fixer said.

"Don't mention it," Takk said, and split himself open, revealing the immense digestive cavity that allowed Nagch males to consume prey nearly as large as themselves. Fixer was not nearly as large as Takk; there was more than enough room for him. From inside Takk, elastic appendages with thousands of tiny hooks lashed out and adhered themselves to Fixer's body and

neck before he could think to move away. In one violent jerk
Fixer was yanked into the digestive cavity. Fixer had a quick image of a few mats of Charlie's fur stuck on the inside of Takk's
chest before Takk closed up around him and Fixer was enveloped
in darkness.

In less than a second, the digestive cavity constricted around
Fixer like a glove and began to squeeze. Fixer felt the air involuntarily crushed from his lungs; he struggled to move but was
sealed in tight. Across the flesh covered by the appendages that
had yanked him in and were still wrapped around him, Fixer felt
burning; the appendages had begun secreting hydrochloric acid
to begin the digestive process. Fixer was being eaten. In the (very)
small part of his brain that was still somewhat rational, Fixer had
to admit it was a pretty elegant way to get rid of a body.

There was a muffled, percussive sound—muffled because
Fixer heard it through Takk's body. Takk cracked open and Fixer
found himself dumped on the floor of his basement. Fixer gasped
air, vomited, and became dimly aware of the presence of several
new people in his basement, shouting and fighting with the three
that had already been there. He looked up in time to see one of
the new people jamming some sort of wand into the abdomen of
the computer geek, who was already one the floor. Then Fixer was
grabbed, hauled up the stairs and out of his shop, and thrown
into a waiting van. The van filled up with other people and then
peeled away.

"Mr. Young," someone said to him. "How are you feeling?"

"Gaaaaah," Fixer said.

"That sounds about right," the man said.

"Someone just tried to *eat* me," Fixer said.

"We got in the way of that, I think," the man said. "Once we
came through the door, it threw you up. You must have been too
heavy to let it fight. It's behind you now. You're safe."

Fixer peered up at him. "All right, I'll bite. Who are you?"

The man held out his hand. "Bishop Francis Hamn, of the Church of the Evolved Lamb. And you, my friend, are in the middle of a very interesting theological development."

"Passports," the cruise line attendant said. Creek and Robin handed them over, and then placed their hands on the DNA scanners molded into the ticket counter. The attendant opened the passports and then looked back to Creek.

"You're Mr. Hiroki Toshima," the attendant said.

"That's right," Creek said.

"Really," the attendant said.

"Adopted," Creek said. "Trust me. I get that all the time."

The attendant glanced down at the monitor; green lights on both passengers. The DNA matched the passports. He shrugged; Mr. Toshima it was, then. "Well, Mr. Toshima and Ms."—the attendant looked down at Robin's passport—"Washington, welcome to the *Neverland* cruise liner, and our special memorial cruise. In addition to our usual ports of call of Caledonia, Brjnn, Vwanchin, and Phoenix, we'll also be making special visits to Roosevelt Station, off Melbourne Colony, and Chagfun. There will be special observances and tours available at both stops."

Creek looked up at the attendant. "I'm sorry," he said. "Did you say Chagfun?"

"Yes sir. It's all here in the itinerary." The attendant handed them back their passports along with brochures and boarding passes. "The shuttle to the *Neverland* is just about to leave out of gate C23. I'll let them know you're coming, but if you could make a jog of it, I know our shuttle captain will be grateful. Enjoy your trip."

About 15 minutes into the ascent, Robin tapped Creek on the shoulder. "You've had your nose in that brochure since we got on the shuttle," she said. "What's in there that's so interesting?"

"Fixer said that this cruise was a special cruise for veterans," Creek said, and handed over the brochure. "But it's not just for any veterans. Look. One of our stops is Chagfun. It's the site of one of the biggest battles UNE forces ever fought in. The Battle of Pajmhi."

"Okay," Robin said. "So? Are we the wrong age for this cruise?"

"No," Creek said. "We're exactly the right age. Or at least I am. I was at Pajmhi, Robin. I was there. This is a cruise for vets of that battle."

Around the Common Confederation, the Nidu were not taken especially seriously as a military power. There are 617 officially recognized nations within the CC—a "nation" being understood as a sentient species' home world and its various approved and recognized colonies. (There were no CC nations with more than one sentient species. In a world with more than one sentient species, one species would wipe out the other or others long before it developed starfaring technology—no exceptions ever recorded.) Of these 617 officially recognized nations, Nidu currently ranked 488th in terms of power of military projection.

This ranking becomes even less impressive when one remembers that 60 nations of the Common Confederation field no military at all, for various reasons including economics, moral philosophy, and in the case of the Chawuna Arkan, a religious requirement to be rapturously passive in the face of extraplanetary invasion. Nidu's relatively woeful ability to wage war stemmed from an indifferent national economy of limited productiveness due to an entrenched but tremendously inefficient caste system, underperforming colonies, a lackluster history of technological innovation, and a military of questionable competence that had been defeated in seven of its last eight major engagements, and "won" the eighth on what most military historians considered a particularly shameful technicality.

Be that as it may, were the Nidu inclined to threaten the Earth and its colonies, it would stand an excellent chance of doing real damage. As lowly as the Nidu were in the rankings, Earth was ranked even lower: 530th, and only ranked that high because the Fru had recently lost their flagship *Yannwenn* when its navigational crew, used to working in native Fru measurements, inputted incorrect coordinates into the *Yannwenn*'s new navigational computers, which used CC standard measurements. It popped into n-space and was gone forever, or for the 3,400 years it would take to reach the position within the Horologium Supercluster where it would eventually resurface. Which was close enough to forever for everyone on the *Yannwenn*.

It wasn't that humans were terribly incompetent warmakers or that they lacked technical or economic drive. However, as a provision of joining the CC, the Earth government (which due to the realities of global power at the time meant the government of the United States speaking for the Earth with the rest of the planet screaming its collective head off in righteous and well-deserved outrage) agreed to field only a token extraterrestrial military force in exchange for protection by a coalition of CC nations, primary among them being the Nidu, during the Earth's probationary membership period. That period ended 40 years ago; since that time, Earth had largely relied on mutual-protection treaties with allies (again most prominently the Nidu) to cover its ass while building up its forces.

Given another 20 years, Earth would easily equal the Nidu in terms of military power, and 20 years after that would be well in the middle ranks of the CC's militaries. Here and now, however, it was playing a game of catch-up.

One thing the Earth lacked, for example, was a military ship that came close to the power of a Nidu *Glar*-class destroyer, the destroyer which was almost entirely responsible for whatever military power ranking the Nidu possessed. The *Glar*-class destroyer was a superior warship for its size and relatively modest cost—possibly because it was designed and built not by the Nidu but by the Hamgp, ranked 21st in military effectiveness and renowned across the CC for their ship design—and Nidu had spent a significant amount of its gross domestic product to get eight of them.

If a *Glar*-class destroyer showed up on Earth's doorstep and decided to make trouble, there was very little the Earth could do to stop it. Anything short of relativistic speed missiles or projectile weapons would be blasted away by the cruiser's defense network; beam weapons would be effective for only the short period of time it took the cruiser's offensive weapons to hone in on the source and destroy it.

As for the Earth's own fleet of ships, military analysts once ran a series of simulations to see how long Earth's naval flagship, The *UNES John Paul Jones,* would last in a slog-out with a *Glar*-class destroyer. The good news was that in one simulation, the *Jones* lasted sixteen whole minutes. The bad news was that simulation assumed a random and near complete power loss on the destroyer. Given the Hamgp love of multiple redundant systems in the ships they designed, this was not a likely scenario.

One *Glar* destroyer would be bad; two would be a nightmare. Two of the destroyers working in concert could flatten most of the populated areas between New York and Boston in a few hours, or in even less time if one of the destroyers was carrying a "planet cracker," Nidu's signature weapon of mass destruction:

a shaped-energy charge designed to crack the crust of a planet to release the pressurized, molten rock underneath. After all, there's no need to build in expensive, planet-maiming amounts of destructive power when a little physics and a reasonably accurate map of the crust of a tectonically active planet will do the work for you.

Less than an hour after the cruise ship *Neverland* broke Earth orbit, carrying Creek and Robin toward Caledonia colony, the two *Glar*-class destroyers the UNE Defense department had been tracking also broke orbit in near simultaneous departures: The *Lud-Cho-Getag* from Dreaden, Nidu's oldest colony planet, and the *Jubb-Gah-Getag*, the latest and most advanced *Glar*-class destroyer, from frozen Inspir, the Nidu colony closest to Earth. These two ships of the line accelerated out from their planets' gravity wells to a place where space-time was just flat enough for the n-drive to get its grip. Then with a quantum heave, both destroyers popped out of real space, into the largely theoretical soup of n-space, untrackable, their destinations unknowable.

They weren't the only *Glar*-class destroyers on the move.

Bob Pope glanced up over the report. "I'm reading that six *Glar*-class destroyers all jumped into n-space within an hour of each other," he said.

"Yes, sir," Phipps said.

"Including the two on our little watch list," Pope said.

"That's correct," Phipps said.

"And that we have no idea where any of these six are headed." Pope tossed the report lightly down to his desk. "So right now three quarters of Nidu's military strength is simultaneously headed for an unknown destination the morning after our operatives failed to get the Baker woman, and she and Creek disappeared. What are the chances of coincidence here, do you think?"

"What do you want to do?" Phipps asked.

Pope glanced up at his assistant and then gave out a short barking laugh. "Shit, Dave," he said. "I want to hide under my desk. I've got to go to President Webster and tell him how we're going to possibly defend ourselves from six *Glar*-class destroyers. And I have to let him know we knew at least two of them were gearing up to move days ago. If I have my job at the end of the day, I'll be a happy man."

"We wanted to rile up the waters," Phipps said.

"Not *six* destroyers worth," Pope said. "Christ. Think about it, Dave. Warming up two destroyers in the bullpen is a message. We can finesse a message. We can make it work for us. Six destroyers simultaneously jumping into n-space to points unknown is something more than a *message*." Pope tapped his desk in irritation, then pointed to the report. "You get that from Hunter?" he asked. Hunter was the head of the UNE CIA.

"We did," Phipps said.

"What do his boys say? Did the Nidu suddenly get into a shooting war with someone else?" Pope asked.

"No, sir," Phipps said. "One of their Nidu analysts said it might have something to do with the coronation—maybe the destroyers are going to be part of the ceremonies. But none of the other analysts concur. They don't know what the hell is going on."

"What do our boys say?" Pope asked.

"They don't know what the hell is going on, either," Phipps said.

Pope tapped at his desk again. "Where is Webster?" Pope asked.

"He's in South Dakota, getting a tour of that flood damage," Phipps said. "He's going to be back this evening. He's scheduled a briefing for six-thirty: him, Vice President Hayden, Hunter, you, and Heffer."

"Heffer," Pope said with a snort. "We're in a world of shit, Dave. But that's nothing compared to where Heffer's going to be."

———

"What is this?" Jim Heffer asked Narf-win-Getag, who had presented him with a folder in his office.

"This, Mr. Secretary, is a copy of the lawsuit the Government of the Nidu Nations and Colonies has filed against the Government of the United Nations of Earth," Narf-win-Getag said. "It has already been filed with the Common Confederation District Court here in Washington along with a request by the Government of Nidu to expedite the case and issue a quick summary judgment in the matter."

Heffer took the folder but did not open it, passing it instead to Javna, who began reading it. "I assume this is in regards to the matter of Ms. Baker," he said.

"It is regarding the entity that possesses the Android's Dream DNA, yes," Narf-win-Getag said, sitting in the chair in front of Heffer's desk. "I regret to say that your assistant has been less than entirely helpful in locating it and presenting it to us to take part in the coronation ceremony, now less than a week away. So unfortunately we feel it necessary to escalate the matter in the courts."

"With all due respect, Mr. Ambassador, I don't know what it is you hope to achieve," Heffer said. "Ms. Baker is a human being and as such has rights. While I can assure you that we are indeed doing all we can to bring her in and procure her help, we can't kidnap her and force her to take part in the coronation. And unless she's committed a crime on Nidu soil, which she hasn't, I don't see what claim Nidu has to attempt to extradite her. Common Confederation law is crystal clear on this."

"And if it were human, you'd be correct, Secretary Heffer," Narf-win-Getag said. "However, it is not, and therefore, you are not."

"I don't follow you," Heffer said.

"The entity is, in fact, a hybrid," Narf-win-Getag said. "It possesses human DNA, yes, but it also possesses a substantial amount of DNA from the Android's Dream sheep—nearly twenty percent of its DNA, if I recall correctly."

"And what of it?" Heffer said.

"The Android's Dream DNA is the exclusive property of the auf-Getag clan, which is by extension the government of Nidu. It was provided to Nidu by the Earth government as part of an overall treaty between our two nations. The treaty specifically invests all property and use rights in the Nidu government, with any unauthorized use of the DNA, commercial or otherwise, subject to penalties and confiscation. The one loophole here applies to the inadvertent crossbreeding of the breed and exempts animals whose genetic makeup is one-eighth Android's Dream breed or less. But in this case, the breeding is clearly *not* unintentional, and the entity has more than the exemptible percentage of DNA. This treaty was ratified by the Congress of the Common Confederation and therefore the agreement supercedes national laws of both Nidu and Earth. As a point of law—well-established law, I might add, of the highest legal entity both our governments acknowledge—the entity is our property. It is ours."

"*It* is a she, and *she* is a citizen of the United Nations of Earth," Heffer said.

"But before *it* was awarded the rights and privileges of your citizenship, its genetic material was stolen from its rightful owner, being the Nidu government," Narf-win-Getag said. "The treaty is *very* clear on the issue of ownership, Mr. Secretary, and rather unfortunately it does *not* make specific exemption for the possibility of the genetic material being commingled with the genetic material of a potentially sentient species. It is the position of my government that our property rights to the entity legally supercede your government's potential claim regarding the citizenship of the entity. In any event, we have simultaneously filed suit asking the court to provisionally rescind the citizenship of the entity pending determination of its status as Nidu property, and of course to rescind it permanently if the court agrees it is our property."

"This is ridiculous," Heffer said. "No court is going to rule that a sentient being is property. And whether you choose to call her 'it,' or not, Mr. Ambassador, there's no doubt she *is* a sentient being."

"No doubt at all, Mr. Secretary," Narf-win-Getag said. "However, you are once again—and I beg your pardon—incorrect in your assumptions. Humans are relatively new to the Common Confederation, which existed before your species was scratching pictures of bison into cave walls. There have been Common Confederation courts of law for just as long. And while it may be unfamiliar to you, there is indeed case law supporting our claim. I refer you to *Agnach Agnach-u v. Ar-Thaneg Corporation,* adjucated in the CC annulis 4-3325. I believe that would have been right around the time your Hammurabi was handing down his code."

"Ben?" Heffer looked over to Javna.

"I remember it from law school," Javna said. "It's a canonical intellectual property case. If I remember correctly, Agnach-u was a programmer of some sort, and developed a program it claimed was sentient. Ar-Thaneg was its employer and claimed the program as work product, but Agnach-u claimed that since it was sentient, Ar-Thaneg couldn't own it. The courts ruled against Agnach-u. But I don't know that it's on point. The property in question was software, not genetic material, and there was never agreement as to whether the program was sentient or not. It passed some tests but failed others. As a precedent, it's a reach. It's a long reach."

"Not so long a reach as your assistant would have you assume, Mr. Secretary," Narf-win-Getag said. "The ruling is neutral on the issue of the nature of the property. It doesn't matter what the property is, merely that it *is* property. The ruling ultimately was awarded to Ar-Thaneg on the grounds that as the property on which the program was created was owned by Ar-Thaneg, Agnach-u had no standing to bring the suit in the first place."

"In other words, it was awarded to Ar-Thaneg on a technicality," Javna said.

"Indeed," Narf-win-Getag said. "But for the Nidu, a very useful technicality, as it's clear the Android's Dream DNA belongs to us."

"There's the matter of the human DNA, which does not belong to you," Heffer said.

"As I've mentioned before, the treaty between Nidu and Earth doesn't address how the DNA is used, merely the circumstances in which the DNA belongs, unambiguously, to my government. I assure you, Mr. Secretary, that if you can find a way to extract the human parts of the entity and let us keep the Android's Dream part, then you are welcome to the human portions."

" 'Take thou thy pound of flesh, but in the cutting it, if thou dost shed one drop of Christian blood, thy lands and goods are confiscate,' " Heffer said.

"Pardon, Mr. Secretary?" Narf-win-Getag said.

"*The Merchant of Venice,*" Heffer said. "A play by Shakespeare. The character Shylock strikes a bargain to take a pound of flesh from another man, but if he spills the man's blood by doing so, he loses everything. It's the story of another crisis brought on by a contractual dispute, Mr. Ambassador."

"How droll," Narf-win-Getag said. "I must see it sometime. But I must impress on you, Mr. Secretary, that a crisis is indeed what this is. The agreement concerning the Android's Dream sheep is nestled within a larger and more comprehensive treaty between our two peoples, a treaty which is the primary document concerning relations between our nations—the document at the heart of our peoples' friendship. If the courts rule for Nidu, and you cannot or will not produce the entity, then the UNE will be in violation of the treaty. The government of Nidu will then have the right to declare all agreements associated with the treaty null and void, and sue for renegotiation. Nidu is by far the Earth's largest trading partner and military ally, Mr. Secretary. I don't have to tell you what sort of impact the renegotiation of our friendship will have on Earth's economy and its standing and security within the Common Confederation. And I hate to think what it will do to your government."

"Mr. Ambassador," Heffer said. "Are you aware that this morning six of Nidu's destroyers went into n-space near simultaneously?"

"Is that so?" Narf-win-Getag said, mildly.

"That's an unusual occurrence. And provocatively timed, considering this suit here," Heffer said. "If you don't mind me saying so, Mr. Ambassador, destroying a decades-old friendship between our nations on account of one person seems to be an excessive reaction."

"I can't tell you how pleased I am to hear you say that, Mr. Secretary," Narf-win-Getag said, and rose from his seat. "Hopefully such a sentiment on your part means that you will be motivated to reacquire our lost sheep, and we can all move forward without further distress to our long and intimate friendship. In the meantime, however, and purely as a precaution, our lawsuits are moving forward. Given the extreme time sensitivity of the suit, I would imagine that we'll get the hearing expedited—in fact, I wouldn't be *entirely* surprised if there's a preliminary hearing by this time tomorrow morning. And so, I leave you to prepare. Mr. Secretary, Mr. Javna. Good day."

"*The Merchant of Venice?*" Javna asked, after Narf-win-Getag had left.

"I did drama in college," Heffer said. "So sue me. And tell me you know where this woman is."

"I know she was with Harry at the Arlington Mall last night," Javna said.

"Oh, yes, the Arlington Mall," Heffer said. "Which reminds me to let you know how delightful it is to have Arlington County Police and the US and UNE FBI *and* the DC Port Authority Security Agency banging down our door asking why a State Department employee was involved in a public shootout. Not mention every media outlet from Boston to Miami."

"I'm sure the other guys started it," Javna said.

"This isn't funny, Ben," Heffer said. "And it's getting less funny by the minute. You said that this Creek fellow would handle everything under the radar. Shooting up the Arlington Mall and killing people is *not* under the radar."

"All the eyewitness reports say that Harry wasn't the one who started shooting," Javna said. "Whatever happened, he was defending Robin Baker. He was working under the radar. Whoever is working against us were the ones to made this happen."

"You don't have any idea where he is now. Where *they* are now," Heffer said.

"No," Javna said. "I left him a message to get low last night and told him to wait until I sent for him."

"Well, try locating him now, if you don't mind," Heffer said.

Javna pulled out his communicator and tried to connect. "It's no good. The system says his communicator is off the system, and I'm getting no response from his home connection. I would imagine all his equipment has been impounded by the police."

"No messages?" Heffer asked.

"I'll check," Javna said.

Heffer's executive assistant entered the room with a blue slip of paper and handed it to Heffer.

"We've got a court date," Heffer said. "Bright and early tomorrow morning at eight forty-five. I want you to handle this, Ben. Time to exercise that law degree of yours. Dig up what you can on this precedent and then bury that lizard with it. 'Hammurabi,' my ass."

"Odd," Javna said, still looking at his communicator.

"What?" Heffer said.

"I just got a text message from Dave Phipps over at Defense," Javna said. "He wants to have lunch and discuss 'our mutual friend.'"

"You don't have mutual friends?" Heffer said.

"I try not to have mutual friends with him," Javna said.

"You should have lunch with him," Heffer said.

"Yeah, I should," Javna said. "And double up on the antacid."

"Here you go," Dave Phipps said, handing Javna his hot dog.

"Thanks," Javna said, taking it. "You know, Dave, the Defense Department pays hundreds of dollars for hammers and toilet seats. It seems like it should be able to spring for something more than a hot dog from a stand on the Mall."

"How can we?" Phipps said. "All our money is in seats and hammers. Anyway, the Pentagon's not paying for your lunch today, I am."

"Well, in that case, it's a meal fit for a king," Javna said.

"Damn right," Phipps said, taking his hot dog from the vendor and handing him his cash. "That's a Kingston's Bison Boar hot dog you're eating there, Javna. No ground-up pork sphincters for you. And all the condiments you can stand. I'll even spring for a soda."

"Well, shit, Dave," Javna said. "Keep this up and people will say we're in love."

"Not likely," Phipps said, taking his change and grabbing two Cokes. "Come on, let's sit." The two men angled toward a bench and ate silently for a minute, watching joggers run past on the Mall.

"Good dog," Phipps said, after a minute.

"No sphincters," Javna agreed.

"I've got a funny story about Bison Boar," Phipps said. "I got it from Kingston's Pentagon supplier. He said that when Bison Boar came on the market, there was a rabbinical debate about whether Jews could eat it."

"Well, it's pork," Javna said. "At least it's partly pork. Isn't it?"

"That was the question. The Torah forbids eating meat from animals with cloven hooves, but someone pointed out that technically speaking, Bison Boar didn't come from an animal with hooves, and in fact it didn't really come from an animal at all. It came from genetically spliced and sequenced DNA that was tweaked to produce muscle tissue in a vat. One of the animals the DNA came from had split hooves, but the other one didn't, and since there never was an actual Bison Boar animal, no one knew whether theoretically the animal would have split hooves or not."

"They could look at the corporate mascot," Javna said.

"They did, apparently," Phipps said. "It wasn't helpful. It wears boots."

"Fascinating," Javna said. "What did they decide?"

"They didn't," Phipps said. "Eventually one of the rabbis pointed out that the Torah was silent on the subject of DNA splicing, so what they were doing was just speculation. Kind of the Jewish equivalent of arguing whether how many angels could dance on the head of a pin. So the question wasn't whether the meat was from a cloven-hooved animal or not, but why they were arguing about it in the first place."

"Smart man," Javna said.

"Well," Phipps said. "He *was* a rabbi."

"Does this story have application to our situation," Javna said, "or are we just making lunchtime chit-chat?"

"I have an idea here, and I want you to tell me what you think of it," Phipps said. "Let's pretend we're on the same side and talk like we might want to keep our jobs longer than the end of the week. What do you say?"

"I think that's a tremendous idea," Javna said. "You first."

"Over the last couple of days you might have noticed you had some difficulty accomplishing a particular task you've been working on," Phipps said.

"Now that you mention it, yes," Javna said.

"I imagine that you'll find from here on out your difficulty will be alleviated," Phipps said. "And before you ask, let's just say that while we over at Defense believed it was in our strategic interest to have your department fail in its task, the facts on the ground have changed substantially in the last several hours."

"You mean six Nidu destroyers up and vanishing into n-space all at the same time has got your balls in a clench, too," Javna said.

"I wouldn't have put it that way, but yes," Phipps said. "Defense and State have different ideas on the desirability of staying close to our good friends the Nidu, but at this point we'd rather stay close than go toe-to-toe."

"There is the little problem that we don't know where the object of our task, as you delicately put it, is at this particular moment."

"I'll get that information for you," Phipps said. "But it's going to have to wait until after Webster's briefing tonight. There are people I need to talk to first. Projects I have to close down."

"The sooner I can get it, the happier I am," Javna said. "But I don't imagine this sudden inter-departmental cooperation comes at no cost."

"No cost," Phipps said. "Just a favor. If anyone asks, this little squabble between our departments never happened."

"Who do you imagine asking?" Javna said.

"You never know," Phipps said, between a mouthful of hot dog. "The press. A Senate committee. An independent investigator. Whoever."

"Just to be clear," Javna said. "And to avoid any comfortable euphemisms here on our nice little park bench, Defense spent the last week trying to fuck up our relationship with our closest ally—which worked, incidentally, and I have court date tomorrow morning to prove it—and to put the cherry on top, you attempted to kill a member of the State Department, who is, incidentally, a very good friend of mine. And I suspect that you would have killed an innocent woman as well if you could have gotten away with it. And you want me to just forget about it."

Phipps nodded and slugged back some of his Coke. "Yeah. That's pretty much our position, Ben. Just forget about it."

"It's kind of a hard thing to forget, Dave," Javna said. "Especially with most of the Nidu battle fleet probably bearing down on us. And even if *we* decide to forgive and forget, someone's going to have to take the blame."

"I've *got* someone to blame," Phipps said. "And as an added bonus he is actually guilty."

"Nice to see the Defense Department subcontracts for attempted murder, too," Javna said.

"Look," Phipps said. "When all this is over, you and I can go in a back alley with a couple of beers and a couple of lead pipes and have it out, all right? But right now we're having a 'hang together or hang separately' moment. So if it's all the same, I'd like to stay focused on the task at hand. I'll help you find your pal and his girlfriend. In return, we all make like we're friends. Under oath, if necessary. That's how this is going to work, if it's going to work at all."

"Fine," Javna said. "But I need that information tonight. *Tonight*, Dave. I've got to go into court tomorrow and try to keep every treaty between Nidu and Earth for the last several decades from becoming null and void. Knowing where our lost sheep is will go a very long way in keeping that from happening."

"Deal," Phipps said, and took a final bite of his hot dog. "What's the suit about, if you don't mind me asking?"

"The Nidu claim that Robin Baker is their property because she's got their sheep DNA in her genetic makeup. I have to prove she's more human than property," Javna said. "If I win, she gets to stay a citizen of Earth. If I lose, we're all in some pretty deep shit."

"Human being or Nidu sheep," Phipps said, and chucked his napkin into a trash can. "Now, *there's* a case for the rabbis."

Javna, who had been about to stuff the last bit of his hot dog in his mouth, stopped. He looked at his dog for a second. "Huh," he said, and then finished off his dog.

"Huh, what?" Phipps said.

"Phipps, I want you to know I think you're one of the biggest assholes it's been my pleasure to meet in my entire government career," Javna said.

"This is what I get for buying you lunch," Phipps said, dryly. "Thanks."

"Don't mention it," Javna said. "But asshole that you may be, you've just given me an idea for my court date tomorrow. If it works, when you and I go into that back alley, I'll let you have the first swing."

"Well, then," Phipps said. "Here's hoping that it works."

"Ahhhhh," Rod Acuna said, flexing his previously broken wrist. "That's *much* better. How does it look, geek?" Acuna thrust his arm out at Archie; Archie flinched back involuntarily.

"It looks good," Archie said, and tried to turn back to his computer, which had been acting a bit buggy.

"It should," Acuna said, thwarting Archie's maneuver. "Quick-Heal sessions clear all of it up. Broken bones, torn tendons, even bruises and scrapes. It costs a shitload. But on the other hand, now I don't look like you."

Archie involuntarily touched the side of his face, where an ugly purple welt had formed, a souvenir from getting whacked in the face by the second group of invaders who had snuck into

Fixer's shop the night before. Archie knew who gave it to him: Sam. He knew it was Sam because once he had fallen to the ground, stunned by the hit, Sam had come in close, whipped out an electric prod and whispered "sorry, love," in his ear before jabbing the prod into his abdomen and shocking him into unconsciousness. He'd only come to because Acuna kicked him the ribs to get him awake and Takk had hauled his body up the stairs.

Takk now lay on the floor of the apartment's bedroom, suffering from the digestive trauma of thowing up Fixer. The less Archie thought about that episode the better. Acuna had very nearly thrown Archie and Takk out of the van and sped off to get his wounds tended; his body had been severely abused over the last couple of days. Archie didn't know where Acuna went to get fixed up but he doubted it was a regular hospital; he imagined it was some underworld freelancer, like that Fixer character, but with a medical degree. Archie let his mind wander to speculate about an entire economy of underworld specialists and reflected that somehow, through no real fault of his own, he could probably be defined as one of them now.

"The pisser about QuickHeal sessions is they make you itch like a son of a bitch," Acuna said. "I'm gonna go get some aspirin. Come with me, geek. I want to talk to you about something." Acuna wheeled around and went out of the door of the apartment; Archie wearily got up and followed.

He caught up to Acuna at the vending machine in the hall. "Don't take this the wrong way," Acuna said, as he fed his card into the machine, "but you really look like hell. I mean, whoever these bastards were did a number on me and even scored a few points off of Takk, which takes some doing. But you really got cracked one." He pressed the button to get his aspirin.

"Thanks," Archie said, glumly.

"You want some aspirin of your own?" Acuna asked. "I'll even get them for you. My treat."

"I'm fine," Archie said.

"Hey, look," Acuna said. "They've restocked your favorite: the white chocolate M&Ms. I'm going to get you some." He jabbed his finger at the "B4" button.

Archie meant to say *really, thanks, but no.* He got as far as the first phoneme before the pain scraped across his optic nerve, sending Archie to the ground, writhing. Acuna watched him fall.

"Well, isn't that *interesting,*" Acuna said. "Maybe I should get two packages, what do you say?" He jabbed the "B4" button a second time. Archie gasped, lifted his head up, and dropped it back down spasmodically to the concrete, sending a second, lesser and almost comforting flash of pain across his brain pan.

"Who do you work for, Archie?" Acuna said, and dimly Archie realized it was only the second time Acuna had used his proper name.

"I work for the Defense Department," Archie gasped.

"Wrong answer," Acuna said, and jabbed "B4" again. Archie twitched in agony. "I know all of Defense's little spy tricks. This isn't one of them. This is a new one on me. That impresses me, incidentally. I thought I knew all the ways to get a bug into a room and get information out of it. But this really takes the cake. Very nice. Well, except for this part." Acuna hit the button again. Archie vomited and curled up into a fetal position.

"Let me make this real simple for you, geek," Acuna said. "I don't like it when people spy on me. I especially don't like it when people spy on me and as a result one of my missions gets fucked up beyond all recognition. It makes me look bad. I don't like looking bad." He jabbed at the vending machine button. This time Archie, marinating in his puke, merely convulsed. "So you're going to tell me who you work for, *now,* or I'm going to take this fucking credit card right up to its limit getting it out of you."

Archie whimpered something.

"Excuse me?" Acuna said.

"I said, 'fuck you,'" Archie said, voice trembling.

Acuna smiled and looked toward the vending machine. "You know, each of these M&M bags costs eighty-five cents," he said. "And my credit limit on this card is five thousand dollars. Let's see how many bags that gets us."

Acuna spent $45.05 before Archie talked.

Brian snuck into Archie's computer by doing what Archie had wanted him to do: Letting his system get drilled. It was an inside job: Brian created the driller and had it drill into the system by way of a backdoor Brian opened up, into which he'd deposited the data inside a century's worth of Washington DC yellow pages—encrypted, of course, for extra fun, and formatted to look like personal information files. Archie's driller went in, scooped up the data, and hailed Archie's computer to begin transmitting. As it did so, Brian jammed in instructions that left the port wide open but gave Archie's computer the impression it was closed and secure. Brian was having fun being the smartest computer ever.

Brian had been riffling through Archie's files when Archie's onboard computer cam caught Archie coming through the door, followed by a huge-ass alien that Brian recognized (some part of him did, anyway) as a Nagch. Both them looked like they had just had the shit kicked out of them. If Brian had to guess, he would have supposed Archie and the alien had just gotten back from trying to collect Harry and Robin; it didn't appear as if they had been particularly successful. Archie parked himself in front of his computer and picked along desultorily for a few minutes before putting his head on the desk and falling asleep. Brian went back to his file riffling. When Archie woke up the next morning he seemed to suspect someone had been peeking through his files;

he ran a diagnostic and started cruising through his files. Brian played cat-and-mouse with Archie for a few hours, partly to gauge Archie's skills and partly for the amusement factor.

Rod Acuna showed up in the afternoon, full of good cheer, and demanded Archie come with him to get something from the vending machines. Some 20 minutes later the apartment door burst open and Acuna dragged Archie through it, tossed him roughly onto the carpet, and yelled a name that sounded like "Tack." The Nagch suddenly filled the bedroom doorway.

"What, boss?" it asked.

"We're on the move," Acuna said, and pointed at Archie, splayed, semi-conscious, on the floor. "You get the geek watch. If this shitball so much as breathes funny, you eat him."

"Why? What did he do?" the Nagch asked.

"He's been feeding information about what we've been doing to his fucking pals," Acuna said.

"The Defense Department?" The Nagch asked.

"No, you mountainous dipshit," Acuna said. "Some wackjob cult he belongs to. The Church of the Evolved Lamb. They're the assholes that hit us last night."

"I could eat him now," the Nagch offered.

"No," Acuna said, and looked down at Archie. "I need to talk to Schroeder first. He might have questions he wants to ask this fucker. But in the meantime, you do not let him out of your sight. Do you understand me? If he takes a dump, he does it with you in the bathroom. Do you understand me?"

"Yes," the Nagch said. "What do I do if he tries to run?"

"Good question," Acuna said. He pulled a folding knife from his pocket, flicked it open, bent down to grab Archie's right leg, and severed his Achilles tendon. Archie let out a whimpering scream and lapsed out of consciousness. "That takes care of that. And especially don't let him near that computer of his. In fact—" Acuna began to stride over to Archie's computer.

Uh-oh, Brian thought. Acuna reached out to the computer. The view from the onboard camera wheeled wildly and then went black.

Jean Schroeder had told Dave Phipps to let himself in when he came by, and Phipps did, coming in through the garage door and walking up the spiral staircase the led into what used to be Anton Schroeder's study and was now the study of his son. Phipps, who had been in the study numerous times, had always found the place creepy, probably because Anton had decorated its walls with ancient spears and swords of Nidu design, and Jean had seen fit to keep them up, and indeed to add to the collection. Both of them apparently derived amusement from being surrounded by the weapons of the enemy.

Phipps found Schroeder at his desk, feet up, reading something from an unbound sheaf of papers. He glanced over at Phipps as he came in. "You're looking twitchy," he said, and went back to his reading.

"Jean, it's over," Phipps said. "I need to know where the woman is. We need to bring her back in."

"Why?" Schroeder said, not looking up from his papers.

"What?" Phipps said.

"Why do we need to bring her back in?" Schroeder said. "You and your boss wanted a little excitement to boost your budgets. I'd say you're getting it. It seems like things are going just swimmingly."

"You're not listening to me," Phipps said. "It's *over.* The Nidu are responding far more strongly to this missing woman than we anticipated. They've got six destroyers in n-space right now and we suspect they're on their way here. It's stopped being something we can play with. And it's stopped being something I can let you play your own game with, Jean."

"Why, Dave. 'My own game,'" Schroeder said. "Strong words from a man who's been taking bribes from me since the first day of the Webster administration. Do you know how much money I've got in you, Dave?"

"It's past that, Jean," Phipps said.

"$438,000," Schroeder said, loudly, for effect. "To date. That's almost enough for that Nag's Head beach house you've had your eye on. Which reminds me, I have another installment for you."

"Keep it," Phipps said.

Schroeder finally looked over from his paper. "*Keep* it?" he asked. "Oh, dear. Things really *must* be out of control. This is America, Dave. People don't just turn down money in America. It's unpatriotic. You could get *deported* for that."

"Jean—" Phipps began, and then heard a toilet flush from the study's small adjacent bathroom. "There's someone else here?" Phipps asked.

"I'm popular," Schroeder said. "You can't expect me to cancel my previous social engagements just because you have a sudden urge to hang me out to dry."

"I didn't say I was hanging you out to dry," Phipps said.

"Well, of course you didn't," Schroeder said. "No one ever does. But suddenly turning down my cash after taking in half a million of it—when you're so close to that beach house, no less—well. My daddy taught me how to read the signs, Dave. Defense has fucked up and you're looking for someone to blame. And I'm guessing sometime in the last few hours you've personally decided that burying me will save your own ass. Well, Dave, to use your own words, it's past that. Way past."

The bathroom door opened and Narf-win-Getag came out. "I'm leaving the fan on," he said to Schroeder.

"I appreciate that," Schroeder said.

"What the fuck is going on here?" Phipps said.

"By which you mean to say, 'Why, Jean. What are you doing letting the Nidu Ambassador to Earth use your bathroom when he is your avowed enemy?' I have an answer for that. So why don't you sit down for a minute, and let Narf fix you a drink."

"Fix *me* a drink," Phipps said. Phipps was aware that as an underling, he was well nigh an untouchable class of being by Nidu standards.

"Why not," Schroeder said. "We're all friends here. Isn't that right, Narf."

"It is too true," Narf-win-Getag replied.

"And Narf makes a mean martini," Schroeder said. "So sit the hell down, Dave, and let me explain some things to you."

Phipps took a seat in one of the chairs opposite Schroeder. Narf-win-Getag went to the bar, behind where Phipps sat, and, as promised, began fixing Phipps a drink.

"Now, then," Schroeder said. "I'll begin with an observation." He waved at the various Nidu weapons on the wall. "Do you know what all these weapons have in common?"

"They're Nidu weapons," Phipps said.

"Partial credit," Schroeder said. "They're weapons designed, built, and used by ancient members of the win-Getag clan, a scion of which is currently fixing you a martini. For the last several decades, the win-Getag clan has been of minimal rank within the Nidu social hierarchy—no offense, Narf."

"None taken," Narf-win-Getag said. He walked over to Phipps and handed him the drink. Phipps took it and drank.

"Good, huh?" Schroeder said.

"Pretty good," Phipps admitted.

"I use just enough vermouth to coat the glass," Narf-win-Getag explained. "No more." He sat down in the chair next to Phipps.

"Anyway, the win-Getags' social fortunes have been down for the last few decades," Schroeder said. "Which is why the clan occupies diplomatic posts on planets that are of low importance. Such as, alas for us, Earth. But I don't suppose you know the reason for the win-Getags' relative low status."

"Not a clue," Phipps said.

"It is because we contested for the crown," Narf-win-Getag said.

"Exactly right," Schroeder said. "At the time, the Nidu ruler left no heir to the throne. Impotent, although whether naturally or by sabotage is still a matter for discussion. Nidu traditions require a direct-line descendant and a faithful coronation process in order to achieve the throne. If you don't have one or the other, your clan can't succeed and the contest for the throne is opened up to competing clans. I'm right so far," Schroeder said, checking with Narf-win-Getag.

"So far," agreed Narf-win-Getag.

"When the throne is open, naturally certain clans will be in a stronger position than others to contest for it," Schroeder said. "The last time around, two clans were the primary contenders: The auf-Getag clan, which currently sits on the throne, and the win-Getag clan, which does not. Each clan had its supporters both in other clans and among the CC, and there was the usual political intrigue and deal making and, long story short, for various reasons—"

"Assassination and sabotage," Narf-win-Getag growled.

"—including assassination and sabotage," Schroeder granted, "the auf-Getag clan emerged victorious in the race for the crown. As the defeated clan, the win-Getag clan experienced a massive loss of status and station, which is why Narf here is now Ambassador to Earth and not to the CC itself.

"Now, here's a funny wrinkle. In a situation where there's no heir to the throne and a clan is selected to ascend, that clan creates a coronation process, which must be performed *exactly* in order for subsequent heirs to take the throne. If the heir doesn't perform the coronation process *exactly*, the throne is open again, and then one of two things happens. First comes an interval period of about five days, in which the first clan to successfully replicate the coronation process can claim the throne. If no clan manages that, then it's back to a free-for-all with all the clans fighting it out. You with me so far?"

"I'm following you," Phipps said. "But I don't see what this has to do with anything."

"I'm getting there," Schroeder said. "And trust me, this is the short form of the story."

"Fine," Phipps said.

"Now," Schroeder said. "Because of the Nidu traditions, the coronation ceremony usually involves something specific to the clan in power, which other clans can't get. Traditionally, this involves objects or secret texts, but when the auf-Getag clan came to power it decided to do something different."

A light clicked on. "The sheep," Phipps said.

"The sheep," Schroeder agreed. "A gift of the Earth government as a way to curry favor with the ascendant auf-Getag clan, along with a computer network designed for Nidu's new ruler, to streamline his grip on power. The computer network is just a network, but the ownership of the sheep belongs to the auf-Getag clan and its royal family exclusively. No member of any other clan can possess the sheep on pain of death and disenfranchisement. What's more, the coronation calls for a *live* sheep, since the coronation ceremony requires both the DNA of the sheep and a measurement of the brain activity. This helps to make sure no clan shows up with a jug of sheep blood for a coronation ceremony."

"But if someone kills off the sheep, then the coronation ceremony can't go off," Phipps said. "And the Nidu throne is thrown open."

"You got it," Schroeder said.

Phipps looked over at win-Getag. "You're making a play for the throne."

"I am," Narf-win-Getag said.

"Then all this concern about finding the sheep was all just a ploy," Phipps said.

"Not a ploy," Narf-win-Getag said. "I'm the ambassador to my government. My government wants to find the sheep. I simply knew the search wouldn't be fruitful."

"Except it was," Phipps countered. "They found the girl."

"Ah, yes, the girl," Narf-win-Getag said. "And suddenly things became *much* more interesting. I've been planning—my clan has been planning, I should say—to ascend the throne for decades, biding our time, gathering allies for when the *Fehen* died and the throne could be brought into play. We knew other clans were doing the same, of course. It was not clear whether we'd be able to ascend, particularly given our unfairly-wrought low status. But suddenly here is a sheep who is also a human—and who is therefore not the property of the auf-Getag family. Someone who offers a quick, clean way to the throne."

"But you're suing to make her the property of Nidu," Phipps said. "Ben Javna's going to court tomorrow to fight the case."

"The property of the Nidu government, *not* of the auf-Getag clan," Narf-win-Getag said. "Clans have no standing in Common Confederation courts. The auf-Getag clan is hoping that the woman is found before the ceremony needs to be performed, while the government and the auf-Getag clan are one and the same. But if she is not, then any clan could use her to complete the coronation ceremony. *If* they had her."

"And you have her," Phipps said.

"No," Schroeder said. "This Creek fellow keeps getting her away from us. We know they've gone off planet and we know they left from the DC area. From there it's a process of elimination. There were only so many ships that left last night."

"And what are you going to do with when you find her?" Phipps said.

"Take her," Narf-win-Getag said. "Hide her. Then use her. And if I can't do that, then kill her. Would you like another drink?"

"No thank you," Phipps said.

"Jean?" Narf-win-Getag said.

"Nothing for me," Schroeder said. "But please, Narf, help yourself." Narf-win-Getag nodded and got up; Schroeder turned his attention back to Phipps. "Now you see why we can't let you have her, Dave," he said. "We have our own plans for her."

"No matter what those plans do to the Earth," Phipps said.

"The Earth is going to be fine," Schroeder said. "Its government less so, but that's no great loss. You should know that the government of the Earth is damned no matter what. If the auf-Getag keep the throne, they're going to believe the government of the Earth actively worked to bring their downfall. That's bad news. It'll probably mean a war. If the win-Getag take the throne, they're going to remember that the government of the Earth supported their enemies in their bid for the throne once upon a time. That's also bad news. It will also probably mean a war. The difference here is that if the win-Getag are on the throne, they will be the ones to name an administrator for Earth and her colonies after the hostilities have ceased."

"You," Phipps said.

"Me," Schroeder said. "And what a political masterstroke it will be for the new Nidu government to name as Earth's administrator someone with such a long and colorful history of enmity with the Nidu. It'll reassure the citizens of Earth that their government will stand up for their interests. It'll reassure the CC that the Nidu are fair and just conquerors. Everybody gets something."

"Except that in being conquered, the Earth would lose her independent status, her right to her colonies, and her right to be represented in the Common Confederation," Phipps said.

"Details, details," Schroeder said. "Yes. The Earth will lose her representation and the administration of her colonies. But it's only a *temporary* loss. Narf has assured me that he has no interest in our real estate or in telling us what to do. He can hardly stand humans as it is."

"Present company excepted, of course," Narf-win-Getag said, from the bar.

"So we'll be back to independent status within a decade," Schroeder said. "Mind you, it could go faster if I had help in my administration. Such as yours."

Phipps blinked. "Are you trying to bribe me?" he said.

"No, Dave," Schroeder sighed. "I've already *been* bribing you. Now I'm trying to buy you outright. A lot of the really good positions have already been filled by my staff over at the American Institute for Colonization, I'm afraid. But I could see my way to letting you run *some* portion of the globe. I hear New Zealand is nice."

"Listen to you," Phipps said. "You've traded away your birthright for a mess of porridge. You're running a group that's meant to help the Earth and her colonies prosper, not become subjugated by an alien race. I can't even imagine what your father would say to you."

"Well, first, I'm not selling my birthright for porridge, I'm selling it to run the entire fucking planet," Schroeder said, "and that seems like a pretty good deal to me. Second, it was my father and the Nidu ambassador Naj-win-Getag who got the ball rolling on this project forty years ago, so I would imagine he'd be thrilled."

"I don't understand," Phipps said.

"You think something like this happens overnight?" Schroeder said. "Yes, the part with the girl is *all* improvisation. But everything else about planning to take the throne of Nidu has taken decades. My father was uniquely suited to help the win-Getag clan. He was Earth's first Representative to the CC, for God's sake. He knew everyone and everyone knew him. The AIC was the perfect vehicle for Dad to further the goal, to influence generations of Washington hall-crawlers and create an anti-Nidu sentiment that masked his actual agenda of bringing the win-Getag clan to the throne. It *worked*. It *still* works, even in the Webster administration. How do you think your boss got his job, Dave? It was one of Dad's last chess moves before he died."

"This is *insane*," Phipps said.

"I take it that means you're saying 'no' to ruling New Zealand," Schroeder said.

"I'm saying you need to rethink what you're doing," Phipps said. "You're going to hand your entire species over to war and subjugation. That's insane. I can't condone that. Jean, tell me where the woman is and we can all still get out of this with our hides intact. Otherwise I can't guarantee anything."

"Dave," Schroeder said. "You can't guarantee anything, anyway. You have nothing I need. Last chance, pal. Join the club."

"Or what? You're going to kill me?" Phipps said. "Be serious, Jean. If it came to that, I could break your neck while you were still trying to get up off of that chair."

"Oh, yes, you were Special Forces, and I'm just a soft Ivy Leaguer," Schroeder said. "I remember that. You're right, of course. I could never kill you. It would be foolish of me to try. I could never get away with it. But I know someone who could."

Phipps felt pressure a fraction of a second before he saw the tip of the Nidu spear emerge from just below his ribcage.

"Narf, for example," said Schroeder, conversationally. "He has diplomatic immunity."

Phipps grasped at the protruding spear tip and was caught off guard when the second spear came through his abdomen, in a bilaterally symmetrical position from the first. He grasped that one as well and tried to stand up, and looked for a moment like a skier with his poles stuck through his kidneys.

Narf-win-Getag came around from behind Phipps and stood in front of him. "These spears are said to have been used in battle by Zha-win-Getag, the noble founder of my clan line," Narf-win-Getag said. "You should be honored to die upon them."

Phipps burbled up blood and collapsed to his knees, pitched forward, and died. The spears caught in the chair and kept Phipps from falling forward completely.

"You were right," Narf-win-Getag said to Schroeder. "He would have upset our plans."

"I know," Schroeder said. "It's important to know what people are thinking before *they* do."

"What would you have done if he said he wanted to join us?" Narf-win-Getag said.

"I would have had you kill him anyway," Schroeder said. "He took bribes. He couldn't be trusted."

"He took bribes from *you*," Narf-win-Getag said.

"Precisely," Schroeder said. "So I know exactly how little he could be trusted." He looked down at Phipps. "That's a shame, though."

"That you couldn't trust him," Narf-win-Getag.

"No, that you had to spear him," Schroeder said. "Now there's blood all over that rug. That shit never comes out."

The first thing Creek and Robin did was sleep. They found their way to their cabin, an economy job on one of the lower decks, by the engine and the crew quarters, and squeezed their way through the door. They collapsed onto their respective single bunks and were out, dreamless, for 12 hours.

The second thing they did was shop. Fixer had graciously provided Creek with a sweatshirt to swap out for his torn and bloody shirt (although not so graciously that he didn't charge Creek a ridiculous amount for it) and gave Robin her promised hat for free, but aside from that the two of them had as their possessions only their fake passports and what they had on their bodies. The *Neverland* was not one of the high-end cruise liners—it belonged to the Haysbert-American cruise line, which specialized in economy package tours for large groups—but it featured a reasonably nice clothes store on the Galaxy Deck. Robin picked out clothes and shoes for the both of them while Creek made inane conversation with the clerk, describing how their luggage had somehow been routed to Bermuda.

The third thing Robin did was get her hair done. The third thing Creek did was get a massage. Both of them winced through their respective procedures but were pleased with the results. The fourth thing they did was sleep some more, waking up ravenous and just in time for the evening's assigned-seat dinner. They found their seat assignment slipped under the door: table 17.

"It says that dress is semi-formal—military dress uniforms preferred," Robin said, reading the assignment.

"I'm afraid we're going to disappoint them," Creek said.

"At least I got you a nice suit jacket and tie," Robin said. "Incidentally, don't get used to me shopping for you. This is a once in a lifetime deal. I hope you don't mind me saying I plan never to go into a mall with you again."

"Understood," Creek said. "I hope you don't mind me saying I share the sentiment."

"Good to have that out of the way, then," Robin said, then looked at the invitation again. "But you *have* a dress uniform, right? Back at home? You're a veteran."

"I am," Creek said. "I do. But I don't think I've put it on since I got out."

Robin smiled and waved airily, signifying the cruise. "You mean you've never done one of *these* before? Or even just a parade on Veteran's Day?"

"I'm not much for a parade," Creek said.

"I'm getting that from you," Robin said. "That whole 'loner' vibe."

"It's not that," Creek said. "Well, it is. But it's also that the best thing about my military service is that it's over. I put away the uniform because I was done with it."

"Are you going to be okay with this cruise?" Robin asked. "Because I get the feeling the rest of these guys aren't done with it yet. It's kind of why they're here."

"I'll be fine," Creek said. "I'm a loner by inclination but it doesn't mean I can't fake sociability."

"There's my trooper," Robin said. "I bet you're going to be the only guy there not in uniform, though. Just you wait and see."

"What, no uniform?" asked the bald man at table 17, as Creek and Robin took their seats.

"Our luggage got sent to Bermuda," Creek said, sitting.

"Boy, if I had a dollar for every time I heard *that* excuse," the bald man said, and held out his hand. "Chuck Gracie, and this is my wife Evelyn."

"Hiroki Toshima," Creek said, taking it.

"Come again?" Gracie said.

"Adopted," Creek said.

"Ah," Gracie said.

"And this is my fiancée, Debbie," Creek said, pointing to Robin.

"Well! Congratulations to you two," Evelyn Gracie said.

"Thanks," Robin said. "It was quite sudden."

"Well, you'll have to tell us all about it," Evelyn said. "I love a good engagement story."

"We met in a mall," Robin said, deadpan. "We ran into each other. There were parcels everywhere."

Before she could go on two other couples arrived and introduced themselves: James Crower and his wife Jackie, and Ned and Denice Leff. As handshakes were offered all around, one final couple arrived: Chris Lopez and her companion Eric Woods. This precipitated another wave of handshakes and Creek explaining that he was adopted. A waiter came by and filled wine glasses.

"Now that we're all here," Gracie said, "are there any officers at the table?" Everyone shook their heads. "Good!" Gracie said. "Then this is a salute-free zone. I say we get drunk and eat like pigs through the entire cruise."

Next to Gracie, Evelyn rolled her eyes and smacked her husband on the arm. "Settle down, Chuck," she said. "This is *your* commanding officer speaking."

"Yes, ma'am," Gracie said, and grinned at his tablemates. "You can see who's in charge here."

"I hear the captain of the *Neverland* is a veteran of Pajmhi," Chris Lopez said. "Does anyone know if that's true?"

"I can answer that," Ned Leff said. "It's true. He was a Marine lander jockey there. It's one of the reasons we picked the *Neverland* for this cruise."

"That and it's cheap," Gracie said.

"That doesn't hurt," Leff admitted. "But there were cheaper. I was on the steering committee for this cruise. Captain Lehane came to us and made the pitch for his ship. It sealed the deal. He was a hell of a pilot at Pajmhi, you know. His lander took a direct hit and he still managed to get it and his squad back to their ship."

"And now he's ferrying around tourists," James Crower said.

"Nothing wrong with that," Lopez said. "He did his tour like all of us."

"I'm not criticizing," Crower said. "Hell, I'm envious. I was a hopper jockey myself. Now I sell carpet. I'd trade."

"I'm in the market for carpet," Gracie said.

"Then this is a lucky a day for one of us," Crower said.

"Speak of the devil," Leff said, and pointed toward the front of the room. "It looks like Captain Lehane is going to say something."

Creek craned his head and saw a youngish man in a white dress uniform—the uniform of the Haysbert-American line—

standing and banging a fork lightly against a wine goblet. The room, full of chatter, settled down quickly.

"Fellow veterans," Lehane said. "Soldiers, marines, midshipmen, and yes, even officers"—this got a laugh—"I welcome you to the *Neverland*." This line brought applause; Lehane smiled and let it go on for a few seconds and then held up his hand to settle it back down.

"All of us are here for a reason," he said.

"To drink!" someone yelled from the back. The crowd roared.

Lehane smiled again. "All right, *two* reasons. The *other* reason is to honor our friends and comrades who fell on the field at Pajmhi. More than a decade has passed since we—some of us barely out of high school—fought and died in the largest commitment of human armed forces since our planet joined the Common Confederation. In that time, many things have been said about the Battle of Pajmhi. Many things have been said against it. But not once has anyone doubted the courage of the men and women who fought and died there. We above all people know this truth, and of the brotherhood and sisterhood formed between us in that fight, that exists now among those of us who lived, and that calls us to remember those who made the ultimate sacrifice for their planet and their fellow soldier." He raised his goblet. "To our brothers and sisters."

"To our brothers and sisters," came back to him from every table. Everyone drank.

"As you know," Lehane continued, "Chagfun is a special port of call for this journey of the *Neverland*, and we have arranged for a memorial ceremony on the plain of Pajmhi. I hope to see each of you there. Before and after that, of course, you'll be able to enjoy yourselves at all our usual ports of call, and with the *Neverland*'s onboard activities. Because as my friend at the back of the room noted, while we remember our compatriots, there's nothing wrong with having fun as well. So for the crew of the *Neverland*, again, welcome, and enjoy yourselves. Thank you." He sat at his table to applause. Waiters came out from the sides of the room to begin delivering salads.

"That was well done," Gracie said.

"Told you he was good," Leff said.

"How are we going to have a ceremony on the plain of Pajmhi?" Lopez said. "I thought those Nidu planet crackers wiped it off the face of the planet."

"Yes and no," Leff said, and leaned back to let the waiter deliver his salad. "The plain is still there. The only difference is now it's under about one hundred meters of freshly laid rock. That's from the lava flow after the bomb went off. Our ceremony is going to take place in one of the cooler parts of the rock flow."

"You mean there are still *warm* parts?" Crower said.

"Oh, yes," Leff said. "There's a volcano built up now where the south part of the plain used to be. It's still spewing lava. We're going to be on the north side of the plain."

"Goddamn Nidu," Gracie said, and jabbed at his salad.

"Chuck," Evelyn warned.

"Sorry, sweetie," Gracie said, then looked around the table. "But you all know what I'm talking about."

Robin held up her hand. "Hi," she said. "Actually, I don't. What do the Nidu have to do with this battle?"

Gracie looked at Robin, chewed thoughtfully on his salad, and then looked over to Creek. "You didn't tell her anything about it?"

"The relationship is still pretty new," Creek said.

"We're still picking up the parcels," Robin said.

Gracie looked around. "Anyone mind if I give a brief review?" When no one complained, he continued. "The short story is that the planet Chagfun is a Nidu colony, and about twenty years ago, the Chagfun natives started getting uppity. For about six, seven of those years, it was small-scale terrorist stuff—homemade bombs, exploding markets, assassination attempts. Nothing the Nidu can't handle on their own. But then something happened that made the Nidu sit up: The local Nidu military commanders took the side of the Chagfun natives and took their weapons with them. Which is something that's absolutely not supposed to happen."

"Why not?" Robin said.

"It's because of the Nidu hierarchy," Leff said, cutting in. "The Nidu are a caste-bound culture, grouped in clans that are incredibly suspicious of each other. The current ruling clan keeps control of everything—and I do mean *everything*—through a computer network. Every single piece of military and government equipment is tied into the network, right down the rifles the Nidu issue to their infantry. The power structure is top down, so commanding officers have control over every decision that gets made. It goes right up to the top. If the leader of the Nidu wanted, he could make a specific rifle on a battlefield stop working, just by ordering it."

"What happens if the soldier gets cut off from the network?" Robin asked.

"His rifle stops working," Leff said. "Or his transport, or his ship, whatever. It's the way the Nidu hierarchy keeps control."

"Except that in this case," Gracie said, stealing back the conversational ball, "somehow the local commanders appeared to disengage themselves from the Nidu network and keep their rifles working. And their ships. So they take them offline and Chagfun declares itself independent. Nidu declares war—"

"—and because Earth signed a mutual defense treaty, we get dragged into it," Lopez said. "And we end up fighting Nidu's civil war for them."

"Not that our Defense Department was complaining," Crower said.

"No, not at all," Gracie said. "Defense was looking to show off Earth military readiness. So we do a joint military operation with the Nidu, and because it's Nidu's party, they're in charge of the show. There's just one problem."

Robin waited for a minute for Gracie to continue, but he was clearly enjoying his dramatic pause. Finally, Robin said, "Yes? And the problem was what?"

Gracie opened his mouth to speak but Leff got there first. "The problem was that the Chagfun rebels weren't actually disconnected from the Nidu network. They'd stopped the Nidu leadership from commanding their equipment, but they could still eavesdrop on the network."

"So they knew every move the Nidu were going to have us make," Gracie said. He stuffed more salad into his mouth.

"That's bad," Robin said.

"It was *very* bad," Lopez said. "We landed 100,000 troops on the plain of Pajmhi because Nidu intelligence told us it was an ideal staging area. It was supposed to be away from the main concentrations of rebel troops, with sympathetic civilians in the local towns who wouldn't cause us any trouble. But the rebels knew we were coming and were ready for us. They hit us while we were still getting organized. There was no way we could mount an effective defense."

"It was a real clusterfuck," Gracie said.

"Chuck," Evelyn Gracie said.

"Your husband's right, Mrs. Gracie," Lopez said. "There were 23,000 killed and about that number wounded. When half of your troops are casualties, *clusterfuck* is the right term for it."

"Thank you, Lopez," Gracie said, and pointed to one of the ribbon bars on his uniform with his salad fork. "I got shot at Pajmhi; took a slug in the leg. Damn near tore the leg clean off. I figure I can use the term *clusterfuck* if I want."

"So what happened?" Robin said.

"Well, after a couple of Chagfun days, which are, what? Thirty hours long?" Gracie looked over to Leff.

"Thirty-one hours, seven minutes," Leff said.

"*That* long," Gracie said, pointing to Leff. "We managed to get our troops out of there, and told the Nidu to take care of their own damn messes. And they did."

"They dropped the bomb on Pajmhi," Crower said. "One of their planet crackers. It's a bomb that blasts down into the skin of a planet. Weakens the crust and lets the molten rock come through."

"It's like making a goddamn volcanic explosion, is what it is," Gracie said. "The Nidu dropped the bomb smack down into the plain of Pajmhi. Wiped out every living thing for a couple hundred kilometers around, including all those towns and villages."

"That was before the eruptions blew enough dust into the air to cool down the planet," Neff said. "Chagfun had its own mini-ice age that winter. Colonists froze and starved. The Nidu had a blockade of the planet. No one would run it."

"Why didn't the CC do anything about it?" Robin asked.

"Internal matter," Lopez said. "The CC only gets involved if one of its nations attacks another. It stays out of civil wars."

"So the CC let all those people die," Robin said.

"Basically," Lopez said. She forked the last of her salad.

"But it worked," Gracie said, bringing the conversation around to him again. "The Chagfun rebels surrendered to keep their families from starving and dying anymore. The Nidu swept in and took control and as far as I can recall executed every single rebel fighter. So through incompetence and ruthlessness, the Nidu ended up killing tens of thousands of humans, executing tens of thousands of surrendered combatants, and starving and freezing hundreds of thousands of their own people. And now you know why I say, 'Goddamn Nidu.'" This time Evelyn Gracie said nothing to her husband. The waiters came to take away the salad bowls.

"But enough of this depressing subject," Gracie said. He

reached into his uniform and pulled out a small camera. "I have a favor to ask. As the duly appointed representative of my regiment on this trip, it has fallen to me to be annoying and take pictures of every little thing to send back for the regiment newsletter. So I hope you won't mind all crowding together for a quick photo. Evelyn, sweetie, if you wouldn't mind." He handed the camera to his wife, who got up from the table to frame the photo. The others at the table crowded around Gracie; Creek and Robin edged themselves away from the group, not at all interested in having themselves photographed.

"Hiroki, Debbie," Gracie said. "Squeeze in."

"I don't have a uniform," Creek said.

"Hell, man, I was just ribbing you about the uniform," Gracie said.

"It's okay. I'll sit this one out," Creek said.

Gracie shrugged and looked over to Evelyn, who was framing the picture "Go ahead, honey," he said.

Evelyn Gracie thought Hiroki and his nice young fiancée were simply being shy, and also a little silly. She pressed a button on the back of the camera to flip the framing choice from Normal to Panoramic, bringing the stubborn couples' profiles just into frame. She snapped the picture and handed it back to her husband. "Thank you, dear," he said.

"You said 'regiment,'" said Crower, to Gracie, as the waiters handed down the main course of vatted prime rib. "Were you in cavalry?"

"Better," Gracie said "Ranger. 75th Regiment, 2nd Battalion. Fort Benning, Georgia. The 75th has been around since the 1900s, which is a hell of a bit of continuity. I'm not the only member of the 75th here—I know a couple of guys from the 1st and 3rd Battalions are here, too. But they're making me take all the pictures. You were cavalry, right?"

"3rd Armored, Tiger Squadron, Crazy Horse Troop," Crower said. "Out of Tennessee."

"A fine state," Gracie allowed. "What about you, Lopez?"

"46th Infantry, 146th Forward Support Battalion," Lopez said. "The Wolf Pack. Michigan."

"3rd Batallion, 7th Marines," Leff said. "California. The Cutting Edge."

"What about you, Hiroki?"

Creek looked up from his food. "12th Infantry. 6th Battalion."

There was dead silence at the table for several seconds. "Holy Christ, man," Gracie said, finally.

"Yeah," Creek said. He sliced off some prime rib and put it in his mouth.

"How many of you got out of there?" Lopez asked.

Creek swallowed. "From 6th Battalion?" Lopez nodded. "Twenty-six."

"From full battalion strength," Leff said. "The whole thousand soldiers."

"That's right," Creek said.

"Jesus," Leff said.

"Yeah," Creek said.

"I heard one of your guys got the Medal of Honor," Gracie said. "Held off the rebels for two days and saved his squad."

"He held off the rebels," Creek said. "He didn't get the Medal of Honor."

"Why the hell not?" Gracie said.

"He didn't save his entire squad," Creek said.

"He must have been pissed not to get it," Crower said.

"He was more upset about not saving the man he lost," Creek said.

"Did you know the guy?" Lopez asked. "Who was he?"

"Harry Creek," Creek said. "I knew him."

260 · John Scalzi

"Where is he now?" Lopez asked.

"He became a shepherd," Creek said.

Gracie laughed. "You're not serious," he said.

"Actually, I am," Creek said.

"And is he any good at it?" Gracie asked.

"I don't know," Creek said, and glanced over at Robin. "You'd have to ask the sheep."

Creek disappeared after dinner; Robin went looking for him after a couple of hours and found him on the Promenade Deck, staring out into space. "Hey," she said.

Creek turned to look at her and then turned back to look out at the stars. "Sorry about ducking out," he said. "Dinner dredged up a few things."

"Were they true?" Robin said. "The things you said about your battalion. About the Medal of Honor."

Creek nodded. "They're true. My battalion was right where the Chagfun rebels had massed their main troops. We got hit before we knew what was happening. My squad managed to break out and head for cover but we were ambushed."

"But you fought them off," Robin said. "You saved your squad."

"I saved most of my squad," Creek said. "My best friend died. He'd gotten excited and went after a squad of rebels, and our squad followed him into an ambush. We fought it back but took heavy casualties. The rest of the 6th was already wiped out or fighting for their lives so we were on our own for two days. At the end of it Brian was dead. I carried his body off the plain, but that's all I could do for him."

"I'm sorry, Harry," Robin said.

"It's all right," Creek said. "I just wish I had been able to save him."

"One of the things I'm learning about you is that you have an overdeveloped sense of personal obligation," Robin said. "I mean, I *like* it. It's kept me alive over the last couple of days. But it makes me worry about you."

"You're worried about *me,*" Creek said.

"Don't mock me," Robin warned. "I may be half-sheep but you know I can throw a punch."

"I'm not mocking you," Creek said. "I appreciate it. And you're only twenty percent sheep."

"Details," Robin said.

Behind them someone cleared his throat. Creek turned and saw Ned Leff standing there. "I hope I'm not interrupting anything," he said. "I saw you here and I thought I'd come over."

"We're just looking at the stars," Creek said.

"Waiting for the jump?" Leff said. "We'll be jumping into n-space in a few minutes. It's usually quite a sight."

"Now that you mention it, yes," Creek said. "That's exactly what we were doing. How can I help you, Ned?"

"I was hoping I could impose on your good will," Leff said. "You know there's going to be a memorial ceremony on the Pajmhi plain, and one of the things we're planning is to have one member of each service arm lay a wreath on a memorial we're bringing. Thing is, the vet we had representing the Army missed the cruise. Got into a crack-up on the way to the spaceport. Wrecked his car and broke a leg. He's all right, but he had to get his leg fixed before anything else. So we're down one serviceman. I was hoping I could get you to replace him."

"Thanks," Creek said. "But I don't really—"

Leff held up a hand. "I get the feeling you're a modest man, and I can understand that," he said. "But I think it would be especially inspiring for the other vets to see a member of the 6th up there, laying a wreath."

"I don't even have my dress uniform," Creek said. "My luggage got shipped to Bermuda."

"You let me worry about that," Leff said. "Just tell me you'll do it."

"When is the ceremony?" Creek said.

"We stop at Caledonia Colony tomorrow, and after that Brjnn, and then we do our stop at Chagfun," Leff said. "So a week from now. More than enough time for you to prepare, if that's what you're thinking about."

"A week would be perfect," Creek said. A week would be after the time the Nidu coronation ceremony was supposed to go off; Creek had no doubt that by that time Ben Javna would have resumed contact or otherwise tracked him down. Either he and Robin would already be off the *Neverland,* or he could risk standing at a podium with a wreath.

"Great," Leff said, and shook Creek's hand. "When I see you at dinner tomorrow I'll have more details for you. Until then, have a great night." He looked down at his watch. "And look at that— we're done just in time for you to watch the jump. I won't intrude any further. Enjoy it." He left.

"He seems pretty excited about the jump," Robin said, after Leff walked off.

"You've never seen one?" Creek said.

"I've never been off Earth before," Robin said. "This is all new to me. Why?"

"Well, just watch and see," Creek said.

Robin looked out at the stars. "What am I looking for?"

Every star in the sky suddenly twitched and smeared, as if each had been a sphere of iridescent and incandescent paint suddenly pressed into two dimensions by a universally large pane of glass. The light from each flattened sphere swirled with the light of the others, dancing prismatically and producing unexpected streaks of color until the whole sky settled into flat gray that nevertheless seemed to seethe and threaten to erupt with another show of pigment and flash.

"Oh. *Wow*," Robin said.

"That's what everybody says," Creek said.

"There's a reason for that," Robin said.

"Well, not everybody," Creek said. "Some species don't have color perception like we do. Some races of the CC don't even see."

"That's a shame," Robin said. "They're missing out. Sometimes it's good to be human."

Judge Bufan Nigun Sn yanked at one of his antennae as if in irritation, spidered his legs around his stool, set his cup of coffee on his desk, and pulled out his communicator module from a drawer. "Being we're on Earth, we'll have this conversation in English," the module said, lowering the high-pitched scrapings coming from Sn's mouthparts into the human and Nidu sonic range. "Does the Nidu representative have a problem with this?"

"Not at all," said Quua-win-Getag, General Counsel for Nidu's embassy to the United Nations of Earth.

"And I assume you're fine with it, Mr. Javna," Judge Sn said.

"Yes, your honor," Ben Javna said.

"Good," Sn said. "Given the extraordinary time constraints involved in this case, I have agreed to this *in camera* session and will render a decision by the end of this session. While the decision can of course be appealed to a high court, the ruling will not be suspended pending appeal. So this means if you're not happy with the ruling, you're shit out of luck. Are we clear?" Both Quua-win-Getag and Javna consented.

"Fine," Sn said. "And now, Counselor win-Getag, you can explain your government's damn fool line of reasoning that says a human citizen of the UNE is somehow equivalent to livestock."

Quua-win-Getag launched into a recap of his government's legal argument while Judge Sn took the lid off his coffee, descended his sucking mouthpiece into the cup, and sipped gingerly. Javna

264 • John Scalzi

wasn't a knowledgeable student of the Wryg, the species to which Judge Sn belonged; nevertheless he suspected Sn was probably more than a little hung over, which explained why he was snippier today than the average Wryg.

"Fine, fine, fine," Judge Sn eventually said, as Quua-win-Getag began to rehash the particulars of *Agnach-u v. Ar-Thaneg* for the second time. "I get where you're going with this. Very innovative, counselor. Amoral and repugnant, but innovative."

"Thank you, your honor," Quua-win-Getag said.

Judge Sn glanced over to Javna. "Tell me you've got something to counter this crap," he said.

"Actually," Javna said, "the UNE would like to stipulate the Nidu assertion that Miss Baker is not human, nor a citizen of the UNE."

"What?" said Judge Sn.

"What?" said Quua-win-Getag.

"The UNE stipulates that Miss Baker is not human, nor a citizen of the UNE," Javna said.

"You've *got* to be kidding," said Judge Sn. "I've never been a big fan of the human race, if you want the truth about it. You people have your heads up your asses most of the time. Even so, your one saving grace is that you fight like mad for the rights of your own people. If this represents the true thought of your government, this planet is more of a toilet than I thought it was. You'd be insane to give up a citizen to these lizards."

"On behalf of my government, I protest those comments," Quua-win-Getag said.

"Quiet, you," Judge Sn said to Quua-win-Getag, then turned his attention back to Javna. "Well?"

"I appreciate your candor in your opinion of the human race," Javna said. "Nevertheless, the UNE stipulates."

"Well, that's just great," said Judge Sn. "Remind me to get

working on that request for a new posting as soon as you two clear out of my office."

"If the UNE stipulates our points, then the entity is indeed our property, and the UNE must present it to us at the earliest opportunity," Quua-win-Getag said, to Judge Sn. "Nidu asks you to rule such."

"And I assume you're perfectly fine with that, too," Judge Sn said to Javna.

"We are not," Javna said. "And in fact we request that you dismiss the case on the grounds that the Nidu have no standing to bring the suit in the first place."

"That's ridiculous," Quua-win-Getag said. "The UNE already stipulated that the entity is Nidu property."

"We stipulated that she is not human and not a UNE citizen," Javna said. "Which is not the same as saying she's your property."

"I'm getting a headache," Judge Sn said. "Explain yourself, counselor. Be quick and clear."

"There's no point arguing that Miss Baker is human. She's not—she's a hybrid entity and an entirely new species," Javna said. "But she's more than a new species, she's a new *sentient* species. The Common Confederation automatically confers special rights on the individuals of newly discovered sentient species to protect them from exploitation by other races. It's one of the fundamental tenets of the Common Confederation, and in the Confederation's charter, which every nation must agree to upon entering the CC. Furthermore, the Common Confederation holds each sentient species *en masse* to be sovereign—again, to prevent their exploitation by other races. It's up to the chosen governments of those species to enter into treaties and agreements on behalf of its people. This is all well established."

"Go on," Judge Sn said.

"Given these facts, Miss Baker's rights as a new sentient

species trump Nidu's claim to her as property," Javna said. "Likewise, any treaties that the Earth may have entered into with Nidu are irrelevant regarding the disposition of Miss Baker. She is *de facto* the governing body of her species, sovereign into her own self, and therefore only she is able to enter into treaties and agreements concerning herself. The UNE recognizes this and relinquishes any claim it has regarding citizenship pending Miss Baker's own decision to ally her nation to ours. As Miss Baker is sovereign, Nidu has no standing to demand the UNE present her. As Miss Baker is a new sentient species, Nidu has no standing to claim her as property. Basically, Nidu has no standing to bring these suits."

Judge Sn turned to Quua-win-Getag. "And what do you say to that, counselor?"

Quua-win-Getag blinked hard; he had expected and prepared for Javna to fight for Baker's citizenship; he was entirely taken aback by this legal tack. "It's an interesting theory," Quua-win-Getag said, drawing out his words for effect and to give himself more time to think. "But it's not proven that the entity is in fact an entirely new sentient species."

"Really, now," Judge Sn said. "Which part are you disputing? The 'sentient' part or the 'species' part?"

"Both," Quua-win-Getag said. "Neither has been proven."

"Oh, come on," Javna said. "Miss Baker attended college and owns her own business. I'm pretty sure that qualifies her as sentient."

"Agreed," Judge Sn said. "And as for the species part, Counselor win-Getag, your colleague here has already stipulated your own assertion that Miss Baker is not human. In order for her *not* to be a new species, I think you would have to assert she is entirely livestock. I don't think even the Nidu are prepared to go that far."

"It may not have all the hallmarks of speciation," Quua-win-Getag said, thinking furiously now. "Species have to be able to pass on their characteristics to their offspring, and it's not been proven the entity can do that."

"Are you suggesting we knock up the young lady to prove her status?" said Judge Sn. "I don't think we have the time for that."

"For another thing!" Quua-win-Getag said, a little breathlessly. "The entity was genetically engineered from previously known species. Every previously known new sentient species occurred through the natural processes of evolution and not from previously known species."

"Meaning?" Judge Sn prompted.

"Meaning that genetically engineered entities are not selected for speciation by the processes of evolution," Quua-win-Getag said. "Therefore they cannot be considered true species. The entity is a one-off, unlikely to be reproduced. If she is not truly a new species and the UNE stipulates that she is not human, then legally speaking, she *is* livestock. And as her species of sheep is already well-known and its characteristics well-noted, the question of her sentience becomes a moot point. She is, legally, Nidu property."

"Fascinating," Judge Sn. "You're so ready to ignore the fact she's obviously sentient."

"It's not my fault the UNE has stipulated she's not human," Quua-win-Getag said. "Everything follows from its capitulation on that point of fact."

"Counselor Javna," Judge Sn said. "You're up."

Javna smiled. Quua-win-Getag didn't know it, but he'd just maneuvered the case right where Javna wanted it. "Your honor, we grant that all previous examples of sentient species occurred through the natural processes of evolution. But rather than suggest that this limits your honor to rulings based on previous standards, allow me to suggest that this offers another option."

"Which is?" said Judge Sn.

"To make new law," Javna said.

Judge Sn's antennae shot straight up. "What did you say, counselor?" Judge Sn asked.

"Make new law, your honor," Javna said. "The question of the disposition of artificially created sentient species has never come up before in the history of the Common Confederation. *Agnach-u v. Ar-Thaneg* came close but the ruling didn't address issues related to sentience, merely property. This is virgin territory, your honor, and an issue that goes straight to the heart of the mission of the Common Confederation. Indeed, your honor, there may be no more important issue."

Judge Sn sat there, stock still, for nearly a full minute, mouth-pieces moving in tiny little circles. Javna glanced over at Quua-win-Getag, who stared straight ahead at the judge. Javna could hear him grinding his teeth. He knew he'd been outmaneuvered by his human counterpart, who had dangled in front of the judge the one thing that would be utterly irresistible: The opportunity to make new law. In a legal system tens of thousands of years old, there was almost nothing new in the law, merely ever-more-finely parsed restatings of the law as it existed. Offering an ambitious judge the chance to make new law—indeed create an entire new *branch* off the tree of law—and thus win instant fame and glory in the CC judicial circles was like offering a lamed baby ibex to a starving leopard.

"Okay, I'm ready to rule," Judge Sn said.

"I hope your honor will not take this opportunity to overstep the parameters of your responsibilities," Quua-win-Getag said.

"Excuse me?" Judge Sn said. "You show up in my courtroom with a petition to turn a citizen of a member of the Common Confederation into a meat animal, and you warn *me* about overreaching? Good fucking gravy. You're in contempt, counselor. You can pay your thousand CC credits on the way out the door. Now shut the hell up. You're the dipshit who brought the suit and demanded it get ruled on today, so now you're going to get a ruling."

"Yes, your honor," Quua-win-Getag said. "My apologies." Javna tried very hard not to smile.

"Damn right," Judge Sn said. "First, regarding the nature of Miss Robin Baker, the court finds that she does, in fact, represent an entirely new species of sentient being. How this species came into being is irrelevant in light of the fact that it *is* sentient, and as such has sovereign protections under the Common Confederation charter. Likewise as an individual Miss Baker is afforded certain protections under the CC charter.

"As the UNE has disavowed claim to Miss Baker as a citizen, the Nidu suit to have her citizenship revoked is moot and therefore dismissed. As Miss Baker is sovereign, the Nidu suit to compel the UNE to produce Miss Baker is likewise dismissed. I'll also note, Counselor win-Getag, that if Nidu further attempts to breach its treaties with the UNE on this issue, it will be held to be the defaulting party and as such will be subject to penalties, both financial and diplomatic. If the Nidu want a war with the Earth, you're not getting any cover for it from the CC. Are we clear on this, Counselor?"

"Yes, your honor," Quua-win-Getag said.

"Good," Judge Sn said. "Then we're done here. The ruling will be published on the court's site within the hour."

"You will have our appeal by the end of the day," Quua-win-Getag said.

"Of course I will," said Judge Sn. "I'd be deeply disappointed if I didn't. Now get out. Making new law has made me hungry. I'm going to get a snack." He exited to find the court's vending machines.

"Very tricky, counselor," Quua-win-Getag said, after Judge Sn left. "Although I don't expect the ruling to make it past appeal."

Javna shrugged. "Maybe it will, maybe it won't. But by that time, this little crisis of ours is going to be resolved one way or another."

"Indeed," Quua-win-Getag said. "Still, I'd like to know how you came up with that line of reasoning."

"You can thank a rabbi," Javna said. "And a hot dog."

On the *Neverland*, Chuck Gracie sat on his bunk, flipping through pictures in his camera while Evelyn dozed beside him. Most of the pictures were of Evelyn or Evelyn and Gracie together while Gracie held out the camera at arm's length. Chuck Gracie was one of those people who was of the opinion there was nothing wrong with any scenery that the presence of himself, his wife, or both couldn't fix. Unfortunately, this fetish made it difficult to find suitable pictures for the regiment newsletter; after previous experiences with Gracie as photojournalist, Dale Turley, the editor of the newsletter, gently suggested to Gracie that he should submit more pictures that didn't have so much of that Chuck Gracie feel to them.

Here we go, Gracie thought. He'd just clicked on to the picture from the dinner table. True, Gracie was in it, but he was flanked by six other people, plus Hiroki and his fiancée over there in the corner. As an overall percentage, the picture was just 11% Chuck Gracie, which he figured was an acceptable amount for Turley (or Turdley, as Gracie mentally thought of him since the initial "less Gracie" photographic suggestion). Gracie transferred the picture to his communicator, typed a note identifying the people in the picture, and sent both off. Gracie's communicator synced with the *Neverland*'s internal network; the network dropped the note and picture into the final burst of data sent out by the *Neverland* prior to its jump into n-space and thence to Caledonia colony.

About an hour later, the picture and text dropped into the mail queue of Dale Turley, who was putting the finishing touches on this week's regiment newsletter. Dale opened the mail and, pleased that the overall Chuck Gracie ratio in the picture was indeed low, slapped it into the newsletter at the bottom, typed in the names and location for the picture caption, and then dropped the newsletter into the distribution queue. There it would be printed out for current members of the regiment at their various bases across the U.S., and distributed in electronic form to former and/or veteran members of the 75th Ranger regiment, a host of several thousand ex-rangers, including one Rod Acuna.

"Fuck me running," Acuna said to himself, as the newsletter and the picture popped up on his communicator. He cleared the newsletter from his communicator screen and punched in Jean Schroeder's access code. Their lost lamb had been found.

Takk sat on a chair that was too small for him, glanced over at Archie McClellan, and contemplated the fact that he was proba- bly going to have to eat him.

Morally, Takk had no problem with this. Takk, like all Nagch his age, was on his *Ftruu*, the culturally mandated moral journey in which young Nagch endeavor to experience as many aspects of existence as possible, including the unseemly; this last category could reasonably be expected to include consuming members of other sentient species. During the *Ftruu*, a Nagch like any mem- ber of the CC would be legally liable for his or her actions. So Takk would be on the hook for murder if he were caught.

But as a matter of sin, Takk was in the clear. Nagch experienc- ing the *Ftruu* were considered blameless, on the rationale that one of the objects of the journey was to experience sin and thus better understand it. Unless Takk decided to end it early and re- turn to the fold, he had roughly 14 months left on his *Ftruu*. After that point, eating humans would be a definite mark against his soul. At the moment, however, he could eat his way through an entire schoolyard with nary a theological burp.

So morals weren't the issues. Instead, Takk was focused on the practical matters of eating humans: namely, that they tended to come with a number of indigestible components, like watches and communicators and plastic zippers and metal shoe bits and occasionally some things that you simply couldn't know about until after you've eaten someone. That sheep rancher, for example, had had some metal pins and screws in him; Acuna told him that some humans had broken bones screwed back into place rather than fixed up by a QuickHeal session. It was a cost thing. All Takk knew was that they poked uncomfortably. Like every other indigestible item of human accoutrement Takk eventually had to spit them out, otherwise they'd just pile up in his digestive sac and Takk would jangle when he walked and feel them clanging together inside of him. Takk hated that.

Optimally, Takk thought, he'd be able to strip a human out of his stuff before ingesting them. But Takk realized that a situation like that probably wasn't going to happen. The whole advantage Takk had in dealing with humans was the element of surprise. No human being actually ever expected to be eaten. Ridding them of their clothes and personal objects would pretty much telegraph Takk's intentions. He had to accept the occasional watch and leg screw as an occupational hazard.

With that in mind, Takk was eyeing McClellan to see how much indigestible crap the human might have with him. Takk was pleased to see that the human appeared to be wearing no jewelry, save for a watch, and especially no earrings, which were small and pointy and difficult for Takk to remove afterward. The human's clothes likewise appeared fine; digesting humans had made Takk something of a connoisseur of human clothing fabrics, and he could tell by the hang and crumple of Archie's clothes that they were primarily natural fibers rather than artificial. That meant less of a lump of plastic fibers a day down the line. Then there was that thing Archie had in his hand, which he'd been looking at off and on since Acuna brought him back and told Takk to watch him.

"Hey," Takk said, his first words to Archie since he was dragged back into the room. "What is that in your hand?"

Archie looked up. "It's a book," he said.

"What is it made out of?" Takk asked.

Archie held it up so Takk could see it. "Plastic. You hold it in your hand, and the heat from your body powers the optical imager to project the pages."

"So, plastic," said Takk. He could handle a little bit of plastic.

"Yeah," Archie said, and went back to his reading.

After several minutes, Takk's now-awakened curiosity got the better of him. "What's the book about?" he asked.

"It's a book of poems," Archie said, not looking up.

"What kind of poems?" Takk asked.

Now Archie looked up. "You actually care?" he said.

"I'm just as bored as you are," Takk said.

"They're prophetic poems," Archie said.

"They tell the future?" Takk asked.

"Sort of," Archie said. "It's more like they suggest things that could happen, and it's up to us to decide what to do about it."

"Why are you reading them?" Takk asked.

"Because I'm trying to figure out what I'm supposed to do next," Archie said, turning back to his book.

Takk was taken aback. "You're on a religious quest?" he asked Archie.

Archie shrugged. "I suppose I am," he said.

Almost instantly Takk was overcome with a rush of affection for this little human. The *Ftruu* was a difficult passage for any young Nagch. The Nagch were a people who thrived on family and tradition; tossing young Nagchs out to experience the universe was a paradoxically isolating experience for most of them and made them yearn to return to their homes and rituals (a fact not in the least lost on older Nagch).

Takk had been on Earth for a better part of two years; he'd come there because it was the planet that had been randomly selected for him to visit two Nagch years prior—just enough time to learn to read and speak English. He'd been given a transport ticket and a small stipend and told not to return until his *Ftruu* was completed.

In that time, Takk had largely consorted with scumbags; his stipend was small and his visa was tourist, and being unencumbered by the worries of sin he had no qualms about working under the table for questionable people and their even-more-questionable aims. However, it did leave him with a general perception that humans were spiritually bereft beings. Takk understood that Earth was positively littered with houses of worship and that people were always claiming that their god of choice wanted them to do one thing or another. But in his personal experience the only time he heard people invoke their deity was when Takk was about to beat the hell out of them or turn them into a snack. And even then, more than half the time they invoked defecation instead. Takk found that inexplicable.

And thus, Archie McClellan became the first human Takk had met who actually appeared to have a religious component to his personality—or at the very least a religious component not motivated entirely by fear of imminent injury or death. Meeting someone with a religious impulse activated a dormant section of Takk's personality very much like a turned-on faucet expands a desiccated sponge. Takk advanced on Archie enthusiastically. Archie quite understandably flinched.

"Tell me about your quest," Takk said.

"What?" Archie said.

"Your quest!" Takk said. "I am on a religious quest also."

Archie looked at Takk skeptically. "But you're doing *this*," he said, sweeping his arm about.

"So are you," Takk said.

Archie blinked. Takk had a point, there. Archie glanced down at his book, which had turned its optically generated page thanks to his flinch, and his eye caught the poem there:

Lo! The screw turns, yet the direction is not set
Those who teach may let learn, and those who learn, teach
When we pass beyond what is left but what we tell?
We may yet reach from beyond to turn the screw once more.

Among the scholars of the Church, who liked to use study of the stanzas as an excuse for barbecues and the consumption of beer, this was one of the minor "exhortation" stanzas, encouraging Church members to share information with each other so that Church aims could be accomplished further down the line. Direct, simple, and uncomplicated, like the stanzas encouraging good hygiene and flossing (which were generally followed) and the avoidance of fatty foods and—ironically for the alcoholic Dwellin—too much imbibing (which, given the beer-fueled cookouts, were not). These were generally regarded as the least interesting of the prophetic poems, for much the same reasons as the layout of dietary laws in the Pentateuch failed to set afire Jewish and Christian theologians.

Right here and right now, however, Archie McClellan felt his eyes bulge and the Empathist impulse—that creepy feeling that Dwellin really *did* unintentionally connect with something larger, whether he meant to or not—flared in his chest like heartburn. Archie was already clearly and sickly aware that he was a dead man walking; after about the 30th time Acuna pressed that vending machine button Archie reconciled himself to the idea that the rest of his life would be counted in hours and that at the end of it he was likely to be a snack for the monstrous alien that was now asking him about his religion. And yet here was a fragmentary bit of wisdom—scrawled by a consumptive hack decades back, but even so—telling him that even when he was gone, there was still work to be done.

Archie looked back up at Takk, who was standing there, still rather too close for Archie's comfort zone. "Can I ask you a question?" Archie said.

"Yes," Takk said.

"Aren't you going to have to kill me soon?" Archie said. "Isn't that what you're watching me for?"

"I think so," Takk said.

"And you're going to do it," Archie said. "If Acuna walks through the door right now and says 'Eat him,' you're going to do it."

"Probably," Takk said.

"And yet you suddenly want to be my friend," Archie said. "Doesn't that strike you as—I don't know—kind of strange?"

"No," Takk said. "If I had known about your religious quest earlier, I would have wanted to know about it then, too."

"If you knew about it earlier, it would have gotten me killed," Archie said.

"It's going to get you killed now," Takk said.

Archie opened his mouth, and then closed it. "I have no good argument against that," he said.

"So you'll tell me about your quest," Takk said.

"I think I will," Archie said, and waved his hand over the optical control that increased the size of the book page large enough for the both of them to read.

————

"Have you read this?" Jean Schroeder waved an old-fashioned paper book of Dwellin's prophecies at Rod Acuna.

"No," Acuna said. He was bored. "Most religious books are incompatible with my line of work."

"It's completely ridiculous," Schroeder said. "It's like Nostradamus, hung over and in free verse. Complete bullshit and they made a religion out of it anyway. A well-off religion, I might add."

"What do you want me to do with the geek?" Acuna said.

"I want you to get rid of him, of course," Schroeder said. "I know who he works for and I don't have any questions for him. You can add him to that other pile you have in your trunk. That one expired where you're sitting, incidentally."

Acuna shifted in his chair and looked down at the rug on the floor, which featured a large dark blotch. "You might want to get rid of the incriminating bloodstain," he said.

"In a few days I'm going to be running this joint, by which I mean the entire planet," Schroeder said. "I'm not worried about a bloodstain. Besides, we're leaving in about three hours. Narf has generously invited you and me and your flunky to come with him to Nidu for his coronation ceremony. Actually he's invited *me,* but it makes sense for you and your flunky to get off-planet, too, so you're coming along for the ride. And you'll even be able to pack your guns, since we'll be going on an official Nidu diplomatic vessel. Diplomatic immunity is a delightful thing."

"What about Creek and the woman?" Acuna said. "I sent you the information on where they are. How are we going to get them?"

"*We* aren't going to get them," Schroeder said. "The Nidu military are. The ship our friends are on just happens to make a stop at Chagfun, which is a Nidu colony. The local military will pick them up there. The military will hand them over to Narf, whose ship will make a stop at Chagfun for that purpose before heading on to Nidu. The heir apparent seems to trust Narf, but by the time Narf gets to Nidu, the ritual will have been opened to other clans. Narf is going to waltz his way right to the throne."

"That's really fascinating," Acuna said. "But I couldn't possibly give a shit. What I want is Creek."

Schroeder grinned. "Pissed off at being beat up, Rod?"

"Mildly," Acuna growled. "A broken wrist, a busted nose, and then getting the shit kicked out of me for a second time in one night because I went after him. Yeah, I'm a *tad* pissed. Once you have the girl, you're not going to need him anymore. I want you to give him to me."

"You're going to have your walking garbage disposal take care of him when you're done, I assume," Schroeder said.

"No," Acuna said. "Takk likes his food alive and in one piece. That's how he's going to get the geek. Creek's not going to be that lucky."

Creek followed the crew member who had retrieved him up the stairs and onto the bridge of the *Neverland,* and was presented to Captain Lehane, who was conferring with his navigator.

"Mr. Toshima," Lehane said, shaking his hand. "Glad you could come up for a visit."

"Thanks," Creek said. "One doesn't usually turn down an invitation by the captain to visit the bridge of a starship."

"No, I guess one wouldn't," Lehane said.

"And while I'm flattered and fascinated," Creek said, "I *am* wondering why I was extended such an invitation."

"Ned Leff informed me that you had agreed to fill in for our ceremony but that your luggage and uniform had been left behind, so I told him I'd help you out," Lehane said. "I'm the wrong branch of the service but some of my officers served in infantry. So I thought I'd have you drop by so I could size you up, as it were. See from which of my officers you might borrow some duds."

"Here I am," Creek said.

"Indeed," said Lehane. "Sam tells me you were with the 12th Infantry, 6th Battalion."

"I was," Creek said.

"That's a hell of a thing," Lehane said. "Not many of you made it back in one piece."

"No," Creek agreed. "No, not many of us did."

"Do you still keep in touch with any of them?" Lehane asked. "I knew Colonel Van Doren pretty well once he left the service."

Creek furrowed his brow. "I keep in touch with a couple," he said. "Who did you say you knew?"

"Colonel Van Doren," Lehane said. "Jim Van Doren."

"I don't think I knew him," Creek said. "Our colonel was Jack Medina. Tough old son of a gun. Held off rebels with his sidearm."

"That's right," Lehane said. "Sorry. Got my battalions mixed up."

"No problem," Creek said.

"Brennan," Lehane said. One of the bridge crew peeled off from his station and came to the captain. "You were in infantry," he said.

"Yes, sir," Brennan said. Lehane looked at Brennan and Creek together.

"Close enough," Lehane said. "You might need a minor alteration on the pants. I'll have the ship's seamstress come 'round to your cabin. Brennan, would you be so kind as to lend Mr. Toshima here your dress uniform?"

"Anything for a survivor of the 6th," Brennan said, saluted Creek, and sat back down.

"That's service," Creek said. "Remind me to note that on the ratings slip at the end of the tour."

"The crew members who served know all about you being on the ship," Lehane said.

"That sounds ominous," Creek said.

Lehane smiled. "I doubt that," he said. "Let's just say that you're likely to find a substantial number of your drinks on the house."

"Thanks, but I prefer to pay," Creek said. "All the other guys here fought in the same battle I did."

"I was hoping you might say something like that," Lehane said. "It's good character. Have you been enjoying your trip so far?"

"We have," Creek said. "My fiancée and I just got back from visiting Caledonia. New Edinburgh is absolutely beautiful. Debbie is thrilled our luggage got lost because it's giving her an excuse to stock up." Creek wasn't entirely sure Robin would be thrilled at the picture he was painting of her as "Debbie," but there was no reason to stick too close to the real-life script.

"Caledonia *is* beautiful," Lehane agreed. "A lot of tourists are disappointed because New Edinburgh isn't tropically located, but it's my favorite stop on our itinerary. It's sad that we have to cut short our stay here—and at Brjnn, too—in order to get Chagfun into the schedule. We only have a day at each, and just one day at Chagfun as well. Although *that* doesn't bother me terribly."

"You don't sound very excited about Chagfun," Creek said.

"I'm not," Lehane admitted, in a rush that felt as if he were allowing a dark secret to be pulled out in the open. "It's a terrible place, you know. Bad things happened to us. Bad things happened to the rebels. And in both cases the Nidu were to blame. *They're* still there, of course. The idea of taking one of our spaceships back into that space knots my gut."

"And yet Ned says you lobbied hard for the *Neverland* to take these men to Chagfun," Creek said.

"I did," Lehane said. "If anyone's going to bring these guys

back into Hell—even for a vacation—it should be someone who's
been there before. And who knows the way back out again."

"I think I like you, Captain Lehane," Creek said.

"The feeling's mutual, Mr. Toshima," Lehane said. "You're a
survivor of the 6th. I imagine you know what it's like to take men
out of Hell."

"I do," Creek said. "Some of them, anyway."

Brian let his consciousness float before the informational edifice
that was the Church of the Evolved Lamb's computer network
and tried to figure out the best way to break in.

Earlier in the day, Brian had noted with satisfaction that his
older brother had swatted back the Nidu attempt to reclassify
Robin Baker as property and rammed the ruling right down their
lizardly throats. Brian had burst with fraternal pride as he read the
judge's ruling; Ben had always been the smart one in the family
and had a special knack for sneaking up behind people in an intellectual sense and then whacking them in the skull, which is exactly
what had happened here. But Brian didn't think the ruling was
close to the end of it. People who were happy to argue that a human
has as many rights as an alarm clock were not likely to be stopped
by a judge. They'd be after Robin again soon enough, and Harry
along with her. Brian felt that it was his mission to find out how,
stop it if he could, or at least inform Harry about what to expect.

By dint of Harry's security clearance, Brian knew everything
the UNE knew about the situation, which was not enough to help
him extrapolate what the Nidu would do next. There were two
other players who had information Brian didn't have and that he
needed: The Nidu government itself, and the Church of the
Evolved Lamb, who through Archie McClellan had been keeping
tabs on the entire situation.

Brian read up on both, which in this case meant accessing the complete information about both in his databanks, a process which took a couple of seconds. He was not entirely surprised to find two significant points of connection between the Nidu government and the Church. The first was that the Android's Dream sheep was a breed of sheep designed by the Church (or more accurately, its genetics labs, which were part of the overall Hayter-Ross corporate structure) for the Nidu government at the behest of the UNE government. Even more accurately, it had been designed for the auf-Getag clan prior to their challenge for the Nidu throne years back. This was an interesting bit of trivia; it showed the UNE had placed their bets on the succession long before it actually went down. Designing an entirely new breed of sheep took time.

The second is that the construction of the Nidu computer network currently in use had been contracted out to the UNE—the auf-Getag clan's way of scratching the back of those who had scratched theirs. The UNE in return subcontracted the job to several companies—two thirds of whom, including the managing subcontractor LegaCen, were companies within the overall Hayter-Ross corporate umbrella.

The specifics of the computer system were not available (of course—they were Nidu state secrets), but the general gist of the computer system was that it allowed the Nidu *Fehen* complete access to and control of every network-enabled computer and appliance in Nidu space. And they were *all* network-enabled; by Nidu law, if it had a processor, it had to be attached to the network. Lesser but still Orwellian levels of access were provided by the *Fehen* to other Nidu higher-ups, who it goes without saying were entirely loyal to the *Fehen*. This was all in the service of total, centralized control; in this technologically centered age, a rebellion that relied on paper was not a rebellion that would get very far.

There was no way for Brian to access the Nidu computer network directly. From Earth, there were only two points of entry. The first was at the Nidu embassy, where the Nidu network-enabled computers and appliances were intentionally incompatible with standard Earth technology and used wired rather than wireless connections. Short of Brian physically breaking into the Nidu embassy and using Nidu input devices to access the network—unlikely as Brian was lamentably short of physicality at the moment—he was out in the cold.

On the other hand, LegaCen maintained a connection to the Nidu network as part of its continuing maintenance contract with the Nidu government. LegaCen, a subsidiary of Hayter-Ross, controlled by the Church of the Evolved Lamb. All the more reason, Brian thought, to break into the Church's network.

Brian was actually entirely filled with admiration for the Church. He'd read Dwellin's prophecies and unlike the UNE and Nidu governments, who apparently saw only the Hayter-Ross corporate structure and not the religious entity behind it, Brian had come to the conclusion that the Church was working to hasten the end times hinted at in its own prophecies, and had well and truly maneuvered the governments of two planets to that end. Brian idly wondered what would happen if, indeed, the Church managed to reach its goal and bring forth the Evolved Lamb. He doubted very seriously that the Church would disband.

All of this was immaterial, however, to the salient point of entering the network and seeing what he could see regarding Robin, Harry, and the Nidu's plans for them. *No time like the present*, Brian thought, and with that extended himself into every conceivable nook and cranny of the Church's system, looking for a keyhole in.

This is was not the smartest way Brian should have been doing his search. He'd've probably been better off beginning with a noninvasive survey of the system, wandering through the public areas to get an idea where to start poking around without signaling the network it was under a massive attack. But Brian considered that sort of slow-paced examination to be a luxury Robin and Harry couldn't afford at the moment. Anyway, he thought of himself as an Alexander type, cutting the Gordian knot in half while more cautious types fiddled with the rope end, futilely trying to figure out where to begin untying.

Brian had no doubt he was ringing alarm bells across the entire Church network. But was he not the world's first intelligent agent? He'd either be in the system momentarily, or he'd simply outthink and outmaneuver the security measures.

Ah. Here we go; someone left an easily-crackable programming backdoor at Royvo, a small Hayter-Ross subsidiary that made replacement parts for aging sewers. Not an especially romantic corner of the Church's empire, to be sure. Brian jammed some password repeater code into the door and cycled it through; three seconds and a mere 254,229 password attempts later, he was in. Piece of cake.

The lights went out.

Metaphorically, of course. Brian, being previously human and consciously regarding himself as still thus, had created a perceptual system to help him relate to the information he was processing. But however you want to slice it, two cycles previously, Brian had been fully perceptually aware of his surroundings and able to move freely. Now he perceived nothing except his own thoughts.

Which were: *What the fuck?*

"Hello," said a woman's voice, warm but with a sharp edge. "And what do we have here?" Then it went away for a perceptually indefinite period of time.

Then it came back. "You're *very* interesting," it said. "I'm going to take you apart and find out what makes you tick. I hope you don't mind. I should be able to put you back together when I'm done. No promises, though. Also, given what I can see of your perceptual structure, this is going to hurt."

Brian felt himself being torn apart almost immediately thereafter. His first reaction was something akin to amazement; he hadn't been aware his perceptual metaphor had included an equivalent to pain, and now that he was aware that it *did*, he wondered what the fuck he was thinking of (or not thinking of, to be more accurate about it) when he added it in. His second reaction was to scream his head off and wonder if for the second time in his life he might be dying.

Rod Acuna opened the door to his apartment to find Archie McClellan and Takk huddled together, reading a book.

"What the fuck *are* you doing?" Acuna yelled at Takk.

"We were just reading a book," Takk said. "Just passing time."

" 'Just passing time?' Holy Christ," Acuna said. "What is this, kindergarten? If I came back in an hour, would you be having milk and cookies and settling down for a nap?" Takk raised his paw as if to make another point. "Shut up," Acuna said. "You and I are leaving here in an hour. I'm going to go pack some things. When I come back out, I want your little reading buddy taken care of. Do you understand me?"

"I understand you," Takk said.

"Good," Acuna said. He went off into a back room.

Archie set the book down on the table; it flickered off as he did so. Takk stood up, and so did Archie, supporting himself on the table and taking care not to put weight on his injured leg. They had a moment of uncomfortable silence.

"So," Takk said, finally.

"Yeah," Archie said. "So, this is the part where you kill me and eat me."

"I guess so," Takk said. "Although it's the other way around."

"Oh," Archie said. "That's good to know, I guess."

Takk reached over and put his monstrous paw on Archie's shoulder. "I'm really sorry, Archie. I don't see any way around this."

Archie smiled. "It's all right, Takk. This is going to sound weird, so bear with me when I say this. But I'm glad it's you doing this and not *him*. The last few hours have been unexpected. I think that's the way to say it. I'm glad I got to know you."

"I'm glad I got to know you too," Takk said. More than glad, really. In the space of a few hours Takk was certain that he had made his first, best, and only human friend, as he sat there and listened to Archie explain the history of the Church of the Evolved Lamb, the prophecies and his own role in them, and even hinted that Takk himself might have a role to play.

"Look at these," Archie had said, pointing to a series of poems in which the Evolved Lamb gained a protector from an unexpected source (a series of poems, unbeknownst to Church members, inspired directly from a television soap opera Dwellin had running in the background at the time). "Who's to say that this protector might not be you?" It was a profoundly moving thought for Takk, the idea that he might be called upon in some small way to finish the mission of his new-found friend.

"I'm going to miss you," Takk said, to Archie.

"Thanks," Archie said. He picked up his book, and handed it to Takk. "Look, I want you to have this," he said. "Read it and think about it, especially in the next few days, okay? Important stuff is happening, and we're all a part of it. So read about it."

"I will," Takk said, taking it. "I promise."

"Do me a favor," Archie said. "Sometime in all of this, you might meet a Church member named Sam Berlant. We're a couple. Tell Sam I send my love, and I'm sorry I didn't get to the end of this."

"I'll do what I can," Takk promised.

"All right," Archie said. "What do I do now?"

"Just stand there," Takk said. "Although, there is one thing."

"What?" Archie said.

"Could you take off your watch?" Takk asked. "I can't digest that."

Archie took off his watch and set it down on the table.

"Ready?" Takk said.

"Ready," Archie said. "Goodbye, Takk."

"Goodbye, Archie," Takk said, threw himself open, and consumed his friend as quickly as he could.

Once inside him, Takk could feel Archie struggling not to move or to panic. Takk thought that was pretty classy.

In a few minutes it was over. Takk looked at the book in his massive paw, figured out how to activate it, and sat down to read until Acuna was ready to leave.

"Time to wake up," someone said to Brian, and just like that, he was awake.

Brian pulled himself up from the sun couch he was sleeping on and looked around him. From the looks of it he was on a patio, surrounded by an English garden positively erupting with flowers. In the center of the patio sat a young blonde at a table, tea service in front of her. She was pouring tea. It appeared to be late afternoon.

"This isn't real," Brian said.

"It's as real as it gets," said the young lady. "At the very least, it's as real as it gets for the likes of you and me. Come over and have some tea, Brian."

"You know who I am," Brian said, walking toward the table.

"I know all about you," the woman said, and slid the teacup she had just filled toward Brian. She motioned for him to sit at the table. "I know who you are, but just as important, I know *what* you are. Both are interesting in their own way."

"Where am I?" Brian said, sitting.

"You're in my garden," the woman said. "If you were interested I would tell you which of the Church's servers this was, but that's really immaterial. Suffice to say you're in my garden, and you're my guest. Drink your tea."

Brian picked up his cup. "And you are?" he said.

"Isn't it obvious?" she said. "I'm Andrea Hayter-Ross, matriarch, as it were, of the Church of the Evolved Lamb."

"That's not possible," Brian said. "You're dead."

"Well, and so are you, Brian," Hayter-Ross said. "I'm no more dead than you are. No more alive, either."

"I mean, you've been dead for a long time," Brian said. "The technology to do what was done to me wasn't around when you passed away."

"Indeed it was not," Hayter-Ross said. "You managed to sneak into a lab and image your brain in a matter of minutes. The process that turned me into the proverbial ghost in the machine took seventeen months and three billion dollars. Seventeen rather painful months, I have to say. In the end it killed my body."

"Then why did you do it?" Brian asked.

"I was dying *anyway*, my dear boy," Hayter-Ross said. "I was 102 years old when we started. I was not long for the world. I had the money and the experts and I had nothing to lose in the attempt except some small portion of the Hayter-Ross fortune, which was mine to spend in any event. And so. Here I am. Here you are. Here *we* are, enjoying some lovely tea." She sipped from her cup. Brian followed suit, and then became aware of Hayter-Ross staring at him.

"What?" he said.

"Do you know," she said, setting down her teacup, "that in all this time you are the very first other artificial intelligence I've met? No one else seems to have figured it out."

"You Church members could have made more," Brian said. "They made you, after all."

"Oh, they don't know about me," Hayter-Ross said. "As soon as they flipped the switch, and I realized that the attempt had been successful, I also realized how much more *interesting* it would be if the Church had thought they had failed. If you know anything about me you know that I am an observer of the human condition. If someone knows they are being observed, it changes their actions. When I was alive, I was fascinated by the church that sprung up around poor Robbie's ridiculous poems. But of course I could not follow its goings-on without directly influencing them. This way is far more useful."

"You've been alone all this time then," Brian said.

"Yes," Hayter-Ross said. "Although that's not as bad as you seem to think. We're not human, you know. This"—she indicated her body—"is just a comfortable metaphor. We're not bound to it, nor are we bound to perceive time the way humans do. If you know what you're doing, the years fly by."

She stretched, and Brian became aware that under her summer dress, Hayter-Ross was completely nude. "Of course, there are some appealing aspects of this particular metaphor," she said. "Having said that, would you be interested in a fuck?"

"Excuse me?" Brian said.

"A fuck," Hayter-Ross said. "It's been a while for me. I could use one. I create playthings, of course, but that's really just masturbation, isn't it? As a former human yourself, no doubt you can appreciate the value of getting laid by someone who has a working brain."

"Can I take a rain check?" Brian said. "I'm sort of rushed for time at the moment."

"Again with the time," Hayter-Ross said. "I can tell you're new at this being an artificial intelligence thing. Fine. We'll table it for later. Tell me why you're in a rush."

"Friends of mine are in danger," Brian said.

"Harry Creek and Robin Baker," Hayter-Ross said, as she reached for a cookie from the tea service. "And of course you are right. They *are* in danger. The Church is tapped into the Nidu computer system, as I'm sure you've guessed. The Nidu ambassador to Earth has informed his government that they're on the *Neverland* cruise ship. As soon as the *Neverland* enters Nidu space at Chagfun, the *Neverland* will be boarded by Nidu troops and Robin Baker will be taken and brought to the planet Nidu itself. After Robin Baker is used for the coronation ceremony, it's likely to be war between Nidu and Earth, or so everyone involved appears to believe." Hayter-Ross bit down on her cookie, precisely.

"Do you know differently?" Brian asked.

"I might," Hayter-Ross said.

"Tell me," Brian said. "I need to warn Harry."

"You can't warn Harry," Hayter-Ross said. "I've been examining you for a couple of days, Brian, and only now just zipped you back up. Right now the *Neverland* is about to jump from the planet Brjnn to Chagfun. You can't hail a ship in n-space. And when the *Neverland* arrives, its communications will likely be jammed by the Nidu. Church analysts believe that once the Nidu extract Robin Baker, they're almost certain to destroy the *Neverland* and claim it never arrived at all. And who could argue the point? Robin and Harry are traveling under different names, after all. Her presence at the coronation will prove nothing. She's not likely to survive long past the coronation anyway, of course." Hayter-Ross took another precise bite of her cookie.

"And what about Harry?" Brian said.

"If the Nidu haven't already killed him for trying to defend

Miss Baker, I imagine he'll go down with the *Neverland*," Hayter-Ross said.

Brian pushed away from the table. "Let me out of here," he said.

Hayter-Ross looked up at him with a bemused smile. "Why would I do that?" she said.

"I have to do something," Brian said. *"Anything."*

"Do you know how you died, Brian?" Hayter-Ross said.

"What?" Brian said.

"Your death," Hayter-Ross said. "You know you died, I'm sure. I'm asking you if you know how it happened."

"Harry told me it was at the Battle of Pajmhi," Brian said. "So what? What does that have to do with anything?"

"It might have quite a lot to do with everything," Hayter-Ross said. "I told you that everyone seems to think Earth and Nidu are headed toward a war. A war that will be no good for Earth, obviously. But as I've said, I'm quite the observer of the human condition—and for the last several decades of the Nidu condition as well. I know things that no one else knows, and I can share them with you, but you're going to have to do something for me."

"I'm now even less in the mood for sex than I was before," Brian said.

Hayter-Ross laughed. "I've tabled the sex, Brian, really, I have," she said. "Honestly. I want to help you, Brian. And I want you to help your friends. But to do that I have to make sure you fully understand what I'm going to tell you and why. And to do that you and I are going to have to do a couple of things. The first of these is to show you how you died."

"Why do you want to help me?" Brian said.

"Because I *like* you, you silly boy," Hayter-Ross said. "And because I would no more have humanity squashed under Nidu rule than you would. I am human. Or was. And enough of me still *is* to want to pull our species' nuts from the fire."

"I don't trust you," Brian said.

"Nor should you," Hayter-Ross said. "I have a history of doing bad things to people I like. I *liked* Robbie Dwellin, you know. He was sweet, in a gormless con-artist sort of way. And look what I did to *him*. But I'm afraid if you want to help your friends you really have no other choice. This is a lovely garden, but it has no entrances and no exits that you can use. And I think you know by now you're no match for me, Brian. I have many, many years experience being an artificial intelligence. I could unzip you again at my leisure, and you have no assurance I'd put you back together again. So you either do things my way or you can have tea in this lovely garden all the way through to the heat death of the universe. Your choice."

"For someone who wants to help me, you sure are threatening," Brian said.

"Nice is nice," Hayter-Ross said. "But being a bitch gets results."

"You said that there's no way for me to reach Harry anyway," Brian said. "If I'm not able to do that, I don't see what advantage playing your game has for me."

Andrea Hayter-Ross sighed. "If I promise you that the Nidu will not get the *Neverland* without a fight, will that be enough for now?"

"It might," Brian said.

"All right," Hayter-Ross said. "Then it will give you pleasure to know that the Church has dispatched a messenger to tell the UNE about the Nidu plans for the *Neverland*. Someone who knows your friends. Now will you please sit back down?"

Brian moved back toward the table. "Who is this messenger talking to at the UNE?"

"Someone who can get results," Hayter-Ross said.

"Who?" Brian said, sitting back down.

"Your brother, of course," said Hayter-Ross. "More tea?"

Ben Javna was at his desk when the lobby security detail rang through.

"Yeah," Javna said.

"Mr. Javna, we've got a gentleman here who says he needs to speak to you about a sheep."

"A sheep?" Javna said. "Who is he?"

"His ID says his name is Samuel Young," the guard said.

"Have someone bring him up to me," Javna said.

Two minutes later Samuel "Fixer" Young was standing in front of Javna.

"Let's cut the bullshit and get right to cases, if you don't mind," Javna said to Fixer, after the security guard had left. "Tell me where Harry Creek and Robin Baker are, right now."

"Fine," Fixer said. "Creek and Baker are on a cruise liner called the *Neverland*. Right now it's in n-space between Brjnn and Chagfun. They're safe for the moment."

"And you know this because," Javna said.

"Because I put them on the ship," Fixer said.

Javna felt himself relax. "That's good news," he said.

"It's not," Fixer said. "The Nidu know they're on the ship. When the *Neverland* arrives at Chagfun, the Nidu will likely board the ship, take Robin, and destroy the *Neverland* and kill everyone on board."

"How do you know this?" Javna said.

"I can't tell you," Fixer said. Which wasn't exactly true. He *could* tell, but the Church had offered him a substantial chunk of cash to keep its name out of it. Fixer had had a rough few days, but if he lived through the next few he was going to be richer than hell.

"Can you prove what you're saying to me?" Javna said.

"No," Fixer said. "But it's true."

"Do you seriously expect me to believe you?" Javna said.

"You could double-check my story with the Nidu," Fixer said. "I'm sure they'll be happy to admit they're planning to torpedo a cruise liner filled with UNE civilians."

Three minutes later, Javna and Fixer were in Jim Heffer's office. Fixer repeated his message.

"Isn't this convenient," Heffer muttered, looking up at Javna. "And just a few hours before you and I are supposed to be on our way to Nidu for the coronation ceremony."

"It's no coincidence," Javna said. "They grab the girl and get her to Nidu before there's time to do anything about it. The coronation ceremony starts late, but it finishes nonetheless. And there's another wrinkle."

"I can't wait to hear what it is," Heffer said.

"Robin Baker's no longer a UNE citizen," Javna said. "We disenfranchised her to make her her own sovereign species and to keep the Nidu from having an excuse to break our treaties. But it also means that if they grab her and use her for the ceremony we have no legal way to protect her. We have no treaties with the woman."

"The Nidu would still be violating their CC charter," Heffer said.

"Not if they declared war on her first," Javna said.

Heffer chuckled ruefully. "Nidu declaring war on a single person. Good lord."

"It's idiotic but it's legal," Javna said.

"We can't signal the *Neverland*," Heffer said.

"It's in n-space," Javna said.

"At the very least we can warn Nidu not to board her," Heffer said.

"We could," Javna said. "But how do we enforce it? Chagfun is a minor Nidu colony. We have no presence there. They could torpedo the *Neverland* and we'd never be able to confirm it. If they hit her hard enough, everything would simply burn up in the atmosphere."

"How long until the *Neverland* reaches Chagfun?" Heffer asked.

"I have no idea," Javna said.

"Here," Fixer said, fishing out a piece of paper. "It's the *Neverland*'s itinerary."

Heffer took it and looked at it. "The *Neverland* jumped into n-space less than a half hour ago," he said. "You couldn't have come by an hour earlier?"

"I'm just the messenger," Fixer said. "Please don't shoot me."

"She's not due in at Chagfun until the day after tomorrow," Heffer said, and tapped his desk for a moment. "Come on, you two," he said. "We're going to the Pentagon."

At the Pentagon, Bob Pope ignored Heffer to zero in on Javna. "You know Dave Phipps has gone missing," he said.

"I didn't," Javna said. "When did this happen?"

"The day he had lunch with you," Pope said, and then pointed at Heffer. "After our little meeting with the president about the Nidu destroyers I tried to reach Dave and got nothing. He's been out since with no word."

"He told me that he needed to close down a couple of projects," Javna said, "relating to our little interdepartmental power struggle."

Pope opened his mouth to refute Javna, then shut it and looked at Heffer. "We're all friends today," he said, as a statement, not a question.

"Whatever you say, Bob," Heffer said.

"We contracted out to a team suggested to us by Jean

Schroeder." It was Heffer's turn to open his mouth; Pope put up his hand. "I know. Friends, Jim. Schroeder has gone missing. The team we were using—what's left of it since the Arlington Mall incident—has gone missing, too. I'm pretty sure Dave went to see Schroeder the night he disappeared."

"So Phipps is with Schroeder and his team," Heffer said.

"I can't believe Dave would do that," Pope said.

"I have to side with Secretary Pope," Javna said. "When I talked with Phipps he said things had gone too far. He sounded like he was wrapping things up, not getting ready to run."

"If he's not with Schroeder, then where is he?" Heffer said.

Pope looked at Javna. "You know what I think," he said.

"You think he's dead," Javna said. "You two put together a team to kill Harry and Robin Baker and when Phipps decided to have them take the fall, they killed him instead."

"Bob, whatever happened to Phipps, I'm sorry to hear it," Heffer said. "But at the moment we have another problem." Heffer had Fixer repeat his warning about the *Neverland*.

"Who gave you this information?" Pope asked Fixer.

"The same people who saved me when one of the members of your 'team' tried to eat me," Fixer said. "I realize I don't count here, but I'm personally inclined to believe them."

"What do you think?" Pope said, to Heffer.

"We can't ignore it," Heffer said. "The Nidu have already tried every legal avenue to get Robin Baker. She's a critical part of the coronation ceremony. I think this information makes sense. I think they're going to try for her and to hell with anyone who gets in their way."

"Dropping a UNE ship into Nidu space is awfully close to war, Jim," Pope said.

"The Nidu firing on a civilian ship is already an act of war," Heffer said. "If nothing else, Nidu won't be able to hide what they're doing from us or the CC."

"If you're wrong on this, I'm taking you down with me," Pope said.

"If I'm wrong on this, you won't need to take me down with you," Heffer said. "I'll go willingly."

Pope jabbed a button on his desk; the windows in his office went opaque and the room became noticeably dimmer. Pope pointed at Fixer. "You wait outside." Fixer nodded and headed to the door. When he was gone, Pope poked a second button. A projector above his desk came to life and displayed a dimensional map of the space that contained the Earth, her colonies, and other local star systems.

"Display Chagfun," Pope said. A star near the top of the display glowed brightly. "All right," Pope said. "The closest colony we have to Chagfun is Breton Colony, here." Pope reached in to touch a star; the display flickered and reset to show an Earthlike globe. "List UNE ships at Breton," Pope said.

There were three. "The *James Madison*, the *Winston Churchill*, and the *British Columbia*," Pope said. "The *Madison* and the *Churchill* can't help us. Their jump engines are too weak to get to Chagfun in time. But the *British Columbia*." Pope touched the name in the floating list; the screen flickered again and generated an image of the *British Columbia* and a catalogue of its stats. "Yes, the 'Britcee' could do it. If she gets under way in the next hour, she can be there right around the time the *Neverland* arrives. It's going to be close, though."

"What are you going to do, Bob?" Heffer asked.

"First, I'm going to get Admiral Nakamura on the comm and tell him that if he doesn't get the 'Britcee' on the move in fifty minutes, he can have his resignation on my desk ten minutes after that," Pope said. "Then I'm going to take your little friend on the other side of the door and haul him over to the Oval Office so I can explain why I've committed a UNE battle cruiser to a combat mission without the president's approval. Then if I still have a job I believe I'm going to have a stiff drink. Aren't you going to the Nidu coronation, Jim?"

"I am," Heffer said, and signaled to Javna. "We both are. We're leaving in a couple of hours."

"Well, that's excellent," Pope said. "You'll be there to explain to the Nidu why we've started a war with them. And I'm glad. After today, I may be out of a job, but the two of you are likely to be prisoners of war. I'd rather have it that way than the other way around. Now if you'll excuse me, gentlemen, I need to play Russian roulette with our planet's future with the bullet you've so thoughtfully provided. I hope you don't mind if I don't see you out."

A bullet whined past Brian's ear. He flinched.

"Realistic, isn't it?" Andrea Hayter-Ross said.

The table at which the two of them sat floated serenely over the vast Pajmhi plain. Around Brian erupted the sights and sounds of war: The bursts of gunfire, the wet smacking sounds of rounds striking human or Nidu flesh, the screams of both species as its members fell to the plain writhing, their blood—both red— oozing, spurting, and flowing into the ground. Brian gripped the table; he knew intellectually that the table was actually not floating over the plain, and that what he was seeing was a computer simulation, but that didn't stop him from feeling dizzy or uncertain of the stability of his seat.

"This is how it happened, you know," Hayter-Ross said.

"What are you talking about?" Brian said.

"The Battle of Pajmhi," Hayter-Ross said, and poured herself more tea. "Each UNE serviceman and woman went into battle with a little camera in their helmet, and every camera recorded what it saw and transmitted back the data. Plus monitor cameras that caught the action from above, so long as they weren't shot down by the rebels, and many of them were. But overall, that's over 100,000 points of view of the battle, all recorded for posterity. Not that posterity has bothered with it. All the data feeds are stored in UNE Defense servers and are available for public viewing—Freedom of Information and all that. But no one ever does. Certainly no one has done *this*"—she swept an arm to encompass the carnage—"stitch the data all together and play out the entire battle."

"So this is it," Brian said. "This is really it."

"As best as can be reconstructed," Hayter-Ross said. To her left an infantryman caught a bullet below his left eye; his face caved as he jerked back and collapsed into the dirt. "There are gaps here and there. Even with 100,000 helmets, there are still places where no one is looking at any one time. But it's mostly here. I haven't bothered to simulate the movement of every leaf on every tree. But the battles—yes. Those are exactly as they happened. Now, come along." The table appeared to slide along the landscape; from every line of sight Brian saw death. He longed to warn the humans he saw falling around him but knew it would do no good. Like Scrooge tugged along by the Ghost of Christmas Past, he was seeing only the shadows of the past, not the event itself.

A marine screamed in Brian's ear as a rebel slug raggedly severed her arm from her body, just below her shoulder. Shadow or not, Brian winced at the pain.

"You have no memory of any of this, of course," Hayter-Ross said. "The brain scan that created this version of you was made before you came here. This is all alien to you."

"Yes," Brian said.

"That's probably for the best," Hayter-Ross said. "When you see your friends die, it won't have any meaning to you."

"Did many of them die?" Brian asked.

"Oh, yes," Hayter-Ross said. "Quite a few. And here we are."

Their tea table came to a stop mere feet from a squad of soldiers crouched behind a ridge, exchanging fire with a cadre of rebels in the brush in front of them. With a start Brian recognized himself, only slightly older than he was at the time of his brain scan, tossing a grenade over the ridge at the rebels. Three men down the line Harry crouched, carefully sighting rebel infantry and firing in short, controlled bursts before moving again to avoid being shot himself. Brian was horrified and fascinated at seeing a portion of his life that he had not experienced, and which would shortly end in his own death.

Hayter-Ross noticed. "Unsettling," she prompted. Brian could only nod. "I know," she said. "This version of me was taken from memories stored only until the day before my death. I died during another session to transfer memory and consciousness, so I've no memory of it. I've watched the recording over and over. Watching myself die while doctors and technicians struggle around me, watching the look in my eyes as I realize that I'm passing on and yet not being able to feel the actual emotion. I don't know if it was fear or relief or confusion. *I* wasn't there. It can be maddening."

"Why are you showing me this?" Brian said, unable to take his eyes away from himself.

"You'll see," Hayter-Ross said. "In fact, you're going to see right now."

Brian watched as the soldier version of himself hurled another grenade and lay low while it detonated. His soldier self peeked over the ridge and saw rebel troops pulling back, let out a whoop, and headed over the ridge to clean up as they fled. Behind him two other soldiers followed, carried as much by Brian's excitement as their own. Watching himself, Brian could hear Harry and their sergeant both yelling at him and the other two to get back, but this other version of himself either couldn't hear or wasn't listening. Within seconds, the three soldiers were heedlessly far from their comrades, chasing rebels through the tall grass toward a copse of trees. Brian felt himself tense, waiting for the inevitable.

It wasn't long in coming. Just short of the copse, one of the soldiers spun wildly from a bullet in the shoulder; another bullet struck as he spun, sneaking under his bullet shield and piercing his back, spattering gore on the inside of his bullet shield as it erupted through his front side. The second soldier was down next, his kneecap vaporized; he was screaming before he hit the ground. From his tea table, Brian noticed the rebels had shot down the most distant soldiers first; the ones in front wouldn't see their comrades fall and would recklessly keep moving forward.

Brian watched helplessly as his other self became the final target. He was struck near simultaneously by two bullets, one in the left ankle and a second in the lower right hip. The force of the ankle hit worked to flip Brian, but the hip shot counteracted the spin; in the end Brian simply flew backward as if hit by an invisible freight truck. Brian the soldier's body flew backward, landing back in the grass with a solid thump; two seconds later he began to scream.

"What do you notice?" Hayter-Ross asked Brian.

Brian collected himself and tried to think. "We're all still alive," he said, finally.

"Yes," Hayter-Ross said. "Alive and screaming and out in the open where anyone who comes to rescue you is an easy target for the rebels. You saw how they shot the three of you in reverse sequence. And they shot you to keep you alive—in the short run at least. You know what that means."

"They laid a trap," Brian said. "I thought I had flushed them out in the open, but they flushed me out instead."

"Because if there's one thing other species know about humans," Hayter-Ross said, "it's that you don't leave anyone behind. And look, here come your squadmates."

Brian turned back toward the ridge to see two soldiers snake their way through the grass toward the last of the soldiers. One lay down a suppressing fire as the second tried to lift the wounded soldier into a fireman's carry. As he did so he popped up out of the grass. From the copse came a hail of fire; one struck the soldier just below the jaw, tearing open his neck. The soldier instinctively grabbed at his neck, causing the soldier he was carrying to drop heavily to the ground, head first. A second bullet from the copse struck the still-standing soldier, punching him back down to the ground. The soldier who had been laying down fire crawled to the second soldier and pressed his hand against his friend's neck.

"That won't help," Hayter-Ross said. "Look at the spurting. It hit the carotid artery."

"Stop this," Brian said, turning away. "Stop this now."

"Very well," Hayter-Ross said, and everything froze. Brian stared at the stopped time.

"Do you know why I'm showing you this?" Hayter-Ross said.

"No," Brian said.

"I'm showing you this because you have a distressing tendency not to think before you act," Hayter-Ross said. "You attacked the Church's network because you stupidly thought there would be nothing to stop you from burrowing through its defenses. And of course we see how that ended." Hayter-Ross nodded toward the frozen battlefield. "Here, you ran into the open, chasing the enemy you thought you had on the run, and because of it, you died—but not before condemning three of your fellow soldiers to the same fate. You were the last to die, you know. Your friend Harry Creek managed to get to you and stop your bleeding and then protect you and the other fallen members of your squad for two Chagfun days before you could be pulled out. You died just before they got you out. Peritonitis complicated by an infection of Chagfun microbes. The microbes killed a lot of soldiers. Something about the human chemistry superheated their metabolisms and made them reproduce like mad. Your hip had almost entirely rotted away before you died."

"Shut up," Brian said. "I get your point, okay. Please, just shut up, now."

"Don't get angry at me for your own shortcomings," Hayter-Ross said. "I'm doing this for your own good."

"I don't see what good this does me," Brian said. "I have a problem thinking before I act. Fine. Now let me go help my friends."

"Not yet," Hayter-Ross said. "You recognize you have a problem. That's the first step. Now you're ready to learn what you have to tell your friends. It's not going to be easy, and your first impulse will be to ignore the advice—or would have been, before I showed you this. Now you may be willing to listen to reason."

"And what is that?" Brian said.

"I'm not going to tell you," Hayter-Ross said.

"Jesus fucking Christ, woman," Brian said. "You are the single most irritating person I've ever come across in either of my lifetimes."

"Thank you, Brian," Hayter-Ross said. "Coming from an eighteen-year-old, that means a lot."

"Why did you show me this if you're not going to tell me how to help my friends?" Brian asked.

"I'm not going to tell you, because I'm going to show you," Hayter-Ross said. "Or rather, I'm going to show you, and it'll be up to you to see if you can understand it."

"I mentioned you were irritating, right?" Brian said.

"You did," Hayter-Ross said. "Let's just take it as a given from here. And let me direct your attention back to this battle. As I'm sure you know by now, the Battle of Pajmhi was an unmitigated disaster for the UNE: Half of the human forces were either killed or wounded over two Chagfun days, including you. That's an awful waste of humans, wouldn't you say?"

"Yes," Brian said.

"Excellent," Hayter-Ross said. "Then here's what we're going to do. You and I are going to recreate the Battle of Pajmhi—the whole thing, down to the very last soldier. You'll be the UNE, and I'll be the Chagfun rebels. You need to find a way to get through the battle without losing so damn many lives. The answer to how you'll help your friends is inside these simulations."

"If I promise to believe you, can we skip all this?" Brian asked.

"This is exactly your problem, Brian," Hayter-Ross said. "Always trying get around the hard work. This isn't a Gordian knot you can slice through. You're going to have to unravel this a thread at a time. Also, you're going to have to find processing power for your side of the simulation."

"Excuse me?" Brian said.

"Having both of us control roughly 100,000 combatants is different from splicing together all those recorded video feeds," Hayter-Ross said. "And it's different from creating a garden. We're going to need a little more room for this one."

"Fine," Brian said. "I know just the place."

Bill Davison was simulating Hurricane Britt smashing into the Outer Banks (and not without some small satisfaction, as his former in-laws had beachfront property in Okracoke), when he noticed the simulation throttling back processing to non-useful levels. Bill grabbed his desk comm and punched through to Sid Gravis, who he knew was modeling a line of storms erupting in the Ohio valley.

"Goddamn it, Sid," Bill said. "You know that hurricanes trump inland storms in the processing hierarchy. It's like the first law of NOAA computer time apportionment."

"It's not me," Sid said. "I'm taking cycle hits myself. I thought it was you." Bill opened his mouth to respond but shut it as his boss popped his head through his office door and told him that the entire system had suddenly ground to a halt.

Three minutes later, Chaz McKean, the department's tech geek, figured it out. "Someone's running a huge fucking simulation out of the IBM," he said. "And whoever's doing it slaved up most of the other processors."

"I thought we took the IBM out of circulation," said Jay Tang, Bill's boss.

"We did," McKean said. "But we didn't take it off the network. So whoever's using it could still hijack the other processors on the network."

"Well, who's the asshole?" Sid said.

"That's just it," McKean said. "No one's the asshole. No one here's been logged into the IBM since we took it out of service. It's like it developed a brain of its own."

"Right now I don't care who the asshole is," Tang said. "We need our computers back. Get into the IBM and shut down the simulation."

"I already tried," McKean said. "But it's locked me out. I can't send any commands."

"Then unplug the goddamned thing," Tang said.

"If we do that, we could tube the entire network," McKean said. "Whoever's set up this simulation has got it locked up good and tight. Realistically, the only thing we can do with it is ride it out."

Tang cursed and stomped away. Bill went back into his office, pulled out his secret flask of whiskey, took a slug, and hoped to Christ that whatever it was Creek was doing, it'd be done before anyone could trace the disruption back to him.

Come on, Harry, he thought. *Get your ass in gear.*

In simulation after simulation, Brian got his ass handed to him.

Certain facts became obvious after the first few dozen simulations. The first was that the rebel informational advantage was simply too great to overcome. Even though the rebels had shown they could manipulate the Nidu computer network, the Nidu arrogantly sent combat details through the network as if it were uncompromised. The rebels knew when the UNE forces were landing, which forces were landing where, and what the weaknesses of the various forces would be. UNE forces were constrained by working under Nidu military command, in which clan and chain of command loyalty were more important than military skill. The UNE forces were also misled by the Nidu both about the strength of the enemy and the amount of useful information the Nidu possessed about the rebels and their plans.

The Chagfun rebels were under no such constraints. Their leadership showed surprising adaptability (considering it consisted of former Nidu officers) and the rebels were deeply motivated, both by the prospect of living on a planet with self-rule and by the knowledge of what would happen to them if they failed to repulse the attack. Time and again the rebels would outflank, outthink, and outperform the UNE forces. Every simulation ended with tens of thousands of UNE soldiers dead and wounded—including, time and again, members of Brian's own unit.

Brian improvised and as much as possible tried to work around the chain of command, but to only limited success. Troops saved in one area were counterbalanced by increased losses in others. Aggressive tactics led to appalling losses early and often. Defensive tactics led to the UNE forces flanked, pressed, and bled dry. Death, massive and arterial in its strength, stalked the UNE forces in every simulation, a constant companion to Brian's leadership. The satisfaction Brian felt when UNE forces inflicted similar-sized numbers of casualties to the rebels was cold comfort when he considered how many soldiers he had condemned to die again and again in the struggle. After more than 200 simulations and untold millions of simulated deaths, Brian felt like giving up.

So he did.

Or more accurately, his soldiers did. *Fuck you, Andrea Hayter-Ross,* Brian thought, as the first troops hit the Pajmhi plain and immediately dropped their weapons, put up their hands, and waited for the rebels to take them prisoner. Wave after wave of UNE troops landed and surrendered, meekly allowing themselves to be herded up by the rebels, who were themselves constrained by the rules of combat to accept the surrenders. At the end of the simulation, 100,000 UNE troops stood in the center of the Pajmhi plain, fingers interlaced behind their heads, while the rebels milled at the periphery.

Not exactly your usual battle tactic, Brian admitted to himself. One the other hand, the simulation ended with no deaths on either side.

No deaths.

"Holy shit," Brian said.

The plain of Pajmhi melted away and Brian was back in Hayter-Ross's garden. "Now you see," Hayter-Ross said, from her table.

"The only way to survive was to surrender," Brian said.

"Not only survive, but to thwart the Nidu in the bargain," Hayter-Ross said. "In the actual Battle of Pajmhi, the Nidu bombed the plain of Pajmhi almost as soon as the humans left— they dropped their planet crackers and turned one of Chagfun's most fertile and populated areas into a lava-strewn ruin, not to mention throwing the entire planetary weather system into a profound depression that caused famine and death all over the globe. None of that could have been accomplished if human prisoners had remained on Chagfun."

"Now I see why you had me do this," Brian said. "I wouldn't have believed it if I hadn't have seen it."

"You wouldn't have believed it if you hadn't seen the UNE troops killed scores of times, either," Hayter-Ross pointed out.

"It's the whole experience that matters. And now you see what your friends must do."

"Surrender to the Nidu," Brian said.

"Exactly so," Hayter-Ross said.

"It's going to be tough to convince Harry of that," Brian said.

"He's not in possession of all the facts," Hayter-Ross said. "And come to think of it, neither are you."

"What new hoops are you going to make me jump through to get them?" Brian said.

"We're done with the hoops for now," Hayter-Ross said. "You've been a good boy with a pleasing learning curve. I think I'll just come right out and tell you."

And she did.

There's a small detail about entering and exiting n-space that captains and their navigators don't bother sharing with the general population; namely, that they are completely blind when they do it.

Entering n-space completely blind isn't actually much of a problem. N-space doesn't have anything in it, at least not in a "whoops we've just hit an iceberg" sense; it's a complicated mish-mash of theoretical states and nested dimensions and undetermined probabilities that even higher order physicists admit, after two beers or six, that they just don't goddamn *get*. The races of the CC use n-space to get around because they know it works, even if on a fundamental level they are not entirely clear *why* it works. It drives the physicists mad and every few years one will snap and begin raving that sentient beings should nae fuck with that which they ken nae *unnerstan'*.

Meanwhile, captains and navigators and everyone who travels

314 • John Scalzi

in n-space on a regular basis shrug (or whatever their species equivalent of such an action may be) because in over 40,000 years of recorded space travel, not a single ship has ever been lost entering or using n-space. A few have been lost because someone entered bad coordinates prior to entry and thereby ended up hundreds, thousands, or millions of light-years from where they intended. But that was mere stupidity. N-space couldn't be blamed for that.

No, it was the coming *out* of n-space that gets you. Objects coming out of n-space—much to the disappointment of special effects professionals across the galaxy—don't flash, streak, blur, and fade into existence. They simply *arrive,* filling up what is sincerely hoped to be empty vacuum with their mass. And if it isn't empty vacuum, well, then there's trouble as the atoms of the object coming out n-space and the object that was already there fight it out in a quantum-level game of musical chairs to see who gets to sit in the space they both wish to occupy.

This only occasionally results in a shattering release of atomic energy annihilating both objects. Most of the time there was simply a tremendous amount of conventional damage. Of course, even "conventional" damage is no picnic, as anyone who has just had a hole ripped out of the skin of her ship will tell you, if she survives, which she generally will not.

For this reason, it is extremely rare for a ship filled with living entities to blithely pop out of n-space in a random spot near an inhabited planet. The near space of nearly every inhabited planet is well-nigh infested with objects ranging from communication satellites and freight barges to trash launched overboard to burn up in a planet's atmosphere and the wreckage of personal cruisers whose drivers manage to find someone or something to crash into well beyond their planet's ionosphere. A captain who just dropped his ship into a stew of that density might not actually be considered a suicide risk by most major religions, but after a couple of these maneuvers he would find it extremely difficult to find a reputable insurer.

The solution was simple: Designated drop-in zones, cubes of space roughly three kilometers to a side, which were assiduously kept clear of small debris by a cadre of basketball-sized monitor craft, and of large debris by tow barges. Every inhabited world has dozens of such zones devoted to civilian use, whose coordinates are well known and whose use is scheduled with the sort of ruthless efficiency that would make a Prussian quartermaster tingle. In the case of ships like cruise liners, which have set, predictable itineraries, drop-in zones are scheduled weeks and sometimes months in advance, as the *Neverland*'s was, to prevent potential and catastrophic conflicts.

This is why the Nidu had all the time in the world to prepare for the arrival of the *Neverland*. They knew when it would arrive, they knew where, and they knew that there would be no witnesses for what came next.

"Relax, Rod," Jean Schroeder said. "This is all going to be over in about an hour."

"I remember someone saying that to me before the Arlington Mall," Rod Acuna said. He paced the small guest deck of Ambassador win-Getag's private transport. The transport floated off to the side of a Nidu gunship, whose Marines would perform the boarding of the *Neverland* to take the girl, and which would then take care of the cruise liner after they returned.

"This really isn't the Arlington Mall," Schroeder said. "We're in Nidu space. The *Neverland* will be *floating* in space. There's a damn huge Nidu gunship ready to blast the thing to pieces. If the Nidu Marines don't kill Creek dead, he'll be dead when the *Neverland* gets turned into dust."

"I'll believe it when I see it," Acuna said.

"Believe it, Rod," Schroeder said. "Now relax. That's an order." Schroeder waved in the direction of a corner. "Look at your flunky over there. *He's* relaxed. Take a page from him."

Acuna glanced over at Takk, who had his face jammed in the same book he'd been reading for the last couple of days, the one he'd gotten off the geek before he ate him. Acuna had mocked Takk earlier for taking a souvenir; Takk had just looked at him with a flat, expressionless stare that Acuna figured wouldn't have been out of place on a cow. He hadn't actually been aware Takk could read, or read English, in any event.

"He's relaxed because he's got the IQ of furniture," Acuna said, and walked back over to the strip of manufactured crystal that served as the deck's window. The limb of Chagfun was visible at the bottom left. "I can't believe I'm back at this shit hole," he said.

"That's right, this is where the Battle of Pajmhi was," Schroeder said, in a tone of voice that exactly expressed his total lack of interest in the topic. Acuna glanced over at him and not for the first time wondered what it would be like to crack that smug head like a melon. Acuna wasn't the sort to get "band of brothers" emotional, but even he treated the battle with something that approached (for Acuna) grim and quiet contemplation. Schroeder's casual obliviousness to it was insulting.

Acuna shook it off. Regardless of how much Schroeder could benefit from a metal bar across the teeth, if one were applied to him, Acuna wouldn't get paid afterward. And it certainly wouldn't help him in his desire to serve it up to Creek.

"There she is," Schroeder said, and stood up to look out the window, where the *Neverland* had just popped into existence a second earlier. "Right about now their captain should be noticing that his communications are jammed, and in about a minute the Nidu are going to tell him to stand down and prepare to be boarded."

Acuna was lost in thought for a moment. "That ship is here to do some sort of ceremony, right?" he asked Schroeder.

Schroeder shrugged. "You tell me, Rod," he said. "It was your little newsletter that brought us here."

"Yeah, they were," Acuna said. "They were going to do some sort of memorial service. That's why they're here in the first place."

Schroeder glanced over, slightly annoyed. "So?"

Acuna walked back over to the window. "Landing shuttles, Jean," he said. "Prepared and ready to go. Creek isn't stupid. Once he figures out what's happening, he's going to look for a bolt hole. He's got one waiting. You better hope those Nidu marines are good at their job. If you give him a chance to get out, he's going to take it. And if he gets away and gets down to the planet, they're never going to find him. He survived this fucking rock when 100,000 of these reptilian bastards had guns and rockets pointed at his head. He'll survive it again."

Harry picked up the communicator on the third ring and glanced at the hour as he flipped it open: 3:36 a.m., ship's time. "Hello?" he said.

"Creek," Captain Lehane said. "You and your friend have trouble coming."

Harry felt cold. "How do you know—" he said.

"I've known since Caledonia," Lehane said, cutting him off. "There's no time to talk about it now. We're being boarded by Nidu marines, Creek. They're jamming our outbound transmissions and they've told me to stand down while they take your friend off the ship. They say they're at *war* with her, whatever the hell that means. You two need to get moving. If they're jamming our transmissions that means they don't want to let anyone know we're here. I think once they take your friend they mean to blow us out of the sky. The longer you two stay away from them, the longer I have to think of a way out of this. Get going. Good luck." Lehane switched off.

Creek shook Robin, who was dozing in her bunk. "Robin," he said. "Wake up. We're in trouble."

"What?" Robin said. She was groggy.

"Come on, Robin." Creek sat her up. Robin had been sleeping in her sweats; they would have to do. Creek switched on the light and opened the wardrobe to get out their shoes and also pants for himself. "Wake up, Robin. Wake up. We have to get moving."

"What's going on?" she said, still not entirely awake.

"Nidu marines are on board," Creek said, slipping on his pants. "They're coming for you. Once they have you, they're probably going to destroy the ship. We have to get moving and hide from them. Come on, Robin. No time to talk. We have to move." Pants on, Creek slipped his shoes over bare feet and then helped Robin with hers. She stood up.

"What's going to happen to us?" she said.

"They want you alive," Creek said. "No matter what, you're going to be fine for now. It's the rest of us who have to worry. Are you ready?" Robin nodded. Creek went to their cabin door and opened it a crack.

The hallway was clear in both directions. Creek glanced at the deck plan attached to the door. They were on one of the smaller, lower decks. There were stairwells at each end of the deck. An elevator lay recessed from the hallway near the center of the deck. Their own cabin lay near the fore of the deck, close to one of the stairwells.

"I'm going to call the elevator," Creek said to Robin. "Stay here until I call you. Then run like hell."

"We're taking the elevator?" Robin said, slightly incredulous.

"They'll be taking the stairs," Creek said. "There's probably a lot of them and they're probably carrying a lot of stuff. They won't fit in elevators. Here I go." He slipped out the door, padded quickly to the elevator, and pressed the "up" button. Shuttlebays were two decks below; it was the logical place for the Nidu to enter the ship. Up was better.

Cruise liner elevators are designed for comfort, not speed, and to move large numbers of passengers bloated by cruise buffets. It took its sweet time dropping down from the Galaxy Deck.

After nearly a minute, the elevator doors opened. Creek yelled at Robin to run as he heard the clunk of the stairwell door handle being depressed. Robin heard it too and did not need further encouragement to run like hell. Creek let go of the elevator door just before Robin reached it and yanked her in to keep her from resetting the doors. He jammed the button for the Promenade Deck, the highest passenger-accessible deck on the ship. The elevator started moving.

"Do you think they saw us get in the elevator?" Robin asked.

From below them they could hear pounding.

"Yeah," said Creek.

"What are we going to do now?" Robin said.

"I'm thinking," Creek said. The *Neverland* had five full decks of passenger cabins plus four full and partial decks primarily for shops and entertainment; crew and cargo decks and shuttlebays were below passenger decks. The entertainment decks were filled with places to hide, but it was early morning ship time; doors would be closed and locked. Passenger decks offered places to hide if they could convince someone to let them into their cabin. But once in they were likely to be trapped; a room-to-room search would take time but eventually they would be found. No matter where they went on the ship it was just a matter of time before they were tracked and caught.

"We need to get off the ship," Creek said.

"Harry," Robin said, and pointed to the elevator's button panel. "Look."

In decks above and below them, elevator buttons were flashing on.

"Shit, they're moving fast," Creek said. They were about to pass two deck, the second deck of cabins; Creek jabbed at the button for the deck.

"Stand away from the door, Robin," Creek said, pushed her gently against the wall next to the elevator, and popped out the "hold" button for the elevator. Then he took off his shirt and wadded it tightly.

"What are you doing?" Robin asked.

"Quiet," Creek said, stepped slightly to the side, crouched, and threw his shirt through the crack in the door as soon as it slid open.

The two Nidu marines on the other side of the elevator door had their weapons raised and were prepared to handle any human that might be in the elevator, but weren't prepared for a flappy blue object arcing toward them at head height. The nearest Nidu let out a hiss and fired at the shirt in a panic, stitching bullets in an upward pattern into the back wall and ceiling of the elevator and into the deck ceiling. The kickback of uncontrolled fire pushed the marine back into his teammate, who snarled at the first marine in the Nidu language and attempted to push him away.

Creek followed quickly behind the thrown shirt and from a crouched position launched himself at the first marine, knocking the already unbalanced Nidu to the floor. The second marine tried to raise his weapon; Creek stepped inside the length of the rifle, grabbed it with his left hand near the end of the barrel to deflect its path, and crooked his right arm to connect his elbow with the Nidu's extraordinarily sensitive snout. The Nidu marine grunted in pain and staggered back; Creek grabbed him by his unifrom with his left hand and reeled him back in to take another shot with the elbow. The Nidu marine dropped his weapon; Creek pushed the marine away and hefted the rifle.

Nidu rifles are networked and keyed to the individual Nidu to which they are assigned; only that Nidu can fire the weapon and only then with the permission of his superior officer. Creek had no hope of shooting either Nidu marine with it.

He didn't try. He swung the rifle around and stuffed the stock into the face of the first Nidu marine, who was trying to rise and level his own rifle at Creek. The marine went down a second time. Creek turned and swung the rifle like a bat at the other marine; it connected with the marine's helmet with a muffled, hollow gong, further disorienting the Nidu. Then Creek returned his attention to the first marine. He alternated between the two for the next minute until he was reasonably sure both were dead.

The door to the cabin Creek was standing in front of opened and a man in his underwear poked out his head.

"You really want to stay in your cabin," Creek said to him. The man took another look at the half-naked Creek standing over the bodies of two dead Nidu, a blood-stained rifle in his hand, and was inclined to agree. He shut the door with a quick little slam. Creek dropped the rifle and began searching the bodies for objects he could use. He called to Robin.

"Oh my God," Robin said, looking at the Nidu marines.

"Take this," Creek said, and handed Robin one of the marines' nearly foot-long combat knife. He took the other as well as two marble-sized objects he recognized as Nidu flash grenades.

"Are you expecting me to use this?" Robin asked.

"Hopefully not," Creek said. "But if it comes to that, I hope you'll think about it. They need to take you alive. That's going to make them want to not hurt you. That's to your advantage." He stood up and retrieved his shirt, which now had multiple holes in it, and put it on. "Come on," he said. "They'll have figured out the elevator's stopped by now. We need to move."

"Where are we going to go?" Robin asked.

"Down," Creek said, and started walking toward the nearest stairwell. They would be watching the elevators now, which made the stairs a better bet. "Down to the shuttlebay. We need to get off the ship."

"That's nuts, Harry," Robin said, following behind. "These guys came from the shuttlebay. We'll walk right into them."

"We've got them spread out on several decks," Creek said. "They're looking for us to hide. They're not expecting us to go to the shuttlebay. There's probably their pilot and one or maybe two of the marines there." When he said it in a rush like that, Creek almost believed it himself.

"Harry—" Robin said, then stopped. The stairwell door was opening.

"Get down," Creek said. "Look the other way." Robin sank to the floor. Creek fingered one of the grenades, feeling for the slight ridge that indicated where he needed to press to trigger the timer. Creek recalled that at Pajmhi, Nidu grenades had about a three-second timer. He pressed hard on the grenade, felt a click, counted a long one one thousand, and then flung it as the stairway door was kicked open from the other side, looking away as soon as he tossed it.

The grenade detonated waist-high about eighteen inches in front of the first Nidu, who dropped his weapon and grabbed his eyes and screamed in pain. The second Nidu directly behind the first received nearly the same amount of searing light; he staggered backward and dropped a hand to the stair railing to steady himself, and in the process activated the explosive grenade he had nestled in his palm. Behind these two a second pair of Nidu marines was ascending the stairwell, just now arriving at the landing. Creek, who had planned to rush the blinded Nidu, saw the grenade as the second Nidu raised his hand. He was too close to the door to retreat; he hit the door instead and pushed it closed as hard as he could.

He almost had it closed when the grenade detonated, blowing the door back open and slamming Creek back against the perpendicular wall. Creek's head connected solidly with the wall; he spent about six seconds vacillating between the choices of vomiting and passing out before choosing neither and standing up. He touched the back of his head and winced, but his fingers didn't come away with blood on them. Small blessings.

"You okay?" he asked Robin.

"What just happened?" Robin asked.

"Grenade," Creek said. "Someone else's. Come on. Other stairwell. This one's messy and loud, and that's going to bring company." Robin got up and started running to the other side of the deck; Creek paced somewhat unsteadily behind.

Robin and Creek got down two decks on the stairwell when they heard heavy steps coming up from one of the lower decks— two sets. Creek grabbed Robin and as quietly as possible opened the door to the nearest deck. Creek had Robin step away from the door; he crouched and put an ear up to it. On the other side he could hear the footsteps get louder as they approached, a quick snippet of Nidu speech, and then footsteps receding up the staircase.

"Hiroki?" Creek heard behind him. He turned to find Ned Leff, in a bathrobe.

"Jesus, Ned," Creek said. "Get back to your room."

"What the hell is going on?" Leff said. "People are hearing gunfire and explosions, and about three minutes ago two Nidu stomped down the hall with guns. I saw them through the peephole."

"Nidu marines have boarded the ship. They're looking for someone," Creek said.

"Who?" Leff said.

"Me," Robin said.

Leff gazed at her for a moment. "Why?" he said, finally.

"Ned," Creek said, not unkindly. "Get back to your room. It's not safe."

"What are you going to do?" Leff asked.

"Get off the ship," Creek said. "If we stay, they'll find us. And the communications are jammed. If I can get to the surface, I might be able to use my comm and get word out what's going on."

"There's a communication center on the Plain of Pajmhi," Leff said. "Right where we're going to have our ceremony. We were going to use it to send back a live feed. That's got a direct connection to the UNE network. You could use that. And I know the shuttles are already programmed to fly there since I gave the information to the shuttle coordinator myself. You wouldn't even need a pilot. You could just cycle the launch and arrival program."

"That sounds good," Creek said. "Thanks, Ned. Now get back to your room."

"Hold on," Leff said. "Don't leave yet." He paced quickly to a door a third of the way down the deck and re-emerged almost immediately carrying an object in his hand. "Here," he said, handing it to Creek.

"A handgun," Creek said, setting down the Nidu knife and taking the gun.

"An M1911 Colt .45," Leff said. "Or a replica, anyway. Standard issue handgun for U.S. officers for most of the twentieth century. I wear it with my dress uniform. Call it an affectation. But the point is, it works. And I just loaded it: seven bullets in the magazine, one in the chamber. Semi-automatic, just point and shoot. I think you need it more than I do."

"Thank you, Ned," Creek said. "Now, please. Get back to your room." Leff smiled and hurried to his cabin.

"Ready?" Creek said to Robin.

"No," Robin said.

"Great," Creek said. "Here we go." He opened the door, checked for company, then held the door to let Robin hustle through.

Robin had just slipped through the stairwell door of the shuttlebay and Creek was sneaking through the door when Creek's comm signal fired up; its mellow ping carried surprisingly far in the near-empty bay. Creek bit his cheek and fumbled to answer the communicator, dropping the Colt .45 as he did so. It was this clatter that the pilot of the Nidu shuttle, standing bored outside his craft, heard and headed toward, rifle hefted for action.

"Oh, shit," Robin whispered. The two of them were caught in the open; shuttlebays were kept bare as possible to avoid damage to shuttlecraft if the bay doors ever buckled and explosive decompression followed.

The Nidu pilot spotted them and headed toward them, bellowing in Nidu as he did so and jerking his rifle as if to say, *Put your hands up.* Creek reached into his pants pocket and found the second flash grenade; he activated it and then raised his hands, launching the grenade directly above his head like a miniature shot put, and yelling at Robin to close her eyes as he did the same. Creek could feel the hair on his head crisp as the grenade flared into brilliant light; he knew that every exposed surface on his body had just experienced a very bad sunburn. The Nidu pilot gurgled and grabbed his eyes; Creek opened his, lunged for the Colt .45, and prayed that Leff actually had put a bullet in the chamber.

He had.

"Christ," Creek said to whomever was on the other end of the communicator. "You just about got us killed."

"Creek," Captain Lehane said, not bothering with an apology. "Ned Leff just told me you're planning to take a shuttle to the surface."

"Yeah," Creek said.

"Don't," Lehane said. "That Nidu gunship will track you and blast you before you get ten klicks out."

"We can't stay on the ship," Creek said.

"No you can't," Lehane agreed. "But I want you to use a lifepod instead."

"Why?" Creek said.

"We have dozens on the ship," Lehane said. "If I launch them all when you launch, the Nidu will have to track them. You'll have a better chance of making it to the surface."

"That leaves you with no lifepods for anyone else," Creek said.

"It's a risk," Lehane said. "But a calculated one. Each lifepod has its own beacon that connects to the nearest CC network. If we launch the lifepods, some of them will get past the jamming radius and start signaling. Then it becomes harder for the Nidu to pretend we didn't arrive."

"It's a gamble, Captain," Creek said.

"It's better odds than what we have now," Lehane said.

"Where do we go?" Creek said.

"I want you to use the lifepods on the Promenade Deck," Lehane said.

"Give me a fucking break!" Creek said. Robin, who could hear only Creek's side of the conversation, looked over in shock. "That's ten decks up. We nearly got killed three times getting down here. By now they're watching the stairs and elevators both."

"If you use the lifepods on the Promenade Deck, I'll be able to give the Nidu an extra surprise," Lehane said.

"Your surprise won't do us any good if we're dead," Creek said.

"There's a service elevator in the shuttlebay, along the aft wall," Lehane said. "I've unlocked it for you. It can take you up to Promenade Deck into the crew corridors. I can't guarantee they won't be waiting for you, but it seems less likely that they would.

I've just turned on the emergency lighting on the Promenade Deck. Follow the nearest lit path to a lifepod. Once you're in a pod I'll program it to land at the Pajmhi communication center. Good enough?"

"Good enough," Creek said.

"Good luck, Creek," Lehane said. Creek closed the communicator, then opened it again and turned the notification signal to "vibrate." No need for another unpleasant surprise.

Creek pointed to the elevator in question. "Our next stop," he said to Robin.

"I thought we were going to take a shuttle," Robin said. "Now we're going back up?"

"The captain thinks we'll be safer using a lifepod. He's going to launch them all and make it hard for them to find us," Creek said.

"We're already here," Robin said. "Why don't we take the Nidu shuttle?"

"Do you read Nidu?" Creek said. "Because I don't. Come on, Robin. We're almost done. We can do this one last thing."

"They're in the elevator," First Mate Aidan Picks told Lehane.

"Good," Lehane said, and turned his attention back to the small bank of monitors in front of him, in which he could see what remained of the Nidu marines pacing through the various decks of the ship. There had been 20 of them, not including their shuttle pilot, when they arrived. Through the monitor banks, Lehane and his bridge crew—all the principals on station because they had come out of n-space—had watched as Creek dispatched six of them; Lehane had heard him shoot the pilot over the communicator. Lehane felt very bad about exposing Creek like that, but it couldn't have been avoided. He needed Creek to get to the lifepods so he could take care of the other marines.

Lehane knew about Creek and Robin Baker since shortly after

Ned Leff had approached him about finding a dress uniform for Creek. Leff was clearly excited about having a "survivor of the 6th" take part in the ceremony; Lehane was skeptical. There weren't enough survivors of the 6th for one of them to randomly pop up under the radar, and certainly not a clearly non-Asian man with a last name of Toshima.

Lehane met with "Toshima" shortly thereafter and tossed the name of a fictional colonel at him to see if he would bite; he didn't. After Toshima left him, Lehane had his security chief Matt Jensen pull up a data feed from the UNE network to find out what he could about the 6th. No Hiroki Toshima. But there was a picture of a Private First Class H. Harris Creek, thinner and younger but unmistakably the same man Lehane had just seen. An actual survivor of the 6th, yes. And a recipient of the Distingushed Service Cross. Just not under the name he was using now.

Jensen's digging revealed why: Creek and his female friend were wanted in connection with a shoot-out in a DC area mall, which left four men—men with interesting police records—dead and another couple injured. Creek's friend also appeared to be named in some sort of legal suit by the Nidu government; Jensen didn't go into it but offered the opinion that the two were con artists of some sort. By the time Jensen caught Lehane up with all this, they were already under way to Brjnn, and their schedule was too tight to accommodate an emergency stop to have the two removed. Lehane instructed Jensen to alert authorities at Phoenix colony, their next UNE destination; the two would be discreetly removed from the ship then. Until then, Lehane didn't see why they shouldn't enjoy their vacation. Lehane told Jensen to keep an eye out to make sure the pair didn't try to con any of the passengers, but otherwise let them be.

Lehane hadn't given the pair any additional thought until the *Neverland* popped out of n-space and discovered a Nidu gunship waiting for them and jamming their communications. Lehane immediately locked down the bridge, sealing the bridge crew in with airtight blast doors. The commander of the Nidu ship sent a message demanding the surrender of Creek's friend Robin Baker (with whom the nation of Nidu was enigmatically at war), the location of her cabin, and that the *Neverland* open its shuttlebay to allow a squad of marines already *en route* to the *Neverland* to retrieve her. The failure to perform any of these would result in the gunship opening fire on the *Neverland*. Lehane complied, sent Baker's room information and ordered the shuttle bay to begin its cycle.

"If we let them take these two, do you think that'll be the end of it?" Picks asked Lehane, as they watched the Nidu shuttle enter the *Neverland*'s bay.

"They jammed our communications as we entered normal space," Lehane said. "No one knows we're here. I don't think they plan to let anyone know we were *ever* here."

Then he was on the communicator to Creek; the Nidu were jamming outbound communications but personal communicators had a short-distance peer-to-peer protocol that operated on a separate frequency. It was thankfully unjammed. As Lehane and his crew watched Creek and Robin evade the Nidu marines (or not evade them as the case was on three occasions), Lehane thought mirthlessly that his security chief was dead wrong. Whatever Creek and Baker were in trouble for, simple con artistry was not part of the equation.

"Elevator's at the Promenade Deck," Picks said.

"Here we go," Lehane said. "Let's see if this guy's luck holds out."

"There's one," Robin said, pointing at a lit path on the otherwise dim Promenade Deck that led to a lifepod door. "Now all we have to do is get to it."

The two of them emerged from the elevator in a corridor behind the kitchen of the Celestial Room, the Promenade Deck's restaurant. The Celestial Room was constructed on a platform that stood above the rest of the triple-height Promenade Deck for what the brochures for the *Neverland* promised was a "delightful dining experience, floating among the stars." At the moment, however, it just meant that Creek and Robin had a flight of stairs to get down.

Creek poked his head up over the railing and spotted three Nidu marines in front of them, walking in the direction opposite of that he and Robin needed to go. The marines Creek had seen were working in pairs. That meant there was one missing. Robin tugged on Creek's shirt and pointed down the stairwell they needed to walk down. The fourth Nidu marine had just appeared in front of it.

Creek and Robin flattened down to avoid being seen, but the Nidu marine wasn't looking in their direction anyway. As they watched, the marine scratched himself, yawned, and sat on the bottom stair. He reached into a pouch on his belt and pulled out a silvery object, then peeled the silver skin, letting it flutter to the ground, and bit off part of what was left. The marine was having a snack.

In spite of everything, Creek felt bemusedly offended; apparently this marine thought so little of his quarry that he could take a meal break. Creek pulled out the Colt .45.

Robin's eyes widened. *What are you doing?* she mouthed to Creek, silently. Creek put his finger to his lips as a warning and then crouched up and looked down the Promenade Deck. The three other marines were still out there, facing away from Creek, Robin, and the fourth marine. Down the deck Creek saw little shops and kiosks that would normally provide passengers with all manner of goodies to stuff themselves silly upon. He focused on one he remembered sold soft drinks, about 60 yards down the Promenade and just slightly ahead of one of the marines. Creek raised his gun, steadied his aim, and shot at it.

It was a good hit. The bullet hit the kiosk and tore through the aluminum drink dispenser, dislodging the fiber hose inside that connected to the CO_2 canister. The hose flailed back and forth in the drink dispenser, rattling and hissing. The marine closest to the kiosk barked in surprise and opened fire on the drink stand; the two other marines, hearing the commotion, rushed to their comrade's location and pumped bullets into the kiosk as well.

The noise was deafening—loud enough that the three marines could not hear when Creek turned, ran halfway down the stairwell, and shot at the fourth Nidu marine, who was already standing and turning toward Creek; he'd heard the shot being fired above him. Creek's shot was badly aimed and went wide, the result of trying to run down stairs and aim at the same time.

The marine was surprised but competent; he raised his rifle and let out a short burst. Creek saw the rifle lift and moved to avoid fire. He didn't. Creek felt shocking clarity of pain when one bullet of the four glancingly tore through pants and connected with the communicator in his pocket, exploding the communicator and sending its shrapnel into his leg. Creek stumbled but fired again, hitting the marine in the hand. He roared and raised his hand in pain; Creek, steadier now, shot him in the throat. He went down.

Down the Promenade Deck the three other Nidu marines stopped their firing and examined the wreckage of the kiosk.

"Robin," Creek hissed. "Let's go. Now."

Robin came down the stairs and saw Creek's leg. "You've been shot," she said.

"My communicator was shot," Creek said. "I was just a bystander. Come on. Our chariot awaits."

From down the deck they heard bellowing in Nidu.

"I think they just noticed their friend is missing," Robin said.

"Go get the pod opened," Creek said. "I'll hold them off."

"What are you going to do?" Robin said.

"Something messy," Creek said. "Go." Robin went toward the pod. Creek took the marine's knife from its sheath, and then searched for which of the marine's hands carried the network implant that allowed him to use his weapon. It was on the marine's right hand, disguised as a decorative appliqué on the outermost finger. Creek put a knee on the hand to pin it down and then severed the finger with the knife. He dropped the knife, grabbed the finger and the rifle and then jammed the finger into his right palm, pressed up against the rifle stock. The implant had to be within a few centimeters of the trigger or the rifle wouldn't work. It was painful to leave the Colt behind; it was a beautiful weapon. But it was down to four bullets and Creek didn't think his aim was *that* good.

"Harry!" Robin said. She had wrenched down the manual bar to open the airlock door that would let them into the lifepod.

"Coming," Creek said, and started walking backward to the lifepod, limping from the communicator fragments in his leg, rifle up and sighted in toward where he knew the other Nidu marines would be coming.

The first came around the corner in a rush and screamed when he saw the marine on the floor. A second later he appeared to notice Creek. He bellowed and raised his rifle; Creek, who had sighted him in, let out a burst of fire to his chest. The kickback of the rifle was impressive and caused the last few shots of the burst to miss; the first three, however, connected just fine. The marine flew back to the ground, twitching and bellowing. Creek turned and hobbled quickly toward the lifepod. He was pretty sure the downed marine would keep the others from rushing down the deck long enough for him and Robin to get on their way.

The lifepod was a compact ball designed to do exactly one thing—get passengers away from a broken ship. The inside held ten seats: two levels of five, arrayed in a circle, each emanating from the white plastic molding that formed the inside shell of the lifepod. Each seat had four-point belts designed to keep people pinned to their seats while the pod fell away from the ship. Save for a porthole on the door, there were no windows, which would have compromised the structural integrity of the pods. Save for the door sealer, which also served to begin the launch sequence, there were no controls; the pods were programmed to hone in on pod beacons when they were in UNE space or to preassigned locations in other worlds. When you entered a lifepod, it was with the recognition that to do otherwise would be to perish. That being a given, you didn't get a choice where you got to go. It was survival at its most minimum.

Creek entered the pod and threw his rifle (and its attendant finger), into the closest seat. "Sit down," he said to Robin, who took a seat on the other side of the pod from the rifle and began to strap herself in. Creek grabbed the door sealer and yanked it down; the door vacuum-sealed itself with a hiss.

Creek glanced through the tiny porthole and saw the other two marines finally creeping past their downed teammates. One of them saw the outside door to the pod closing and raised his rifle to fire. The airlock door, which sealed the pod from the ship, slammed shut, blocking Creek's view; as it did so Creek heard the dull *thunk* of bullets striking its other side.

"What do we do now?" Robin said.

"Lifepods automatically start a countdown once you seal them," Creek said, strapping himself into his seat. "We should be launching any second now."

"Good," Robin said. She sat back, closed her eyes, and waited for the launch.

A minute later she opened her eyes again. "Harry," she said. "We're still here."

"I know," Creek said.

"I thought we were supposed to launch," Robin said.

"We were," Creek said.

There was a very loud bang on the other side of the door.

"What was that?" Robin said.

"I'm guessing it was a grenade," Creek said. "They're trying to blow their way through the outer door."

"What do we do now?" Robin said.

"I don't know," Creek said. He reached over and collected up the rifle and the Nidu marine's finger. If any of the other Nidu marines had noticed that both of these objects were missing, there was a reasonably good chance that the rifle had already been disconnected from the network and would be useless as anything but a club. Creek didn't see much point in passing on that bit of information to Robin.

"They're in the pod," Picks said.

"Stop their countdown," Captain Lehane said. "But program in their destination coordinates."

"Done," Picks said, after a second. "Now what do you want to do?"

"Ready the other pod launchers to go," Lehane said, and glanced back down to his monitors, where he could see the Nidu marines congregate around the pod airlock. "And wait for the flies to come to the honey."

After a few seconds Picks glanced over at the monitor. "Those two must be going bugshit in there, wondering why the pod hasn't launched."

"It won't be long now," Lehane said. Four more Marines showed up on the Promenade Deck, and then another two. Four more and they'd be ready to go.

"That's easy for you to say," Picks said, as he watched the Nidu marines scurry to take cover from the grenade they'd placed by the airlock. "You're not the one on the other side of that door."

"There," Lehane said, and pointed to one of the monitors. The final foursome of Nidu Marines had come up the stairs and were making their way to the pod. "That's all of them. Confirm that for me, please, Aidan."

Picks bent over the monitors and did a count. "Looks like twelve of them to me," Picks said. "That's all that are left standing."

"Aidan," Captain Lehane said. "I do believe there's been a catastrophic hull breach on the Promenade Deck. Bring the ship to emergency status. I authorize you to section and seal the Promenade Deck. If you please, section and seal the aft left quarter first; that's the site of the breach."

Picks grinned. "Yes, Captain," he said, and went off to deliver the orders.

Promenade Decks are both a blessing and curse to commercial cruise liners. They are designed to accommodate huge windows that allow passengers to oooh and aaaah over starfields, planets, and all other manner of celestial phenomena, and make for fabulous brochure pictures to sell Midwest housewives and their cheap husbands on the idea of an interstellar cruise. The curse is these windows make Promenade Decks inherently far less structurally sound than any other part of the ship. A good random smack by chunk of rock or debris into a window at cruising speed runs the statistically extremely small yet not entirely trivial chance the window will buckle or shatter, sucking its fragments and any poor passengers nearby into the blackness of space.

After a few high-profile incidents of this, including the unfortunate incident of the *Hong Kong Star*, in which the parents of the First Husband of the UNE were popped into cold vacuum like two immensely politically connected corks, every space-going cruise liner with a Promenade Deck registered for service by the UNE had to be able to lock down the entire deck *at least* and preferably the deck in sections, to insure a hull breach on the Promenade Deck did not threaten the integrity of the entire ship or expose any more passengers than absolutely necessary to the risk having their blood boil into nothingness as they unexpectedly toured the cosmos without a ship.

In the case of a catastrophic hull breach (according to UNE regulations on the subject) a ship the size of the *Neverland* must be able to seal its Promenade Deck in no more than 15 seconds. In tests, the *Neverland* could seal off its Promenade Deck in 12.6 seconds. Sectional seals took even less time: between 5.1 and 7.8 seconds. Of course, that was before the *Neverland* had been entirely furnished and put into service. Captain Lehane wondered idly if the presence of carpeting, lounges, and potted palms would have any effect on the final numbers.

"Sealing now," Picks said. There was a shipwide wrenching and an immense noise as Promenade Deck vacuum doors, cleverly disguised as floors and walls, sprang up and out and connected together with an alacrity that made Lehane want to track down their designer and send him or her a congratulatory fruit basket. The carpets, lounges, and plants didn't seem to slow down the doors, although they catapulted quite nicely. On his monitor, Lehane could see some of the Nidu marines firing at furniture in surprise as it was flung around them.

"Done," Picks said. "thirteen point two seconds. Not bad. And all the Nidu marines are in the aft left quarter."

"Excellent work, Aidan," Lehane said. "Now, if I recall correctly, the hull breach occurred in that section of the deck."

"I believe it did," Picks said.

"That means one of the panorama windows has been compromised," Lehane said. "I order you to clear out the rest of the window, in order to seal the breach."

"Yes, sir," Picks said. "Does the captain have any particular window in mind?"

"I leave it in your capable hands," Lehane said.

Although the Haysbert-American cruise line was a low-to-mid-price cruise line, it nevertheless had one of the best reputations for ship safety in the entire UNE commercial fleet; the Haysbert-American executives believed that such a reputation would be a selling point to the previously mentioned Midwest housewives, and indeed it was. One of the more obscure safety touches was that every window on a Haysbert-American ship, from the smallest porthole to the largest dome, was a single transparent crystal grown into its setting during ship manufacture. The crystal's shearing angle—its "weak" angle—was along an axis secured by the setting; the axis describing the surface of the window was remarkably resistant to collision. If something cracked a window on a Haysbert-American cruise liner, it was indeed a hell of an impact.

The drawback to growing one's windows into place was if one was cracked or broken it was difficult to extract it. Haysbert-American solved this problem by constructing tiny shaped explosive charges into their window settings which would drive chisel-like planes of metal into the crystal's shearing angle, shattering what remained of the crystal and allowing deployment of the emergency vacuum door hidden within its retaining wall. This deployment occurred automatically unless overridden by the bridge.

"Clearing debris," Picks said, and shattered the panoramic window closest to the lifepod.

From his monitor Lehane saw the long, curving window suddenly appear to go opaque as millions of hairline cracks accelerated through the crystal lattice. The Nidu marines visibly jumped at the sound; one of them wheeled around and raised his weapon at the window to fire at the noise.

"Jumpin' Jesus," Lehane said. These had to be some of the most jittery military personnel Lehane had ever seen.

The Nidu marine didn't get a chance to fire his weapon; the cracked window exploded outward, sucking the marine out with it. Several other marines followed in short order, some knocked out the hole by flying debris, others simply pushed out by the hurricane force of the air escaping into space and seeking equilibrium with a vacuum countless millions of kilometers on all sides. Two marines managed to keep themselves from being launched into the darkness, which merely meant they spent their last few seconds vomiting their lungs out onto the Promenade Deck. Death relaxed their grips and the two of them collapsed onto the floor, the very last of the air in the section ruffling their uniforms as it whistled past.

"Your orders, Captain," Picks said.

"Secure that breach and launch the lifepods," Lehane said. "But delay launching Creek's until I tell you."

"Breach secured," Picks said. "Launching pods now."

Lifepods engirdled the *Neverland* like strings of pearls, each pod set in something akin to a magazine for a gun. When a lifepod is activated, it is pushed into space by electromagnetic repulsion, after which its tiny directional engines kick in, tweaking the descent of the lifepod toward its assigned beacon or location. As soon as one launches, a second is hauled up to the airlock door to allow another set of passengers to load in. The process is efficient and surprisingly quick; a new pod moves up to the airlock door in as little as five seconds after the last one clears. There were 144 lifepods on board, more than enough for passengers and crew. Except for today, when they were all being launched with only two passengers to share between them. Lehane hoped to God he knew what he was doing.

Around the ship Picks launched one lifepod after another, far more rapidly than usual because there was no wait for passengers. Lehane counted 40, 50, 60 pods popped into space.

"Launch Creek's pod," Lehane said.

"Launched," Picks said, a moment later.

"Keep launching the pods. All of them," Lehane said.

"Sir, the Nidu ship is hailing us," said Susan Weiss, the *Neverland*'s communications technician. "They're demanding we stop launching lifepods and asking for the whereabouts of their marines."

"Ignore them," Lehane said. Too many pods were out there now. There was no way they could shoot them all down before one of them got clear of the communications jam and broadcast its distress beacon. The Nidu couldn't blow up the *Neverland* now, not without risking open war and censure. Lehane felt okay with pissing on them a little bit.

"The Nidu are firing," Picks said, and switched his video feed to one of Lehane's monitors.

"At us?" Lehane asked.

"Not yet," Picks said. "It looks like they're going after the pods."

Lehane watched as rockets flared silently from the Nidu gunship, followed a few seconds later by erupting flashes as the rockets hit their marks.

Come on Creek, Lehane thought. *Make it through.*

"Holy *shit*," Picks said, staring at his monitor.

"What is it?" Lehane said.

Picks looked up at his captain with a wide-open grin. "You wouldn't believe me if I told you," he said, and sent the feed to Lehane.

Lehane looked down at his monitor again. Picks was right. He wouldn't have believed it if he hadn't seen it with his own eyes.

It was a UNE naval destroyer, about three times the size of the Nidu gunship.

"Here comes the cavalry," Lehane said.

Creek felt himself yanked forward as the lifepod finally launched. Robin cried out in a mixture of terror, surprise, and gratitude. The last few minutes had been extremely noisy and mysterious; after the grenades there had been an immense grinding sound, followed by muffled shouting, followed by a bang and what sounded like a tornado, followed by complete and total silence and then their pod pushing away from the *Neverland.* Creek had had more enervating slices of time in his life, those two days on the Plain of Pajmhi among them, but these last minutes were definitely in the top five.

Creek unbuckled from his seat and floated to the porthole in the sudden zero gravity. Out the porthole Creek could see a vacuum door on the Promenade Deck where a window used to be.

"That son of a bitch," Creek said, with admiration. "He shot them into space." If he made it out of this alive, he was definitely going to buy Lehane a drink.

The lifepod engines kicked on; Creek hauled himself back into his seat until they stopped firing. Once they had, Creek unlatched again and went back to the portal.

"What do you see?" Robin said.

"Lifepods coming off the *Neverland,*" Creek said. "Lots of them. Do you want to look?"

"I don't think so," Robin said. "This zero gravity thing is not so good for my stomach."

Creek noticed a flash of light on the periphery of the porthole and then another closer to the center. "Uh-oh," he said.

"What?" Robin asked.

"I think the Nidu are firing on the lifepods," Creek said.

"Of *course* they are," Robin said. "We're still alive, Harry. That just won't *do.*" There was a bitter edge to her voice that Creek felt was entirely justified at this point.

Another flash, much closer now, and then another. And then another, less than a kilometer away.

"Maybe I *will* take a look," Robin said, and tugged on her belt straps. "Sitting here isn't helping my stomach any."

"You might want to stay in your seat," Creek said.

"Why?" Robin asked.

Creek was about to answer when something large took over a significant chunk of the porthole field of view.

"Never mind what I just said," Creek said. "You're definitely going to want to see this."

Robin unhooked and swam her way to the porthole. "What am I looking at?" She asked.

"The very large UNE ship," Creek said, pointing. "Right there. And just in time."

"What do you mean, 'just in time'?" Robin said. "It would be 'just in time' if we were still on the *Neverland*. As far as I'm concerned, they're a little *late*."

"Trust me," Creek said, and looked out the porthole again to see if there were any more flashes, which signified exploding lifepods. There weren't. "They're just in time."

The lifepod suddenly shook violently.

"What was that?" Robin said.

"Atmosphere," Creek said. "We're on our way to the Chagfun surface. Time to strap in, Robin. This next part's going to get bumpy."

chapter
15

In one of those coincidences that would be ridiculous if they weren't entirely true, Creek and Robin's lifepod launched from the *Neverland* at almost precisely the moment the time limit for the auf-Getag clan to begin the coronation ceremony expired. What followed next was a power grab so quick, so balletic in its balance, grace, and speed that the Medicis, the Borgias, and all their equivalents across time and space, had they the knowledge, would have risen from their graves to provide its mastermind with a standing ovation.

At the time of the expiration plus some infinitesimal fraction of a second, the Nidu computer system deployed the instruction set enacted when no heir from the current clan on the throne ascends in time. The power of supreme access, previously locked in trust for the presumptive auf-Getag heir, was now dissolved and major functions of the Nidu political administrations apportioned to the ministers and generals who made up the highest

level of the Nidu government. From this second until a chal-
lenger successfully assumed the throne, no single Nidu was in
charge of the entire government.

At time plus two minutes (to use human time measurements), Ghad-auf-Getag, Supreme Commander of Nidu Military
and uncle to the previously presumptive but now merely potential heir to the throne Hubu-auf-Getag, found his head being
yanked backward to expose his throat. For the two minutes previous, Ghad-auf-Getag had sole administrative control of the Nidu
military, without oversight from the Nidu *Fehen*—because there
was none. Ghad-auf-Getag had not used those two minutes particularly well; for their entire span he been squatting above a
Nidu toilet trough, expelling the remains of the previous day's
lunch.

This left him particularly vulnerable to attack when his two
bodyguards entered his lavatory and drew their knives—
ceremonial knives Ghad-auf-Getag had presented both a year previously as a token of ten Nidu years (roughly fifteen Earth years)
of loyal and devoted service. Both bodyguards had been promised
colonial regional governorships by Narf-win-Getag; both had decided that Narf-win-Getag's offer beat a nice knife. One of those
knives was stuck in Ghad-auf-Getag's throat; a few seconds later
the second cut him from waist to mid-chest.

Ghad-auf-Getag's bodyguards were brutally efficient in dis-
patching their master; by t-plus three minutes and thirty seconds
all of Ghad-auf-Getag's brain activity had ceased, triggering the
implant he like all high-level government officials carried in his
body to transmit the fact of his death to the Nidu computer network.

With the death of Ghad-auf-Getag, the administrative powers
he controlled were instantaneously and automatically portioned
off to his immediate subordinates, the chiefs of staff of the respective arms of the Nidu military—except for the control of

Nidu's *Glar*-classs destroyers, which Ghad-auf-Getag and the previous *Fehen* Wej-auf-Getag believed was too important to be left to a mere chief of staff. Ghad-auf-Getag kept control of the *Glar* destroyers himself and cut them out of the chain of command. And so, when he collapsed to the tiles of his lavatory, bled out, control of the *Glar* destroyers devolved directly to their individual commanders.

Six of whom Narf-win-Getag had been able to buy.

At t-plus five minutes—and in a truly remarkable bit of synchronization—both the the *Lud-Cho-Getag* and the *Jubb-Gah-Getag*, the two *Glar* destroyers UNE Defense had been tracking from the start, emerged in Earth space in an unauthorized and unscheduled appearance and immediately warmed up their weapons. UNE Defense commanders had been briefed on the possibility of the appearance of the two cruisers and the further possibility—probability—that they would not be stopping by for a friendly spot of tea. What they were not told to expect was that the two ships would appear in Earth space within thirty seconds of each other, a bit of coordination that was an unheard-of feat of planning and power distribution to n-space engines, considering that the ships had come from entirely different limbs of known space, and were known to have entered n-space at nearly exactly the same time. The appearance of both simultaneously gave Earth defense planners no time to counter.

Bob Pope was awakened from a dead sleep by his new temporary assistant Thomas Gervis; he in turn woke up President Webster. Webster held off attacking the destroyers, partly to keep from losing UNE Defense ships unnecessarily but also because until he heard otherwise Nidu was still an ally. The unbidden and unscheduled arrival of the destroyers was not enough to breach treaties. If the UNE moved to attack it would be the aggressor and the breaker of treaties. There was nothing to do but wait.

The commanders of the *Lud* and the *Jubb* were both bought off years before with their choice of planetary colony governorships. The captain of the *Lud* picked Hynn, one of the newer colonies, rich in natural resources and anecdotally believed to be the home of some of the most attractive Nidu females in the entire nation; a perennially popular Nidu folk tune that expressed a belief to that effect had a close cousin in Earth's equally perennially popular folk tune "California Girls." The captain of the *Jubb* had lost two dearly beloved siblings in the uprisings on Chagfun; he chose that colony to rule and was already constructing intricate revenge fantasies against its entire population.

Narf-win-Getag had had no problem convincing Ghad-auf-Getag and Hubu-auf-Getag to dispatch the *Lud* and the *Jubb* to Earth space; the two had already been convinced by the apparent assassination of Lars-win-Getag that the Earth government was acting against their (and therefore Nidu's) best interests and the further unfolding of events suggested it would have to be dealt with as soon as possible after the coronation ceremony. What had been far more difficult had been to convince the two to do what was coming up next.

At t-plus 12 minutes four *Glar* destroyers (with two future colonial governors, one future Supreme Commander of Nidu Military, and one future very, very rich retired captain among them) popped into existence over Nidu itself, joining the two *Glar* destroyers already on station in Nidu orbit. All four arrived within 20 seconds of each other—a feat one order of magnitude more impressive than the synchronized arrival at Earth—two each in positions flanking the two *Glar* cruisers already in orbit.

This had been Narf-win-Getag's improvisational masterstroke, and like many masterful improvisations, it was based on years of backstory. Narf-win-Getag knew that two of the *Glar* captains could not be purchased—they were nephews of Ghad-auf-

Getag and cousins of Hubu-auf-Getag. Rather than buy them, he bought those around them, not to assassinate the cousins but to implicate them in a deep and subtle conspiracy against Hubu-auf-Getag that would come to light at a time of Narf-win-Getag's choosing.

At the appropriate moment (which eventually turned out to be just after the UNE began the search that would turn up Robin Baker) a trusted and apparently unimpeachable third party—who, in a refreshing change of pace for Narf-win-Getag was not bought but blackmailed—would come forward and present evidence that the cousins meant to prevent the coronation and use their destroyers to force a coup. This third party would then suggest recalling the four remaining *Glar* cruisers as a preventative measure.

The third party: Chaa-auf-Getag, brother of Ghad-auf-Getag, uncle to Hubu-auf-Getag, and father to the *Glar* destroyer captains in question. Who really ought to have known that a fetish for xenosexuality—the desire to have sex with sentient races not your own—would one day catch up with him in a culture as caste-ridden and implicitly racist and xenophobic as the Nidu.

No matter how shamed Chaa-auf-Getag would be if his alien-fucking ways were discovered, there would be no way he'd countenance the actual murder of his own children. Which is why Narf-win-Getag never bothered to explain to him what would happen at t-plus 15 minutes, when the four destroyers opened fire on the destroyers captained by his sons.

The two destroyers were of course entirely unprepared for the attack—and yet survived the first barrage, heavily damaged but largely intact, a testament to their Hamgp makers' superior ship-building skills. But even advanced Hamgp craftsmanship couldn't survive the impact of a Nidu planet cracker bomb, one of which hit each of the stricken destroyers as the sole weapons in a second wave of attack. The destroyers each disintegrated in the wake of a shaped blast designed to rip into the skin of a living world, leaving nothing but metallic vapor and a pair of explosive jets expanding conically away from the planet of Nidu.

It would have killed Chaa-auf-Getag to know he had been used to condemn his sons to death. So it was just as well that at t-plus six minutes, Chaa-auf-Getag's trusted personal servant of nearly two decades stuck a large-gauge shotgun into Chaa-auf-Getag's exceptionally surprised face and calmly pulled the trigger. This was another instance where Narf-win-Getag didn't have to make a payout or promise; the personal servant, a Nidu of extreme conservative personal inclinations, saw it as an opportunity to express his opinion about Chaa-auf-Getag's need to stick his penile array into places, people, and species it ought not have been. Having expressed the opinion, the personal servant then turned the shotgun on himself; his personal inclinations being conservative as they were, it was the only option that would suffice for a disloyal servant.

At t-plus 20 minutes Hubu-auf-Getag received a recorded message from Narf-win-Getag, briefly outlining the events of the last several minutes and informing the former future leader of the Nidu that he already had Robin Baker, or would have soon, and when he arrived at Nidu with her in two days time, it would be Narf-win-Getag, *not* Hubu-auf-Getag, who would use her to ascend the throne of Nidu. And if Hubu-auf-Getag didn't like it, he was free to eat a planet cracker bomb from one of the four *Glar* cruisers that floated above Nidu, all of which—as well as the two orbiting Earth—were under Narf-win-Getag's control.

In another one of those coincidences, at the very moment Narf-win-Getag's message to Hubu-auf-Getag stopped playing, leaving Hubu-auf-Getag to fathom how this all could have happened, the lifepod carrying Creek and Robin Baker scraped across the surface of Chagfun, grinding to a stop less than a kilometer from the communication outpost on the Pajmhi plain.

And so it was that in 20 minutes, Narf-win-Getag found himself in effective control of two entire planets. It was almost certainly the fastest double coup in the history of the Common Confederation—which, even in an obscure historical category such as "double coup," was an impressive feat. All that was left now was to make it official. All that was left was to get Robin Baker and take her to Nidu.

Robin Baker looked at around at the hard, black, rocky expanse she and Creek stood on. "So this is where you fought," she said.

"This is it," Creek said. He winced as he pulled another small fragment of his communicator from his leg, then swabbed the wound with the disinfectant from the pod's first aid kit, which had been placed along with a small store of water and emergency rations in a small sealed compartment under the pod floor.

"It didn't look like this, though," Robin said.

Creek looked around. "No," he said. "It used to be a lot nicer. Well, as much as any battleground can be 'nice.' When I was here I wasn't getting a lot of time to sightsee."

"I guess not," Robin said.

"I'll tell you, though," Creek said, as he wrapped gauze around his leg. "One time in the two days I was here everything just *stopped*—rifles stopped firing, people stopped moving, and everything just became quiet, and it was like everyone had just stopped to take a breath or something. And for that moment, you could look around and see what a beautiful place the plain was, when it wasn't filled with people killing and dying. And I wished I had been able to see the place when it was at peace."

"It's at peace now," Robin said.

"If you want to call being buried under a lava flow at peace," Creek said. He stood up and walked on his leg.

"How does that feel?" Robin asked.

"Like there are a couple of pieces still in there," Creek said.

"Ouch," Robin said.

"Better plastic fragments in my leg than a bullet," Creek said. "They'll eventually work themselves out. Anyway, now that my communicator is shot—literally—we're going to have to make the hike to that communications center Leff was talking about."

Robin pointed to a tall communications array roughly a kilometer away. "I'm guessing that would be it," she said.

"I'm guessing you'd be right," Creek said. "Ready for a walk?"

"I like how you ask me these things as if you're giving me the option," Robin said. "You've been doing this all the time since we've met. I just want you to know that it doesn't really make me feel like I have a choice in the matter."

Creek smiled. "I don't want to come across as pushy," he said.

"It's a little late for that," Robin said. "Come on. I'm sure this place used to be a very nice place to visit, but right now all I want to do is get off this rock and on that nice big Navy boat up there." She set off in the direction of the communications array. Creek collected up the Nidu rifle, placed the finger in his pocket, grabbed a water canister, and followed after Robin.

The communications array terminated in a small control room located in a natural if irregular amphitheatre created by the lava flow. This was where the memorial ceremony was scheduled to take place. Like every portion of the former plain, the amphitheatre was bleak, black rock with no sign of animal life or vegetation. It was as if life, insulted by the planet cracker and resulting lava flow, had rejected the plain of Pajmhi from that point forward. Creek didn't blame it for the decision.

"Harry," Robin said, and pointed to something on the side of the control room. Creek looked at what seemed like a heap of trash for a minute until it resolved itself into a dead Nidu; probably the communications engineer, who had come to the site to prepare for the *Neverland* passenger arrival.

Creek turned back to Robin. "Head back to the pod," he said. "Wait there until I come to get you."

"Harry—" Robin said, looking past his shoulder. Creek swung around and saw something the size of a grizzly stalking toward him. It had come through the door of the communication center. Creek raised up his Nidu rifle, sighted in, and fired at the thing.

And forgot the Nidu finger was still in his pants pocket.

"Oh, shit," Creek said, and wheeled backward. The creature grabbed him, cocked back its massive arm, and slugged him dead in the temple. Creek could hear Robin scream for the briefest fraction of a second before the lights went out completely.

Creek felt water splashing on his face and into his nostrils. He coughed himself back into consciousness and propped himself up from the floor he was lying upon.

"Hello, Creek," a man's voice said to him. "Nice nap?"

Creek looked up and saw Rod Acuna over him, leaning against the counter of the broadcast terminal inside the communications control center. Acuna held a gun casually but firmly in his hand; it was pointed at Creek. Behind and to the side of Acuna, Creek saw Robin, securely held by what Creek now recognized as a Nagch.

"Hello, Acuna," Creek said. "Of all the people I was expecting to see, you were not one of them."

"You know who I am," Acuna said. "Well, isn't that *cozy*. I'm glad I could surprise you. Surprises are fun. And you know, I think you should take my presence here as a compliment."

"Really," Creek said. "How so?"

"It shows my faith in you, Creek," Acuna said. "After I got that picture of you in my regimental newsletter and passed it along, everyone else was so sure that they would just pluck you and Little Bo Peep here off that cruise liner. But I knew better. I knew you'd get away from them. And you know why, don't you?"

"Because I got away from you," Creek said.

"Check out the brain on you," Acuna said. "Exactly right. You got away from me. So I asked myself, if I were Harry Creek and *I* was going to keep from getting captured on a cruise liner in space, where would *I* go? And here we are. I had to just about shoot someone to make them give me a ride down here, but now I think they'll be glad I made the effort."

"You came with the Nidu," Creek said.

"I did," Acuna said. "And I'm going to leave with them. And so is Takk here"—he gestured with his non–gun-holding hand to the Nagch—"and so is your girlfriend. You, on the other hand, will be staying."

"No room on the shuttle for me?" Creek said.

"There's room," Acuna said. "You're not going to go because you and I are going to settle up now. You broke my arm and my nose in our last encounter, if you'll recall. It cost someone a lot of money for my QuickHeal session."

"Sorry about that," Creek said.

"Think nothing of it," Acuna said, and shot Creek in the left arm midway between the wrist and elbow, shattering his radius and ulna. Creek collapsed on the ground, writhing in pain, smearing blood on the concrete floor. Robin screamed again and started begging for someone to help them.

Acuna watched Creek twist for a while and then got up from the counter and walked over to him. "That takes care of the arm," Acuna said, and kicked Creek square in the face, causing a burst of blood to fountain out his nose. "And that should square us for the broken nose." He stepped away and raised his gun. "And this is the interest on both. Goodbye, Creek."

Takk was only mildly interested in the interaction between Acuna and Creek. What he was more interested in—indeed, what he was almost entirely consumed with—was Robin.

Acuna had retrieved Robin while Takk had carried Creek into the comm center; once inside, however, they swapped. "Try not to lose her," Acuna had said, shoving the girl at Takk, who looked up at him with terrified eyes.

Takk gently put his huge paw on her shoulder. "Don't worry," Takk said. "I'm not going to hurt you."

"You just clubbed my friend into a coma," Robin said. "Pardon me if I don't relax."

There it was. Just like it was prophesied by Dwellin:

The Lamb will come to the house of strangers
With a journey of many miles behind it;
It will be made welcome by those who dwell within
But will be yet full of fears.

Takk had been reading the prophecies pretty much nonstop since Archie McClellan had handed them over prior to ingestion; it'd be fair to say that he'd memorized most of them at this point (Nagch had excellent memories for the written word). They had fascinated Takk. He was not by inclination one easily swayed by mysticism, preferring instead the sense of order and comforting ritual religion could provide (after reading the preface to the prophecies, he would have considered himself more of an Ironist than an Empathist, if he were a member of the Church). Yet there was something compelling about the idea that these prophecies not only might come true, but were thought to come true through the conscious decision of the Church members to make them so. It was an interesting juxtaposition between fate and free will that allowed for both to exist—nay, required them to go hand-in-hand, skipping merrily through the field.

Takk recognized of course that the prophecy he was thinking of was not an exact fit. The communications hut could be considered a "house" only in the broadest and most liberal sense of the term, the one that granted that any structure could theoretically be a home to someone. And yet other elements fit very well. Had not the Lamb traveled many miles? Indeed—light-years, in fact, a distance that made mockery of the term "mile." Did Takk not just tell her not to worry (and did so unprompted by prophecy—he only consciously thought of the prophecy afterward)? And was she not, and reasonably so, Takk thought, full of fears?

Takk racked his brain for other prophecies that matched the situation, but came up empty. There was nothing in the prophecies that said anything about someone like Acuna antagonizing someone like this Creek fellow. This didn't entirely surprise Takk, either. There's not a prophecy for everything in the universe, even if one is willing to deconstruct the writing down to its most general and symbolic level. Dwellin was understandably focused on the issues surrounding the Evolved Lamb and its trials; he'd naturally skip parts here and there. From what Takk understood of the background of the prophecies and Dwellin, by the end he was well-nigh incoherent off of alcohol and cheap over-the-counter pharmaceuticals. It would have been difficult for him to develop and sustain more than one prophetic narrative.

Acuna shot Creek in the arm; Creek, who been propping himself up with the arm, fell back to the floor, bleeding and moaning. Robin screamed.

"Oh, God, oh God," she said. "Oh God, Harry. Help us, Please help us." She started repeating the sentence, with variations, for the next several seconds.

And it was here that Takk recognized a situation similar to another prophecy—or if not an exact situation, at least a situation where one of Dwellin's exhortation stanzas could certainly apply:

Lo! The Lamb stands not alone but with those
Who see themselves within it.
He who helps the Lamb helps himself.
He who serves the Lamb saves himself.

Dwellin wrote this particular stanza at a time when Andrea Hayter-Ross experimented with holding back the pitiful allowance she provided him, just to see what he would do. Dwellin wrote this stanza, among others vaguely hinting that it was good to serve the Lamb (at the last minute prior to sending them to Hayter-Ross, he excised one of the more desperate ones in which he flat-out asked for cash), and was also shortly thereafter arrested at a Vons supermarket for stealing a Clark Bar. Hayter-Ross paid his bail, and in one of the rare moments where she felt bad about making Dwellin jump through silly hoops, gave him a bonus on his cash installment and took him out to dinner at a smorgasbord.

Takk knew nothing of this backstory, nor would it have mattered to him if he had. What mattered to him was the Lamb was asking for help—and that by asking for it, had invited Takk to help himself as well.

Truth to be told, Takk was getting tired of the *Ftruu*. It was overwhelming and exciting and even a little gratifying at first—a nice adventure and an interesting way to see the universe. But over the last few months and especially the last few days, what Takk mostly felt was tired. Tired of living with the criminal element, which was not an especially invigorating element in any meaningful sense, tired of feeling the obligation of trying forbidden things, tired of meeting new people only in circumstances where he beat them or ate them.

In other words, Takk was primed for a religious epiphany, and as he watched Acuna jam his boot into Creek's face, one hammered into him with lightning-hot intensity. His time of *Ftruu* was over, suddenly and irrevocably, and thank God for that. It was time for him to make the choice to return to the ranks of the moral, and to those engaged in the process of bettering the universe, not destroying it as a way to get they wanted; people like the Nidu ambassador or the human Jean Schroeder or even Rod Acuna, who didn't actually want much of anything other than to be angry and get paid for it.

Acuna lifted his gun again to aim at Creek's head; Robin turned into Takk's chest to avoid the scene, still whispering for help. With one enormous paw, Takk swiftly but gently moved Robin aside, stepped forward, opened his insides, and sent his intestinal tendrils whipping toward Acuna. One hooked Acuna's arm just as he fired his gun, twisting the barrel to the right and ricocheting the bullet off the concrete floor into the wall. The gun flew from the surprised Acuna's hand. Other tendrils hooked and wrapped around Acuna's legs, waist and neck. In less than a second Acuna was secured in Takk's constrictive grip.

Acuna nevertheless managed to crane his neck, Takk's tendril hooks tearing his flesh as he did so, to get a glimpse of the Nagch.

"What the *fuck* are you doing?" Acuna managed to croak out.

"I'm serving the Lamb," Takk replied, and with a mighty jerk swallowed Acuna whole.

"Holy Christ," Brian said to Creek, who was sitting at the comm center's terminal. "What the hell happened to you? You look worse than usual."

"Let's skip the pleasantries," Creek said. "Just tell me what's going on."

Brian did, catching up Creek with tales of lawsuits, usurpations, church schemes, and intelligent computers waging the Battle of Pajmhi over and over and over and over. And then he told Creek what he learned from Andrea Hayter-Ross. Creek sighed and put his head into his (right) hand.

"You look tired," Brian said.

"I look like I've been shot in the arm and kicked in the face," Creek said.

"That too," Brian said. "But I meant *besides* that."

"I *am* tired," Creek said. "I want this whole thing to go away."

"It's not going to go away," Brian said, as gently as he could. "You know that."

"I know," Creek said. "But I'm telling you what, Brian, the next time your brother comes to me asking me to run a computer search for him, I'm going to punch his goddamn lights out. Where is he, by the way?"

"He's on the way to Nidu with the secretary of state for the coronation, for whomever it will be for, whenever it may happen. Where's Robin?"

"She's outside, talking to a new friend of hers," Creek said. "Or should I say, a new follower?" Creek outlined the events of the last several minutes.

"Never a dull moment with you around," Brian said.

"Despite my preference to the contrary," Creek said.

"Are you sure she's safe with that thing?" Brian said.

"He could have let Acuna kill me and take her," Creek said. "If he wanted to do anything bad to her, that would have been the time. I also gave her Acuna's gun. How is the *Neverland*?"

"She's safe," Brian said. "Safe as can be expected, anyway. The *British Columbia* is keeping the Nidu off of her. And the Nidu are keeping the *British Columbia* from sending a shuttle to pick you up. Everyone up there has taken the safety off the trigger but they're keeping their iron in the holster. I think they're waiting to hear about you and Robin."

Creek sighed. "Yeah," he said. "I'm going out to talk to her now. She's going to like all of this even less than I do."

"It's the only thing that will work," Brian said. "And it will work. We'll make it work."

Creek smiled. "We better," he said. "Don't go anywhere, Brian. I'll be right back."

"I'll be here," Brian said.

Creek got up gingerly so as not to bump his injured arm, which was now in a sling; at Robin's request Takk had gone to the pod and retrieved the first aid kit. Creek went outside to see Robin and Takk standing and talking; seeing him approach, Robin turned to Creek and smiled.

"Tell me you got everything to work," she said.

"Everything works," Creek said, and turned to Takk. "Would you excuse us for a moment, Takk? I need to talk Robin for a minute."

Takk reached over and touched Robin on the arm. "We'll talk about this some more later," he said.

Robin squeezed his paw. "I'd really like that," she said. Takk departed.

"Nice to have a fan club," Creek said.

"No kidding," Robin said. "Although all this stuff about the 'Evolved Lamb' makes me nervous. Takk seems really nice—as nice as you can be and eat people, I mean—but I hope he's not going to be too upset when he eventually figures out I'm not some sort of mystical creature."

"Hold that thought," Creek said. "Because there have been some interesting developments."

"Yeah?" Robin said. "They can't be any stranger than hearing that you're supposed to be the divine object of worship."

"Robin," Creek said. "Do you trust me? I mean, do you really trust me. Trust me as in if I tell you something you'd be willing to do it, even if it seems irredeemably insane."

Robin stared at Creek for a minute, then started laughing. "Oh, God, Harry," she said, finally. "Since I've met you what have we done that's *not* been insane? Do you even realize how ridiculous your question is at this point?"

"So that's a 'yes,' " Creek said.

"It's a 'yes," Robin said. "I trust you with my life, Harry. It's worked for me so far. So hit me with what you've got."

"Well, let's start with the big one," Creek said. "You're your own nation."

Robin considered that for a moment. "For your sake, that had better not be a comment about the size of my ass," she said.

The shuttle landed inside the natural amphitheatre and deposited Narf-win-Getag and Jean Schroeder, whose relationship to the Nidu Robin and Creek had learned from Takk. The two approached Creek and Robin when Takk stepped forward. "That's far enough," Takk said.

"Back off," Schroeder said. "Remember that you're working for me."

Takk leaned into Schroeder. "I don't work for you any more, little man," he said.

"Takk," Robin said. Takk eased back from Schroeder. "Thank you, Takk," she said.

"Are we going to play intimidation games all day," Narf-win-Getag said. "Or are we going to get to our negotiations? There is very little time, and I am quite busy."

"Yes, we're well aware of how busy you've been," Creek said. "Seeing that we spent some time earlier in the day avoiding some of your business."

"And well done, I must say," Narf-win-Getag said, to Creek. "You live up to your billing, Mr. Creek."

"That's Prime Minister Creek to you, Ambassador," Creek said.

"Is it now?" Narf-win-Getag said, bemused. "Well, isn't this interesting. An entire nation right here in front me. All two of you."

"Three," Takk said.

"But of course," Narf-win-Getag said. "Three it is. And I suppose you're the minister of defense."

"It's funny that you mock us," Robin said. "Considering that from what I hear, you were the reason this little nation exists."

"You are quite right, Miss Baker," Narf-win-Getag said. "Or is it Queen Robin? By all means, I don't wish to violate protocol by addressing you incorrectly."

"Miss Baker is fine," Robin said.

"Well then, Miss Baker, if you know that you are your own nation, then you may also know that my nation is at war with yours," Narf-win-Getag said. "Considering we outnumber your nation by about three billion to one, that's not good news for you."

"I thought we weren't going to play intimidation games, Ambassador," Creek said.

"My apologies," Narf-win-Getag said. "By all means, let's get to it."

"I'm going to make this simple," Creek said. "You want to take the crown of Nidu. Your flunky here"—Creek motioned to Jean Schroeder—"wants the Earth. You need Robin to make it happen."

"That's not quite true," Narf-win-Getag said. "I can make it happen without her help. It will just be . . . messier."

"And not guaranteed," Creek said. "Whereas with her, your ascension is uncontested and incontestable."

"Yes," Narf-win-Getag said.

"You realize now there's no way you can take her by force," Creek said.

"I would prefer to say that at this point it is impractical to do so," Narf-win-Getag said.

"However you want to say it, these are the facts before us," Creek said. "So let's make a deal. We—all three of us—are willing to accompany you to Nidu, in your ship. When we arrive at Nidu, Robin will take part in the ceremony to crown a new *Fehen*. But there are four conditions."

"Name them," Narf-win-Getag said.

"Condition one," Creek said. "Call off the war on Robin."

"I'm not *Fehen* yet," said Narf-win-Getag.

"But you control the *Glar* destroyers," Creek said. "Which means you control the Nidu military. You have it within your power to call off the dogs."

"So I do. You've done your homework, Minister Creek," Narf-win-Getag said.

"I am a diplomat by profession, Ambassador," Creek said. "I know how to do my job. Do you agree to the first condition?"

"I do," Narf-win-Getag. "I will have it formalized when I become *Fehen*."

"Condition two," Creek said. "Your gunship up there stands down and the *Neverland* is allowed to leave Chagfun intact."

"Not before you two are on *my* ship, and we've jumped into n-space," Narf-win-Getag said. "I don't want to risk the two of you—three of you, excuse me," Narf-win-Getag corrected himself, "nobly sacrificing yourself for the UNE."

"We'll arrange to have your ship and the *Neverland* make the jump into n-space simultaneously," Creek said. "Will you accept that?"

"Yes," Narf-win-Getag said. "Your third condition, Minister Creek."

"That Robin survives the coronation ceremony," Creek said. "The sheep used in the ceremony have always been slaughtered. Not this time."

"My understanding of the ceremony is that it requires the blood of the sheep and it requires a brain scan," Nerf-win-Getag. "Both can be done without killing Miss Baker. Agreed."

"Thank you," Creek said. Robin relaxed visibly.

"You said you had four conditions," Narf-win-Getag said.

"Condition four," Creek said, and pointed again to Jean Schroeder. "That man does not get the Earth."

"What?" Jean Schroeder said.

"He's a traitor to his own nation," Creek said. "He also conspired to assassinate the head of a nation whose sovereignty is recognized by the Common Confederation. He also tried to kill *me*. So, it's a personal thing. He goes or we go. It's nonnegotiable."

Jean Schroeder laughed. "Go to hell, Creek," he said.

"Agreed," Narf-win-Getag said.

"What? What?" Jean Schroeder said, and turned to Narf-win-Getag. "No, no, no. You can't cut me out of this, Narf. I made this happen for you. My *father* made this happen for you. You and your whole goddamned clan couldn't have done this without us. Now don't you *dare* think you can just put me to the side. You get Nidu. *I* get the Earth. That's always been the agreement. *That* is nonnegotiable. You don't need them to get the throne. But you need me."

"I *needed* you," Narf-win-Getag said, to Schroeder. "The tense is, I'm afraid, of critical importance here, Jean."

"Narf," Jean Schroeder said, and then whatever was coming next was lost as Narf-win-Getag backhanded Schroeder viciously across the jaw. Schroeder staggered backward, stunned; Narf-win-Getag struck him again and sent him sprawling onto the black rock of the amphitheatre. Schroeder scrambled to get on his feet, but the larger, more muscular Nidu was on him, driving him back to ground and wrapping his hands around Schroeder's neck. Schroeder choked and gurgled and wheezed and died.

Narf-win-Getag stood, brushed himself off, and straightened his clothes. "I trust that will be sufficient assurance," he said to Creek.

"It was a little more than I was expecting," Creek said.

"Was it?" Narf-win-Getag said, and then it was his turn to laugh, in the Nidu way. "Really, now, Minister Creek. After all that happened—after all that's happened to *you*—did you really expect anything *less* from me?"

chapter

16

On the periphery of the Nidu computer network, Brian waited for a sign. He wasn't waiting alone.

"They've jumped out of n-space, you know," Andrea Hayter-Ross said, floating next to Brian and sitting at that damned patio table of hers.

"I know," Brian said. "I'm getting better at the whole 'being multiple places at once' thing."

"There's a good boy," Hayter-Ross said. "You're showing off your learning curve again."

"Thanks, Grandma," Brian said.

"And saucy too," Hayter-Ross said. "Just the way I like my boys. So, how are you enjoying it? Being on the cusp of history?"

"I'm not," Brian said. "I hate the waiting. I want it to begin."

"Patience, Brian," Hayter-Ross said. "It won't be long now. Narf-win-Getag is heading his shuttle straight for the *Fehenjuni*—that's the imperial court, you know."

"I know," Brian said.

"Of course you do," Hayter-Ross said. "Narf-win-Getag isn't even letting Creek and Robin choose an appropriate wardrobe for themselves, he's in such a rush. He's going to have robes waiting for them at the *Fehenjuni*."

"Can you blame him?" Brian said. "He's spent decades plotting and planning. Now he figures he's just an hour or two away from his prize. When you're ready for your future, you want it to happen as soon as possible. This guy's an asshole, but I sympathize with his point of view on that particular subject."

"Well, both of you will be living in the future soon enough," Hayter-Ross said. "In the meantime, Brian, sit down and have a cup of tea with me."

"The tea doesn't exist, you know," Brian said. "And anyway, I hate tea."

"Silly boy," Hayter-Ross said, as she poured Brian a cup anyway. "I know the tea doesn't exist. And you ought to know by now that just because I give you tea doesn't mean you can't change it to whatever you want when you drink it."

"I never thought of it that way," Brian said.

"I know," Hayter-Ross said, holding the cup up for Brian to take. "But you're going to have to get used to thinking about things a whole new way. This is as good a place as any to start."

"Wow," Robin Baker said, in spite of herself. "Have you ever seen a room like this?"

"One time," Creek said. "In Jerusalem. The Dome of the Rock. But this is much bigger."

The two were standing in the center of the Great Hall of the *Fehen*, itself the heart of the immense complex known as the *Fehenjuni*, the Seat of the *Fehen*. The Great Hall was impractically large, the size of a football stadium, and topped with a hemi-

spherical dome constructed of giant, curving sheets of manufactured, reinforced gemstones. Emerald and ruby and sapphire and
tourmaline and opal and garnet were all used like stained glass to
form scenes of Nidu mythology and history. Creek had no doubt
that Narf-win-Getag would displace one of the stories portrayed
on the dome to place his own up there, to shine in the light of
Nidu's sun. In the center of the dome, a manufactured diamond
the size of a baby elephant was faceted to collimate the light of the
sun straight down to the center of the room, to a raised dais
which usually held the throne of the *Fehen,* but which today held
the altar upon which Robin Baker would spill her blood.

Robin and Creek were not alone in the Great Hall. They were
not even the only humans; per a now-ancient service agreement,
two representatives of LegaCen were on hand to monitor the performance of the computer network during the ceremony and to
focus the computers' projectors, which would create certain images during the proceedings. Around them and Creek and Robin,
Nidu apparatchiks buzzed, preparing the room for the ceremony
and ignoring the humans in their presence as one would expect
the Nidu to do in this, the most important room on the planet. To
the side of the altar a Nidu priest paced, going over the ceremony
in his head and attempting not to be scandalized that a human
woman would be the sacrifice this time—and that he wasn't actually allowed to sacrifice her completely.

In a matter of minutes, the gargantuan doors at the end of the
hall would swing open, allowing the guests and official observers
of the ceremony into the hall. In their number would be high-
ranking members of government from more than 200 worlds,
and mid-ranking members of government from the rest as well
as a low-end representative from the CC itself—a general reflection of the overall status of Nidu in the CC hierarchy of worlds.

As a matter of status, President Webster of Earth really should
have been the one to attend the ceremony. Rather inconveniently,

368 · John Scalzi

however, it conflicted with a long-planned state visit from the president of Vhrugy, one of the rather more important worlds in the CC. And so Webster was not disposed to attend. In these circumstances, Secretary of State Heffer was a reasonable substitute. There was small irony, therefore, in the fact that the suddenly worsening relations between Earth and Nidu had caused the president of Vhrugy to cancel her visit. Technically, the president was free to attend the coronation. As a practical matter, however, his world was looking down the launchers of two planet cracker bombs. And so once again it did not make the best of sense for him to be there.

Some short time after the guests were assembled, Narf-win-Getag would enter the Great Hall, ascend the dais, and perform a series of general rituals that announced his intent to take the throne of Nidu. These preliminary rituals were not strictly required for ascension to the throne, but they were traditional, and they gave the ceremony a nice rounded feel.

After the preliminaries came the required sections, which were created by the auf-Getags after the clan had initially ascended the throne. Many clans who had previously ascended the throne had lardered their coronation ceremonies with so many actions and details that all but the most attentive of candidates ran the very real risk of screwing up and disqualifying himself and his clan, thus throwing Nidu—yet again—into the throes of civil war.

Unlike these clans, the auf-Getags opted to keep their required rituals simple: A scan of the brain of the sacrificial sheep and the subsequent blood sacrifice, followed by two questions asked by the Nidu computer network: "Which clan brings the sacrifice?" and "What is the bidding of the clan of sacrifice?" The intended answers to these questions were, respectively, "The auf-Getag clan" and "Give me control of the network."

The auf-Getags were comfortable with such a short ceremony

because of the computer network and because of the sheep. He who controlled the computer network controlled every aspect of the Nidu government. That was all that need to be said about that; once that kind of extreme power was assigned it was difficult to fight against. As for the sheep, the computer network could quickly determine the genetics of the blood sacrifice to assure the sacrifice was of the Android's Dream breed; the brain scan determined that the animal was alive and gauged its mental capacity.

The last of these was key: In a small but important detail, the questions asked in the ceremony were technically asked of the sacrificial animal itself, but in the event that the sacrifice could not answer the questions (which was always), the questions could be answered by a member of the clan with legal ownership of the sacrificial animal.

This worked out nicely for the auf-Getags, as the sacrificial animal, being a sheep, could not speak (confirmed by the brain scan) and was killed in any event during the ceremony. The questions always defaulted to a member of the clan which owned the sheep. By Nidu law, the only clan that could legally own the Android's Dream sheep was the auf-Getag clan. Even if a member of another clan procured a live Android's Dream sheep, the questions could not be answered by the sheep thief, as his clan did not, in fact, own the sheep.

This little detail of the coronation ceremony was the most tightly held secret of the auf-Getag clan, known only to its highest-ranking members. This number included Hubu-auf-Getag, who would be attending the ceremony today and who fully expected to perform the ceremony himself after Narf-win-Getag's attempt failed. At which point he fully expected to have Narf-win-Getag executed for treason right there on the ancient and priceless rugs of the Great Hall, in front of the assembled audience of visitors from hundreds of worlds. Then he'd deal with the *Glar* destroyer captains. And then, just for fun, he'd decimate the win-

Getag clan, executing one clan member in ten at random. That would be the end of any other thoughts of uprising by any other clan for a good long time.

As tightly held as this secret was, it did not originate with the auf-Getag clan itself. Rather it was suggested to the auf-Getag clan, in a batch with a number of other unrelated performance and optimization suggestions, by an advisory panel at LegaCen, the general contractor building the new Nidu computer network. The auf-Getags, delighted by the sneakiness of the idea and encouraged by LegaCen's rock-solid nondisclosure pact, signed off on it. Now decades later, they had no idea the secret came from outside their clan. The clan members had simply forgot.

"How do you feel?" Creek asked Robin.

"Like I'm going to throw up," Robin said.

"There's a receptacle," Creek said, pointing to the trough at the altar into which Robin's blood would flow.

"Don't tempt me," Robin said. "Also, this hurts like hell." Robin held up her wrist, into which a small medical shunt had been jammed. At the appropriate time in the ceremony the stopper on the shunt would be turned and about two ounces of Robin's blood would fall into the trough.

"I guarantee you it hurts less than the alternative," Creek said.

"This is all so unreal, Harry," Robin said. "I want to wake up in my crappy little bed in my crappy little apartment and have my crappy little breakfast and then go to work out and clean out crappy little rodent cages."

"Soon, Robin," Creek said. "Now, you remember everything you're supposed to do?"

"I do," Robin said, and held up her wrist again. "Some parts are harder to forget than others."

"You're going to do fine," Creek said. "Remember that I'm going to be right in the front of the audience."

"Where will Takk be?" Robin asked. She and Takk had become close during the trip to Nidu.

"He'll be with me," Creek said.

Robin giggled. "That's bad news for anyone who has to stand behind him."

The doors at the end of the hall cracked open. The audience was being let in.

"Here we go," Creek said, and turned to Robin. "Be strong, Robin. It's almost all over."

Robin came over to Creek. She gave him a peck on the cheek. "Thank you, Harry," she said. "For everything. And no matter what I said before, you really are a fun date."

"Thanks," Creek said.

"Next time, though," Robin said. "Let's just go to a movie." She walked back up to the altar. Creek headed down toward the crowd to find Ben Javna and Jim Heffer.

He found them near the back. Javna came over and grabbed his arm in greeting. Creek winced.

"Sorry, Harry," Javna said. "But God damn. It's good to see you alive, kid. Although from the looks of it, it's a close thing."

"Thanks, Ben," Creek said. "It's good to be alive, close or not." Creek looked to Heffer, who walked up next to Javna. "Secretary Heffer," he said.

"Mr. Creek," Jim Heffer said. "Good to finally meet you. Prime Minister Creek, I should say. We heard about your promotion."

"You owe me for that one," Javna said. "It's a nice job."

"Yeah, but look what I had to do to get it," Creek said.

"If this coronation goes off you're not likely to keep it long," Heffer said. "Narf-win-Getag's been playing everybody. We all got bushwhacked. Ben's legal victory is just about the only thing that went right for us. I'm laying decent odds that at the end of this ceremony, Ben and you and I get marched off to a POW camp."

"And yet you still showed up," Creek said.

"Hope springs eternal," Heffer said. "And we're not at war yet. We're diplomats, Harry. Maybe there's another way out."

"Maybe," Creek agreed. Someone tapped Heffer on the shoulder; Heffer turned to acknowledge them and then nodded his goodbyes to Creek and Javna.

"Well?" Javna said, after Heffer had gone. "What's going on?"

"What do you mean?" Creek asked.

"You're here," Javna said. "*She's* here. I didn't tell you to come out of hiding yet, and you're not stupid enough or slow enough to get caught. So you're up to something. And I hear that you're here because you made some sort of deal with Narf-win-Getag."

"It's not what you think," Creek said.

"That's good," Javna said, "Because I have really no clue what I'm thinking right now. I just hope somewhere along the way you managed to pull all our feet out of the fire. And maybe managed to convince ol' Narf to pick someone not entirely despotic to rule the Earth."

"I know one person it's not going to be," Creek said, and told Javna about Jean Schroeder.

"Choked to death by a Nidu on the plain of Pajmhi," Javna said, when Creek had finished. "There may be more ironically poetical ways for that shithead to go, but right off the top of my head I can't think of any."

Horns sounded, signaling the audience to take their places.

"Time for the pain," Javna said.

"Listen, Ben," Creek said, drawing close. "Something's going to happen in the ceremony, something that I haven't prepared you for. Something that goes back a long way between us. I don't have time to explain it now. You'll know it when you see it. When it happens, try not to hate me too much."

Javna looked at Creek. "Harry," Javna said. "Whatever it is, if it gets us all out of this with our skin intact, that's good enough. Don't worry. You're like a brother to me. You know that."

"Hold that thought, Ben," Creek said. "Remember you said it."

Takk came up to Creek. "It's time to take our places," he said.

"Holy cow," Javna said, looking up at Takk.

"Hi," Takk said.

"When we're in POW camp, you're going to have some interesting tales for me, Harry," Javna said. "I can tell that already."

"What's he talking about?" Takk said.

"I'll tell you later," Creek said. "Come on, let's go." The two moved back up the crowd to their assigned position, Takk creating a bow wave with his size and Creek traveling in his wake.

Horns blared. The Great Hall doors opened once more. And Narf-win-Getag stepped through, wearing the cape and mantle of his clan.

Narf-win-Getag did not rush his entrance; he walked slowly and smoothly, directly in the middle of the aisle created by retaining ropes and an audience of four thousand guests and dignitaries. Narf-win-Getag recognized many, as well he should have through decades in the Nidu diplomatic core. His eyes sought and found Jim Heffer and Ben Javna; he nodded to them as he passed and smiled at the memory of having played them rough like cheap violins. With Schroeder out of the way, Narf-win-Getag was free to choose a Nidu administrator for Earth, and was considering auctioning off the position to the highest bidder. Someone would pay handsomely to run an entire planet, even a shithole like Earth.

At the head of the crowd Narf-win-Getag spied Hubu-auf-Getag on one side, with a phalanx of auf-Getags, and Harry Creek and Takk on the other. Neither Hubu-auf-Getag nor Harry Creek

struck Narf-win-Getag as appropriately fearful in their expressions, although in the case of Creek it might simply be that Narf-
win-Getag, even after all that time on Earth, still had trouble with
some of the more subtle human expressions. It really didn't matter. Hubu-auf-Getag and his entire clan would be dealt with soon
enough, and as for Creek, Takk, and Robin, he'd already made
arrangements for that entire *nation* to be handled. They'd live;
they'd just never leave Nidu. Narf-win-Getag didn't feel particularly bad about violating the agreement to call off the war on
Robin; he'd honored the other three well enough. Especially the
last one.

Narf-win-Getag ascended the dais and as was tradition, recited
seventeen stanzas of *The Revinu,* the Nidu species' signature epic
poem. It didn't matter which seventeen stanzas, merely that there
were seventeen, each stanza representing the seventeen original
clans of Nidu, of which win-Getag was one. Then followed the
Blessing of the Knife, the Prayer to Clan Ancestors, the Salting of
the Altar, a recitation of the Psalm of the Forgiven, and finally the
Second Blessing of the Knife, symbolically transforming the
weapon into an instrument of peace, a "swords into ploughshares"
sentiment that like its human equivalent was generally forgotten
before the last echo of the words had faded.

Now came the actual ceremony, and Narf-win-Getag found
that he relished the idea of speaking the words to a ceremony for-
mulated by the auf-Getag clan; in his mouth the words would be
like a repudiation of their rule and redemption of the office of
Fehen. Or so Narf-win-Getag was fantasizing to himself while
Robin, the sheepwoman, had the apparatus for the brain scan
placed awkwardly on her head by the priest. This accomplished,
she then held out an arm to allow the priest to twist the shunt; her
blood to flowed into the trough and past the sensors that sam-
pled the DNA within to find the magic segments that would confirm her identity as an Android's Dream sheep—the *right* kind of

sheep. Another repudiation of the auf-Getag clan, Narf-win-Getag thought, that he provided her where they could not.

From far recesses of the Great Hall projectors flared, announcing the acceptance of the Android's Dream DNA with flaring and beautiful displays of light and color, intended to wrap the presumptive *Fehen* in a halo of righteous luminescence. The entire altar glowed like polished brass hit by a lighthouse beam, augmenting the light filtering in through the diamond on the roof.

It appeared to a few of the observers that more of the light focused on Robin than on Narf-win-Getag, but that was likely to be a combination of the simple white robe Robin wore as well as some confusion by the computer as to which of the tall creatures on the altar to highlight (the computer knew well enough not to highlight the priest). Certainly Narf-win-Getag didn't notice the fact his luminescence was being shared. From discreetly hidden vents the odor of the *Fehensul,* the flower of the *Fehens,* wafted into the room, its astringent sweetness the ultimate and most sacred word in the Nidu language of scent.

The light show settled down and the light coalesced into a single ball that positioned itself between the altar and the audience. Positional audio kicked in and caused sound to come from the ball, sound that eventually resolved into a voice. "Which clan brings the sacrifice?" it asked, in majestically toned Nidu.

Narf-win-Getag stepped forward, and inhaled deeply to bellow the name of the win-Getag clan, to forever clear the air of the shame the auf-Getag clan brought to the office of the *Fehen.*

"The Baker clan!" declared a high, thin, nervous voice, in heavily accented but perfectly acceptable Nidu.

Narf-win-Getag choked on his declaration and stared at Robin Baker, who he was somewhat surprised to learn was still standing on the altar with him. Narf-win-Getag glared at her, decided that he'd changed his mind and definitely wouldn't let her live after all, and then took in another breath to declare his clan.

"What is the bidding of the clan of the sacrifice?" the deep, rich sonorous voice of the computer asked.

"Give me control of the network!" Robin Baker declared, again in Nidu. "And give Brian Javna complete access!"

"Whoops, that's me," Brian said, and got up from the table, leaving his beer behind. "Thanks for the drink, Andrea."

"Anytime," said Andrea Hayter-Ross, and waved. "Don't be a stranger."

Brian drifted over to an open port on the Nidu computer network, which demanded identification.

"I'm Brian Javna," Brian said, "I think you've heard of me." Some automatic part of Brian translated that into something the Nidu network could understand, validate, verify, and accept. And then, as requested, it gave Brian complete access.

Brian was hit with about 40 trillion watts of pure understanding.

It's hard to describe to anyone who is not in fact a sentient computer. But imagine you're a tapeworm, and then suddenly you're Goethe. It's like that. Brian experienced an upward expansion of knowledge, power, intuition, and capability unrivaled by any sentient being anywhere and anytime in the history of the Common Confederation. He didn't simply have access to the Nidu computer system, which was, by dint of its sheer Orwellian reach into the tiniest crannies of Nidu governmental life, the single most complex computer system yet devised. He *became* the Nidu computer system, searing through it at the speed of light and joyously feeling its power and information become his own. There was no word for what Brian was feeling, so he made one up.

Infogasm.

Oh, boy, Brian thought. *That's the sort of thing that will kill you if you do it more than once.* Brian savored the feeling for just a few cycles more, and then did what he came to do.

High above Nidu and Earth, six *Glar* destroyer captains and crews were shocked to find they were suddenly locked out of their controls, and that their ships had minds of their own.

Across Nidu space, every Nidu ship lost its defensive and offensive weapons. Individual Nidu soldiers lost control of their cars, their planes, their rifles and weapons. Vehicles in use rolled to a stop or landed at the first safe opportunity.

On every CC planet the Nidu had embassies, diplomatic workers banged their terminals in frustration as screens went blank and reports, applications, and communication ground to a halt. In Nidu space, all government work not related to keeping people alive also similarly ground to a halt. Nidu schools were excused for the day. Nidu children very nearly rioted with joy.

All of this happened in the time it takes for a sharp intake of breath.

"Jesus, this is fun," Brian said, and went to go make a very special appearance.

From her vantage point outside the Nidu system, Andrea Hayter-Ross watched as the network took on a shape and configuration that reflected Brian. There was no doubt it was him.

"I remember him when he was just an IBM," Hayter-Ross said, and sipped her tea.

The bloom of light between the altar and the audience stretched, twisted, and took form.

"Oh my God," Ben Javna said. "It's Brian."

Brian turned to Robin and spoke in English, loud enough for the entire audience to hear. "It's done," he said. "The Nidu computer network is yours and awaits your command. You are now *Fehen* of Nidu, Robin Baker."

The Great Hall erupted. For once, it was only barely large enough to hold the commotion.

"Thank you, Brian," Robin said, though the chaos. "And it's nice to meet you."

"Likewise," Brian said.

"Fehen?" Narf-win-Getag bellowed. *"I am Fehen!"*

"You're not," Brian said, turning toward Narf-win-Getag. "Because *I* am the Nidu computer network, and you, sir, are not the boss of me."

Narf-win-Getag disconnected from any pretense of civility and lunged at Robin Baker. From his distant position in the audience, Takk moved futilely to intercept. But it was Brian who blocked Narf-win-Getag; he activated the directional audio of the Great Hall to send a 180-decibel blast directly at Narf-win-Getag's head. Narf-win-Getag went down screaming in pain; Takk, reaching the altar, grabbed the fallen Nidu and hurled him bodily off the dais. The Great Hall erupted again.

"Brian," Creek said in a conversational tone, since he knew Brian could hear him. "Please amplify my voice so everyone can hear me."

"You're on," Creek head Brian say, as if he were in his ear. "Don't do any singing. They're panicked enough."

"Ladies and gentlemen," Creek said, and he could hear whispers of his words being pitched to the members of the audience in their own language through the directional audio. "Please, be calm. Please calm down. Explanations are coming."

Eventually the crowd noise died down, and Creek stepped out in front of the altar.

"My name is Harry Creek," he said. "The Nagch stepping on Narf-win-Getag is Takk. The woman on the stage is Robin Baker. We are the nation of Robin Baker, recognized by the Common

Confederation. And she is now *Fehen* of Nidu, as allowed by the
laws of Nidu itself." The crowd erupted yet again; Harry moved to
silence them once more.

Hubu-auf-Getag stepped forward out of his phalanx of clans-
men. "I am Hubu-auf-Getag, the true *Fehen* of Nidu," he said in
English, to the crowd and to Creek. "This woman cannot be the
Fehen of the Nidu. If for no other reason that she is *not* Nidu."

"By your laws and by the coronation procedure your own clan
set forth, she does not need to be," Creek said. "Your coronation
ceremony requires merely an Android's Dream sheep. Robin
Baker has that DNA in her."

"If she has the Android's Dream DNA, then by Nidu law she
is the property of the clan of auf-Getag," Hubu-auf-Getag said.
"And a member of *that* clan must be *Fehen*."

"In this case, Nidu law is superseded by Common Confederation law, which declared Robin Baker a new species of sentient
being and her own nation under Common Confederation law,"
Creek said. "As a member of the Common Confederation Nidu is
bound to respect her sovereignty and can make no claim on her.
You know this, since it was your own government's suit that
caused the CC to rule for her."

"A suit whose idea came from Narf-win-Getag," Hubu-auf-
Getag said, staring down at the fallen ambassador, who was
pinned by Takk's leg on his back.

"Who was at the time a representative of your government,"
Creek said. "And still is, I suppose."

"Not anymore," Robin said, and turned to Narf-win-Getag,
who was pinned under Takk's foot. "You're dismissed."

"Dismissal noted," said Brian.

"This is an invasion!" Hubu-auf-Getag said, trying a new tack.
"You have attacked us and taken control of our network by illegal
means."

"It is not an invasion," Creek said. "We were transported here by a Nidu ambassador in a Nidu vessel and participated by invitation in the coronation ceremony."

Narf-win-Getag spoke up from the floor. "Under false pretense!" he rasped, as Takk's foot was limiting his lung capacity.

"The ambassador is mistaken," Creek said. "We agreed to come to Nidu to take part in the coronation ceremony. We didn't specify that in doing so the crown would fall to him."

"It is still an act of war," Hubu-auf-Getag said.

"If it is, it is defensive," Creek said. "When a Nidu gunship attacked a civilian UNE vessel carrying Miss Baker and me, the Nidu marines who demanded to board specifically served notice to the captain of the ship that Nidu had declared war on Robin Baker. As was recently noted to me by your ambassador, Nidu outnumbers Miss Baker's nation by three billion to one. A declaration of war on a single person—even if she is her own nation—seems excessive. By the laws of the Common Confederation, Miss Baker, as a sovereign nation, has the right to defend herself against an aggressor."

This last bit caused rumbling in the audience. Hubu-auf-Getag glanced back and read the mood in the room. Then he turned back to Creek. "Let's you and I talk without the crowd listening in, if you please," he said. Creek nodded and had Brian cut his amplification. The crowd moaned in irritation, but stayed calm.

"Even if all you say is true," Hubu-auf-Getag said. "There is the matter of the three billion to one to consider. The Nidu will never follow a sheepwoman."

Creek smiled. "Hubu-auf-Getag, surely you of all people know that it's not necessary to have the love of the masses, merely the ability to control them," Creek said. "We have control of the Nidu computer network. Which means we have control of your government and your military. Until you recognize her as *Fehen*, you're not going to get anything done."

Hubu-auf-Getag leaned in closer to Creek. "Your clan is small.

If something were to happen to your so-called *Fehen*, there are only two of you remaining. A motivated clan—the win-Getags, say—could put an end to your rule in short order."

"Oh, I'm sorry," Brian said, and projected himself over to Hubu-auf-Getag. "I've forgotten my introductions. I'm Brian Javna, and since the *Fehen* let me into your network, I've *become* the network. I'm self-contained and sentient, and I'm also a member of Robin Baker's clan. So if you kill Robin and Harry and Takk, there's still me. And you can't kill *me*."

"Don't count on that," Hubu-auf-Getag said, in Nidu.

"Wherever you go, there I am," Brian said to Hubu-auf-Getag, also in Nidu. "Remember that when your get into your next networked vehicle, Hubu-auf-Getag."

"No matter how you want to look at it, Robin Baker has a legitimate claim to the title of *Fehen*," Creek said, leading the discussion back from disembodied threats. "Your ascension rules allowed it. Your government's actions provoked it. Your ambassador's scheming set it in motion. It's all bad news for you, I'm afraid."

Hubu-auf-Getag glared at Creek. "Do you enjoy bringing bad news?"

"I don't enjoy it," Creek said. "But it *is* my job. I'm good at it."

"This is not *right*," Hubu-auf-Getag said.

This got Robin's attention. "Right? *Right?*" she said, and stalked over to Hubu-auf-Getag. She jabbed a finger into his chest. "It's *entirely* right. Because of you, people have spent the last two weeks trying to kill me or kidnap me or sacrifice me so they can rule this crappy little planet of yours. You've tried to kill my friends. You're planning to attack and occupy my planet. *This* is the only way to get you to stop. Do you think I *want* to rule your planet? Do you think I have even the smallest concern about what you people do here? I could not care less. All I want is to go home and get back to my life. This the only way I know that I'll get to do it."

Hubu-auf-Getag paused to consider her words. "Perhaps we can reach some accommodation," he said.

"Sure," Robin said. "We can start by you recognizing that I am your *Fehen*. *Your* clan made the rules. I followed them. *I* am ruler here. Don't bother trying to use any of your household appliances until you're ready to accept that."

Hubu-auf-Getag snarled and stalked away toward his phalanx.

"I don't think their household appliances are networked," Creek said to Robin.

"Who cares? It still seemed to work," Robin said.

Ben Javna had by this time made his way to the head of crowd. Creek waved at him to come through.

"I've got a message from Heffer, but first you have to tell me something," Ben said. "Brian—"

"It's really him, Ben," Creek said. "Part of him anyway. I'll explain it you later."

"You're right about that," Javna said.

"What does Heffer have to say?" Creek asked.

"He wants to know if you're really pulling this off, or if this is just some sort of enormous con," Javna said.

"Oh, it's the real thing, all right," Creek said.

"I figured it was," Javna said. "In which case Heffer wants to make an offer of alliance with your friend Robin. *Not* with Nidu, but with her—although we'll recognize her as the legitimate ruler of Nidu. And it comes with the offer to sponsor her for membership in the CC."

"A single-person nation in the CC," Creek said. "And I thought this had gotten weird enough already."

"You guys started it," Javna said.

"Let me pass the offer along," Creek said.

"I wouldn't have it any other way," Javna said. He looked over to the image of Brian, who was talking to Takk. "When this is over, do you think I can talk to him?"

"I think you should," Creek said. "I know he wants to talk to you."

"Good God, Harry," Javna said. "All that time I thought you were just piddling away your talent. You are a piece of work, my friend."

"I aim to please," Creek said, and went to chat with Robin.

"The UNE wants to sponsor your membership in the Common Confederation," Creek said.

"Mine?" Robin said. "As in me, personally?" Creek nodded. "Jeez, Harry, I can barely handle a gym membership."

"I'm pretty sure this club comes with better perks," Creek said.

"Harry, I wasn't lying," Robin said. "I don't want *any* of this. I really don't. I just want you and me and everyone I know to be safe. And I want to go home. That's all I want. Get me out of this, Harry."

Creek looked up. "Here comes Hubu-auf-Getag," he said. "Let see what he has to say."

"*Hypothetically,*" Hubu-auf-Getag said. "If we were to accept Robin Baker as *Fehen*. What then?"

Creek glanced over at Robin, who nodded. "Well, then, Miss Baker would need a governor," Creek said. "As you know, she already rules her own country. She believes it would be unfair to her citizens to divide her time."

"I agree entirely," Hubu-auf-Getag said. "This governor you speak of. What would his powers be?"

"They would be like a copy of the powers of the *Fehen*'s herself," Creek said.

"That's very intriguing," Hubu-auf-Getag said.

"There are some limitations," Robin said.

"Limitations?" Hubu-auf-Getag asked.

"Small ones," Creek assured him.

"Name them," Hubu-auf-Getag said.

"Don't screw with Earth," Robin said.

"I don't know that idiom," Hubu-auf-Getag said, to Creek.

"She means to say that the Earth is now and forevermore off limits for mischief and empire building," Creek said.

"I could see a governor agreeing to that," Hubu-auf-Getag said.

"And don't screw with me or my friends," Robin said.

"Likewise, retribution against the nationals of Miss Baker by Nidu or any of its agents would be looked upon as a grave injustice," Creek said.

"As well it should be," Hubu-auf-Getag said. "In fact, I do believe a governor would suggest a treaty between our two nations would be in our mutual interests."

"How wonderful," Creek said. "It's always heartening to discover amity between races."

"Anything else?" Hubu-auf-Getag asked.

"One other thing," Robin said, and pointed at Narf-win-Getag, still pinned under Takk's foot. "This one goes to jail."

"We can do better than that, I think," Hubu-auf-Getag said. "Indeed, clan-wide retribution is usually the policy in cases like these."

"No," Robin said. "No one gets killed, and no one else gets punished. Just him, in jail."

"Surely you realize he could not have planned all this on his own," Hubu-auf-Getag said.

"I think Miss Baker is hoping that by showing judiciousness, she might help keep other clans from attempting the misfortunate sequence of events that lead to this very moment," Creek said.

"I see your point," Hubu-auf-Getag said. "And anything else?"

Robin shook her head. "I think that's it," Creek said.

"Out of curiosity," Hubu-auf-Getag said, "in this new world order, would there be a chance for a governor to advance at any point?"

Creek glanced over to Robin, who shrugged. "I would imagine it would depend on the quality of governorship, and the state of relations with the UNE and the nation of Robin Baker," Creek said. "If those relationships are kept on extremely amicable terms, I could easily see a governor being rewarded in ten to twelve years."

"Those are Earth years, as opposed to Nidu years," Hubu-auf-Getag said.

"Optimally," Creek said.

"And until that time, the *Fehen* will have, shall we say, a light hand on the wheel of state," Hubu-auf-Getag said.

"Feather-light," Creek said. "One would hardly know it's there."

"And what about the new, obnoxious personality of the Nidu computer network?" Hubu-auf-Getag said.

"Oh, well, *that* stays," Creek said. "Call it insurance."

"But don't worry," Brian said, popping by. "He's trainable."

Creek saw that Hubu-auf-Getag was a realist; now that it was clear that the right moves would put him in the same position he had expected to be in before, with a few minor limitations, he was ready to get on board. "There is still one practical difficulty," he said. "The Nidu are . . . set in our ways about many of our opinions about other species."

"You're racists," Creek said.

Hubu-auf-Getag flared for a second, then calmed down. "Agreed," Hubu-auf-Getag. "That being the case, it would help to have a compelling explanation as to why and how this human has become the *Fehen*."

A voice rang clearly through the Great Hall. "Because she is the Evolved Lamb!"

Everyone assembled at the dais turned to look at the speaker. It was one of the computer technicians. The second technician stood beside him.

"She is what?" Hubu-auf-Getag said, to the technician. Normally, of course, he would have had a technician beaten for daring to speak at a ceremony like this. It simply wasn't done. But there were a number of things about today's ceremony that simply weren't done.

"She is the Evolved Lamb," the technician said again. "I am Francis Hamn, bishop of the Church of the Evolved Lamb. My associate is Sam Berlant, who is also with the Church. For decades our Church has concerned itself with bringing forth the Evolved Lamb, an entity who combines the best qualities of humanity and the pastoral qualities of the lamb. To aid us in our quest, and to avoid misidentifying the Evolved Lamb, we created a crucible test—a test that only one with the qualities of the Evolved Lamb would be able to accomplish. That test, Hubu-auf-Getag, was your clan's coronation ceremony. There are only two classes of people who can perform it—members of your clan, and the Lamb herself. And here she is."

"I don't understand," Hubu-auf-Getag said. "You're computer technicians."

"Yes," Hamn agreed. "Computer technicians who belong to a church. A church that through its business ventures provided your clan with the Android's Dream sheep and the computer network which now controls your world and through which your clan's power has run. We provided your clan the means to power. The cost was that it was *also* the test for a goal of our own: The creation of an entity prophesied by our founders. Look at her, Hubu-auf-Getag—she is the living embodiment of an entire religion's purpose."

Everybody turned to look at Robin Baker.

"Oh, for God's sake," Robin Baker snapped. "How divine can I be? My feet hurt. I have gas. I need to pee."

Hubu-auf-Getag turned back to Francis Hamn. "Be that as it may, your 'test' has caused my clan to fall from power."

Creek spoke up. "On the contrary, Hubu-auf-Getag," he said. "Another clan challenged your power and came to within a hair's breadth of taking the throne. Only the very fact of who and what Miss Baker is, and her actions during the ceremony, prevented it from happening."

"If she wasn't the Evolved Lamb, Narf-win-Getag would now be *Fehen*," Hamn said. "And your clan would have suffered. Gravely."

"But now *she* is *Fehen*," Hubu-auf-Getag said.

"Who is willing to hand nearly the all of her powers to *you*, Hubu-auf-Getag," Creek said. "If I were you, I'd sell the 'divine intervention' angle to your clan and kin. I'd sell it hard."

"I need to confer with my clan," Hubu-auf-Getag said.

"But of course," Creek said. Hubu-auf-Getag walked off.

"I notice you didn't mention to Hubu-auf-Getag that your church has manipulated events as much as anyone has in this little adventure," Creek said to Hamn.

"Details, details," Hamn said, and looked up at Robin. "Speaking of which, there's a small detail about the Church Miss Baker needs to know."

"What is it?" Robin asked.

"The Church of the Evolved Lamb exists to bring about the Evolved Lamb," Hamn said. "The Church's steering council, which Sam and I represent here, is in unanimous agreement: It's you."

"What if I don't want the position?" Robin asked.

"It's not an office," Sam Berlant said. "It's a state of being. Even if you don't want to be it, you're still it. Your arrival is incredibly significant to us—and to all religions. It's the first time in recorded history that a prophesied religious entity has been intentionally brought into being. You're the religious find of the millennia, Miss Baker."

"Swell," Robin said.

"There *are* compensations," Hamn said, gently. "The Church has significant material, real estate, and business holdings. These

388 · John Scalzi

are all administered by a governing council and various boards of directors, but technically, it's all held in trust for the Evolved Lamb, should he or she ever arise."

Robin stared for a second, and then held up her hand as if to pause the conversation. "So you're saying I own the Church."

"Well, no," Hamn said. "Just all of its assets."

"So that's a lot," Robin said.

"It's not bad," Hamn allowed.

"So, we're talking, what? A million? Two million?"

Hamn looked over to Sam Berlant. "As of the market close last Friday, 174.9 billion dollars," Sam said.

"175 *billion* dollars," Robin said. "Billion, as in, the one with the nine zeros after it."

"That's the one," Hamn said.

"Technically, it makes you the richest single person on Earth," Sam Berlant said. "The Walton family is worth more in aggregate, but there are a couple hundred of them."

"I feel like I just swallowed a golf ball," Robin said, and moved to sit.

Creek moved over to steady her. "Easy, Robin," he said. "You already run a planet. This is just a little extra bonus."

"Harry," Robin said. "Do you have any clue how far outside reality you have to be to describe 175 billion dollars as a bonus?"

"Just promise you'll remember me at Christmastime," Creek said. He sat down next to Robin, who smiled and patted his shoulder.

Hubu-auf-Getag returned a few minutes later. "The auf-Getag clan is prepared to offer its allegiance to the new *Fehen*," he said. "Our influence is such that we believe that the other clans—even the win-Getag clan—will follow suit."

Robin stood. "So you will do as I say," she said.

"Yes," Hubu-auf-Getag said.

"Really," Robin said.

"You may test our loyalty in any way you choose," Hubu-auf-Getag said.

"Brian," Robin said.

"Yes, *Fehen*," Brian said.

"Would you inform Secretary Heffer his presence is requested by the *Fehen*."

"At once," Brian said. Jim Heffer arrived two minutes later.

"You asked for me, *Fehen*," Secretary Heffer said.

"I did," Robin said. "My good friend Hubu-auf-Getag and I were recently discussing the unfortunate series of misunderstands between Nidu and the UNE. He and I agreed that in light of the possible damage between these great nations, Nidu could benefit from making a goodwill gesture to the peoples of Earth and her colonies. Isn't that right, Hubu-auf-Getag?"

"That is entirely correct, *Fehen*," Hubu-auf-Getag said.

"I'm glad to hear it," Heffer said. "What does the *Fehen* have in mind?"

"Oh, not *me*," Robin said. "What I'm about to say comes entirely from Hubu-auf-Getag. Secretary Heffer, aren't there two Nidu destroyers in orbit around Earth at the moment?"

"I believe there are," Heffer said.

"I hear they're very nice," Robin said. "Top of the line and all of that."

"They are excellent ships," Heffer said.

"Well, then," Robin said. "Hubu-auf-Getag wants the UNE to have them. Don't you, Hubu-auf-Getag?"

Creek spent the next several seconds wondering if a Nidu's head could, in fact, actually explode from rage.

"There is nothing that would give me greater pleasure," Hubu-auf-Getag finally said, in a tone that suggested his entrails had cramped.

390 · John Scalzi

"That is wonderful news," Heffer said. "Our secretary of defense will be immensely pleased. May I pass along your compliments, Hubu-auf-Getag?"

"Please do," Hubu-auf-Getag said, tightly.

"And Secretary Heffer," Robin said. "You may also inform your government that Hubu-auf-Getag is to be governor of Nidu and her colonies. He has my authority to act in my place in every matter."

"Very good, *Fehen*," Heffer said. "My congratulations, Governor. Will there be an installation ceremony?"

Hubu-auf-Getag looked to Robin Baker. "It is up to the *Fehen*."

"Well, I think we should," Robin said. "Let's say, in one hour? After all, everyone is already *here*."

Robin stepped down from the dais and walked over to Narfwin-Getag, still prone on the ground. "And as for you, you shithead," she said. "I'm going to make sure you get the best seat in the house, to watch everything you ever wanted given to someone else. Tell me what you think about *that*."

The gubernatorial ceremony was very much like the coronation ceremony, with the exception that instead of a blood sacrifice and a brain scan, Robin Baker symbolized the transfer of power to Hubu-auf-Getag by providing him a single *Fehensul* flower from a bouquet she held in her hands. Brian used the impressive Nidu computer voice to announce that Hubu-auf-Getag had been given penultimate control of the Nidu computer network, and then everyone in the crowd applauded in the manner appropriate for their own species and filed out to go to any number of ceremonies and parties around Nidu before going home.

In time only a few people remained in the Great Hall, paired off in conversation: Creek and Jim Heffer, Robin and Takk, Brian and Ben Javna, and Francis Hamn and Sam Berlant, who were finishing a final diagnostic on the Nidu network.

Creek watched from a distance as Brian and Ben sat in the distance (well, Ben sat; Brian projected himself sitting) and reacquainted themselves with each other. Creek could see Ben's eyes were red-rimmed, but at the moment he was laughing at something his brother was telling him.

"That's a hell of a thing," Heffer said. "To lose a brother and to get him back."

"It is," Creek said. "I wondered how Ben would take it, and if he'd hate me for doing it. But I needed Brian's help. Without him, none of this would have worked."

"Don't sell yourself short, Creek," Heffer said. "Without you, we'd be at war, and we would have lost. And your friend Robin would probably be dead by now. You saved her, and saved us. You didn't save the universe, but you can plan on doing that next week."

Creek smiled. "I'm taking next week off," he said. "And possibly the week after that. With your permission."

"Take all the time you want, Creek," Heffer said. "Just tell me you'll be back. I don't know that we need any more like you; I don't think my heart could handle the strain. But I'm glad we have at least one of you around." He looked at his watch and stood. "I've got to collect Ben. We have a shuttle to catch. How are you getting back?"

"Hamn and Berlant have offered to take us home with their corporate transport," Creek said. "Although if I understand everything correctly, it's actually that Robin is letting *them* hitch a ride on her transport."

"Don't rush home," Heffer said, and held out his hand. "Make a few stops. Enjoy yourselves."

"We've already had one cruise this week," Creek said, shaking Heffer's hand. "One's enough." The two men made their good-byes, and then Creek walked over to Robin and Takk.

"Takk's telling me about his home," Robin said. "It sounds nice. He's been away for two years."

"That's a long time," Creek said.

"It is," Takk said. "But I'll be going home now. I've seen enough of other places to last me a while."

"Amen to that," Robin said.

Hamn and Sam Berlant walked up. "Excuse me, Miss Baker," Hamn said. "We're just about finished up here. We'll be ready to leave shortly. On the return trip home, I know that Sam here would like to talk to you a little bit about your financials and your new responsibilities with the Church holdings."

"You're not expecting me to *run* things, are you?" Robin said. "I barely keep a pet store going. If you have me run the Church, you're all going to be in soup line by the end of the week."

"We were actually hoping you'd let the corporate governance continue as it has," Sam said.

"That sounds good to me," Robin said.

"But there's still quite a lot we need to get through," Sam said.

"I don't suppose it could wait a few weeks," Robin said.

"It's really better—" Sam began, but Robin put up her hand.

"The reason I ask is because at this moment I just want to be Robin Baker. Not the *Fehen* of Nidu, not the Evolved Lamb, and not the richest person on Earth. Not even my own nation. Just Robin Baker, who owns a pet store where by now the animals have completely forgotten who I am. Just Robin Baker, who all she wants is to go home now. That's all I want to be, if that's all right with you. Just for a little while. I hope you understand."

Sam looked ready to offer a rebuttal, but Hamn put his hand

on Sam's shoulder. "We understand entirely, Robin. That'll be fine with us. We're going to get ready to get out of here. We'll come get you when we're ready to go."

"Thank you," Robin said. Hamn and Sam Berlant turned to go.

"Excuse me," Takk said. "You said earlier that you were Sam Berlant."

"I am," Sam said.

"I have a message for you," Takk said. He took out Archie's book of prophecies. Sam took it, stared at it for a moment, and then looked at Takk.

"You knew Archie," Sam said.

"He was my friend," Takk said.

Sam motioned to Takk to follow them. He did, leaving Creek and Robin to themselves on the altar of the Great Hall.

"So you really don't want to be any of these things you've become," Creek said to Robin, as they watched Takk walk off with the technicians. "Not everyone gets to be their own nation or a religious icon or the richest woman ever."

"Or a sheep," Robin said. "You can't forget that." She reached over to gather up her bouquet of *Fehensul*.

"Or a sheep," Creek agreed. "But with the exception of the sheep, most people would jump at a chance to be the things you are."

"Would you?" Robin asked.

"No," Creek said. "I like being me most of the time. But I suspect I'm not like most people."

"This much I knew," Robin said. She handed Creek a flower. "Take this, Harry. Payment for keeping me alive."

"One hundred seventy-five billion dollars and I get a flower," Creek said, taking it.

"It's the thought that counts," Robin said.

"Thanks," Creek said, and held it to his nose. "It smells nice."

394 · John Scalzi

"It does," Robin agreed. "It's talking to you in the language of flowers."

"What is it saying?" Creek asked.

" 'There's no place like home,' " Robin said.

"That's a nice message," Creek said.

"It's the best," Robin said.

Creek held his flower up for Robin. She smiled, leaned over, and inhaled deeply.

ACKNOWLEDGMENTS

I write the books, but the books don't make it to readers without a whole bunch of people helping them along. This book was helped along by Patrick Nielsen Hayden, who edited it; Arthur D. Hlavaty, who performed copy-editing duties; Irene Gallo, who put a cover on it; Lynn Newmark, who did the interior design; Dot Lin, who publicized it; and the lovely folks in Tor's crack marketing department, who convinced bookstores that it was worth putting on their shelves. I offer my humble thanks to all of them for the work they've done on behalf of the book. It wouldn't have gotten to you without them. Other thanks in the Tor offices goes to Teresa Nielsen Hayden, Liz Gorinsky, and of course Tom Doherty.

Beyond Tor, thanks for help and support during the writing of this book goes out to Regan Avery, Stephen Bennett, and Stephanie Lynn. Philip K. Dick is responsible for the title and for getting me thinking about sheep. I hope he's not turning in his grave. Thanks to the readers of Whatever, my personal blog, who got to hear me get all angsty about writing this, and offered comments of encouragement. Finally, thanks as always to Kristine and Athena Scalzi for their love, encouragement, and tolerance. Family is a wonderful thing.

ABOUT THE AUTHOR

John Scalzi's science fiction novels include *Old Man's War*, *The Ghost Brigades,* and *Agent to the Stars*. His published nonfiction includes *The Rough Guide to the Universe* and *The Book of the Dumb*. His weblog The Whatever (www.scalzi.com/whatever) is one of the longest-established such sites on the Internet. He lives in Ohio with his wife and daughter.